The Memoirs of Elizabeth Frankenstein

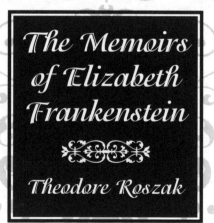

The Memoirs of Elizabeth Frankenstein

Theodore Roszak

RANDOM HOUSE

NEW YORK

Library of Congress Cataloging-in-Publication Data
Roszak, Theodore
The memoirs of Elizabeth Frankenstein / Theodore Roszak.
p. cm.
ISBN 0-679-43732-0
I. Title.
PS3568.O8495M46   1995   813´.54—dc20   94-43985

Manufactured in the United States of America on acid-free paper
Book design by J. K. Lambert
2 4 6 8 9 7 5 3
First Edition

Unable to endure the aspect of the being I had created, I rushed out of the room and continued a long time traversing my bedchamber, unable to compose my mind to sleep. At length lassitude succeeded to the tumult I had before endured; and I threw myself on the bed in my clothes, endeavouring to seek a few moments of forgetfulness. But it was in vain: I slept, indeed, but I was disturbed by the wildest dreams. I thought I saw Elizabeth, in the bloom of health, walking in the streets of Ingolstadt. Delighted and surprised, I embraced her; but as I imprinted the first kiss on her lips, they became livid with the hue of death; her features appeared to change, and I thought that I held the corpse of my dead mother in my arms; a shroud enveloped her form, and I saw the grave-worms crawling in the folds of the flannel. I started from my sleep with horror; a cold dew covered my forehead, my teeth chattered, and every limb became convulsed: when, by the dim and yellow light of the moon, as it forced its way through the window shutters, I beheld the wretch—the miserable monster whom I had created.

MARY SHELLEY

Frankenstein: Or The Modern Prometheus

AUTHOR'S NOTE

In the original version of *Frankenstein*, Mary Shelley used herself as the model for Elizabeth, the tragic fiancée of Victor Frankenstein. Yet it was not to Elizabeth that she entrusted the telling of the tale; for this she chose the Arctic explorer Robert Walton. Male voices—the voices of Walton, Victor, and the monster—dominate the story. Elizabeth is allowed to speak only through a few scattered letters. Even when it came to publishing the book, Mary proved to be self-effacing. Although she was as liberated a woman as her mother, Mary Wollstonecraft, the Western world's first feminist, Mary agreed to remove her name from the title page. Her publisher considered the novel too shocking to be attributed to a female author. Published anonymously in 1818, *Frankenstein* was thought by many readers to have been written not by Mary, but by her husband, Percy.

I have long felt that the *Frankenstein* Mary most wanted to offer the world lies hidden in an under-story that only Elizabeth could have written. This retelling of the tale parallels the original version, but views the events as only Elizabeth could have known them. In placing an alchemical romance at the center of the novel, Mary Shelley was delving deeper into the psychological foundations of Western science than she may consciously have realized. In her own time, she could not have known the more exotic sources of alchemy; but her intuitive insight into what alchemy reveals about the sexual politics of science has proven to be astonishingly correct. I hope that, speaking here as the bride of Frankenstein, she will at last find the voice she was not free to adopt in her own day.

THEODORE ROSZAK
Berkeley, California, 1994

CONTENTS

PREFACE TO THE MEMOIRS OF ELIZABETH FRANKENSTEIN

by Sir Robert Walton, F.R.S., O.B.E.

London, 1843

Many readers will know me solely as the man responsible for introducing Dr. Victor Frankenstein to the world. In the fall of 1799, while serving as ship's naturalist on a voyage of exploration to the Arctic regions, I participated in rescuing a stranded traveller who had lost his way in the polar seas. Adrift for days upon an ice floe, the poor wretch was nearly dead from hunger and exhaustion when we brought him aboard our ship. This was Victor Frankenstein—who, upon being revived from his comatose condition, proceeded to recount the macabre chain of circumstances that had brought him to this lamentable pass. Desperate to have the record of his misadventures preserved, he pressed me to take notes as he spoke, a request I could hardly deny to one so close to death.

Thus, by an unaccountable turn of fortune, it fell to me to chronicle Frankenstein's story from his own lips. I alone in all the world learnt of his crimes against nature from the man himself; I alone knew the suffering they had wrought upon him; I alone witnessed the remorse etched upon his features. His was indeed the aspect of a condemned soul crying out for a redemption that could never be his. It was as an act of charity that I did what Frankenstein begged me to do in his final hours. Still, all the while I sat at his bedside, my scientist's mind struggled with a single question. *Where was the tangible proof for anything he reported?* How could I be certain these were not the ravings of a broken mind?

And then, when Frankenstein finally lay dead, I found myself confronting the unnatural being he had fashioned with his own hands; I spoke to it face to face; I heard the low, bestial rasping that was its voice; I felt the dread menace of its presence; and at last I watched in amazement as it took up its maker's corpse and carried it out across the ice-bound wilderness for cremation.

Only then did I believe.

I will frankly admit that I rue the day that fate saddled me with the reputation I now must bear. For I believe I can say without risk of immodesty that my own researches into the natural history of the polar regions represent a substantial contribution to modern science. I therefore have not easily resigned myself to the fact that my identity in the eyes of the world turns upon this single fortuitous circumstance in which it was my rôle to function as amanuensis to one who will be remembered always as a madman and a criminal, if not an enemy of God.

I might at least have hoped that, upon publishing my conversations with Frankenstein, I would be rid of the man and free to resume my own career. But this was not to be. Instead, having gone to such lengths to preserve his memory, I found myself the reluctant trustee of a terrible but inescapable burden. I felt impelled to do all that lay within my power to make certain the moral of his story should be made indisputably clear. For there are lessons in this matter that I would not see lost on my colleagues in the scientific fraternity. Prisoner to my own conscience, I felt that every detail of Frankenstein's work must be preserved—not least of all the story of the man himself. I found myself asking how so gifted a mind had lost its way and debased its genius. Along what paths and under what influences had he been drawn to his tragic vocation? If I could answer these questions, the credibility of Frankenstein's tale and the moral horror of his deeds might be greatly enhanced.

But *was* there more to be told than the man had himself revealed to me?

It was not until the late summer of 1806 that political conditions on the continent of Europe once again became peaceful enough to permit an extended enquiry into the background of Frankenstein's narrative. In that year, during the brief interval of peace in southern Europe that followed Napoleon's triumph at Austerlitz, I was free to travel extensively in the region of Geneva, the Frankenstein family seat. During those unsettled years Geneva and the entire Vaud had been freshly annexed to the Napoleonic empire. But alas! the revolutionary forces unleashed by the invasion of the Emperor's Grand Army had made short work of the city's municipal records, as they had of its aristocratic families. The Swiss merchant dynasties had been driven into exile and their properties roughly expropriated, with little concern for historical materials. The few distant members of the Frankenstein clan I located in the region proved reluctant in the extreme to discuss their relative; he was seen by one and all as a blot on the family's honour best expunged from memory. Similarly, at the University of Ingolstadt, Frankenstein's alma mater—not far from the battlefield at Jena where Napoleon's forces were already gathering for their epic confrontation with the armies of King Frederick—I discovered that his principal mentors had died or departed; the school itself had been closed, a casualty of the troubled times. I was on the point of giving up all hope when I uncovered the whereabouts of Ernest Frankenstein. This, the last surviving member of the family, was then living in a remote village high in the Jura; reluctantly he admitted to possessing certain papers relevant to his brother's history. A slow-witted man, now deeply embittered by the loss of his family estates, Ernest would part with the documents only for a price. In his suspicion, he would not permit me to so much as handle the material until I had first placed money in his hands—and even then he would reveal only the first few pages, holding the remainder tightly in his grip as a miser might clutch his last coin. But what he showed me was enough; I needed to do no more than translate the first several lines, and I was eager to pay what the man asked—which was but a small fraction of their worth to me.

Following the sale, Ernest displayed a smug amusement at what he took to be my gullibility. "It's just the Gipsy bastard's rubbish, that's all you've bought for your money. Much good may it do you, Mr. Busybody!" I permitted the man his ignorant satisfaction and quickly departed, almost giddy with my sense of triumph. For what this poor simpleton had delivered over to me were the writings and papers of Elizabeth Lavenza, Frankenstein's adopted sister and later fiancée. I could not have hoped for a more precious find.

Readers of my original account will recall that this most unfortunate of women, Victor Frankenstein's life-long love and fond companion, met her death on her wedding night, murdered by the very fiend her husband had created. Clearly Ernest Frankenstein had no idea of the value these papers might have. I realised as soon as I laid eyes upon them that here might lie the key to Frankenstein's tragedy. For there are *three* voices that must be heard if we are to understand this extraordinary history accurately. The first is that of Frankenstein himself; this we have, in the man's own words as I took them down verbatim. The second is that of his monstrous creation, both as the fiend's words were quoted by Frankenstein and as then spoken to me by the creature itself while it confronted me over its creator's corpse. But here at last was the voice of one who knew Frankenstein more intimately than any other: Elizabeth, the third and (so I thought at the time) only innocent member of the unholy trinity.

Thus, with the exuberance of true discovery, I returned to England to complete the story of this remarkable man—just as the fragile peace of Europe was again shattered by the clash of great armies.

I soon learnt my task would be far from easy. After several readings, I realised that Elizabeth Frankenstein's memoirs provided more insight than I had at first recognised, possibly more than I would ever have invited. For this was no mere supplement to Frankenstein's accounts; her testimony was of the tale's essence. Indeed, I soon had reason to fear that these pages might conceal greater depths of meaning than I had the capacity to elicit.

I will now for the first time admit that Victor Frankenstein confided more to me than I have thus far revealed to the world. In his original narration, he had touched upon certain subjects that I did not see fit to include in my published accounts. He had, for example, talked at some length—often in an almost hallucinatory manner—about his early alchemical studies and about the rôle his fiancée had played in these experiments; but his remarks were obscure and frequently too unsavoury for my taste. Much of this talk I attributed at the time to his feverish state of mind. Though I dutifully noted down his words, I had already decided, even as I sat at Frankenstein's bedside, that these outpourings, filled with rambling confessions of self-loathing and remorse, should never become public knowledge. They might, after all, be no more than the guilty rantings of a dying soul. I therefore elected mercifully to suppress what he told me of certain demeaning uses to which he had subjected the woman he claimed to love. I did so out of profound concern for this hapless lady's reputation. For even if what Frankenstein reported should be true, I had no wish to recount the aberrant acts that she, in her moral weakness, might have been forced to perform as partner to Frankenstein's so-called "chemical marriage." I took Frankenstein at his word when he averred that he and he alone was responsible for Elizabeth's corruption. He asserted not once but repeatedly and with the most ardent emphasis that she was but the passive recipient of the indecencies he inflicted upon her.

To this day, I have tried always to regard Elizabeth Frankenstein as the victim of her fiancé's twisted ambition. But gradually, as my studies of the strange lore that surrounds Elizabeth's life have deepened, I have grown steadily less certain of her moral character. I could never have guessed that I should discover this seemingly guileless young woman dabbling in rites that our Christian forefathers assumed were long since purged from memory. Nor could I have imagined her voluntarily delving into the erotic practices that constitute the dark side of alchemical philosophy. After a time, I could no longer tell which of these two—Victor or Elizabeth—had debauched the other. Was it possible, as certain passages in this text suggest, that Elizabeth, far from being a reluctant participant in her lover's unnatural pursuits, was to some degree their initiator? Given what I have learnt from her own accounts, I must conclude that what I would once have found unthinkable is indeed true. Frankenstein was not alone in perpetrating the obscenities he confessed to me; he had a willing accomplice, whose culpability is little short of his.

Most unsettling of all is the evidence one finds in these pages of the Baroness Caroline Frankenstein's rôle in the lives of both her son and her adopted daughter. If these memoirs are to be believed, this shadowy woman, whom Victor Frankenstein chose to leave all but anonymous in his original narrative, would surely rank as the most grotesque human phenomenon I have encountered in a lifetime of travels and uncommon adventures. *If*, I say, the words upon these pages can be believed. But can they? For as long as a reasonable doubt clouded the facts, I hesitated to accept the veracity of what Elizabeth Frankenstein reports of her foster mother; it was easier by far for me to label Elizabeth a shameless liar or to attribute what she says to the derangement of her faculties than to credit the possibility that there was ever so depraved a soul as the mother who gave Victor Frankenstein birth. Yet here, too, my research has yielded incontrovertible evidence that Lady Caroline Frankenstein was in fact guilty of all that these memoirs recount.

Thus, after forty years of scholarly toil, I am at last left to ask: Must it once again be my rôle to vex the mind of my fellow man with a story of unredeemed decadence? For as I ruminate among these documents, I see that Frankenstein's crimes—perhaps committed with the complicity of his bride—were more heinous than I had surmised. The monstrosity he fashioned in his profane pursuit of God-like power was but the final act in a succession of moral transgressions. Though I believed for a brief interval that Frankenstein merited compassion as a tragic soul, I have lived to realise that his memory deserves to be buried in obscurity—and even more so, the name of his bride. I confess that I was at several points sorely tempted to cover over her rôle in these matters, lest I should be responsible for bequeathing such an example of female degeneracy to posterity.

What was it that at last rescued me from this state of irresolution? One thing only. My steadfast allegiance to the ideal of scientific objectivity. This alone, the cherished habit of a life-time spent in the service of truth, strengthened me in an endeavour that moral revulsion might have persuaded me to abandon. In that spirit I lay this report before the world, confident that a candid public will not mistake my true purpose, which is the defence of Reason and the vindication of Moral Rectitude.

Part One

Belrive, August 30, 1797
Dearest Victor:

I take up my pen in a dark hour.

The happiness I have so long awaited is now at last to be mine; in another hour I will become as much the wife of your flesh as I have been the wife of your soul these many years. But that jubilant realisation comes to me veiled by the shadow of death. I cannot tell when or how I must die; but the knowledge that it must be soon presses in upon me like a suffocating hand. The road we shall travel to our long-delayed wedding night has been so tortuous, I only pray that we will at last be granted a single hour of joy.

I need not tell you why I am so certain of this dread fate; you were the first to hear my sentence of death pronounced, and you, even better than I, know why I stand condemned. A vengefulness that has attained diabolical invincibility hovers over our marriage. I know that you would gladly give your life to preserve mine; but (my dearest, forgive me for saying so!) I know your love is neither strong enough nor true enough to stand against this evil. Do not—I beg you!—see in this any lack of faith on my part in the sincerity of your devotion. Read my words, rather, as an expression of my greater faith in the justice of God, Whose Law you have profaned. For this evil is, after all, a thing of your own making. Mourn me if you must—but think of me afterwards as the blood-sacrifice your sin required.

Know that I blame only myself for the wrath that is now to be visited upon us. Once——you remember the moment, and know that it was no more than a moment——I turned from you in horror; in that moment, you felt my loathing and rejection. Brief as that instant was, I see now that it impelled you along the path toward those unhallowed arts that became your vocation. Had my devotion proved constant in that hour, had I been able to forgive and to strengthen the momentary weakness of the flesh that overcame you——had I, in short, been the true partner in our mystic marriage that you so deeply needed ——doubtless we should have remained the lovers, fellow-workers, and spiritual companions I believe a Divine Providence intended us to be. Was my frailty in that moment any less than yours?

Now, therefore, in these last months, I have set down what is as much the story of your life as it is of mine. I have told the tale as if it were written for an audience of strangers, though it is to have but a single reader. All that I have unwisely kept secret from you, every unspoken word of anger and reproach, every wound of the spirit that I hid from view, I here commit to writing for your instruction. There is nothing more to do than to attach this final letter. Are the words I write in such haste coherent? . . . I think they are coherent. It is difficult . . . my mind has of late been so distracted. The iron voice spoke again last night. It does not let me sleep.

I will finish now, for I must go be married. Dearest love, dearest enemy, when this comes to your hand, accept it as the half of you that you did not know and could not know, the half that was——

Your Loving Bride
Elizabeth

I Am Born into Exile

Then are nights that bring me the same evil dream over and again; they have done so for as long as I can remember.

I am as if divided in two. Two pairs of eyes, two sensibilities. As if from a distant height I see the bed on which the tormented woman lies, torn by the anguish of a difficult birth. I watch how she writhes in terror of death, like a wounded soldier wallowing in his own blood on the field of battle. Horrible it is to watch her suffering; but more horrible still to see the creature that bends above her. Scarcely human in appearance, it, as much as the pain she suffers, is the source of her fear. Its hands reach out—and I understand the cause of her alarm; for *these are not hands;* they are the claws of a predatory bird: falcon or eagle. The bird-man's talons rake the woman's helpless flesh, leaving behind a scarlet tracery. They plunge into the hollow of her thighs, tearing at the tortured portals of her sex. All the while, outside the window, lightning like the wrath of God sets the sky afire, throwing her form into hideous relief, the ghost-white light making her pale face terrifying to behold. I want to go to her, to take her in my arms and share her tribulation.

But now there is *another* me. I am the powerless, unformed babe that lodges inside her anguished body. I see a distant light; I struggle to reach it, crawling laboriously through a tunnel whose sides are warm and moist. All about me I hear a pulsing rumble, as if I had been swallowed by a great beast that has begun to digest me. I approach the light, panic seizes me . . . I cannot breathe, my lungs ache. I must escape!

And then I feel the pain at my temples. I am gripped and tugged at; the pressure seems to crush my brain. But at last I am free. My face, my body are soaked in blood. Blood everywhere. At my temples, blood. The bird-man has driven his claw inside the womb itself; he has caught hold of me! I see myself dangling in the grip of his talons like a morsel he would devour. I look round and see the crimson and yawning gulf from which I have been disgorged: my mother's sex, trembling like a mute mouth wanting to cry out in anguish. I see her twisted face, its eyes staring at me in accusation. But the eyes do not see me; they see nothing. They are dead—dead eyes in a dead woman's face.

And then I realise: My life has taken a life. I have come into the world a murderer.

This fearful scene returns still to rend my sleep, even though I have long since known it to be only a figment of my childhood imagination. Yet, in another sense, it keeps a truth that only dreams can tell. It recalls the retribution that has awaited me since I first opened eyes upon the world.

For this much I at a later period discovered regarding the facts of my origin. I am the child of a strange and tragic birth. The tide of blood that washed me into the world was my mother's last vital reflex. She died to give her child life. My father was left so distraught by the loss of the woman he dearly loved that he responded almost as if punishing the newborn for the mother's death. He sent me, as it were, into exile. At his bidding, while my mother's body still lay stretched across the bed, the blood not yet washed from it, I was abruptly placed in the care of the midwife who had helped bring me into the world. "Her name shall be Elizabeth, after her mother," he ordered. These were the final words the Romanish woman remembered from that terrible night when she took the place of my vanished mother.

Though she had already four hungry children of her own, this humble soul, whose name was Rosina Lavenza, did her best to fill the place assigned to her; but indeed I might as well have been motherless. A good and caring woman who nursed me at her bosom together with her own infant, she was neither of my social rank nor of my race—as she herself readily gave me to know. The blood I inherited from my father was that of Milanese nobility; my mother was descended distantly from the English royal household. From her I inherited the fair colouring and golden hair that marked me off so dramatically from the swarthy Lavenzas whom I was reared to think of as my kin. Rosina's children, especially, came to treat me with suspicion and contempt; in their eyes, I was destined always to be an intrusive and unwelcome presence, distinguished from them by the delicacy of my features. Though I shared their cramped caravan and wore the same tattered clothing—and though my first language was the Romany dialect of the household— their mother taught them to regard me as someone above their station. "Remember," Rosina instructed her children in my presence, "Elizabeth is a princess. Her father rules all the kingdoms of the South." Though the good woman meant well, my new brothers and sisters were not to be won over by the exalted claims she made in my behalf; indeed, these envious urchins were all the more inspired to treat me with hostility, even calling my parentage into question. Most hurtfully, they told me the shameful secret their mother had confided to them: that I was base-born and had been abandoned. This made me seem, in their naturally resentful eyes, not a person of privilege, but their inferior, and they lost no opportunity to wound me with the accusation of bastardy. Yet they listened with fascination whenever Rosina related her fabulous tales of the father I had never known, stories of his adventures in the lands of the East and across the seas, fantastic accounts of his daring and great wealth.

Perhaps she told these tales in the hope that my father would continue to supplement the stipend he had given her when I was first placed in her keeping. Or perhaps there was another, more ominous reason for these glorified accounts of my lineage. Though Rosina was a kind woman, the paterfamilias of the Lavenza clan was the very opposite. Toma was a dark and brooding man given to drink and possessed of an evil temper; even in my childhood I could see how Rosina trembled with terror in his scowling presence. And frequently I saw marks of ill-use upon her that could not be hidden. Toma treated the children, myself included, no less harshly. Worse, he regarded the sisters I grew up with as his *carnal* property, to be used for the vilest of purposes. The oldest of the girls, some five years my senior, was Tamara, a dark and lovely child, born to be a temptress of men. Her natural charms were hardly lost upon Toma, who was forever fondling her and lavishing unseemly affection upon her. He called her his "little wife," and often she shared his bed when he would not have Rosina there. Nor did the value of her beauty escape the notice of this grasping man. In my innocence I could not have guessed it at the time, but with the bitter wisdom of years I realise that the man was making this child his whore, soon to be sent into the streets to earn him something more than the miserable pittance he gained from his trade as a woodcarver. I can only assume he had similar plans for me, his "golden girl," who, he continually remarked, would grow to be a greater beauty than his own daughter. On one occasion when I could not have been older than five, this wicked man did succeed in cajoling me into his bed. Only Rosina's courageous intervention prevented the success of his designs upon me. She burst in upon him with a knife, pressed it against his throat until it drew blood, and threatened to sacrifice her own life in taking his, should he ever lay a defiling hand upon me.

As beholden as I remain to Rosina for her loving care and protection, she more than anyone was the source of my evil dream. Before I could clearly understand the import of her words, she began to tell me what she remembered of my birth. Whenever she bathed and groomed me, she drew her fingers gently down a scar I bore just at the left temple. Even before I could think of it as a disfigurement, Rosina would bemoan the defect, which she regarded as the one flaw in my fine looks. It was the jagged remnant of some injury I could not remember suffering. "See here, see here," I recall her saying. "Here is where *he* took you. Here is where the claw took you, my poor one. We must take care not to let it show." And then she would arrange my hair in ringlets about my face to veil the mark, making me all the more conscious of the imperfection. Years later, even now, I wear my hair in that same way she showed me, though the scar has long since faded from view. In my infancy, I might have taken it as a game, this hiding of the ugly blemish;

but ere long I came to grasp more fully the meaning of her words. The thought became fixed in me that this mark had been left by some malicious attack: A creature armed with claws had at some time assailed me. I understood no more than this, but the image was horrific enough to find permanent lodging in my inventive revery, where it would in time burrow into my dreams to haunt my sleeping hours. I would wake screaming—hearing, as I thought, the flapping of great, predatory wings above my bed.

What dread reality this fantasy masked I discovered soon enough.

Rosina, as I have said, was a midwife, earning more at her trade than Toma did at his. Expecting her daughters to follow in her footsteps, she was in the habit of taking me and my two sisters with her when she was called upon to attend a birth. Her intention, as she made clear, was that the girls should be from their earliest years accustomed to the harsh facts of childbirth. Before I could fully comprehend what I saw, I was stationed with my sisters behind Rosina as she knelt before the birthing stool to bring a new life into the world. She would show us how she prepared the herbal steam that was to be applied diligently to the thighs and abdomen of the expectant mother. Child though I was, I was shown how to brew a potion that would hasten the labour: several pieces of pungent ergot steeped in a pan of water. The birth completed, I was permitted to hold the newborn still moist and writhing from the womb. I recall the experience as troubling, for often it seemed there was great suffering involved—and I feared that the wailing mother might be in peril of her life.

One episode in particular I recall, for through it I learnt what little I know of my own birth. On that occasion, Rosina had been summoned to the home of a genteel lady whose labour was proving prolonged. As I had seen her do on similar occasions in the past, Rosina patiently kneaded and massaged the woman's belly, applying a salve that soothed the anxious mother-to-be. The other women in attendance had taken up the crooning chant that served to calm the most distraught patients. But when the delivery had at last begun, a strange man burst into the room and proceeded to thrust aside the women who surrounded the birthing stool. He identified himself in a strident voice as a physician summoned to the scene by the fretful father. The doctor refused to let Rosina continue with the delivery, dismissing her imperiously as a "hag." Setting to work, he ordered that the mother be removed from the stool and returned to her bed. Then, turning fiercely on Rosina, he instructed her to make herself useful in the only way she might. "Hold her hands, slut! Keep her still!" he commanded.

Reluctantly, Rosina took a position standing behind the bed, gripping the woman's hands in her own while the physician bent to his task. From his black satchel he removed a selection of clanking metallic instruments: they were hooked and sharp-edged like a carpenter's tools; among them he found two spoon-shaped rods and began to fit them together. At the very sight of this instrument, which I would later learn was called the forceps, Rosina fell to crossing herself and cried out for the man to stop. At which, the physician angrily ordered her from the room, calling her many an offensive name. Rosina in turn bit her thumb at him and, calling out an oath, refused to budge from her place. She positioned herself squarely between the physician and the woman, who was now screaming with an animal terror.

Ablaze with anger, the physician hurled a single word at Rosina. "*Strega!*" he cried. It was enough to crush Rosina's resistance. As she backed away, he called out the word again and again as if he were lashing her out of the room with a whip. "*Strega! Strega! Strega!* Be off with you!" Then, turning back to the bed where the distressed mother lay, he pulled a rolled leather belt from his valise. "Strap her down!" he barked to the remaining attendants.

Outside the door, Rosina took me aside, her face burning hot with rage and insult. "You see what he does? He ties her down and makes her helpless. He takes away the force of the Earth. And then . . . he will use his claw because the baby cannot make its way. He is killing her, the poor woman! He brings her death, not life." Then, taking me to her breast, she moaned, "It was how your own mother was killed—by the claw. They would not let me help her. You see here—you still have the mark." Her fingers were at my temple, tracing the scar just beneath the hair. "Yes, there, my child," she said. "That is what the claw did. It is the Devil's mark upon you. Soon all children will come into the world bearing it. It is a crime against God to take birth away from the women. What does he know, this . . . *man?*"

That night I dreamed for the first time of my dead mother and of the bird-man whose claw had taken her life and marked my flesh.

꽃

Through the first nine years of my life, Rosina struggled valiantly to surround me with the air of a prized possession, perhaps most of all to convince Toma that my safe-keeping might earn the family more than if he should make a strumpet of me. I cannot say how often my distant father contributed to my sustenance during those years—or if he did at all. I remember the man himself from only one occasion, and that a poignant one.

There came a day in my sixth year when a troop of condottieri, fully armed and with banners unfurled, passed through the Gipsy camp outside the village of Treviglio where the Lavenza clan made its home. It was an arrogant band, which rode roughshod over garden plots and sent both children and animals running before it. At its head rode an imposingly handsome man dressed in brocaded silver and a scarlet cloak. He wore a high, plumed helmet, and across his chest many gleaming medallions. The entire encampment was astonished to see him lead his contingent to our wagon, where he drew up his horse and called for my mother by name. When she emerged wide-eyed and trembling, he ordered her to bring me to him. "Come! Come!" she called to me where I played. "It is your father!" I was soon lifted into his arms where he sat mounted at our stairs. He held me in a strong grip for a long while, studying my face with the greatest care. I, looking back, engraved his features on my child's mind. This was the great lord of the South, of whom I had been told so often. And he did look to me for all the world like the kings I knew from fairy lore—a proud man magnificently armoured, deep-eyed and glowering. I can still see his features as vividly as if he stood before me. "Innocent destroyer, remember me in your prayers," I heard him say. "And forgive me. I loved your mother well."

Then, brushing a kiss through my hair, he looped a necklace over my head; the pendant that was attached fell well below my breast, so that I could not see it until he had returned me to my mother's arms. On her he bestowed a jingling pouch and admonished her to keep me in the best of care until he returned.

"He is going to the wars," she whispered at my ear as we watched him ride away.

That was the first and last I saw of him; no report of his fate ever reached me. I cannot even say in what war he had gone to fight. As for the trinket he left with me, it was not destined to be mine for long. Though Rosina did her best to keep it safe for me, within a few days' time Toma had secured it; I did not have the chance to do more than impress its salient features upon my memory. At the time it was given me, I could not have known it was a coat of arms. I remembered only the image: the quartered shield, decorated at the top with a great double axe and a two-headed eagle, and below with winged and dancing lions. This faint and fading image, which was not even substantial enough for me to trace its origin among the noble families of Italy, I nevertheless treasured in the little sketch I made of it after it had been taken from me, for it was to be the only remnant of my true parentage.

Though I had now at last looked him in the face and felt his hands upon me, that one meeting with my father served to make him a darker mystery still. His very obscurity prompted me to weave fanciful tales of my birth and heritage. I dwelt most often on the things that might have been, had my mother lived, had I grown up to become the princess I was meant to be. But sometimes I looked back upon the beginning of my life as a bewildering fall from grace, my father, like the offended Yahweh, banishing the life he had created into the harsh wilderness on the far side of Eden. Why had he condemned me to so low a station in life? Was this my punishment for the rôle I had unwittingly played in taking the life of my mother, the woman he loved so well? Having no one to answer these questions, I lived in a condition of inexplicable abandonment that allowed me to know nothing of childhood's ideal ease and merriment. I was in a sort of Purgatory, waiting for the

Redeemer who would come to harrow this dark dwelling and bring me out of exile.

In my case, the saviour was female.

EDITOR'S NOTE

Midwifery, Witchcraft, and the Disputed Rôle of the Forceps

Tragedy was the alpha and omega of Elizabeth Frankenstein's life; it marked both her birth and death. Indeed, if we can believe her story as she records it, her life was framed at the first and last by murder. But what credence can we give to her foster mother Rosina's account of Elizabeth's birth? The Gipsy was convinced that the physician who brought Elizabeth into the world was responsible for ushering her mother out—and this through the use of the very instrument that may have made the child's survival possible.

We must remember that Rosina's testimony is hardly reliable evidence, emanating as it does from an illiterate woman whose intellectual development is obviously of the lowest order. Moreover, we must bear in mind that all she says rings with what might fairly be called professional bias—that of a midwife who sees in the obstetrical physician a rival to her own livelihood. At one time every town and hamlet across Europe had its Rosina, an untrained woman who lived by a single skill, if skill it can be called. Rumour has it that many of these women were practitioners of the diabolical arts. Thus, in the witch craze of former times, numerous midwives perished, leaving a vacuum in the practice of gynaecological medicine that was to be filled by their male competitors. The hostility that grew up between such village "wise women" and the physicians who were displacing them was understandable enough. In the Inquisitional records, one even finds the women complaining that the charge of witchcraft was deliberately used to discredit them.

To gain a more objective view, we can do no better than turn to one of the pioneers of scientific obstetrics in our own land. At my solicitation, the distinguished physician Thomas Cosgrove has generously consented to contribute the following communication to this study.

My dear Walton,

  The questions you raise regarding the dangers of modern obstetrical proce-dures, I am pleased to say, form no basis for serious concern. Never before our time has parturition, so long the bane of womankind, transpired under more humane and competent conditions. Little more than a generation ago, the preg-nant woman was left to the mercy of untutored midwives who were in most cases no better than bumbling village crones operating under the influence of the grossest superstitions. Their "methods," if they can even be so dignified, were based on a body of ignorance that appalls the enlightened mind.

  One need do no more than describe the practices to condemn them. It was common during these times to allow the expectant mother to assume the major rôle in giving birth, physically exhausted and non compos mentis *as the poor creature normally is in this critical hour. The woman was positioned upright upon a torturous device known as the "labour stool" and then exhorted to expel the fetus by her own efforts! The midwife did little more than catch the newborn as it dropped from the uterus. You can imagine what an intolerable strain this placed upon the delicate constitution of the parturient. Moreover, I have heard that it was standard practice among midwives to sub-ject the new mother to a round of vigorous exercise, following which she was returned to her work in the fields, all in less than a day's time! While peasant women might possess the sheer bovine stamina to bear such inordinate demands upon their already debilitated bodies, women of some refinement would surely be facing a near-fatal risk if they were to undergo so arduous a regimen. As every physician can aver, women for the most part approach their first lying-in with almost no rational understanding of their condition. They are grossly uninformed and therefore understandably fearful; I have attended many a young mother who had no idea where the baby would emerge or what the nature of the placenta might be or what the cramps she suffered might portend. Terror alone places a terrific burden upon the constitution of the primipara, accelerating the pulse, increasing the pressure of the blood, and clouding the con-sciousness. There may be fevers and nausea; many all but swoon, leaving the child they carry in the gravest danger of strangulation. In some cases, the after-birth was only partially removed by the midwife, giving rise to convulsive fevers and death in but a few days following the birth.*

When at last enlightened techniques of delivery were introduced, they came as a blessing to the gentle sex. Placing the mother prone upon the table allows her mercifully to remove herself from all responsibility for the birth. The physical restraint about which you ask is of course necessary to allow the physician to concentrate his entire attention upon his demanding duties. Permitting the distraught woman to flail about would obviously endanger both mother and infant. The first consideration of the trained physician is, therefore, to take the situation well in hand so that the delivery may be efficiently managed.

As for the rôle of the forceps: This instrument has of course become essential to modern childbirth for the most obvious of reasons. The woman prone cannot by her own efforts expel the baby; she requires assistance, especially when there is a transverse or breech presentation. In such cases, where version of the fetus is demanded, the forceps are an absolute necessity. Expertly used they present no risk whatever to mother or child. Though they may on occasion bruise the skull somewhat, these abrasions soon vanish without a trace; laceration of the vaginal tissue is, of course, a more serious matter due to the near-certain infection that will follow. Nevertheless, I believe we can say without fear of contradiction that the invention of the forceps by our own Dr. Chamberlen has been the greatest single blessing the male sex, in its rôle as Homo faber, *has been able to bestow upon the lives of its women.*

It is true that the number of women who expire in childbirth in our day remains worrisomely high. The reason for this is not far to seek. Childbirth brings with it dangers of puerperal fever that cannot be avoided. Over these inherent risks, the gynaecological physician has no power. Both the clergyman and the doctor can agree that the sufferings and perils attendant upon childbirth are quite simply a fact of nature as old and ineluctable as Biblical law.

I cannot tell in what spirit you raise the issue of witchcraft, an accusation frequently directed against midwives. It would be yielding to a superstition as flagrant as the midwives' own to ascribe any truth to this belief. Crones and hags the midwives may often have been, and perhaps many times feeble-minded or encumbered by all manner of arcane lore; but we need believe no worse of them than that they failed to achieve a civilised degree of rational judgement. It is enough that science has liberated womankind from this ancient tyranny over the act of birth; no further sanctions need be invoked against these benighted females than to let them pass quietly into history. Yours Faithfully,

T. Cosgrove, M.D., F.R.S.
St. Giles Hospital, London

I Find a New Mother

Lady Caroline Frankenstein, who was to become both my material and my spiritual benefactress, was a person of the most unusual moral qualities. With me she shared the experience of a tragic childhood. Her mother also had died early in her life, leaving her, even as a child, to tend her widowed father, one Henry Beaufort, through the declining years of his career. A once prosperous Genevan merchant, Beaufort had lost his fortune through reckless speculation, and with it all will to rebuild his life. Morose and self-pitying, he grew steadily more dependent on his loyal daughter, who earned what little she could for their household by menial trades. Her skills, however, did not reach beyond plaiting straw, labour that brought her hardly enough to provide food and shelter. She and her father would surely have sunk beneath the waves of penury had not the Baron Alphonse Frankenstein appeared on the scene like a guardian angel.

The Baron and Beaufort had been friends since their university years. Learning of Beaufort's misfortunes, the Baron, the scion of one of Geneva's great commercial dynasties, had initiated enquiries as to his whereabouts. Finally discovering he was living near Lucerne, the Baron had gone searching for him. There he found his friend on his deathbed in a tiny, ramshackle cabin, his stricken daughter, Caroline, standing watch over him. Within a few days of the Baron's arrival, Beaufort was dead. As a gesture of friendship, the Baron adopted the orphaned daughter into his household. There she soon became the joy of his life. The Baron, who had never married, suddenly found his lonely existence brightened by the high spirits of a gifted and vivacious young woman. Though the girl had been raised in poverty, he discerned in her manner, her bearing, and the graceful facility of her intelligence a natural aristocracy that the accident of birth could not long conceal. Caroline, for her part, came to love the Baron, though more out of gratitude for his kindness than from any more impassioned sentiment. Within a few years, despite the great difference in their ages—for the Baron was the very age of the father she had lost—they married.

Though she was now a baroness, Lady Caroline never allowed herself to forget the hardships of her childhood; all the rest of her life, she continued to spend her earliest hour each morning, before others in the household had awakened, plaiting straw beside the kitchen hearth as she had done in her girlhood when she shared her father's misfortunes—the better to remember the lowly station from which she had risen. Now having the Baron's fortune at her disposal, she was determined to use it for charitable purposes. She became a woman driven to comfort the suffering of others. Orphaned children especially called out to her generosity; for in them she saw so vividly the plight that might have been hers.

In the twelfth year of the marriage, Lady Caroline, the Baron, and their children—for by then she was the mother of two sons—embarked upon a tour that took the family through the north of Italy. For the spring and summer of that year, the family took up residence in a handsome villa beside Lake Como. From there she and the Baron travelled through the surrounding countryside, visiting in turn the many quaint villages of the region. On one such excursion, while the Baron was occupied with business in Milan, Lady Caroline chanced to visit the marketplace in Treviglio where I was often taken with my family to sell the meagre trinkets my father carved, a collection of whistles and dolls and novelties that rarely fetched enough money to keep us fed. For the children, the day was an occasion less for honest commerce than for begging, a skill in which my mother had schooled us assiduously. For that purpose I was dressed to look all the shabbier; my face was blackened with soot, and a dress that was little more than rags was draped over me. As Fortune would have it, Lady Caroline's chaise passed by the fair that day and, seeing me, she ordered her driver to pause. No language can describe what I experienced in that moment when our eyes met. The sensation was one of physical transport, as if I had been lifted from the ground by wings I did not know I possessed. This woman, a complete stranger to me, sat studying me with a warmth and tenderness I had never witnessed. And she was so very striking a woman! If one turned to her expecting to find beauty, perhaps she would disappoint, for her features were not what fashion finds pleasing. Still, they at once commanded attention. Her brow was high and regal, her nose imposingly aquiline, the flesh of her face drawn taut as a mask across high, thrusting cheekbones that lent her the elegance of an Egyptian queen. Her expression possessed a hauteur that could intimidate with a glance. In one gloved hand she held a sprig of green (edelweiss, I think it was) with which she idly stroked her cheek and throat. But it was above all her eyes that were most arresting—narrow and cat-like, their colour a grey-blue as chilly as silver coins in an icy pool. When first I saw them, my childish imagination told me: *These are such eyes as angels have, that can spy into one's very heart.* And I shivered with the thrill of believing that this woman knew me for all that I was. So when she beckoned me to come to her I leapt to respond as if I were her own child.

"Whose girl are you?" she asked, leaning from her coach and using the sprig she held to brush the matted hair back from my brow.

Her Italian was all but courtly in its refinement, but I could tell from her accent that she was French. She was pleased when I answered in her own language—or sought haltingly to do so. French travellers often passed through our village to see the church and inspect the Gipsy fair. Toma and Rosina, who could beg and bargain in several languages, had taught me a sort of gutter French I might use for importuning rich visitors. Indeed, my daily speech was a stew of any and all languages that might prove useful for taking a coin off the passing traveller. People of quality thought it winsome to come upon a Gipsy urchin prattling in their own tongue. "My father is at the wars," I answered brightly. "He is a great prince."

"Is he indeed? I can believe it. You have the look of a royal child."

I both blushed and thrilled at the compliment.

Toma, overhearing, was quick to seize the opportunity. "The girl goes to sleep each night hungry, my lady. She goes cold in the winter."

"Does she? And are you her guardian?"

"Her father, my lady."

"She says her father is at the wars."

"The child makes up such stories. She is my own dear girl."

As Lady Caroline would later tell me, with each word Toma spoke she became more intensely concerned for my fate. I was obviously not of this man's race; she saw that I stood out in this family like gold amid dross. But it was not, she said, my fair face and bright locks alone that set me off; it was the lustre she could discern all about me, a sort of halo shining like sunlight through a veil of haze. There was, as she remembered, a celestial stamp upon me that marked me out not only from the members of this swarthy household but from all others. My "bright spirit," she called it, meaning by these words something I would never fully understand until I heard them from her years later, for the last time, only moments before death stilled her lips forever.

The Baroness feared that I had been kidnapped by this desperate, deceiving man; the Gipsies were burdened with a reputation for abducting children. Was I such a victim? she wondered. "You owe her far better care," Lady Caroline admonished. "As you do all your children."

"True, true!" the man admitted, quailing beneath her gaze. Many times before, I had heard him whine thus, with expert theatricality. "For my sins, for my sins, dear lady! The poor innocent goes cold and hungry because I cannot care for her—or for my other beloved children, as you see. Disease and misfortune have ruined me. Can you perhaps give something to ease our condition? A few poor coins would do."

Fixing Toma with a hard, unflinching stare, Lady Caroline answered with a question. "What will you take for the child?"

Not very convincingly, Toma pretended shock—but then readily fell to bargaining. At last, for a single Venetian ducat he proved willing to part with me. At which point Lady Caroline gazed at him with contempt so cruel that he was forced to wince as if he had been struck with a whip. "I would pay more for a horse that had no pedigree," she said. From her purse she took a golden florin, which she cast at his feet. "I give you this to spare the child the insult."

Never once had Toma thought of asking his wife's permission to conclude the agreement. When, upon hearing that I was to leave with the Baroness, Rosina rushed forward to protest, she was immediately squelched by her husband.

"She has paid gold! *Gold!*"

"Is this your wife?" Lady Caroline asked. Toma could only answer that she was. "I would speak with her," the Baroness insisted.

"The woman is a teller of great lies," Toma protested. "She lies about me. You can believe nothing she says."

"Nevertheless, I will speak with her. Alone." And she stood her ground. Humbling the man with an icy look, she waited for him to draw off.

Toma, clutching the money the Baroness had given him, backed away with a surly growl. "The woman keeps secrets," he muttered. "Even from me. Perhaps this is not my child. How can a man tell?" At last, muttering black oaths to himself, he trudged off toward the market, leaving the two women to converse.

Lady Caroline took Rosina to one side. For several minutes the women spoke together in hushed voices. I could hear nothing of what they said, but I saw the tears welling from Rosina's eyes. And I saw the Baroness reach out to comfort her. What Rosina imparted to Lady Caroline in that *tête-à-tête*, I would not learn until many years thereafter; but I knew it was of me they spoke. Watching from a distance, I noticed for the first time how unusual a figure Lady Caroline cut. She was tall above the average for a woman, and military-straight in her bearing. As for her costume, that was the most curious feature of all. French ladies of fashion I had seen heretofore were always grandly costumed in great billowing gowns and powdered wigs that balanced like towers atop their heads. This lady was nothing like that. Though she rode in a fine coach and was clearly a person of rank, her dress was austerely simple. She wore no wig, nor did she powder her hair, but simply knotted it back in a tight chignon. More striking still, the clothes she wore might have been borrowed from a man: a frock coat and flowing cravat. Even her skirt had a daringly mannish cut to it, for she wore it drawn high enough to reveal her boots. Did she come from a land where the men and women dressed to look alike? I would not realise it until some time later, but Lady Caroline's fashion represented the advanced social views of her time, a belief in the natural simplicity advocated by M. Rousseau, her homeland's most famous philosopher.

At length, the Baroness completed her dialogue with Rosina and, removing the necklace she wore, coiled it into the Gipsy woman's hand.

"Come, Elizabeth," she said to me, leading me back to her chaise. "Would you like to visit my home?"

I looked about in amazement for Rosina, who was scurrying to gather a few scraps of clothing for me to take along. When she returned, her eyes were glinting with tears. Was I to be allowed to go? I asked. She nodded gravely and said, "Yes, go, little one." And she bent to give me a farewell kiss. "Trust in this good lady," she whispered at my ear.

I entered Lady Caroline's coach, struggling to wipe away as much of the grime from my face as I could. I turned to wave once more to my foster mother, whom I would not see again. I have often thanked whatever angels watch over me that, having been—in effect—sold, I was sold to one who intended me only good. For I might easily have been traded like a slave into a life of degradation.

We had barely left the marketplace of Treviglio when the Baroness removed her glove and bent across the aisle between us to run her long, fine fingers over my brow. I realised as she swept my hair aside that she was feeling for the birth scar I bore at my temple. When she found it, her eyes grew still sadder than was their ordinary expression. "Poor thing!" she whispered in a tone that at once brought tears to my eyes. Then, reaching out, she took me in her arms, and I was consoled at once.

I cannot recall that I hesitated for a moment in following where Lady

Caroline led. I had little more than a child's instinct to guide me; but it served me well. My trust in this strange lady was instantaneous. For the first time in my life, I felt that I was among people of my own stock and station. Moreover, I knew in my heart that this woman was in some sense I cannot even now put into words my spiritual mother—one who cared for my soul more than for my body.

How Victor
Entered My Life

On our journey home, Lady Caroline told me something of her other children, the two boys who, as she assured me, would be delighted to have me as their sister. Ernest, the younger, was almost exactly my age; she said I would find him shy and in need of much patience. And so I did; he was a silent and sullen lad whose dullness of wit was a worry to his parents. Being timid as well as backward, he was never far from his mother's side while she was at home. The moment she entered the house, he would rush to nuzzle close to her like a frightened pup at its mother's breast. From the outset, Ernest, in his excessive need for maternal attention, begrudged me my place in the household, a childish envy that would grow into a life-long hostility. In his eyes I would always be the Gipsy foundling who had filched his mother's love from him. His brother, who was older by two years, was different enough to be the member of another family. Though I was too dozy to spy him on the evening of our arrival, he was upon me as soon as I awoke the next day. The shock of that encounter remains vivid in my mind.

By the time we arrived at the Baroness's villa beside the lake, night had fallen and sleep had overcome me. I have not the least recollection of being taken from the coach and transported by waiting servants to the house. My first night in my new home, I was put to sleep unwashed and in my beggar's rags upon a divan in Lady Caroline's bedchamber. I slept well and long, not waking until early the next afternoon. When I opened my eyes, there before me was the most horrific sight I had ever seen: a livid face streaked with blood and lacerated by scars. Two protruding eyes stared at me, alight with menace. The head of the thing was surrounded with feathers. The creature raised its arms into view; where there should have been hands there were pincer-like claws. I thought at once: *It is the bird-man!*—who had but lately begun to trouble my sleep. I rose up in my bed and screamed with panic.

To my amazement, the monster who stood before me burst out laughing. A boy's laugh! *"Non aver paura, piccola ragazza!"* he commanded in a halting Italian. *"Non ti farò male."*

"Are you real?" I asked.

"Of course I am. There. See?" And he stretched out a claw to touch my face. I leapt back and screamed again. By now the Baroness was in the room.

"Stop!" she cried, drawing the monster away from me. "Can't you see you're frightening her?" She sat down to take me to her breast. "Don't be afraid. This is Victor. Do you remember? I told you about him on our way home last night."

"Does he look like *that?*" I asked.

"Of course not," the boy said. "Can you not see it's just . . ."

He groped for the word he wanted, reverting at last to French.

"Yes," the Baroness said, "Victor is just 'pretending.' You have no reason to fear. Come to me," she ordered her son, "and remove this frightful disguise." The boy began at once to rub away the face-paint he had been wearing, and discarded the claw-like gloves that had covered his hands. "Now attend me, Victor," the Baroness continued, bringing him close to her side. I remember how concentrated his attention became when his mother spoke to him, carefully translating each French phrase into Italian so that I might understand. Though he was still half-smeared with the hideous colours of the monster-thing he had seemed to be, Victor's intense respect for her showed clearly. "Elizabeth is to be your sister—and, as I hope, your more than sister. She is my greatest gift to you, a treasure beyond price. You may not yet understand what I mean by this, but in time I trust you shall. She is yours to love and cherish as if she were the partner of your soul."

Victor looked from his mother to me and for long stood staring with the closest scrutiny. Under his gaze, I felt myself flush with embarrassment, for I understood even less than he what Lady Caroline intended by her remarks. Finally, she placed my hand in Victor's.

"I am here to protect you," the boy said at his mother's bidding, as solemnly as if he were swearing an oath. "I will protect you always, little Elizabeth."

"You didn't protect me. You frightened me," I protested, clinging to the Baroness.

For a moment he reddened with shame. But he quickly waved his emotion away. "Oh that. Just a game. It was meant to amuse you."

"I think he killed my mother," I whispered to Lady Caroline as I burrowed deeper into her embrace.

"What's that she says?" Victor shouted with honest shock. "Killed her mother? Whatever can she mean?"

"Bird-man," was all I would say. "Bird-man! Bird-man!"

It was not until later that day that I saw Victor for the first time relieved of his horrible disguise and as God had made him. There could have been no greater contrast between the ugly thing he had sought to make himself, and his own true appearance. For he was, I thought, the loveliest creature I had ever seen, his face so exquisitely-shaped and cherubic that he might have passed for a girl. His hair, though not so fair as mine, was brightly flaxen and wildly curled, having been allowed to grow uncut until it formed a vibrant nimbus about his features. His eyes were his mother's, a silvered ice-blue, wide and penetrating in their gaze. He was the first boy whose beauty I had ever had occasion to remark. After our distressing encounter he behaved humbly and solicitously toward me, as if to convince me at every turn that he was nothing like a monster. Indeed, he seemed to take Lady Caroline at her word that I was intended as a gift for him, a gift he must treat with the utmost courtesy. On the family's last full day at the lake, as we prepared for our departure, he approached me sporting a great proud grin, his hands behind his back.

"This is for you," he announced, holding forth a small package. "I hope you will like it. It is to welcome you to our family."

The parcel he placed in my hand contained a box about the size of a thin book. When I had unwrapped it I saw that it was a flat glass case, and inside it was a large, brilliantly coloured butterfly almost the size of my hand. Carefully mounted on a purple velvet pad, it was so perfectly displayed I wondered at first if it was perhaps a crafted thing.

"Is it real?" I asked.

"Yes, of course it is. It is my finest specimen. Do you understand 'specimen'? *Una cosa morta . . . da studiare?* I caught this last summer and mounted it as you see."

"I have never seen a butterfly so large."

"It is a moth, not a butterfly. It is an *Acher-on-tia a-tro-pos.*" He picked his way carefully through the phrase, clearly hoping that I should be impressed. "That is what scientists call it. Ignorant people call it a death's-head, because of the pattern, you see? I have a collection of over one hundred specimens. But this is my best. Sometimes the wings come apart when you apply the lacquer. But this one is perfectly preserved. That is why I want you to have it."

"How do you find specimens?"

"You must watch carefully all the time. Each needs to be trapped in a different way. You catch moths like this, see? With a net."

"They are not dead when you catch them?"

"No. You catch them live and then kill them. That is the whole point."

"Kill?"

"Yes. *Uccidi li.*"

"Did you kill all your specimens?"

"Of course. That is what naturalists do."

"How did you kill them?"

"Mostly you suffocate them so they will show no marks. *Asfissiare.* You put them in a jar and fasten the lid tightly. *Tu capisce? No aria.* Then you leave them until they are dead, that is all. You can kill anything that way, as long as you can keep it tightly covered."

"What things have you killed?"

"Only mice and insects. And, oh yes, once a snake. Snakes take longer to kill."

"Why did you kill them?"

He shrugged his shoulders, bewildered. "So that I might study them further. When a thing is dead, you can cut it open and look inside to see how it works."

"But why must you study things? Can't you just look at them and admire them? Butterflies—moths—are very lovely to watch when they are alive."

Victor wrinkled up his face in true incomprehension. "What is the point of that? Anybody can just look at pretty things. What does that tell you?" Sensing my uncertainty about the moth he had given me, he asked, "Don't you want it?"

I could hear the hurt in his voice. "Oh, yes, I do. It's very lovely. Thank you, Victor."

And I saw that he was pleased.

When on the following day we were packed to leave, the valise that Lady Caroline had lent me was barely large enough to hold the clothing and trinkets she had hastily purchased for me in the surrounding villages. I, who had been accustomed to running barefoot in the streets, suddenly owned boots and slippers for every day of the week. Even so, she assured me, this overabundant wardrobe was merely provisional; it would be augmented when we returned to Geneva. And then there was Victor's gift, a poor dead creature forced forever to display the beauty that had cost it its life. I knew I should value it above all else, but I had already decided I would try never to look upon it again.

Our journey to the Frankenstein home was the Odyssey of my young life. I had no idea where the place called Geneva might be; I did, however, know that Switzerland lay beyond the mountains that distantly encompassed the entire western horizon of my village. But only now did I realise that the peaks I had espied from Treviglio were but the foothills of what lay beyond. It was not until we were a full day's travel beyond the lakes that the great Alps rose up before us like the battlements of a giant's castle. For days thereafter, the six brawny horses that laboured in the traces of our carriage drew us ever higher into the chill, knife-edged air of the snowbound passages; warm and secure between the plush panels of the coach, I stared in amazement out the windows across glacial vistas so vast, and down crevices so precipitous, that my mind was set to whirling. The disproportionate immensity of all I beheld staggered my imagination; it so far surpassed all conception that only by a supreme effort of the mind could I believe that these mountain heights form a part of the very Earth we tread each day. As we made our way deeper into the Alpine wilderness, the Earth did indeed vanish from sight. For hours at a time, I might see nothing whatever of the world below us or round us through the swirling banks of cloud that filled the ravines and ghostly mists that sealed every window of our coach. At some sharp turnings, the very road we travelled over disappeared; and in its place the sunlight glancing from the hovering spray of waterfalls created rainbow bridges across the chasms. Thus besieged by the vaporous elements, I was inspired to imagine that we were making our way into a celestial kingdom beyond the heavens.

We travelled as only a patrician family might, accompanied through the mountains by a wagon train loaded with luggage and by a dozen burly postillions on muleback. The road before us was endlessly serpentine and exceedingly steep, overhung on one side by half-distinguishable precipices, while on the other was a gulf filled by the darkness of driving clouds and the sound of dashing streams far below. At times, as we slowly ascended, we were enveloped by violent storms that battered our carriage and melted the narrow road away beneath our wheels; then we might have to make our way for as much as a league by mule or on foot, sheltering as well as we could from the inclement weather while our crew laboured to guide and lift our vehicle over the treacherous ground. Sometimes, as the toiling coachmen negotiated their way ever so delicately around the switchback curves and along the narrow ledges that barely creased the walls of the pass, I hid my eyes beneath my blanket, fearing that we might plummet over the crumbling edge of the road and be lost forever.

At other times, the dizzy heights and ceaseless jostling of the carriage unsettled my stomach and made me fiercely ill. But Lady Caroline had brought with her a relaxing potion and chalybeate waters that eased me into sleep. Across the rocking carriage the Baron watched me quizzically, as if he were wondering what manner of little savage his wife had brought into his family. He was a jolly man, shorter than his wife by a full head and quite stout. His high forehead disappeared above his eyes into great, bushy brows that waggled comically whenever his speech grew animated. His protruding nose was as ruddy at the tip as if it had been rubbed into a glow; beneath it sprouted a flaring moustache, which was stiffly waxed and curled at the tips. In the carriage he wore no wig, preferring to wrap his bald pate in a flowing turban. "Never fear, little one," the Baron assured me whenever he saw me take fright. "My drivers are the best in all Europe. They are surer of their footing in these mountains than the ibex." Then he took me on his knee and pointed out the great peaks on each side, giving each its name as if they were good old friends; for he seemed to have walked among them all. For my sole benefit, the Baron diverted our carriage just before we had entered the rock-bound desolation of the great pass named for St. Gotthard so that I might cast one last look upon the valley where I had spent my childhood. "On that side of the pass," he announced, gesturing across the magnificent vista, "you were a beggar. On this side, you shall be a princess. Are these mountains not a fit barrier to mark so great a change in one's life?"

I was soon debarrassed of all my childish diffidence before this warm, jovial man who seemed to have an endless store of games and stories to pass the time. But most absorbing of all were the tales he had to tell of the many ruined castles and hermitages we passed on our way. These remnants of the hoary past that one spies clinging to the mountainsides and summits at every turn had each a history known to the Baron. Child that I was, I could not tell if his reports were accurate, but they were surely enthralling: narratives of the disasters and vengeances of noble households, of conspiracies and counterplots, of duels and villainies— and of supernatural happenings. It seemed there was not a ruin but had its dread curse, its demon, and its haunting.

So cleverly did the Baron spin his enchanting lore that I scarcely realised his educational intent. He was using my childish whimsy to teach me my new language. For he related all he had to tell by translating between the Italian I knew and the high and courtly French I was expected to learn. "The girl knows the Italian of the Renaissance," he announced; "now she shall learn the French of Enlightenment. And so her journey shall recapitulate the progress of Mankind." In this task the Baroness participated too, seeking to strengthen her sons' Italian as well as my French. But none relished the game more than Victor, who hastened to embellish the ghostly tales. He used his slate and chalk to write and draw all that his father related. Where the Baron, pointing out some distant monastic ruin, told of the ghouls that might haunt its churchyard, Victor quickly drew upon his slate the grave, the waning moon, the casket, and the creeping fiend.

"See? He snatches the body. Ah! The body is not dead. It's alive! It reaches out a bony hand. There, see! The hand takes the demon by the throat." And Victor would enact the drama before my amazed eyes, falling to the floor of the coach writhing and gagging—much to the Baron's amusement. Lady Caroline, for her part, found Victor's excess quite unacceptable, and expressed her strong disapproval, fearing that either I or Ernest would be terrified.

"Come now, my dear!" the Baron chided her. "The girl is learning. She will forget never a word of this astonishing narrative. Go to it, Victor! Dramatise! Rhapsodise! Amaze the child!" And he laughed a great full-bellied guffaw. "By God, she will know more French by the time we are home than King Louis himself—for to judge by that great buffoon's conversation, he cannot carry more than forty words in his head."

So this then was my new father, as attentive a parent as I could have wished for. Never once did I detect the least reservation in him regarding my membership in his family; it seemed sufficient to him that Lady Caroline had decided, in effect, to purchase him a daughter without so much as consulting him in the matter. Her happiness was his only concern; and if that meant taking an unscrubbed foundling into his household, so be it. I also learnt the endless joy my new parents took in conversation, for their talk all along the way was of learned subjects. My French was not yet strong enough to follow all they said; but I would have been left far behind had they spoken in any tongue I knew. For they seemed to carry the entire world in their brains, discoursing at large upon the affairs of distant lands and peoples whose very existence was unknown to me. My new family lived on some loftier plane, breathing an air that was as fresh and bracing as the air above these mountain heights. They talked of wars and commerce and religious matters, of literature and philosophy and inventions. Above all they spoke of Nature, and not only of the mighty mountain vistas we saw about us but of the stars and planets that stretched to the end of space. I soon realised that these, too, were part of the world I was entering, for they were the Baron's constant study. I was given to understand that the mule train that followed behind us included, besides wagonloads of books the Baron had purchased in the cities of Italy, a device called a telescope that would allow me to see the most distant stars as if they were right outside my window. All this awaited me at the end of our journey: a new home, a new country, a new universe.

It became my habit, whenever I dozed in the carriage, to lay my head in Victor's lap, where he delighted to stroke my hair and comfort me as I drifted into sleep, and to sing me little rhymes that attached the words of my new language to childish images I have still not forgotten. Of all these jingles, I remember best the one that endured to become an oft-repeated diversion between us. Drawing the coverlet over our heads, Victor would whisper close as he bent above me,

> *The bee bites at thy rosy cheek*
> *The flea feeds at thy ear.*
> *The nasty gnat nips at thy neck*
> *But I would suck thee . . .* here!

And with the ending of each line, he would kiss the part he named, finishing, after a long, teasing pause, with a noisy peck upon my lips, which left me giggling in his embrace. By the time our journey was completed, our companionship was such that we might have been brother and sister all the years of our lives.

Belrive

Tonight, my dear, you shall sleep upon the bones of barbarian kings." So the Baron announced as, after days of jostling travel, our coach at last turned into the winding road that led to the gates of the Frankenstein home.

"Shall I indeed?" I asked, looking to Victor and the Baroness to explain this extraordinary remark.

"You shall. For Belrive is that old and older. Its foundations might have been laid by Charlemagne himself. Yet even deeper than those foundations we have found the skulls of Helvetian chieftains grinning up at us out of the dust. Dark ages, my child, dark ages. The record of folly, ignorance, and savagery all now laid to rest in the mouldering Earth. And good riddance."

Our journey had taken us within sight of many châteaux in the Alpine valleys, some of them fortresses of great age and grandeur, some little more than ruined hulks. Which of these might my new home be like? I wondered with ever greater anticipation as we made our bumping, creaking way through the final mountain passes and at last beheld Lake Leman, crystal-bright and serene, opened out before us. But as if it were hiding from me until the last possible moment, Belrive made itself invisible from the road. All the while we climbed the steep heights leading up from the lake, I could see nothing of the castle; a dark forest of ancient oaks and towering larch shielded it from view. Even when we entered the drive that approached the front gate, the trees bent on either side of the roadway as if to curtain my vision. Then, suddenly we emerged into a sunny garden where close-cropped bushes stood upon the bright velvet lawn like files of soldiers at attention—and I saw Belrive for the first time.

Though it was not so large as some of those castles I had seen along our route, it was nonetheless an overwhelming vista. Its broad rose-trellised façade of polished granite gleamed in the sunlight, standing fully four storeys tall and flanked at either end by lordly towers whose narrow chimneys and bannered peaks soared still another storey higher. There was such a regal air surrounding the pile, I would not have been surprised if one was expected to offer some act of obeisance before approaching.

As we drew near, the Baron proudly informed me that the wing of the mansion I saw spread so graciously before me was his family's addition to Belrive; he and his father had brought "civility" to this ancient war-like site upon whose battlements rusted cannon were still deployed. Indeed, the newer section of the house looked not at all like a castle, but like a stately home, comfortable though vastly oversized in my trifling view; I had seen nothing so large in all my life other than churches meant to hold whole flocks of people. Only when our coach had delivered us into the central courtyard did I realise Belrive's true dimensions and the complexity of its character. For the newer part of the house attached to two far older wings of a distinctly different appearance. "All this we leave to history," the Baron explained with a wave of his hand. "And to the storage of our disused goods."

The surviving antique portion of Belrive retained the sterner aspect of the true fortress it had once been. Here the towers had only narrow defensive slits for windows; broken fortifications lined the roofs between. Over the centuries the weathered stones had put on a thick garment of vines so that the whole now came to seem complacently vegetative, as if perhaps this were some giant plant that had bulged up out of the Earth.

"And does no one live there?" I asked as I descended from the coach, for I was at once fascinated by this brooding ruin.

"Only the vermin, my dear, and the bats in the eaves."

"And the ghosts!" Victor added mischievously, though by now I knew he was teasing.

"Nay, sir," the Baron corrected. "We have left the ghosts behind us on the road. I rent my home to none such. They are banished from the age. Things of the past, things of the past."

I could not imagine ever calling Belrive my "home," so great was the contrast it made with the hovel where I had passed my childhood. Though it was not the family's only abode (there was a *campagne* across the lake, and a chalet in the nearby mountains), Belrive seemed to me as much of a palace as an emperor might need. On every upper floor were spacious apartments, which, though richly appointed and carefully cleaned, were used only occasionally by guests. One of these would now become mine; "Elizabeth's room," as it was to be called. And, so I was promised, it would be outfitted as finely as I desired from floor to ceiling—though with what I scarcely knew. For what acquaintance had I wish furnishings and curtains and beddings? The entire caravan in which Rosina's family lived had been smaller than this one room; and what filled our Gipsy home had been little better than scraps. I had for so long bedded down on straw and coarse burlap that I felt almost mortified to lay my skin against such smooth, freshly-laundered linen. Even had it been unfurnished, I might have found enough in this one room to delight me for weeks, for its vista was endlessly attractive. It allowed me to see at a sweep the cloudy heights of the Jura beyond the lake, and the snowbound pinnacles to the east. With the aid of a spyglass that Victor gave me, I could pick out the sailboats that plied the lake and trace their course back to the distant harbour of Geneva, which rose like a tiny toy city on its hilltop above the ramparts that ringed it. When the wind was in the right direction, I could just faintly hear the bells of its great cathedral; and at night, when the city folk lit their candles, Geneva glowed in the night like a narrow golden galaxy.

There was a long, proud history to this house and its family. The Frankensteins dated far back into the barbaric origins of German history. Their ancient coat of arms commemorated them as legendary dragon-slayers and warriors of the Crusade; their name was listed among those of the Teutonic Knights who had driven off the invading hordes of the heathen East. During the Wars of Religion, the family had fallen upon troubled times. When the Landgraves of Hesse, their long-time liege lords, became champions of the Lutheran cause, the Catholic Frankensteins were forced to flee their ancestral home. Drawing upon marriage ties with the House of Savoy, they found a new home in Collonge as clients of the dukes from whom they received their new baronial title. Belrive, the estate that came with the title, was far from promising. A typical Medieval mingle-mangle of barren and neglected holdings, it sprawled from its abandoned port on Lake Leman far into the wild wastes of the Voirons. Its château was little more than a mouldering heap of stones inhabited by owls and foxes; once a great Savoyard fortress, it could not have defended the road it overlooked from a light spring breeze. Farmed for generations by a backward peasantry that resisted all change, the domain might have yielded nothing more than debts and disputes in the hands of less energetic seigneurs.

But the first of the barons Belrive was a ruthlessly improving landlord. By dint of tireless ditching and hedging, draining and manuring, he reclaimed Belrive's rich vineyards and put a fat flock of cattle out to pasture. Moreover, he was willing to whip his sluggish tenants into new and better ways. He strictly enforced the use of the horse hoe and the winter turnip upon them until he had compiled the richest rent-rolls in the district. Even so, the family might never have risen beyond middling nobility had not the Baron shaken off the prejudice of his class and sent his oldest son into the city to seek his fortune as a tradesman. Apprenticed to one of Geneva's foremost banking houses, François Frankenstein quickly mastered the arts of money-lending. Drawing upon his family connection, he made himself banker-in-chief to the House of Savoy and was soon a prospering patrician.

"Like all their defunctive kind," the Baron delighted in explaining, "the Savoyards loved nothing so much as making war. And why should an honest banker deny them the means of their own destruction? Which is, not gunshot, but money. Money to burn on the field of battle. Oh, they are a fat source of debt, these feudal rogues! My father picked them clean to the bone, so he did—but with the most gracious good manners. He pledged them to usurious contracts while he dined on squab and champagne at their table. For he was, after all, a baron's son and not a mere Genevan money-lender."

Eventually François became himself the Baron—but reluctantly so. For, as I was given to understand, nothing grates more upon the conscience of a true republican Genevan than to don a title, especially when that title derives from such Papist rascals as the Savoyards. There were those among his city colleagues who mocked him cruelly for so doing. "Though if the truth be told," the Baron boasted, "our family's money has done more to defend the independence of Geneva than all the walls our city fathers ever built. For with one tug upon the purse strings, a tactful banker can lead the mightiest of warlords by the nose as if he were a cart-horse.

"By the time he assumed the title, my father was as thorough a bourgeois as the city has ever seen, and French from the neck up—among the first, I would have you know, to subscribe to M. Diderot's great *Encyclopaedia*. It was he, borrowing from M. Voltaire's own coat of arms, who boldly added the torch of liberty to our family crest. And it was I who added the lightning bolt. Can you guess its meaning, child?"

I shook my head. Though I did not say so, I found it a fearful image, for my evil dream was always lit by flashes of lightning.

"It is the symbol of Enlightenment, more so even than the torch, for it is a power of Nature greater than living fire, waiting only for the genius of man to harness it, a design in which I hope to play some part before my days are over."

The Baron would have me make no mistake: for all his aristocratic bearing, he, like his father before him, was a man of the democratic cause. Nothing filled him with greater pride than to rehearse the human benefits he had ushered into the world. He boasted how he had been the principal force behind the great Genevan pumping station that brought clean water to the tops of the highest hills in the district. *"Noblesse oblige,"* he once instructed me even before I knew the meaning of the term, "but follow where this leads, add good hygiene, and you have the shortest way to equality. The alternative is anarchy."

At the time, these great political lessons meant little to me. What use have children for history unless it can be woven into the stuff of fairy tale and fantasy? I judged by what I saw; and what I saw each day on all sides were furnishings fit for royalty. Clearly, the Baron was one of the wealthiest merchants of the city and had built unstintingly to suit his taste. His home contained great state rooms and sumptuous salons where troops of guests might be entertained. In every room there was a stone fireplace cavernous enough for a child to play in; and in the cool of the morning, as if by some fairy magic, these were set ablaze before the family woke. The fairies were the Baron's staff, on hand to wait on the residents of Belrive throughout the day. This bustling contingent of maids and footmen was like a second family sharing our house, ceaselessly attending to their duties. Just as they provided heat in the morning, so they provided light in the evenings, from the great crystal chandeliers that depended from the ceilings like blazing glaciers, each bearing more candles than I could count; even before the darkness descended, these were punctually set alight by those same elves who moved silently and swiftly through the rooms. I thought back to the one poor candle that had lit our family caravan in Treviglio at night, and to the open campfire outside which might be our only warmth.

Wherever one looked in any room, there were works of art fine enough to make our home a veritable museum. There was not a corridor without its statuary, its shelves of antiquities, its array of weaponry and armour, its richly loomed tapestries. The tapestries were a particular fascination; it was the Baron's delight to use the historical scenes they depicted as woven books in which his children might read the wisdom of ages past. Following in his footsteps as he led us about the house, I learnt of the wars of Caesar and Charlemagne and of the great Crusades that had driven the invading infidel from the Holy Land. One tapestry, the largest in the château, told the story of Hannibal, who had led his squadron of elephants through the passes of the Alpine heights. The Baron, who was a singularly patriotic citizen, relished especially dilating upon scenes from Swiss history. From these I learned of the great battles of Morgarten and Näfels, and the heroic victories over Charles of Burgundy that had kept the proud Swiss cantons free over many centuries, and of the legendary William Tell who, because he would not doff his hat to a tyrant, had inspired the nation to rebellion. But more than once the Baron reminded me that, loyal Swiss that he was, he was before that a Genevan; and even before that he was a Frankenstein; and before all else he was a member of "the party of Humanity."

Other tapestries there were that depicted Biblical scenes, showing how Moses had divided the seas, and how King David had danced at the defeat of the Philistines, and how our original mother and father had been tempted by the serpent. But of these the Baron would say nothing, not even when I asked him directly. Instead he offered a forceful disclaimer. "I speak only of *history*, do you understand? Which, as the wise ancients tell us, is 'morality teaching by example.' You will hear no obscurantistic nonsense about miracles and mysteries in this house! Do you follow me, child? Or do you believe the seas might really part themselves to the left and right because some bearded humbug invited them please to do so?" And, flexing his craggy brows, he fixed me with an irate stare that convinced me I had best question no further—even though he followed his make-believe anger with a wink and a great guffaw. "You will learn, miss. You will learn. I can tell: like your mother, you have been blessed with a masculine intelligence that can divide sense from nonsense the way a sharp knife cuts the mould from the cheese. And if you would have miracles, let them be miracles of Enlightenment." Then, bending close, he asked, "Do you know the names of the stars, my child?" When he learnt I did not, he appointed Victor to be my teacher. Victor took up the assignment with zeal, for he relished showing off what he had learnt from his father.

"Father calls the stars the Great Creator's alphabet," he told me.

"Exactly so!" the Baron approved. "The book of Nature is the only holy book we have been given, and all we require. Remember this!"

Victor taught me all he knew about the stars. And when we had studied all that the naked eye can see, he stood me on a chair before the enormous brass telescope the Baron had brought back from Italy and which was said to be the largest in Switzerland. Through this I viewed unimaginable sights: the spectral mountains of the lunar landscape and the moons of Jupiter.

"The marvels you see there, my dear," the Baron told me, "St. Peter himself could not have shown you if he had worn out his knees praying a thousand years. But Signor Galileo, who gave us new eyes to see such marvels, was very nearly roasted at the stake by St. Peter's pompous disciples. Learn this lesson well, I adjure you!"

"Father is a freethinker," Victor informed me one day with no little pride. But that told me nothing, since I had never heard of freethinking. "He was M. Voltaire's guest at Ferney many times. Moreover, M. Voltaire was once Father's guest here at the château—for three days! *Anybody* could visit Ferney; but for M. Voltaire to come to Father . . . this was no small thing." Having no idea who M. Voltaire might be, I was still no wiser. "Father does not believe in Biblical miracles and such," Victor at last explained. "Nor do I. Nor must you."

I assured him dutifully that I would not, but in my secret thoughts I was still the child of my Gipsy mother. Growing up as I had in an unlettered family, I had learnt the rudiments of faith not from erudite texts, but from the murals and statues that decorated the village church to which I was taken every Sunday. Using these inspiring images with all the skill of her people's story-telling wit, Rosina had taught me that miracles were the very meaning of religion. Her humble catechism had put down such deep roots in my memory that I could not imagine what God might be, or why anybody should pray to Him if He could not stop the sun in the heavens or strike down His enemies from on high. Whenever I passed the Biblical tapestries that filled Belrive, it was not the Baron's fine-honed scepticism but Rosina's entrancing fables that sprang to my mind—and never more so than when I lingered to study one hanging in particular. This was a Renaissance weaving that occupied a darkened corner of the gallery outside my room. It showed Our Lord raising Lazarus from the dead. The fallen man, still draped in his winding sheet, was depicted sitting bolt upright in his sarcophagus; more a corpse than a living soul, his flesh was a cadaverous blue and his livid face aghast with amazement. On all sides, those who watched quaked with awe—as I knew I should if I were there.

"Could such a thing ever happen?" I asked Victor one day as we paused before the tapestry. "Do you believe the dead might rise and walk again?"

"If they could, they would not wish to," Victor answered.

"Why not? Would you not wish to escape from the tomb?"

"Never! Dead things rot; the maggots feed on them until they explode and stink. That is why we hide them away in the ground. I have watched this happen many times with my specimens. The picture does not tell the truth about that, for, see! it shows Lazarus whole and well-formed. But if Jesus had resurrected him after four days in the grave, Lazarus would have become too terrible to look upon. He would have hated Jesus for doing such a thing. But, of course, like all miracles, this too is merely make-believe."

I Meet
"The Little Friends"

Yet there were miracles to behold within the very walls of Belrive. These, the works of man rather than of God, the Baron had saved as a special surprise. One morning at the breakfast table, after the plates had been cleared away, he looked across at Victor, rubbed his hands together in anticipation, and asked, "Well, my boy, don't you think it's high time Elizabeth met our little friends?"

The Baroness smuggled a sly wink in my direction, as if to warn me that some prank was afoot.

"Oh, yes!" Victor cried, and rushed to lead the way.

We passed through the library, whose every wall was lined to the ceiling with books and whose floor was cluttered with navigational and astronomical instruments on which the Baron delighted to discourse. But today we did not tarry with these, but marched instead straight to the huge fireplace at the far end of the room and then stopped with our noses pointing at a stone wall. I looked up, frowning, wondering what we were to do next.

The Baron nodded to Victor, who eagerly stepped to one end of the mantel. Reaching up, he placed his hand upon the carved head of a stag. He sought out one prong of the creature's antlers and tugged at it. The prong moved forward like a lever and I heard a sharp report from behind the wall. In another instant, the panel beside the hearth sprang open. Now I saw that this was no wall but a small door, cleverly disguised to blend with the rough stone of the fireplace. Victor grasped my hand and pulled me forward into the passage that was now revealed; so narrow was the space that it was barely wide enough to admit the corpulent Baron, who had to draw in his well-rounded belly as he followed us. "Coming, coming," he called as Victor rushed ahead with me.

We entered a room whose narrow, barred windows were covered by heavy drapes; these Victor hastened to pull aside, revealing a view of the gardens at the eastern side of the château. The morning sun, now halfway up the sky, struck boldly into the room, disclosing a sight that fairly stopped my breath. I stood in the midst of an entire new population! All about me were men, women, children . . . and they were indeed "little friends," for none of them stood higher than my waist. They occupied the tables and shelves on all sides, staring at me with inquisitive glassy eyes. I was surrounded by a gallery crowded with dolls! Every one was exquisitely crafted and elegantly-costumed. There were kings and queens, knights and ladies, acrobats, dancers, and musicians—and a menagerie of animals, some of them fabulously dressed in boots and hats and fine satins. There was a bear garbed like a general, an elephant adorned like an Oriental potentate, a troop of prancing horses, a silver swan floating on a crystal pond, and a family of foxes in dancing shoes, holding hands in a ring.

"Well, my dear, what do you think of our little friends?" the Baron asked.

"They are the most wonderful toys—"

"*Toys?*" the Baron snapped in mock displeasure. "Indeed! They are nothing of the sort. They are living beings like ourselves." His words made me gasp; but I had no idea what to say in response. I turned in complete confusion to Victor, who at once burst out laughing so boisterously he had to bend double. I looked back to the Baron. "Well, *almost* like ourselves," he now added with a wink. "Victor! Shall we bring our friends to life?"

Victor looked this way and that around the room, then selected the delicate figure of a lady seated at a pianoforte. Except for the porcelain texture of her skin, she was remarkably life-like in appearance. She was dressed in rose brocade, with a high, powdered wig upon her head; on her tiny fingers were rings studded with sparkling jewels, and about her throat was a necklace of gleaming pearls. Victor reached under the piano stool; I heard a faint click. And all at once, the tiny woman moved. Her head turned and nodded directly at me. Then her hands moved to the left and right. I saw each finger bend and press as she brushed them lightly one way and the other over the keyboard. And, lo! music filled the room, a gem-like tinkling air I recognised as a lullaby. I blinked in amazement. The tiny pianist cocked her head to listen at the keys, then looked back at me and nodded again daintily. Meanwhile, Victor had moved on. He had stopped at a table where a turbaned blackamoor sat cross-legged on a velvet cushion sucking a hubbly-bubbly pipe; at a touch from Victor, the figure reached to take up a flute and hold it to his lips. A reedy sarabande arose to compete with the pianist's lullaby.

"Put your finger just here," the Baron told me, placing my hand above the holes of the flute. I could feel a tiny draught of air: the black-amoor's breath blowing through the instrument. "There is a bellows here in his chest," the Baron explained, "that will make music as sweetly as any human lung." Behind the blackamoor, a richly inlaid cabinet swung open, and out glided a veiled *danseuse,* who bent and twisted to the exotic strain. On her delicate finger there perched a tiny canary that wagged its tail, opened its beak, and twittered. The little dancing lady attitudinised in a perfectly fascinating manner, but before I could take in the details of her performance, Victor had set several more dolls to working. The elephant bent forward to balance on its tusks, the swan glided forward and back preening its feathers, the horses reared and gamboled, the foxes performed a skipping dance to still another music.

"Well, now," the Baron said, "you see how much more these are than mere toys. These, my child, are automata." He bent low to whisper the words as if they were some awful mystery. *"The very secret of life is in them."* I stared at him in speechless bewilderment. "Perhaps . . . *perhaps* they are smarter than you are, my dear," he continued, tapping his forehead gravely. "You do not believe me, eh? Victor, shall we have Herr Doktor Heinrich join us?"

At once, Victor dashed to a rear shelf and brought back a bearded doll dressed in a scholar's cap and gown. At Victor's touch, the figure sat up tall in its chair and turned its head to left and right.

"Herr Doktor!" the Baron declaimed. "I want you to meet Mlle. Elizabeth. Go ahead, my dear, shake his hand."

And I did, giving the waxy little fingers of his left hand a delicate tug. His right hand, I saw, held a quill alertly positioned above a sheet of paper. The doll bowed and stared up at me. "Now, tell us if you can, Elizabeth," the Baron said, "What is the product of seven and seventeen? Quickly!" And he snapped his fingers in my face once, twice, thrice. Even if I could have done the calculation so quickly, his manner would have stymied my mind. I confessed I did not know; for I had learnt my multiplication tables only up to the fives—and even so, not very securely. "Ah, you see! Herr Doktor," the Baron said, turning to the doll and shaking his hand once again. "Did you hear? *Seven times seventeen.*"

Herr Doktor nodded and winked. With a jerky motion, the hand that held the quill reached to one side to dip the pen-point in a tiny inkpot that rested on the desk across his knees. With consummate precision, Herr Doktor drew "7×17" on the sheet of paper that lay upon the desk. After a moment he added an "$=$." And a moment later the number 119.

"Which is exactly right!" the Baron announced.

At this I gasped with amazement, looking to the Baron and to Victor for a word of explanation. At my side, Victor was unable to restrain a certain cynical merriment; he cupped his hands at my ear to say, "It is the only sum he knows, the stupid oaf!"

The Baron, overhearing, frowned. "Not so!"

"It *is* so!" Victor insisted. "Unless we change his brains."

"His *brains?*" I asked.

"For each sum," Victor explained, "we must take one set of brains out and put in another. See? Here are his brains." And he turned the doll around. Lifting its coat, he showed me what lay beneath: an intricate tracery of wheels and levers and springs.

"Yes, by all means inspect Herr Doktor's brains," the Baron said, "for this is the true miracle." He took a lens from his waistcoat pocket and held it out to me so that I might scrutinise the mechanistical labyrinth that filled the puppet's body. "You see how tiny these works are? You might think that only a spider can spin such a fine fabric. Yet year by year these works grow smaller—as tiny and delicate as the works inside our best watches." He drew out a watch he had often shown me; on its round face it displayed the sun and moon moving with the precision of the seasons. "One day, when we can make the parts small enough, we will pack all possible sums into one set of brains. And perhaps very much more besides. Herr Doktor may one day carry my entire library about inside him. What do you think now, my dear?"

I looked to Victor and back again to the Baron. "But how could that be?"

"If already these little people can write and sing and play, where is the limit, I ask you? We have one little fellow here who plays chess, would you believe it?"

"Only two moves," Victor corrected contemptuously. "He can move his pawn and his knight. And always the same move."

"Ah, but he is learning, he is learning. One day—can you doubt it?— he will surely be able to make three moves, and then four . . . and finally, who can say, eh? Who can say?"

"Did you make all these?" I asked the Baron.

He broke into a hearty laugh. "Lord, no! These are the creations of Switzerland's most gifted scientists. I am no more than their patron."

"They are not *scientists* at all," Victor protested with a surprising show of impudence. "They are only watchmakers."

"Nonsense!" the Baron retorted. "They are practical men of science, true natural philosophers—not such as lose themselves in clouds of theory. One day, I warrant you, they shall be able to fashion living entities so like ourselves that you will not be able to tell if they are human beings or automata." Noting the cross expression that had come over Victor's face, he added, "My son, as you see, questions my prediction. Well, judge for yourself, my dear. See here, what M. Vaucanson has achieved." I was led across the room to a stand beneath one of the windows; it clearly occupied the place of honour among the Baron's exhibitions. Behind us the little dolls continued to nod and dance and play, though I noticed that the elephant had stopped in the middle of a headstand, and the dancing girl was now barely creeping. On the stand before me was the life-sized replica of a duck, so real in appearance that, but for its stillness, one might almost mistake it for the living original. At first I assumed it was a stuffed trophy. But then Victor reached around behind the stand to search out a switch. I heard a sharp click; from the duck a whirring and ticking sound emerged. All at once, the little bird opened its beak and emitted a harsh quack that was very like a true duck's call. Its head turned, its wings fluttered, and it quacked again.

"Go ahead, my child," the Baron said. "Feed him."

"Feed him?"

"Yes, here." And he handed me a few dried seeds from a bowl that lay on the stand. Cautiously I held a seed out to the tiny automaton. The Baron pressed a switch and the beak popped open to receive the food. The next instant the seeds were gone, and the beak clacked up and down as though the duck were eating. "Again," the Baron ordered, and still, "Again." After I had inserted several seeds into the chomping beak, there was another sharp quack. I looked round to Victor to ask, "But where have the seeds gone?"

"Watch!" said Victor, giggling. He pressed another switch; I heard wheels and springs whirring; the duck's wings fluttered, and presently, from its rear area, a tiny pellet emerged. "He shat!" Victor explained with a loud guffaw. "That is where the seeds went—right through him."

"The secret of alimentary chemistry!" the Baron announced. "There! You have observed it before your eyes." Seeing my gaze of blank incomprehension, the Baron bent close to explain further. "Electro-magnetic fluid! The basis of life itself. M. Vaucanson has included it in his invention. He is the greatest natural genius of our time. I prize his creation more than all the rest."

We spent fully two hours that morning exploring the Baron's chamber of marvels. I was shown automata that spoke and sang and performed acrobatic manœuvres; I listened to tiny mechanical violinists and harpists and guitarists. The Baron fairly bubbled with pride as Victor brought out one after another of his father's "little friends" to meet me. "What you see in this room," the Baron informed me, "is our family's most precious possession, the finest collection of its kind in the world. That is why I keep it here in this hidden chamber. But already I am laying plans to build a museum; and then my little friends will belong to the world for all to see and admire. This will be our family's gift to man's deeper understanding of life."

Victor knew all the dolls and demonstrated how they worked, though I could follow little of what he said. "This one," he boasted, taking up a clown that swung on a trapeze, "I have taken apart and put back together." I displayed the amazement he seemed to want. I found him to be more taken with my reactions than with the dolls themselves; for while the Baron beamed with pride to see how I admired his collection, Victor seemed often to be bored.

"I once believed all these dolls were alive," he told me later that day, "when I was a child like you. I was much disappointed to learn how misinformed I was. As you see, Father believes stoutly in the mechanical philosophy; he wishes me to share his conviction. But these are really nothing more than toys, as you said. They are not alive, or anything like it."

"Father believes so."

"But he is wrong! You touched the dolls. They are not made of flesh and blood and nerve as we are. They are only imitations of life made of wood and wire and porcelain. See here, my hand? Even the tip of my smallest finger is more wonderful than all the dolls in Father's museum. Because this is living tissue! It can bleed, it can burn and freeze, it can hurt, it can . . . *feel.* A living thing should be made of flesh, as we are. The dolls play music, but they cannot hear what they play; they dance, but they do not enjoy dancing. Who would want to be a machine—even if you could be as clever as clever can be?"

"But you have told me that living tissue must one day moulder in the

Earth and become hideous. Perhaps then the dolls are a better thing to be, for they shall never rot and perish."

"That is true," Victor answered, pondering my words carefully. "Still I think it would be better to perish than never to have been alive."

"How did Herr Doktor do the sum?"

"Oh, pff! The doll does not truly calculate; it has no brain at all, only gears and springs. It simply draws with its hand whatever number its inner works were created to draw. Sometimes it is 95 or 123 or 437. Father knows beforehand what number it will write on the paper; he sets it a sum that the doll would write anyway. It is just a trick. True science is far more than tricks."

"What is *science*?"

"It is a sea vaster than any man has sailed, as boundless and dark as the universe. When I think of voyaging on that water . . . my head nearly aches with questions." Then, catching himself in a sort of revery, Victor burst into laughter. "I shall tell you what science is *not*. It is not something little girls are suited to know about."

"But why not?"

He squinted at me playfully. "Quick! What is the sum of 150 and 72 and 33? Quick, I say!" And he snapped his fingers at me.

"Oh! I cannot think so quickly."

"There. That is why. You have no head for mathematical calculation. Nor has M. Vaucanson, for all my father's praising him. He is a clever tinkerer, that is all. Life is a greater mystery than any watchmaker will ever construe, that much I know."

"Victor . . ."

"Yes?"

"Would you tell me just one thing I want so very much to know?"

"Yes—what?"

"What is the sum of 150 and 72 and 33? Quickly!" And I snapped my fingers under his nose.

"Why, it is . . ." But before he could work out the answer—for he had as much need as I to reckon the total—I had stuck out my tongue and dashed away giggling, with him in pursuit. When he caught me, as

I wished him to, he wrestled me about roughly and pinned me against the wall, my arms stretched above my head and my breast pressed tight against his. I often teased him like this so he would chase me and hold me and set me all aglow.

"Two hundred and fifty-five!" he answered. "Which is the number of blows I shall give you for your impudence, you little mischief!"

But instead of blows, he pressed a kiss upon me, which I pretended to resist, thus forcing him to hold me more roughly. *Again, again!* I cried inside my mind when he removed his lips. But outwardly I squealed, "Stop! You mustn't!"

"Why do you tell me to stop when it is what you want?" he asked.

"You cannot tell what I want," I protested, struggling free of his grip. "I am not one of your mechanical dolls that you can take apart and know its secrets." But if there was anger in my reply, it was as much at myself as at Victor. For I could not understand this divided feeling, this wanting to say both yes and no.

I was to visit the Baron's private museum many times again; and each time I was shown still more amazements. Yet as wondrous as the Baron's little friends were, it troubled me when he spoke of them as living entities. For these were, at last, lifeless contrivances, which neither saw nor heard nor felt; like Victor, I could not ignore their obvious artificiality. The very fact that they were as life-like as they were made their ingenious artifice the more chilling to me. Could the Baron, in his enthusiasm, truly not tell how great was the difference between these automata and their human model? Was *I* no more in his eyes than a doll that might be disassembled and reassembled by a watchmaker's tools?

These thoughts I often took to bed with me at night, bewildering questions of life and death that surpassed my childish understanding. Then, in the privacy of my own imagination, the little friends took on a more ominous demeanour. I saw them sometimes smiling superciliously at me, as if they were as curious about my inner workings as I had been about theirs. And once I dreamed that they had gathered round my bed, alien and inquisitive intruders, deliberating among themselves.

"How does she *see?*" the lady pianist was asking. "Let us take out these strange glassy orbs she calls her eyes and inspect them."

"How does she speak?" the blackamoor was asking. "Let us take out this flickering little ribbon of flesh that she calls her tongue and examine it."

"And this fluttering heart," another said.

"And these breathing lungs . . ."

I tried in my dream to rise and flee, but discovered they had found some way to immobilise my limbs so that I could scarcely lift them.

"And her blood," another said. "What is that?"

After that night, I did not ask to see the little friends again.

What I Discovered
of My Ancestry

You are a princess in my eyes and always shall be. This has nothing whatever to do with worldly inheritance. Yours is a nobility of soul, not of titles and emblems."

This was Lady Caroline's answer when I first brought up the subject of my parentage. As I grew older, it was inevitable that I should become more inquisitive about the story Rosina had told of my royal lineage. Was there any truth to it at all? Who was the unnamed father I knew only as a "king of the South"? And who was the unfortunate mother I remembered as belonging to English royalty? Since I knew of my birth and parentage only through tales told by an untutored Gipsy mother, all this might have been the stuff of fairy tale. Or it might mean that regal blood ran in my veins.

I was amazed at how lightly my new mother brushed aside these questions—as if she had no interest in stories of high birth. "Perhaps your first mother had need of such flights of fancy in her poor life; I do not. You see, my dear, I, who was born a pauper and have been careful to retain a pauper's eye—I have lived among these titled folk; I have seen them drunken at table, and heard their vicious chattering gossip in the salon, and seen them busy all night with mischief that you are too young even to imagine. I know their true worth. If one could buy any prince among them for what he is *truly* worth, and sell him for what he *thinks* he is worth, one could become richer than Croesus by that single transaction. Let me assure you, if you were an emperor's daughter, that would tell me nothing I wished to know about your goodness of heart. Always remember that all men, though they are everywhere in chains, were born free. In the eyes of heaven, we are equals all. That is the great lesson of our age, though it has yet to be learnt by many of our most celebrated minds. But it shall, it shall! Even if it must be written for them in letters of blood."

Even when I drew for her what I remembered of my father's crest of arms, Lady Caroline showed only mild amusement. Letting her finger lazily trace the double eagle and the winged lions I had crudely sketched, she remarked, "You shall have much to do in your life with fabulous beasts, my dear; but they will be of far greater significance than mere heraldic symbols."

Strange to say, it was my new father who proved the more eager to know the truth of my heritage. Learning of Rosina's tale, he became intensely curious about my family. "It may be that we have dined at this very table with your aunts and uncles and sisters and brothers," he announced one night at dinner. This was entirely likely. A steady stream of titled guests came calling at Château Belrive, which functioned for travelling notables like a hotel on the roads between Italy and France and the German states. I had no idea what their business might be; I know that they often insisted on taking the Baron aside for hours at a time to speak of matters that could be mentioned only behind closed doors. Thus, at our dinner table I had met princes and counts and duchesses, as well as ambassadors and ministers of state and diplomatic envoys bustling between the royal courts of Europe. Any of these might be my relations. Many came from Italy—from Milan itself. Might one of these guests have known my true father or mother or their families?

I later learnt that it was this very prospect—the possibility that people of my own blood might come visiting—that made Lady Caroline so reluctant to enquire into my family background. For what if the Baron should succeed in finding my relations? Would she not have to give me up to them? For this reason (as I later discovered) she swore my father to a solemn pledge that he would make no open enquiry about me, nor announce any speculative conclusions about my ancestry, without first consulting her. He agreed, but remained as fiercely curious as ever, and especially about the possibility that I was related to the English ruling house. "What if this little ragamuffin has a claim upon King George's throne?" he asked only half-jokingly. "The English have replaced an imbecile monarch before this. Perhaps we are harbouring England's destined agent of Enlightenment in our very home. For the child, just as she stands in her shoes, could not make a worse ruler than George Booby."

I was too young to understand the deep implications that underlay what the Baron said about political matters. The revolutionary currents running in Europe were beyond my childish ken; but I could easily understand what it meant to know one's own parents. In time, however, as the passing years made enquiry less fruitful and as I became more and more a child of the Frankenstein family, my history melted back into a cloud of fanciful speculation that was never to be lent the substance of fact. I preferred to think of myself as one who had been triple-born: by my first mother into life, by my second into childhood, and by my third into womanhood.

EDITOR'S NOTE
On the Ancestry of Elizabeth Frankenstein

It was a matter of the greatest curiosity to me to trace whatever might still be discovered regarding Elizabeth Lavenza-Frankenstein's ancestry, especially with respect to her recollection of high birth. Thus, in the summer of 1806, when I was able to undertake my exploratory journeys upon the Continent, I made a point of enquiring into the accuracy of Elizabeth's childhood memories. I had little to go on beyond Elizabeth's recollection that her father was of the Milanese nobility and had been on his way to battle when he stopped at her caravan to bid her good-bye. Unfortunately, the historical archives of Milan, the obvious starting point for my investigation, had been ransacked and largely destroyed by the victorious revolutionary forces that had, in alliance with Napoleon's armies, established the Cisalpine Republic. In this delicate political situation, I found no one in the city willing to discuss the banished ruling household, let alone to admit a family connection with it. I confess that, after a certain point in my enquiries, I sensed that my interest in Milan's *ancien régime* might actually be attracting the suspicion of the town's revolutionary authorities and possibly endangering my safety. One must remember that these were troubled political times.

As for the war that Elizabeth recalled, and which I placed in the early 1770s: this was so unsettled a period of dynastic skirmishing in European affairs that one could hardly tell the wars one from another. Histories of the time do mention that the Duchy of Milan was embroiled in the Russo-Turkish War as the reluctant ally of Austria; I discovered that the Duke had sent his son, Prince Alessandro, into the Crimea in 1773. A visit to the town cemetery revealed a monument commemorating the death of the Prince in the following year. Beyond this, I could find no family records for the man, neither his birth nor his death. A search of the surviving ecclesiastical register at the Cathedral of Milan yielded mention of a marriage contracted between Alessandro and a daughter of the House of Farnese of Parma five years before his demise. The wife's name was given as Juliana, but I experienced little success in tracing her or her family. As for the name Elizabeth, I came upon it nowhere.

But what of Elizabeth Frankenstein's childhood recollection of a coat of arms, a drawing of which she had affixed to her memoirs? What might this distant memory reveal? It was not the device of any Italian aristocratic household I could locate. Upon my return to London, therefore, I hastened to take the little sketch to the College of Arms, whose curator made an instant identification. "The double axe has been placed in the wrong quarter," he observed, "but there is only one crest that combines the axe with the double eagle. It is not Italian but German. The House of Saxe-Gotha, which belongs to our own royal lineage by way of the Hanover succession."

"Can this house be in any way connected to the Duchy of Milan," I asked, "say, as of the late eighteenth century?"

My learned informant puzzled over the point, then shook his head. "Not to my immediate knowledge. But then the German nobility of that era present a peculiarly complex genealogy. There was much inter-marrying."

The crest, then, was from the mother's side, not the father's: an English connection by way of German lineage. With that much of the mystery solved, I left him with the name Elizabeth and asked if he might do his best to trace the matter for me. He agreed, and some weeks later sent the note I here attach.

Sir:

The records of the House of Saxe-Gotha do in fact list a child of Count Albertus of Gotha named Elizabeth. Little is known of her; she died in 1773 at the age of nineteen and was, as far as can be ascertained, unmarried. The Count's biography credits him with diplomatic service from the year 1764 to 1775 at the court of Milan. Beyond this, I can tell you nothing more.

Hoping this information is of some help to you, I remain

Yours faithfully,
D———
Chief Archival Officer,
Royal College of Arms

Though this settled nothing with certainty, it allowed for a plausible hypothesis. Might it be that Elizabeth of Saxe-Gotha accompanied her father on his diplomatic mission to Milan and there became the mistress of Prince Alessandro? In that station she might have given birth to a daughter who was noble of blood but illegitimate. This might explain the young prince's otherwise puzzling decision to send the newly-born child into seclusion with the Gipsy midwife, the better to conceal her existence.

I Find My
Intellectual Companion

More than my home, Belrive was my school. Between the château and the city, there was a constant coming and going of tutors, all for the benefit of the Baron's children, who were meant to become the very models of Enlightenment. Morning and afternoon, as often as the weather permitted, our teachers made their way from the city by coach or boat. Herr Dienheim, a distinguished German scholar who never failed to boast that he was a member of King Frederick's Berlin Academy, taught us the classical languages with a strictness that might have been onerous in the extreme had he not possessed the wit to make our lessons as much a game as a discipline. "Herr Fritz," as Victor slyly called him when he was not within earshot, seemed to have invented a clever trick for remembering every idiom and irregular declension. We learnt music from the elegant Mme. Branicki; she, though now a woman of advanced years whose fingers were less than limber on the keyboard, had performed as a girl prodigy at the courts of Queen Catherine of Russia and King Louis of France. From her we acquired as much history as musicality, and not a little courtly gossip. Mme. Eloise, the Baroness's personal maid, was responsible for my training in French and for my deportment; but her special passion was for dancing, at which she still exhibited the grace of a woman half her age.

In the Baron's view music and dance were all very fine for a young girl to learn for reasons of deportment; but their true value in his estimation lay in another direction entirely. "Harmony, rhythm, counterpoint," he explained, "are *mathematical* arts: calculation put to melody. They prepare the mind to read the eternal laws of nature. That is their quintessential worth." Accordingly, I was brought before Signor Giordani, a Paduan scholar under whose supervision Victor had already progressed in the study of calculation as far as algebra. "The little lady is to learn mathematics?" he asked with great surprise. "Does the Baron mean perhaps arithmetic?"

"Indeed, sir, I do not. For that she already knows. I mean the higher mathematics."

"No, no, no, no, that is not possible," Signor Giordani protested in his chirping Italian tenor. "The female brain, it is devoid of *l'esprit géométrique*. This will be like pouring fine wine into a sieve."

"With respect to that, sir," the Baron replied indignantly, "you may wish to consult my wife, who seems to have little difficulty whatever in reading the treatises of Messieurs Descartes, Pascal, and Lagrange. Perhaps she will be able to convince you of your error."

"Ah, but the Baroness is an extraordinary woman," Signor Giordani protested. "She has the intellect of a man."

"Then let us see if the same may not be true of my daughter, sir," the Baron insisted. "For how can we tell without fair trial which of our women may not be harbouring masculine faculties of mind?"

Signor Giordani reluctantly agreed to his assignment, but I was to prove him a better judge of female limitations than the Baron; in truth I was most ungifted at calculation. While geometry proved well within my aptitude, for it was a science of visible forms that might be drawn upon the page, algebra and the calculus sifted away from me like sand through my fingers, leaving only a few grains behind. When I ashamedly confessed this to Lady Caroline, she showed no great concern. "Apply your mind to what it loves," she said. "The world has more than enough clever calculators in it."

"But the Baron wished me to prove that a girl can be as proficient as a boy at numbers."

At this she was greatly amused. "Oh, did he? Then let me tell you, my dear: the Baron has never been able to find his way through Pascal's triangle, for indeed he has no great head for numbers himself. But I daresay I could teach every maid in the château to do so, including those who cannot read a word."

As important as my teachers were, I learnt far more in the salon and at the dinner table than at my pupil's desk, for at Belrive instruction was constant and as near at hand as the air I breathed. In the travelling season, no transient philosopher, artist, or man of letters crossing the Alpine passes failed to accept the Baron's open invitation. Belrive was the most famous gathering place of great minds in Geneva (and, therefore, the Baron would have insisted, in the whole of Switzerland, for, in his view, Geneva was to the rest of the cantons "as the brain is to the belly"). Here they came to hold forth, to lecture, and to display their mental wares in return for the most generous hospitality short of a royal court.

This was in large measure what made Victor so intolerably smug; he claimed that when he was no more than an infant he had been dandled on the knees of the greatest men of science. I had no idea who the likes of Baron d'Holbach or the Abbé Condillac might be, but I had met the man of whom Victor boasted most and took to be his model in life: Professor Saussure, who was his godfather as well as his life-long tutor. Professor Saussure, a frequent visitor to Belrive, was spoken of across Europe as the greatest of all Swiss natural philosophers. He could discourse on the heavens and the Earth and all that lay between. He was, besides, the most daring of mountaineers, having scaled the most challenging peaks in the Alps, all except Mont Blanc. For the conquest of that forbidding summit, he had posted a prize, which Victor, like all the youth of Switzerland, aspired one day to claim. When Professor Saussure came visiting, Victor might be closeted with him for hours examining the many instruments the professor brought to the château. This remarkable man seemed to spend his life devising machines for measuring everything that I, as a child, found immeasurable. His instruments weighed the air, gauged the moisture of the clouds, computed sunlight, and even calibrated the blueness of the sky. When once, with frank naïveté, I asked why such things needed to be measured at all, I evoked his condescending laughter. "First we measure, demoiselle," the professor answered, "then we master." Another of the professor's inventions was a small glass globe in which were suspended two tiny balls of pith that allowed one to measure electricity. The Baron, who was the professor's patron, regarded Saussure's electrometer as the most remarkable achievement of the century. But so tiny was the spark that flew within the vessel that, even pressing my eye hard against the glass, I could see nothing at all and was left to wonder if perhaps this was a hoax. Why, I wondered, did the Baron think it superstitious to believe in angels that only saints could see, when it was not so to believe in leaping sparks that only professors from the Academy could see?

Much as Victor might admire Professor Saussure, I was deeply thankful that his quality of mind differed greatly from that of his idol. Otherwise he might have been another "clever calculator" and nothing more. But Victor had, in his childhood, discovered a greater teacher than any of the tutors who came calling. And this was Belrive: I mean the house itself, which was everywhere endowed with a magic that called childish fantasy to life. In the Scriptures one reads, "In my Father's house are many mansions." So too Belrive, *my* father's house, was a place of many mansions, intangible chambers of the mind hiding treasuries of knowledge in their every nook and corner. I could scarcely move from one room to the next without finding my imagination taken captive. Most obviously there were the collected masterpieces that filled the house. Much that I know of history and letters still appears before my mind's eye in the shape of the Baron's great tapestries and historical canvases glowing with fancies of the Renaissance. But there were other, subtler occasions for instruction; and these I discovered thanks to Victor, who was eager to reveal the secret resources of the château to me. From him I learnt that there was not a stick of furniture in Belrive, not a cupboard nor a cabinet nor a shadowed cornice, that might not yield amazements—if one had but the fanciful vision to spy them out and the wit to lend them animation. He taught me to make every carving, every filigree, every armorial bearing upon the walls an occasion for rhapsody. This, the habit of imagination, was his greatest gift to me, and in its exercise we first became the intellectual companions we would remain for life.

That the château at night became a place of tenebrous enclaves and gloomy galleries only fed one's fancy more. Painted things and sculptured shapes might then seem to come alive in the flickering candlelight. "See there," Victor might say, his voice falling into a warning hush as we passed along some darkened corridor. And he would point to an ornate lacquer chest imported by the Baron from Tartary or the coasts of Arabia. "Can you see the ogre that lies in wait for us there?" Then, creeping close, he drew with his finger the leering face he had found hidden among the tangled vines. Or perhaps he would pause before an armoire laden with chinaware to light the painted plates with his candle, insisting that we weave stories round the scenes we saw there. "Say what the unicorn is telling the maiden," he would order me, pointing to the depiction of a princess in a garden. "Is he her friend or foe? If she mounts him, where will he run with her?"

There was not a wall or moulding in the castle but had been embellished by some musing artisan to tell a tale. Chivalric episodes—the adventures of knights and their ladies, evil wizards and infidel warriors—were everywhere to be seen, recalling the high days of King Arthur and Count Orlando. If one studied closely, a menagerie of fantastic beasts—dragons and chimeras, minotaurs and gorgons, centaurs and mermen—could be found wandering in the stove tiles and table legs we lived amidst each day. From the chiming clock outside the Baron's library I learnt the Olympian deities whose images marked the hours on its face; and in the marquetry that lined my bedroom shutters I read the legend of tragic Tristram and the fair Iseult that, scene by scene, some nameless craftsman had inscribed upon the panels. How vividly I recall Victor telling me the story, not all at once, but lingeringly over many nights as he carefully traced each picture in the wood and gave the lovers voice. It was the first tale of high Romance I had ever heard; it gripped my heart to know that there could be such love. "And see here," he said as he came to the final panels, "this is Lord Tristram's jealous wife. She wickedly tells the dying knight that the sail she spies upon the sea is black instead of white; and so he thinks his beloved lady will not come, and dies despairing. Listen! You can hear how poor Iseult moans and moans as she holds him in her arms. Her heart is breaking; she cannot live without him; and at last she dies to join with him in death. See here how the trees that grow from their graves braid their branches overhead."

"Would they die for love?" I asked. In vain I tried to fight back the tears his words had summoned up, so feelingfully had he recreated the tale.

Victor, studying me closely, reached out a curious finger to touch the sorrowing drop he spied upon my cheek. "This is merely literature, *piccola ragazza*," he answered. "It needs to be true only for as long as the story lasts." At which I determined I would make the story true again every night of my life, imagining myself as the grieving queen and Victor the dying knight in my arms.

The Evil Pictures

ut of all the works that filled Belrive, none were to have greater influence than the evil pictures. And these, too, Victor brought to my acquaintance.

It was upon an idle winter's day when no tutors could fare the impassable roads from the city. We had passed our time that morning studying the life of Jeanne d'Arc as it was preserved in one of the Baron's tapestries. "She was burnt for a witch," Victor told me. "But then the church changed its mind and named her a saint."

I was prompted to ask: "Do you believe there were ever witches?"

"But there *are*. And I can show you them." At which an impish gleam that I had learnt to dread came into his eye; it was often the prologue to some irksome prank. "Wait here," he ordered and took off at a run, soon to return with a great jangling ring of keys that I recognised as belonging to Joseph, the Baron's major-domo.

"We must return these before Joseph misses them," he informed me with an air of intense furtiveness. With a stealth meant to exaggerate the daring of our adventure, Victor led me to the rear of the château and thence to the oldest tower of the house, an unpopulated ruin (as I thought) whose narrow windows had long since been grown over by vines. Here he struck a flint and lit a rushlight to guide us along the tightly-spiralling stairs. Up and up the cramped and lightless passage we wound, at every landing passing fastened doors, some of whose locks had rusted with age. Lit by our unsteady light, the tower assumed an ever more supernatural aura; but more than I feared any ghosts, I dreaded we might encounter rats or spiders along the way, and kept a wary eye. To my surprise, as ancient and crumbling as the stonework of the tower was, the stairs were swept clean as if they might only recently have been used. Nor did the air, while close, seem as stale as I expected. Clearly others had passed along this way.

When we had reached the top storey of the house, Victor paused and there swore me to secrecy. Only then did he use one of Joseph's keys to open a ponderous door that led into the south wing of the château. I had been told that the apartments here were empty—unoccupied for generations and used only for storage. But I entered with the greatest trepidation, for I had, on several occasions, glancing from my bedroom window, seen someone moving in this part of the house. And after dark I had seen a candle, carried by an invisible hand, glide along the corridors.

Once inside, we passed with the utmost stealth down an unlit hall toward a chamber that was also under lock and key. This door was soon opened; we stepped into the musty interior, whose windows were heavily curtained. There was an air of guilty secrecy about this room that seemed thickly menacing. "Look," Victor commanded in a hushed voice. He drew back a curtain—but only a little, so that I could not at first see more than a row of framed rectangles upon the walls round me; then he uncovered part of one window at the end of the room, allowing a revealing shaft of light to penetrate the gloom. The images that lined the walls captured my attention immediately. I saw wispy figures floating through darkly shaded woods, garbed in pale robes that lent them a spectral aspect. The execution of these canvases, as I would learn in later life, was crude, even primitive in comparison to the Baron's many masterworks. But these, Victor let me know, were not part of the Baron's collection. "He is ashamed of these," Victor whispered as we passed along the line of canvases, many of which hung unframed on the wall. "That is why they are hidden away up here."

It was not, however, the artistic quality of these works that absorbed my attention; rather it was the air of unearthly strangeness that surrounded them. For though I saw in the pictures the mountains and forests that surrounded us, these familiar landscapes took on a peculiar mystery. Mostly scenes of night lit only by some waning remnant of the moon, they were touched with a phantom phosphorescence. And, most arresting of all, through this ghostly light moved robed figures, all of them women as far as I could tell, though their faces were hidden under shadowing hoods. By some magic of the brush, the artist had bestowed an eerie and ominous animation upon them. But what were they doing in this haunted woodland? In one picture, they lay face-down with arms outstretched upon the Earth; in another, they were bent as if in prayer before a painted stump festooned with all manner of trinkets; in another, following behind women playing flutes and drums, they danced hand-in-hand among the moonlit trees, heads thrown back and mouths open to the night sky as if howling. Uncanny the pictures were—but I saw nothing "evil" in them, such as Victor had promised.

"Why do you say they are evil?" I asked.

"Because they are *witches!*" Victor hissed the word in a scandalised whisper. "See here?" And he summoned me over to a set of pictures in which the figures—again all women—were unclothed. I felt a blush come over me; close beside me as I studied the canvas, Victor seemed hardly able to stifle his hilarity at my embarrassment. I had already learnt from the celebrated works in the Baron's collection that a nude body, especially that of a woman, may permissibly be shown in a work of art. But when nudes appeared in such classic paintings, they were well-formed and unblemished, the bodies of goddesses all but marmoreal in their smoothness. In the works I speak of now, the bodies were presented with no hint of either modesty or refinement. On the contrary, these figures were all too realistically depicted, lounging or sprawling with no attempt at modest concealment—and this whether the body was scrawny or obese, deformed or frankly voluptuous. There were old women, crone-like figures with stringy grey hair, and young shapely women giving suck to their babies. There were not a few who seemed to be caressing their own naked flesh and whose limbs were distorted by some transport of ecstasy, which even at that young age I knew to be unseemly. One canvas was painted as if the artist were looking down over the woman's shoulder, viewing the undraped body as a woman might herself see it, the breasts viewed from above, the thighs splayed open, the fingers exploring the shamelessly gaping organ, a sight I had never expected to be depicted. All in all, there was a candor to the work that proved startling and yet fascinating to my young mind.

"Look here," Victor instructed me, pointing to a canvas farther along as if it might be the most shocking of all. But here was a picture I recognized at once, for I had once been part of just such a scene! It showed a full-bellied, pendulous-breasted woman seated on a stool, her head thrown back and face twisted in great physical effort, her legs wide apart in a posture that was vividly familiar to me. Round her stood other women, with towels and basins, one of them waiting to receive the newborn, which must have been on the very point of birth, for the woman was vastly agape. Victor reached out to place his finger on the painted sexual organ that was the centre of the picture. "Do you know what that is?" he asked as if I could not possibly answer yes.

But I did. "She is having a baby," I said with some pride. "I have seen that. The woman opens like that; I have watched this happening."

"You never!" he snapped, disputing my answer.

"But I have! See, the baby comes from there. The midwife is waiting to take it. I have held a new baby in my own hands."

Victor was disconcerted by my response, but did not wish to show it. "Imagine painting *that!*" And he made a sound as if he might be taking sick. Why did he act so? I wondered, but had not the courage to ask.

Our tour of the room was perforce a rapid one. "Never let my father know you have been here," Victor admonished as he led me from the wing.

"But where have these pictures come from? Who made them?"

"Hush!" Victor ordered. "I cannot tell you."

"Will I be able to see them again?" I asked, for I dearly wanted to return.

"Perhaps; but only when I say so."

For days afterwards the pictures floated in my revery; I could imagine the music that filled the scene—the wailing flute and the wild drum. There was an enchantment to the images that thrilled me even in the recollection. What must it be like, I wondered, to frolic to the point of frenzy beneath the moon, to dance naked in the night, to feel the damp Earth against one's flesh? It seemed to me the height of lewdness; yet I was drawn to the clear pleasure of the acts I contemplated. Much as I wanted again to view the pictures, I wanted more to lay eyes upon the living scenes they depicted. Were there people—*women*—who behaved so? Could the artist possibly have painted these pictures from life? And if so, to what man would these women have granted the right to witness their indecorous conduct?

What I Saw in the Glade

Though the Baron would spare no expense on his children's education, at one point he stuck as a matter of principle. Freethinker that he was, he was reluctant to have religious matters included in our instruction. This left the Baroness fearing that her children's moral development might go unattended. At her insistence, Pastor Dupin of the Genevan Reformed Church was invited to visit the château regularly twice each month to offer religious instructions. Though the Baron, who regarded all theology as chicanery, grumbled over this and served notice that he was not apt to be at home when the pastor called, he deferred to his wife's wishes. He consoled himself that, in the hands of the Reformed Church (for which, as a good Genevan, he had a patriotic respect) the young ones would at least not be subjected to any "Jesuitical prating!"

Pastor Dupin was a handsome but stern young man whose perpetually frowning face wrapped him in the mantle of premature age. He seemed always to be playing the dour Calvinistic disciplinarian his superiors at St. Pierre expected him to be. Though he was gentle enough in his treatment of his pupils, neither Victor nor I welcomed his coming any more than did the Baron, for he invariably entered the house like a dark cloud. Oddly enough, Lady Caroline also seemed to have her reservations regarding the pastor, who would not have been our guest at all had she not invited him. It puzzled me that she did not restrain herself from mocking him whenever the occasion arose. Thus, when one or another of the children sulked, she would laugh and admonish us, "Take care! Or you will grow up to be as gloomy as Pastor Dupin!" And she would caricature his scowling look, corrugating her brows and grimacing, which never failed to encourage Victor to carry the sport still further.

As amusing as this was, it left me to wonder how I was expected to take the Pastor's lessons to heart when my mother insisted on reducing the man to a figure of fun. I asked this of Victor during one of our sessions, while Pastor Dupin was away from the room. Why did our mother bring him to the château, if she would ridicule him so freely?

"Can you not tell?" Victor asked. "It is *Francine*. Do you not see that?"

I had of course noticed that Lady Caroline was quite fond of Francine, the Pastor's wife, who always accompanied her husband to the château. Indeed, it was almost as if the Baroness's invitations were meant more for the wife than the husband. But what was I to make of that?

Francine was as bright and cheerful as the Pastor was grave. Moreover, she was a pleasure to behold, for she was the comeliest girl I had ever seen. Because she was a pastor's wife, she was not permitted to adorn or paint herself; her gown was a plain black frock that covered her from neck to ankles, and her gleaming dark hair was tied back in a tight bun. But she was gifted with a beauty that easily shone through the austere style she was obliged to affect. Her features were classically proportioned, and her wide, frank eyes as lustrous as black pearls. There was, moreover, a natural grace in her movements that made her seem almost to glide above the ground. I in particular looked forward to her visits because Lady Caroline had hinted to me that she intended Francine to be my special friend, though she did not say in what respect. Thus, while the Pastor put us through our instructions or walked us about the château to lecture on the Biblical tapestries, Lady Caroline and Francine would sit together sewing, or more often sketching, a pastime at which the Baroness was quite clever. She delighted in teaching the skill to others, and Francine was grateful to learn. Seated with Francine before an arrangement of flowers, Lady Caroline would show her how to apply charcoal or pastels. As they worked, they exchanged confidences *sotto voce*, often laughing at some private joke. From time to time they would retire with their drawing books into some more distant part of the house or into the garden, returning only when the Pastor's visit had ended.

One day, as he often did, the Pastor set us a lesson to study and left us to ourselves. He had no sooner quit the room than Victor stole over to me and plucked me by the sleeve. I looked up to see him signalling me to be silent. He carefully raised one of the windows and lifted me over the sill. Then he moved swiftly behind the nearest hedge and bade me to follow him as stealthily as I could. I kept close behind him as he led me away from the garden and into the nearby woods. There, like hunters on the track of elusive game, we made our way on silent feet into a small, shaded ravine where a mountain stream ran between towering pines. It was a particularly secluded place, which I had never visited before. To reach it, one had to slip sideways through a tight cleft in the rocks; as we squirmed through this passage, Victor turned to place his finger to his lips, bidding me to be silent.

The passage at last opened upon a ledge that overlooked a narrow wooded glade. Victor motioned me to lie flat upon the Earth and follow him as he crept forward to the edge of the rock shelf. The air within the glade was motionless and densely hot under the noonday sun. The harsh odour of the pines was thick all about us. Looking down where Victor pointed, what should I see but the Baroness seated upon a blanket with a basket of victuals at her side. And several paces off I saw Francine, wearing only her shift, wading barefoot in the stream. In the heat of the day, Lady Caroline had also undressed to her undergarments and removed her stockings. After several minutes, Francine returned to where Lady Caroline sat; the two women spoke. They were not far off, but the echoing babble of the stream made it impossible to hear their words. The Baroness gestured toward a tree across the glade that had fallen and lay partly immersed in the stream. Francine moved to seat herself upon it. But before she did so, with one quick gesture she drew her shift over her head and allowed it to fall away to the ground. Now entirely naked, she reached up to untie her hair and shook it free so that it fell about her shoulders and well down her back. I felt myself blush warmly, as much at the casualness of the act as at Francine's nudity. At Lady Caroline's bidding, Francine felt her way along the trunk of the fallen tree, stretching herself as languidly as a sleepy cat, then looked to the Baroness, who directed her to turn first this way then that. Francine, easing her body along the length of the tree, at last found a position to Lady Caroline's liking. With her hair spilled amply about her shoulders and bosom, she folded her arms behind her head and let her eyelids droop as if she might fall asleep. After studying Francine's form for some while, the Baroness took up her drawing pad and began to sketch.

Where he lay beside me on the ground, Victor's concentration was palpably fierce. His eyes were feeding on Francine's body. One might have thought that one as young as I then was, still indeed a child, could not have understood the nature of Victor's transgression. But I did, if only instinctively. My affection for Francine—and, no doubt, a certain womanly sympathy—persuaded me that it was treacherous to approve of his spying; and yet I wanted desperately to know what these two women were about. Torn between curiosity and shame, I blazed with embarrassment, but was fearful to speak, lest any altercation between us be overheard. Instead, I buried my eyes in my hands and waited helplessly. After several minutes, Victor whispered close at my ear, "Look!" When I shook my head to indicate I would not, he pinched my arm until I raised my head.

Lady Caroline, having laid aside her drawing pad, had moved to sit beside Francine, who reclined still upon the fallen larch. As they spoke, Lady Caroline reached out to touch Francine's cheek, and then her hair, combing gently through it. After a moment the Baroness leaned forward to place a brief kiss on Francine's lips, and then another that was not so brief. The kiss lingered long enough to leave me uneasy. Before it ended, her hand strayed across Francine's throat and bosom, at last settling on her breast, cradling it delicately for a moment, rubbing the full palm over its tip, and then gliding downward across her body. A moment longer, and I could watch no more; I scrambled backward as quietly as I could and crept toward the passage in the rock. In a moment I was out of the glade and running back toward the château. I did not care if Victor followed me, but I soon heard his footfalls and panting breath behind me.

When he had caught up with me, he clutched my arm roughly and brought me to a halt. "Why did you leave?" he asked crossly. "They might have heard you."

"You should not have spied on them. That was wicked."

"Oh? And why?"

"You know. You are a boy. You should not watch."

Victor made a wry face. "Shall I tell you something? My mother would not have cared."

"Yes, she *would!*" I insisted, now almost dizzy with confusion and anger. "She *would!*"

Victor answered only with a self-satisfied glance as he raced along beside me. "You wanted to see, too."

"No!" I half-shouted; but I knew he did not believe my answer.

"Now you know why she wishes to have the Pastor visit," he observed smugly.

By the time we reached the château, Pastor Dupin, who had been searching for us, was wholly out of patience. "It was so hot in the room," Victor told him when he chastised us for absenting ourselves from our lesson. At which the Pastor delivered an impromptu sermon we had heard before on the Christian virtues of fleshly mortification. Did we not know how blithely the martyrs of the faith had endured death at the stake? What was an hour in a warm room compared to their blessed agony? Later Victor would remark, "I would rather burn at the stake than hear his witless lecture again!"

Our afternoon adventure left me with many wild and spinning questions. Though I was angry with Victor, I secretly relished the forbidden knowledge he had brought me. I wanted him to tell me more. Indeed, I wanted him to tell me how I should feel, for I assumed he knew. To my surprise, he had as many questions to ask as I.

"Would you like to kiss Francine?" he asked.

"Yes," I said without hesitation, for I had kissed her already—whenever she arrived and departed. "I have kissed her many times."

"Not the way Mother did. Would you like to kiss her like that?"

There I was not sure what to say. "I cannot tell. . . . Maybe."

"And touch her, as Mother did? *There?*" And he reached out a finger to poke my bosom, which was of course nothing like Francine's full breast. "Or *there?*" And he reached to touch me lower down, but I eluded him.

What was I to answer? Did he wish to have me say I disapproved of what our mother had done? I could not bring myself to say either yes or no; both answers caught in my throat. In truth, I was curious to know how Francine's body might feel to the touch, for I knew my own body would soon begin to resemble hers. But Lady Caroline, I knew, had not touched out of curiosity. "She was showing her fondness for Francine. . . ."

"But could you do it? Would you *want* to do it?"

"If Mother does," I replied feebly, but pretending this was the only possible answer. I knew Victor would not challenge the propriety of anything his mother did; but inwardly my mind swam with uncertainty, and I was angry that he made me feel so childishly ignorant.

I Am Invited into
Mother's Workshop

Other questions that careered through my mind were answered quite by accident a few weeks later.

One day, finding myself alone at play, I once again stole up the stairs of the south tower to the topmost storey of the house, hoping I might somehow gain entrance to the wing where the strange pictures were. To my surprise, I found the door unlocked. Entering, I crept along the dim corridor, taking care to step softly across the creaking floor—but before I could find the room I sought, a door along the passage opened and Lady Caroline stood before me.

"Elizabeth?" she said, questioning more with surprise than displeasure, as if she did not trust what her eyes saw. Having no idea what to reply, I stood silent and shamefaced. For several moments she squinted down at me as if I might be some illusion before her. She was dressed as I had not seen her before. Her dishevelled hair carelessly swaddled in a turban, and her feet bare, she was wrapped in a grey smock that covered her to just below the knees. The gown, which was spotted with stains of every colour, was unbelted at the waist and fell open for its full length. I could not be certain in the dim light, but I thought she wore no bodice beneath, nor anything more than her lower petticoat. For several moments she stood gazing at me closely. Then, coming closer, she reached out to touch my cheek, which seemed to satisfy her that I was no apparition. Only then did she draw her gown together and fasten it at the waist. "How do you come to be here?" she asked.

"The door was open."

"Are you exploring, then?" she asked. When I answered timidly that I was, she smiled and continued studying me with the curiously distracted stare that sometimes came into her eyes. At such times, she seemed to be listening meditatively to a voice others could not hear. She might stand that way, lost in her thoughts for many long moments, idly stroking her cheek with the sprig of green she invariably carried. Then at last: "Come," she said.

Once in the room, I realised why Lady Caroline was so underdressed. Being at the top of the house, the chamber was exceedingly close even with the windows thrown open. The abundant dust fairly rushed to fill one's nostrils. But I paid no attention to that, and instead stared about me in wonder. This was a place more like a museum than a household chamber. From all the wainscoting and the ceiling depended fantastic plant and animal forms: stuffed beasts, skeletal remnants, horns, tusks, desiccated skins. There were tables bearing scuttles that overflowed with shells and stones, shelves crowded with inscrutable implements, cabinets cluttered with exotic icons and figurines. In the shadowed recesses of the room I could make out rows of vessels and stoups that held coloured fluids, and in them floating substances I could but dimly discern: vines and tendrils they seemed to be, or the preserved remains of insects and animals. The walls everywhere displayed antique charts and enigmatic emblems, many of them human forms contorted into monstrous anatomies.

Everything in the room was excessively untidy. Moreover, it was filled with acrid chemical odours that tickled my nose. "It is not quite milady's chamber, is it?" Lady Caroline laughed. "As you see, the servants do not clean here; they are not permitted to. I prefer to lock my mess away and be at my ease to go about my work. Ah—what 'work,' you wonder. Well, if you have come so far, let me satisfy your curiosity. It is time you learned."

She led me across the room. There was much to catch the eye on all sides, but it was soon forgot when we turned into an alcove at the far end of the room and there discovered Madame Van Slyke lounging in the plush window-seat. "Welcome, little mouse," she said.

Madame Van Slyke and her husband were visiting notables from Amsterdam; they had been our guests for several days. She was an exotic woman perhaps a few years older than Lady Caroline. To judge from her conversation, one would conclude she had read all the books in the world; she surely spoke every language I had ever heard of, including that of the Algonquin Indians of the New World. Born Hungarian, she claimed to be the incarnation of a Red Indian princess. The Van Slykes, disciples of a great thinker whose name was Baron Swedenborg, had lately created a prodigious stir in Geneva, where they had come to lecture upon the philosopher's astonishing doctrines. It was inevitable that they should be invited to be our guests during their visit.

"So then," the Baron had announced with obvious relish as he welcomed the Van Slykes to our home, "now we shall hear what this remarkable man Swedenborg has to contribute to the great cause of Enlightenment and human virtue."

During the Van Slykes' sojourn at the château, the salon and dinner table bubbled with animated discussions of Baron Swedenborg's teachings, metaphysical discourse that was, needless to say, far beyond my childish comprehension. Lady Caroline seemed entranced by all that she heard; she and Madame Van Slyke were in constant, lively conversation between themselves. But I could see that the ever-sceptical Baron had quickly grown impatient with what he heard. I recall one emphatic exchange in particular, for, much to my surprise, I found myself identified as the "living proof" of Swedenborg's folly. At dinner that evening Father fell to mocking Swedenborg for having predicted that the world would come to an end in the year 1757—and more so for insisting that it actually *had!* even though the prophet himself had lived on several years more. How could the end of the world fail to capture my attention? Especially when the Baron pointed his fork down the table squarely at me to ask, "Do you hear, Elizabeth? Here sits a man who believes the world came to an end before you were born into it. And yet there you sit filling your face with Celeste's excellent dessert. And does it not taste perfectly delicious, my dear?"

"Yes," I answered timidly as all eyes descended upon me.

"There, sir," Father pronounced, turning triumphantly to Mynheer Van Slyke, "you have the argument from *crème moulée*. With every spoon the child places in her mouth she is the living proof of Swedenborg's folly."

But Mynheer Van Slyke, a nervous, wizened little man with chronic catarrh who stared goggle-eyed from behind thick spectacles, was undeterred. He hastened to correct Father. "No, no, sir! You do not understand. The teaching is that the *material* world came to an end in 1757. The *material* world. According to Swedenborg, we have passed over into the realm of Heavenly Man, don't you see? We have all of us been reborn in the spiritual world."

"Ah, well then, sir," Father replied with some temper, "if that is so, I might have saved myself a pretty penny by ordering my spiritual cook to serve you up a spiritual goose. And I daresay I could have afforded you even more spiritual wine to wash it down than you seem to have swilled already. But I wonder if your spiritual belly would then feel half so full as it now does."

Of all the rest that was said, only one matter proved of interest to me. Victor, who as usual pretended he understood everything that passed between the adults, informed me that Baron Swedenborg had, in his lifetime, discoursed with angels and walked in heaven. This moved me to ask Father privately if it was so.

"It is so that the man *said* he did," the Baron answered wryly. "And so does every lunatic one meets beside the road. And there you are. We live in an age of Reason and yet lunacy walks among us still—often on stilts."

Father's relations with Madame Van Slyke were little more agreeable. Though Lady Caroline took to her warmly, the Baron was put off by her assertive demeanour. Worst of all, she dared to criticise Voltaire to Father's own face. "A man of wit," she had pronounced him, "but not half so wise as the sachems of my tribal ancestors whose learning was derived from the true state of Nature." That she should claim a savage people were of superior brilliance to the great Voltaire was more than Father could tolerate. Afterwards I overheard him speak of her as a "brazen she-male." This was the lady who now greeted me in the alcove of Mother's workshop.

"Elizabeth has come to pay us a visit, Magda," Lady Caroline announced.

"Ah, yes! We wondered who might be stealing along the corridor to spy on us," Madame Van Slyke said as she summoned me to her side in the window-seat. "Have you never been to your mother's studio before?" she asked.

"No, I have not. I did not know it was here."

"Then you have much to learn about your mother's gifts. She is among the most remarkable women of our time. I believe that, like the great Swedenborg, she has walked in heaven."

Madame Van Slyke's appearance was as greatly awry as Lady Caroline's. Her hair was undone and lay falling about her shoulders, and she smelled rankly of sweat. She seemed to have exhausted herself in some great exertion, for her cheeks and throat and bosom were brightly aglow and her breath was laboured. I saw her clothes tossed in a heap on the floor, leaving her with only her chemise to cover her; this garment, fragile to the point of transparency, clung to her moist flesh, revealing her great thrusting breasts as if they were wholly naked. But what took my attention even more was the cheroot she raised to her lips to suck upon. It was the sort I had seen Father offer to gentlemen callers; but I had never seen a woman smoke before.

"Your mother has been sketching me," she said. "Would you like to see her work?"

"Yes, very much."

From the corner of my eye I saw Lady Caroline quickly wag her head no. She passed a phrase in German to her friend.

"Ah, yes, of course; then show the girl something more suitable," Madame Van Slyke answered.

Lady Caroline went to a file of paintings stacked against one wall. From it she carefully selected a canvas and placed it upon an easel. "There," she said, "come see." Though the picture was only partially finished, I could see that it was one of the "evil pictures" I had come seeking. There were the same ghostly, robed women roaming a dark wood, this time a circle of them moving hand in hand in a boisterous dance. And at the centre there was a female figure that I recognised at once, even though its face was still a blur. It was Francine unclothed and recumbent as Victor and I had seen her that afternoon in the glade.

"Well, what do you think?" Lady Caroline asked gaily.

"*You* have made this?" I asked in amazement.

"You find it strange that a woman should paint?" she asked with clear amusement, tossing a wink in Madame Van Slyke's direction. "Oh, yes, it is mine. It is my great joy to make pictures—though I am far from a master painter, I realise."

"Come now!" Madame Van Slyke protested. "No man would acknowledge a woman to be a 'master painter,' not even if she were greater than Raphael. *Our* art is not *their* art. And what does it matter what they say? Tell me, Elizabeth, what do you think of Lady Caroline's painting?"

"I think it is quite strange," I answered. "And lovely . . . in a different way."

"Do you truly think so?" Lady Caroline asked, frowning over my remark. "You are very kind to say so."

"The girl has an eye. And a brain," Madame Van Slyke commented. "There is the making of a woman in her."

"But are there really people like those in the picture?" I asked.

"Oh, yes, there are," Lady Caroline answered.

"Are they witches?"

At this she knitted her brows with clear concern.

"Who has told you they are?" Madame Van Slyke asked.

"They look like witches . . . I think."

The women exchanged remarks once more in German. Again Lady Caroline seemed to drift away from me on some contemplative wave.

"Not witches as you know them from fairy stories, my dear," Madame Van Slyke answered. "Do not think of them as such. Think of them rather as *cunning* women."

"Are there people like this in these woods?"

Lady Caroline smiled. "You will one day learn of this, when the time is ripe. Then I shall show you more pictures. Until then, you must respect these rooms as my private quarters—to be visited only with my consent. Do you understand?"

"Yes. But I would like to know more."

"And you shall. But let this for a time be my secret: that you were here with Magda and myself; what we talked of. Do you not also keep secrets?"

She asked as if she knew I did. And of course there was one secret in particular that leapt to mind. "Yes," I answered.

"And I shall respect your secret, I promise."

"Will you ever paint me?" I asked as she led me from her workshop.

"Yes, I shall. I want very much to."

"When will you?"

Again her thoughts seemed to drift. "Soon, I think. When you become one of us."

A few days after this, the Van Slykes' visit ended in near-disaster. Late one night after I had been despatched to bed, I heard voices howling in high dudgeon through the château. I was sure these included the Baron's, whom I had never heard in such a pet. The next morning the Van Slykes departed from our estate under an evil cloud. Though Lady Caroline and Madame Van Slyke embraced warmly before the carriage left for town, the Baron and Mynheer Van Slyke were clearly not on speaking terms; Father would not so much as set foot out the door to bid his guests farewell. Instead I heard him growl, "Good riddance!" as the carriage rode off. "I shall have no more of this Swedenborgian trash in my home. The man is a miscreant and the woman little short of a strumpet." Lady Caroline sought to put in a word in Madame Van Slyke's defence, but the Baron would hear none of it. "In my experience, madam, only a strumpet would so much as remain in the room while such a proposal is made—and only a procurer would offer it. *Ergo* they are trash; the pair of them and their travels will do little more than to corrupt the gullible."

That day a rumour raced through the household that Baron Frankenstein had challenged Mynheer Van Slyke to a duel! Could this be true? Victor affirmed that it was.

"But why?" I asked.

"Because Swedenborg taught that man must take a concubine." It was a favourite way Victor had of teasing me, and one I particularly deplored: to employ words I did not know, then force me to ask for clarification. I confessed I had no idea what a "concubine" might be.

"A sort of second wife that a man can take to bed with him."

"Is that permitted?" I asked.

"Only in the church of the Swedenborgians. And of course among the infidel."

"But why should a man want a second wife?"

"Because, you see, men have exceedingly powerful needs."

"Needs for what?"

"Oh, come now! For the things that are done in bed by men and women. And in the barnyard in plain sight by the animals. You have, I think, observed the bull and the kine doing what they do."

"And if I have, what has that to do with the needs of man?"

"Simply that one woman cannot be enough to satisfy a man's lust; perhaps even several women cannot do so. So men must take concubines."

"And is the same true of women?"

"Not in the least. Women have very little need. Their need is more than satisfied by their husband."

"And men are made to be barnyard bulls? Is this what you have learnt from watching the cattle?" It was the first time I had spoken so impudently to Victor; it was, I discovered, quite enjoyable.

"I have learnt that females are born to be mothers. Their need is satisfied in that way."

"I wonder how you know so much about women's needs, Victor. And Baron Swedenborg too? Or any man?"

He replied with a weary sigh. "It is universally known."

"Is it? 'Universally known' to but *half* the human race? That is strange arithmetic for a mathematician to employ."

"The half may know about the whole."

"The half may *think* it knows. But how shall it know for certain unless it asks? Now, I will tell you what I have learnt from our own kitchen maids: '*Un coq suffit à dix poules, mais dix hommes ne suffisent pas à une femme.*' "

At that he reddened, which brought me greater pleasure still. "I am only telling you what Baron Swedenborg believes," he protested.

"But why was Father so angry?"

Victor openly smirked. "Because—can you believe it!—Mynheer Van Slyke proposed that he might move his residence to Geneva and take Mother as *his* concubine."

"You mean to share his bed?"

"Yes, of course. And in return, he offered Father Madame Van Slyke to be *his* concubine."

I thought of Mynheer Van Slyke with his crooked teeth and sniffling catarrh. I remarked that I could not believe Mother would find much to admire in him.

"Well," Victor explained, "that is not supposed to matter. It is the man's need that prevails—so Swedenborg believed."

"Do you believe such things?" I asked. "Do you wish to have a concubine, or fifty concubines, to fill your bed?"

"Come now! Swedenborg claimed to learn all this from the spirit world. I am a freethinker. How should I take such notions seriously? Moreover, I intend to be a man of science; what need would I have for fifty women?" When he saw me cast him a scoffing glance, he added, "Or for so much as *one?*"

EDITOR'S NOTE
Four Extant Paintings by Caroline Frankenstein

It was not until 1806, the earliest occasion on which I was able to visit Belrive, that I realised with what dark Gothic fancies I had surrounded the Frankenstein family seat. Since it was the house that had incubated Victor Frankenstein's unholy ambitions and corrupted the soul of his bride, I had secretly come to think of it as the quintessence of a haunted Romantic castle.

Only when I laid eyes on what had become of Belrive did I realise what foolish expectations I had harboured. For, alas! it was nothing like. The once-magnificent château had been violated untold times; its treasures had been stripped from floor to ceiling—and virulently so. The very wallpaper had been torn away, and slogans of the Revolution were scrawled across the panelling. Painful to see! Where people of privilege had once dined and conversed in the time of the *ancien régime*, common soldiers now bivouacked. Most of the family property had been vandalised either by revolutionary elements loosed upon Geneva during the turmoil of the Helvetic Republic, or by marauding troops in the wake of the many campaigns that had traversed this disputed terrain. I found the property and grounds being used for billeting a full brigade of Swiss and Milanese mercenaries in the employment of the Emperor. The French commandant in charge, one Marshal Chabânnes, permitted me to explore the château and its outhouses, but gave me little reason to expect that I would find any of the art treasures that had once graced the mansion. These—especially the Baron's highly prized collection of automata—would have vanished, he was certain, in the first of several waves of official confiscation by the Vaudois revolutionary régime. The fate of the automata I had already been able to confirm on my own; several of the devices described by Elizabeth Frankenstein have reappeared in museums and private collections on the Continent and as far away as New York City. I had, however, some hope that family papers might have survived somewhere on the premises, or that I might be able to interview servants who had been in the family's employ. I was mistaken; an afternoon's careful examination of the house yielded nothing of scholarly value. Not even the Frankenstein library had been spared; its shelves were stripped bare. So thorough was the pillaging of furniture and personal effects that I could not even identify the rooms that might have once been used by the principal members of the family. As for the household staff, I was able to locate a few of the younger domestics at other homes in the vicinity; but they either knew nothing of the family's habits or pretended ignorance. The figures who played a greater part in the story—Joseph, the major-domo, and Celeste, the cook—were deceased; Eloise, the Baroness's personal maid, had departed without trace.

I had little choice but to wait for more peaceful times. Accordingly, in the year following Napoleon's defeat at Waterloo, I undertook to advertise for Frankenstein family memorabilia by placing commercial notices in several French and Genevan publications. By an incredible stroke of good fortune, my enquiries were answered in April of 1816. In that month I received a letter from a Parisian art dealer who claimed to be in possession of four canvases signed by "C. Frankenstein." At first, I did not understand what this might mean, so far from my thoughts were the Baroness Frankenstein's paintings. But once I read the brief description contained in the letter, I realised that of course these were the "evil pictures" that figure in Elizabeth Frankenstein's memoir.

I attach the letter, which contains an illuminating assessment of the work by an independent critic who knew nothing of their origin.

Sir:

Your advertisement in Le Courier Français *regarding properties once owned by the family of Baron Alphonse Frankenstein of Geneva has reached my hand. I believe I may be able to satisfy your request. I have in my possession four curious paintings that bear the signature of one "C. Frankenstein," an artist with whose work I am totally unfamiliar.*

The paintings are highly unusual both in subject matter and execution. I cannot frankly say they possess any artistic merit; the work shows little formal training in either anatomy or perspective. Indeed, in both these respects, the paintings display an almost deliberate distortion, producing a repulsively amateurish effect. As abrasive as the artist's style may be, his subject matter is even more rebarbative. I will do my best to describe the canvases; but please understand that I do so reluctantly and only so that you may form some basis for judging whether these are among the works you seek.

The paintings are all of female nudes, posed with one exception out of doors and in a highly provocative manner. If I may be frank: they would fall little short of the pornographic if so many of the figures chosen for depiction were not physically unappealing in the extreme. Indeed, I know of no painter who has been willing to place such malformed female bodies in his work, nor to delineate their anatomy with such repellent frankness. One of the paintings would seem to be an appallingly tasteless study of pregnancy, displaying a group of nudes in various stages of gravidity. Another is a presentation of explicitly Sapphic practices of which I will say no more. A third picture describes some woodland celebration in which the figures are preoccupied; it focuses upon a man-shaped object fashioned of twigs or wicker. I would take this to be the reconstruction of some prehistoric Druidic rite, perhaps a harvest festival. The fourth painting, the most carefully executed of the lot, depicts the gruesome death by drowning of an unidentified nude female.

I will not trouble to tell you here how the paintings came into my possession; I will simply say that I have seriously considered destroying them as artistically worthless, and in any case incapable of public exhibition. Only my curiosity about the artist has delayed the execution of that design. If you can supply any information about M. Frankenstein, I would be most grateful. And I am of course willing to strike a bargain for the sale of one or all.

Sincerely Yours,
Gaston de Rollinat
Galerie Lamennais
14, blvd de Grenelle

As soon as the times permitted, I made arrangements to visit M. de Rollinat, whom I found to be a charmingly cultivated man. He informed me that he had purchased the paintings as part of the estate of a French officer who had apparently collected *objets d'art* indiscriminately while campaigning for the Emperor. M. de Rollinat preferred to go no further into the matter, indicating that he had agreed to purchase the entire estate with no questions asked. He assumed that the paintings, like much of the rest of the Colonel's property, were spoils of war. When he exhibited the works for me in the back room of his gallery, he did so almost apologetically and only after reminding me that I had been given clear warning of their character. "You English," he observed, "may have less tolerance for works of this nature than those of us who deal in the Parisian world of the arts."

The paintings were indeed as amateurishly executed and as blatantly erotic as he had led me to believe. The picture he had referred to as "Sapphic" was especially unsettling. I will limit my description to saying that it showed women indulging in various acts of sexual congress and self-abuse. By that time my research into the Frankenstein memoirs had brought me into contact with certain Hindoo erotic illustrations that softened the shock of these images; even so, I had never, either in art or literature, come upon depictions of tribadic intercourse as graphic as these. With some sense of embarrassment, I felt impelled to justify my interest in the work—but not before M. de Rollinat had agreed to fix a price upon the canvases. I was apprehensive that, should he know more, he might place a higher value upon them. Having struck a bargain that made the four paintings mine for thirty guineas, I then explained that I was involved in research upon the Frankenstein family. These pictures, I informed him, were the work of a woman: Baroness Caroline Frankenstein. The astonishment that swept over him was impossible to conceal. He wondered if I might conceivably be mistaken; he found it difficult to believe that a woman could have executed work as morally rank as this. In any event, if that were true, then I was to be congratulated for having gotten the better of the bargain. For while there was little commercial value in work of this kind on the legitimate market, he was certain that in other less savoury quarters I would have no difficulty finding buyers who stood prepared to bid premium prices for these canvases precisely because they were the work of a sexually deranged woman. I hastened to assure him that I had no interest whatever in trade of that kind.

The paintings remain in my possession, though I, like M. de Rollinat, have found no occasion to exhibit them. Their value, however, has been inestimable in another respect. At least in my eyes, they serve as indisputable physical evidence that Elizabeth Frankenstein's characterisation of Lady Caroline is substantively accurate. The creator of these paintings is surely as deviant a personality as Elizabeth recollects in her memoirs. This much, then, I can offer as proof of the validity of her account.

My research over the years has produced only one more item of Frankenstein family property. The animated duck that Elizabeth mentions seeing in the Baron's collection of automata reappeared just a few years ago, in the summer of 1838. The work of the French inventor Jacques Vaucanson, it can be seen on display at the Vienna State

Museum. The years have, however, taken their toll and the mechanism stands in severe disrepair. Its original genius can only be guessed at.

Of the paintings I acquired from M. de Rollinat, I will briefly mention the picture I found most arresting, since it was destined to play a special rôle in Elizabeth Frankenstein's life. It was the smallest of the four canvases, but the most expertly executed. It showed signs of careful revision. The painting was peculiarly dream-like in its subaqueous mood. It showed the corpse of a nude female submerged in the sea. Wrapped in leaden chains, the young and shapely woman floats head downwards into the oceanic depths; her skin glows faintly in the dark water; her luxuriant black hair spreads over her body like a shroud. There is a sensational touch: a stream of blood issues from her sexual organ, spreading upward to incarnadine all the sea around her. Above the churning surface of the waters, a bird (or so it seemed to be at first) is seen vanishing into the storm-tossed sky. Upon closer study this figure proves to be a winged lion; in its mouth it carries a human form.

I could not remotely imagine what dark sources of mental or spiritual aberration Lady Caroline Frankenstein had quarried to find the images of myth and nightmare she had painted upon this canvas. The picture carried only one elusive hint of its meaning: on the back, the single word "Rosalba" was scrawled in dark paint. The name had even less meaning for me than the picture. Yet when I returned to my home in London, I felt impelled to give the picture a place upon the wall of my study, where it frequently drew my wondering attention. Some instinct was surely at work telling me that this painting embodied Elizabeth Frankenstein's entire tragedy. Though I did not realise it at the time, the remaining years of my life were to be spent deciphering the enigma that I saw each time I raised my eyes and gazed across my study.

The Wilderness

I t was upon my twelfth birthday, three years after the Baroness had taken me into her family, that I learnt there was a greater purpose in my adoption. Though I was still too much a child to grasp the full import of her remarks, I can remember the evening Lady Caroline took me aside at bedtime to tell me how my fate was linked to Victor's. As so often when she talked of her elder son, her eyes took on a shadowed sadness. She spoke searchingly, as if she were seeking her way to islands of meaning that lay scattered across a great pool of silence.

"You have a special rôle to play in our family. The kinship that I would have grow between you and Victor is more than a matter of blood; it will be of a kind for which our world has as yet no name. Let us call it simply a union. There is genius in Victor, a rare gift. He possesses a daimon—or is possessed by it. It arouses a certain wildness in him that must be tamed. His mind can take strange turns. Something asserts itself in him . . . something I have no power . . ." There for a while she broke off and drifted into a pensive interlude. Distractedly, as if she were walking in a dream, she wandered to a bookshelf at the far end of the room. Her hand strayed across several volumes; then, reaching behind, she brought out a book that had been concealed at the back of the shelf. She returned with it and held it out to me.

"You will at first find this demanding, but make it your particular study, my dear. As your French improves, this book may help you understand about Victor."

I opened the book. *Emile* was the title. Though I knew nothing of its content, I recognised the author, at least by name. Jean-Jacques Rousseau had emerged several times in conversation at the dinner table and in the salon. "Conversation," I say—but "battle" would be the better word. M. Rousseau could not be mentioned within the Baron's hearing but that he would seethe with anger. It was the one point on which he and Lady Caroline grew vehement.

"I have heard Father call M. Rousseau a 'shameless savage,' " I observed. In fact, I had also heard the Baron call him a "rascally knave," a "brute," a "barbarous oaf," and a "gibbering ape." I remembered all the phrases because I did not often see the Baron wax so wroth. But "shameless savage" stuck in my mind because he had gone on to say that if M. Rousseau had his way "we would all be swinging naked from the trees." I wondered if this could possibly be true.

Lady Caroline smiled, though a trifle sadly. "Rousseau was the Prometheus of sentiment. Of all the writers of our age, he alone possessed the fire of inspiration necessary to portray those passions that go directly to the heart—and to portray them fearlessly. I believe him to be the philosopher of our future. The Baron disagrees about this, however—and emphatically so. You will hear others say similarly harsh things. To be sure, Rousseau suffered from certain limitations, as great minds often do; in particular, he did our sex many injustices. He did not understand the part that woman must play in defending the life of the passions from the dead hand of Reason. In person, however, he deeply admired women of learning. Perhaps only those of us who had the good fortune to meet him can fully grasp the grandeur of his mind."

"You *knew* him?"

"Only briefly, while he lived near by. I was very young, and he, alas! was very troubled—especially in his relations with women. This was a serious failing in him. One who cannot respect as his equal the woman with whom he shares his life is hardly qualified to speak for humanity, having left half the human race out of account. I am proud to say he found my company soothing to his agitated soul. I used to play for him on the harpsichord. Music was his one solace. The book you hold was his personal gift. It has become a sort of Bible for me. The Baron, however, is infuriated by every word Rousseau ever placed on paper, so I suggest you read this privately. You will not find many copies in Geneva. Along with all Rousseau's writing, *Emile* was burnt by our city fathers in the town square. To his credit, the Baron, despite his feelings, sought to prevent this barbarous act. He offered to buy every copy of Rousseau's work to save it from the flames, but he was not permitted to do so."

"Has Victor read it?"

"He has no need. Victor *is* Emile—or as close to that ideal as I have been able to bring him in his education. I have encouraged certain forces in his soul. I believe it was right to do so. Nature is, after all, our only true guide in life. And Rousseau, I believe, is our only true guide to Nature. *Trust, trust, trust!* he bids us. *Trust* the natural man; for 'God made all things good.' But in Victor's case, the response has been unpredictable. Nature, you see . . ." Here again her thoughts drifted into silence; for many moments she sat stroking her throat with the sprig of green that was placed beside her plate each morning at breakfast. Resuming at last, she said, "You will find Victor at times impulsive, perhaps quite carried away—and at those times he grows unfeeling. Be patient with him, Elizabeth, I pray. Teach him your gentleness; show him your heart. Think of him as something more than your brother, as you are his more than sister."

Though Lady Caroline offered me but fragments of meaning, I understood her thought better than she knew. The wildness she spoke of in Victor was already known to me. I had soon learnt that he was a restless spirit, a born devotee of uncharted places for whom the civilised amenities of life were an intolerable constraint. The very estate we lived upon, vast as it was, confined him as closely as a monk's cell. From his earliest years, Victor had rebelled against its well-tended order, preferring the unruly wilderness of the Voirons, where the Baron's only claim upon the land took the form of half-wild sheep that grazed the high meadows. To this rough and hazardous country Victor, when a mere child of four, had wandered and become lost. Starving and half-frozen, he was found fully three days later in an icy cave at the foot of a sheer cliff; there he had given up his adventure, stopped by a barrier that no mountain goat could have scaled. From that day onward, Victor was a source of unceasing anxiety to his parents and tutors. Until he was at last physically robust enough and sufficiently surefooted to make his way safely over harsh terrain, there was reason to fear that he might once again roam abroad and do himself harm in the mountains he was drawn to explore.

For this reason, Victor was never so gloriously at home as when the family made its seasonal migration to the Baron's chalet across the frontier near Mont Salève. Here he was closer to the mountains, whose aerial summits, draped eternally in cloud and snow, invariably moved him to ecstatic wonder. Even from the chalet, it took hours of trekking to find the haunts where Victor loved most to spend his days—as far up the craggy slopes as our legs could carry us. I was invariably the laggard, unable to clamber as fast as he; at times, when I paused to rest, I would watch his form growing smaller and smaller as he rushed away into the mountainous distance. When I caught up again with him, he might be challenging an impossible granite face or balancing precariously above some crashing cataract. Above all, he adored these desolate places at the brink of winter, when the weather turned stormy; he relished racing against the high winds and being battered by the rains. He longed to be far inside the mountain fastness when the enraged heavens hurled down bolts of fire. Then we would shelter in some cave or under some *couvercle* along the rock façade and watch the storm charge forward like the barbarous horde invading the echoing ravines.

"I would wear this lightning like my crown!" Victor exclaimed, shouting out against the howling gale, which whipped his words away before I could hear more than half what he said. "It is the secret of life itself, this fire."

"What do you mean?" I asked.

"Surely you have heard: in the beginning, there was light. That light was fire—*this* fire. It brought life out of the Earth, I am sure. We are made of this power. It is in us."

The wildness that came over him in those moments was so fierce I became near terrified and needed to reassure myself that this was no more than my boy-brother speaking.

"I never heard that," I protested. "You are making that up."

"Yes. I am making it up. But I know it to be true."

"You cannot make up truth. You must be taught."

"I have been taught. The lightning is my teacher. It is my God."

Secretly I thrilled at the sweeping passion of his words; yet I knew this was blasphemy. And though I could not believe God would take vengeance on a mere boy, I felt instinctively that it was my rôle to rein in the fervor of his declaration. For what if such sentiments, harmlessly conceived in childhood, should take root and grow one day to acquire the power of adult intellect? Thus, whenever possible, I wished Victor to feel something of what I found in Nature, its gentler and more sympathetic virtues. "The mountains," I once told him, "are sleeping giants. I hear them in the night breathing so deeply. Perhaps we are only their dream, a dream of the slumbering Earth."

"Nonsense!" Victor replied. "They are there to be climbed as Father has climbed them. When we stand upon their top, then *we* are the giants."

"Father calls each of them by name like old friends," I reminded him.

"That is just a game he plays with us—like make-believe. The Alps are dead piles of rock, that is all. Someday we shall build cities on their tops. They will all be mastered—and Mont Blanc too. I shall be first to deserve M. Saussure's reward, but I will not accept it. I would not climb for money, any more than he, but only to study the light and air and storm."

Winning M. Saussure's award for the conquest of Mont Blanc had become a favourite fantasy of Swiss youth, and of Victor no less than any of his boyhood companions. Often in their play they would mark out some nearby hillock and rename it after the lordly mount, then vie and fight to be the first atop its summit. I could not share Victor's passion for such a reckless exercise.

"There is so much right here to see," I told him one day while we sat in a quiet meadow. "Just here from where we sit, I can see enough to fill my heart with gladness. And when I listen . . ."

"Yes? What then?"

"Hush! And listen with me. Everything has a voice, everything has a story. The stories hide everywhere. Here in the grass . . . the blades are like so many green tongues. I would rather know the language of the grass than hear the thunder shouting on the tops of the mountains."

In his less impulsive moods, Victor was sometimes charmed by what I said; he tried to learn my gentler way of viewing Nature near at hand. But always he soon grew restless. His mind ran to more savage phenomena: storm, gale, lightning. I had invented but one pastime that appealed to him. We would borrow a boat that lay tethered on one of the mountain lakes and anchor a little way from shore. Then we would lie side by side on the floor of the drifting craft, letting the waves rock us gently. Saying nothing, we would gaze into the bright and fathomless vault of the sky, letting our minds lift away from us like feathers in the wind. "Wait," I would say to Victor, "just a few moments longer." And sometimes he would share my experience. A certain sweet vertigo would descend upon us; the heavens would spin in a drunken whirl, filling with strange hues and wandering lights. And then what pictures came!

Victor relished this sensation, though not quite in the same spirit as myself. It was enough for me to taste the delirious moment; but he always returned to himself filled with questions. What *caused* this queer experience, he wanted to know. It was, he felt certain, some vagrant humour of the brain. Words like this meant nothing to me, except that they left me always amazed at the contrast in our natures. For me it was sufficient to contemplate the magnificent appearances of the world.

"Why do you *wonder* about such things?" I asked.

"Why do you *not?*" he asked in return. "Are you not curious about what happens in here?" He placed his finger upon his forehead. "Where dreams come from, and thoughts?"

"*Come from?* Out of the air, out of nothing."

He guffawed. "That is not an answer. An answer is finding out a secret, don't you know?"

But, I thought to myself, *the Baroness says it is good to have secrets. Perhaps the world must also keep some secrets from prying human eyes.*

What Came
of Child's Play

Victor and I had soon become fast friends and fellow adventurers, roving the lush country round about like innocents in an Eden restored. Once our lessons were finished for the day, we were, from then until nightfall, free spirits at play in the veritable state of Nature. As we were constantly in one another's company, our habits grew ever more trusting and intimate. I was flattered that he came to prefer my companionship to that of the local boys, who less and less visited the estate after my arrival. At first I knew this was because Lady Caroline had so strongly urged him to watch over me so that I should not be continually plagued by Ernest, who, cleaving to his mother whenever she was near, would never be reconciled to my presence in the family; but within our first year I saw that Victor genuinely favoured my company over that of his rowdy playfellows. Quite spontaneously one day he told me, "You have a better head by far than if I were to put all their brains together. You have *imagination*, and they have not."

"What is imagination?" I asked. I was determined to cultivate this faculty if Victor admired it.

"It is an eye of the mind that sees into other worlds. It is more precious than gold, because gold cannot buy it."

"And do I have this eye?"

"Indeed you have. That is why you like to lie dreaming in the boat."

There was a favourite pool we visited that lay smooth and bright as a mirror upon the high meadows. Gazing from its edge across the limpid surface, one stood as if at the centre of two skies, one above and one below. The pool, fed by deep springs, lay within a dell of lawny expanse; here all was inconceivably verdant, adorned through spring and summer with the rarest flowers and odorous with thyme. All about us, the needle-sharp spires of the distant peaks stood like sentinels guarding the solitude of the place, making it all our own. Often, in the milder seasons, we swam there naked like innocent savages, yielding our fine young bodies to the sun and breeze. Victor was not the first boy I had seen unclothed; since my infancy I had many times bathed with my former Gipsy brothers. But theirs had been the smooth and babyish bodies of little boys, displaying as yet no sign of maturity. Indeed, having had no occasion to peer beyond the boundary of childhood, I would not have known such changes were to be expected. It was Victor, a few crucial years beyond me in age, who first served to call my particular attention to the bodily differences between us, or rather to make that difference more than a matter of casual observation. For the two of us were balancing upon that delicate threshold beyond which carnal curiosity, like some imp lying in ambush, leaps out to surprise us and make our maleness and femaleness the stuff of intensest attraction.

One day, after we had finished swimming, we lay for some while stretched out upon the grassy bank to take the sun. Presently, Victor fell into a doze; turning to him, I let my eye browse upon his handsome profile. I lifted myself on one elbow and, whispering at his ear, played out the kissing rhyme he had taught me.

> *The bee bites at thy rosy cheek*
> *The flea feeds at thy ear.*
> *The nasty gnat nips at thy neck*
> *But I would suck thee . . . here!*

And pressing my mouth fast to his, I did not merely peck, but lingered until our lips seemed to melt together into one flesh. When at last I drew away, my mind spun in a dizzy reel and my heart was racing in my breast. Looking down, I was startled to discover that he had become aroused. I had never seen this extraordinary metamorphosis come over the male body before. The jarring disproportion of the change struck me as much as did anything else; this object, declaring itself so obtrusively to the eye, seemed to be wholly out of place. Almost in spite of myself, my eyes surveyed his form, discovering round the base of his penis a light tracery of hair which I had not noticed before. Fixated as I was by the sight with a concentration that fairly burned inside me, I was torn between staring still more closely and looking away. I could not recall that anyone had ever told me it was wicked to gape in this way at a boy's nakedness; yet, in the way that comes inexplicably to children, as a lesson they seem to imbibe from the air round them, I had absorbed the notion that to do so was misbehaving. Perhaps for that very reason, I could not turn my gaze away from the deliciousness of this sight. As attractive as I had always found Victor to be, he was now handsomer still in some new, disturbing way. I saw how articulated his torso had become, showing bands of muscles where once he had been as smooth as a babe. And now his face, when I looked up to see it, had acquired (why had I not noticed before?) the lean definition of an elegant young man's. To be in the presence of so beautiful a person, to be gazing on his nakedness, made my breath catch in my breast—a sort of giddy panic I had never until that moment felt. Sensing my perplexity, Victor, who was not the least dismayed to have my eyes feasting thus upon him, laughed aloud and blithely invited me to inspect his body all I wished; he was in fact taking clear delight in my fascination. "What do you call this?" he asked, pointing to his alerted organ.

There were names I had learnt from Rosina's sons; but I blushed to speak them, for I now realised they were the words a child would use. The occasion called for adult language I had not learnt. So I answered that I did not know what to call this thing.

"I will tell you," he said, almost heartlessly amused at my discomfort. "Boys call this their prick. Can you tell why?"

Blushing still more hotly, I confessed I did not.

"Do you not see that it is like a pike? Hard and pointed as naked steel?"

Had he not described it thus, I would never have thought to see it as so menacing an object. Indeed, it did not look at all weapon-like to me. Quite the contrary—I would have said it was pitifully exposed and delicate. Did he intend that I should take fright? The truth was: I felt grateful that my physique was not burdened with anything so ungainly and so obviously vulnerable.

"I call it my soldier standing at attention," he went on. "He is making ready to do battle." Then, slyly, he asked, "Do you understand what I mean?"

Again I said I did not, and felt embarrassment for my ignorance sweep over me like a searing wave. Even had I known, I would have asked him to tell me, wishing for the excitement that comes of hearing forbidden things. Though I felt ashamed, there was an absolute hunger in me to know what I hoped he would tell me. And this I both suffered and enjoyed. Instinctively I knew I was playing at the edges of a knowledge that parted the child from the adult.

"Go ahead," Victor boldly insisted, "touch him, if you dare! Watch how he springs to action!" He made it sound like another of our games; but I knew this was far more serious than any game. "Go ahead!" he commanded again, a broad, insolent smile upon his lips. "I do not mind; it will do no harm. Take hold of him. Or are you afraid?"

Thus challenged, I reached out and curled my fingers lightly around him. His rigid flesh gave a sudden twitch; I drew my hand away from the reflex as if I had indeed been pricked. At which Victor burst into laughter. "There, you see, he has charged at you!" And springing up, he stood menacingly over me laughing and allowing his projecting organ to sway this way and that before me. "Run, girl! Run! He is upon you!" I rolled to one side, rose, and ran across the open meadow feigning terror, but feeling gleefully vertiginous. My confusion mounted at every stride as Victor closed upon me, laughing boisterously. When he had caught me, he threw me down upon the grass and sat astride my thighs, pressing his still erected member against my belly. "Now!" he proclaimed as if he were delivering an ultimatum and passed his hand swiftly down my body until it lodged between my legs, where he chafed me roughly. At this I screamed in outrage and sought with all my strength to unseat him, though without success. His hand stayed where it was and even burrowed deeper into the soft folds of my body. Suddenly a wave of unaccountable panic swept over me. Something in Victor's manner had shifted; I was not at all sure that he could be trusted.

"I gave you no permission!" I shouted, glaring up at him in angry amazement. But he was unapologetic and pressed further into me until I feared he meant to force himself into my belly.

"Come now!" he answered, perversely amused at my distress. "Be truthful. It pleases you."

"No! I want you to stop." Only when tears of rage flooded from my eyes did he withdraw his invading hand.

When at last he allowed me to sit up, he spoke almost resentfully. "But did you truly find it so distasteful?"

"You were hasty and rough. You have hurt me." I moved well off from him, making ready to run if I must.

"I thought you would enjoy it as much as I," he answered with a puzzled shrug. "I think girls wish boys to be forward with them; I think they want to be forced a little to protect their innocence."

"Why should you think that?"

"You are not the first girl I have touched," he said boastfully.

"Who else have you touched? Tell me! There is no one else. You are lying."

"It's true! I have been with Solange," he answered. "And done as I wished with her." Solange was a buxom, slow-witted girl older by a year than Victor. The daughter of Anna Greta, Lady Caroline's chambermaid, she had been put to work with Celeste in the kitchen.

"Solange! She is brainless as a post!" I saw him smirk at my obvious jealousy. "I do not believe you. When did you have the chance to be with her?"

"In her quarters, when her mother was not there."

"And did you enjoy being with her?"

He shrugged again, as if he placed no importance on the matter. "I was merely curious. I studied her as I might study a book."

"Then your studies taught you very little, if this is how you conduct yourself—like such a ruffian."

"Solange made no protest."

"Because she is your *servant*, Victor! You do not understand that? If she were free to speak her mind to you, that silly great cow, she would tell you differently. But who would care if she protested—or even believe her? You are her master and can do as you would. But you are not mine."

A frown of sincere contrition finally came over his face. "I meant no harm, Elizabeth. I was quite carried away. That happens when a man is aroused."

"As I see you now are not. And so you are a friend and a brother to me again." In the heat of my displeasure, I made this observation only in passing, intending no hurt. But Victor's response to the remark was one of immediate embarrassment. At once he reached to hide himself, as if he were more ashamed that I should see his organ in repose than alerted. *How easily a man may be subdued and shamed,* I thought. *This soldier ready to do battle is disarmed in a moment.* "But I am still your sister," I continued, "even when you are aroused. And not a book to satisfy your curiosity."

"Would you never want me to do it again?"

My mind struggled with his question. "I will not say that. But I will never enjoy what you do without my permission."

A while later, as we made our way home, Victor stopped me when we were in sight of the château. "Never tell!" he implored me, taking a firm grip on my arm. "We will be punished if you tell."

And until I promised, he would not turn me free.

⊱✦⊰

In the woman, nothing so marks the approach of adulthood as the dawning of vanity. In this respect, what happened that day in the meadow worked a curious change upon my childhood habits. Heretofore, I had given no more attention to my appearance than any young girl does. But now the image I saw in the mirror became the tyrant of my waking hours, constantly demanding my service. It was no longer enough for me to glance in the glass to see if I had placed a bow correctly or failed to wipe away a spot of grease acquired at the table. Now I searched every feature of my countenance as if the very act of scrutiny might redraw what I saw before me. And what I saw I much disliked, for I saw myself entrapped in an unspoken competition with the rest of womankind. Every contour of my face seemed imperfect, if not grossly flawed. My cheekbones, once mercifully concealed by the lingering roundness of a child's face, had become far too high and prominent. My forehead was surely too low by more than an inch, a condition I sought to remedy by drawing my hair back until it strained at the roots. This made for little improvement, and besides revealed the birth scar at my temple. This faded blemish, a mark that few might see except upon the closest scrutiny, was nevertheless glaringly apparent in my eyes, and quite unacceptable. Might it be creamed or powdered away, I wondered? And my eyebrows—they were surely too close together, nearly meeting across the bridge of my nose. This, however, was easily repaired by tugging at every offending hair until it came out by the roots. My eyes, though finely coloured I thought, were in danger of growing much too large and the lashes not long enough. The nose between them was utterly characterless, still a tiny nib of a thing, but at least well-proportioned. As for the mouth, it seemed hopelessly ugly—not at all as puckered and full-lipped as I might have wished. Staring still more closely, I detected flaws at every point upon my cheeks and throat and brow: here a pimple, there a freckle, and each seeming to grow more conspicuous every time I looked.

On the other hand, I fancied that my chin was strongly shaped and my neck gracefully balanced upon my shoulders. But when I stepped back so that I might see more, I could hardly stand the sight of myself. For what I saw was a straight, narrow torso, as flat across the bosom as a boy's. Even when I inhaled deeply and thrust out my chest to the maximum, there was only the faintest hint of protuberance. And below, my hips were wholly undefined from my waist; between them, at the juncture of my narrow thighs, my sex was that still of a child, smooth and modest. How much there was of me yet to be shaped!

But by what touchstone of female comeliness was I measuring myself so severely? Was it Solange, whom Victor had made his plaything? I called up her image and frankly prayed heaven I might never look like her. Such sluttishly stout girls, so brazen of manner, invited the contempt that men showed them. No, the true template I had before my mind's eye was Francine, upon whom I had first seen Victor cast his lustful glance. She had become my female paragon, a criterion I knew I could never equal. Yet I knew she took no care whatever for her looks, trusting to plain Nature for whatever appearance it bestowed upon her. Even with her hair tied sternly back and knotted, and wearing not a trace of paint, she radiated beauty. And what I had seen of her naked form had become my ideal of mature womanhood, though again I had no hope I could match the standard.

What children learn most deeply, they need no vocabulary to express. Sometimes the very absence of words makes the experience all the stronger. I had no language to express all I learnt that day at the pond; that would come later; but the emotions that had been set momentarily alight within me were nonetheless an education. Disgust and captivation, trepidation and impertinence, shame and exhilaration had all mingled in the lesson. Thereafter, when Victor and I swam naked together, it was as if another, more exotic climate enveloped us: an electricity that charged the air, surrounding our once-chaste nakedness with honeyed delirium.

Looking back now, I realise that on that day we had both crossed the line that divides innocence from experience. That achingly poignant moment at childhood's end was the beginning of a chapter in our lives that would be the most impassioned and most tragic. Never again would Victor and I be the brother and sister we had been in the past—though brother and sister we would now become in another, more daring kind of kinship. Without realising where our sweetly tempted flesh was tending, we had taken our first, faltering steps toward the chymical marriage.

EDITOR'S NOTE
A Surviving Portrait of Elizabeth Frankenstein

The evaluation the author offers above of her appearance, as seen from the vantage point of her girlhood, is far too unflattering to pass without a corrective comment. I will at this point introduce a contrasting and less subjective image.

Among her papers, Elizabeth Frankenstein preserved a tiny, faded water-colour miniature. Though the work bears no name, it will be identified later in this memoir as her portrait, painted under unusual circumstances in the year 1788. The drawing is of a strikingly lovely woman in her late adolescence. Her hair is natural and unpowdered, tied back into a casual topknot and worn close around the face in ringlets, not the usual

French style of the day. I note that this is the manner of combing Elizabeth mentions as a means of covering the birth scar at her temple.

There is a vividly memorable refinement to the face—the cheekbones high, the chin proud, the lips full. The eyes are frank and penetrating. There is no hint of virginal timidity in the gaze, but rather a vivacity of expression that bespeaks high intelligence and an enquiring mind untypical of her sex—exactly the quality of intellect I should have thought that Victor Frankenstein, as a man of science, would value in his betrothed. The throat and shoulders match the delicacy of the visage, as does the tautness of the young bosom. I could not, indeed, cast my eye upon that fragile throat without ruminating morbidly upon how easily it was crushed in the hands that stopped this lady's life; that act could have been no more difficult than snapping the bones of a songbird.

I will confess that this portrait occasioned great unease during my research. When the true nature of Victor's alchemical experimentation became clear to me, my heart at first went out to the maiden whom he had, as I assumed, seduced into cooperating in his unnatural designs. But as Elizabeth's own rôle in these acts emerged from her memoirs, I found myself increasingly troubled by the terrible possibility that one so young and fair might have harboured such unseemly passions. Since my studies of these papers began, this captivating portrait has been before me constantly, displayed upon the desk where now I write. Not a day has passed but I have scrutinised it yet again, seeking to elicit the true character that lay hidden behind the chaste surface. I have asked, Would not such unnatural desires betray themselves in some shade or nuance, some small hint of a corrupted heart? But I have at last had to yield to the bitter wisdom that teaches us "There's no art / To find the mind's construction in the face."

Was it possible, I found myself speculating, that the cultivation of self-possession and high intelligence in woman must always risk the moral degeneracy that led to Elizabeth Frankenstein's undoing? Is there no way to guarantee that the intellectual development of our companion sex will safeguard its virtue? Or must we regrettably choose between the two? I daresay this will remain among the great conundra of our revolutionary times.

I Learn the
Mysteries of Women

In the weeks that followed, I gave my particular attention to
Solange, studying her every quality. I tried to dismiss her as a
sluttish simpleton; I took wicked satisfaction in the crude peasant
accent with which she spoke, and watched for every coarse trait in
her manners. How disgustingly she reeked of the kitchen! Even so,
though I would not admit to the fact, I burnt with secret jealousy
in her presence. Was this, then, the sort of slatternly wench Victor
desired? I wondered. Was it her vulgarity he fancied: the ribald language she used, the shameless way she displayed her legs and fat
bosom as she worked about the house? What liberties had he taken
with her when he had her alone and at his mercy? Had he truly done
no more than lay an exploring hand on her? Before I fell asleep at night,
I imagined the two of them together as naked as I had been with Victor
in the meadow; but Solange would have permitted him to do what
he wished—and had perhaps enjoyed his wantonness. Was it possible
that she had seduced Victor? I had heard that cunning servant girls
often schemed to gain their master's favour in that way. But then I
could not believe Solange was so clever. Whenever the opportunity
presented itself, I took to giving her troublesome orders that made
her chase and carry for me; I complained aloud that she was stupid
and fumbling. If I could have had my way, I would have banished her
from the house and ordered her to work in the yards where the sun

would turn her milk-white skin brown and the labour would bend her back.

✖

What I had learnt by examining Victor's body that day at the pond was prologue to my own womanhood; I knew I was to undergo an even greater metamorphosis. And would I then look like the many women I had seen when I assisted Rosina at her deliveries, with their stout flanks and drooping breasts? I did not altogether relish the prospect of taking on this womanly figure. Certainly, as the artists portrayed it, it looked to me lumpish and ungainly; I was not eager to give up my lithe girl's body that allowed me to gambol as I pleased, in return for what I feared might be a great sedentary carcass. Yet, despite my misgivings, I longed still more strongly to join Victor in his maturity, expecting I would enter upon secrets that no child can know.

I had some idea what to expect; even so, womanhood came to me with the shock it invariably brings to girls. From my Gipsy sister Tamara, a few years older than myself, I had learnt about the bleeding; yet it is one thing to hear of such a thing and another to suffer it. And when it came upon me, I quite forgot all I had ever been told. I woke one morning to find my nightgown red and sticky. Was I injured? I wondered, and ran at once along the corridor toward Lady Caroline's room. But she was not there; I found instead Anna Greta the chamber-maid at work smoothing the bedclothes. When she turned, I shrank back, both panicked and ashamed. She at once saw what my condition was. "Lord! Don't be frightened, child," she said. "Your mother will explain about this."

She took me to a nearby water closet and gave me what I needed to clean myself. "Wait here," she instructed me gently. "And be calm. You have no reason for shame." And then she sent Lady Caroline to me.

I knew as soon as Lady Caroline appeared wearing a kindly smile that I had no cause for alarm. Her caring presence was enough to lift my spirits. "Do you know what has happened, my dear?" she asked. "You are of age. Something has changed here . . . and here." She placed her hand on my abdomen and bosom. "It is a dark and wonderful change.

You are being remade inside, the way a caterpillar is remade to become a butterfly."

"But must there be blood?" I asked.

"The blood is your strength, as you will learn. Now listen carefully," she instructed me as she took me onto a sofa beside her. Her eyes assumed their remotely pensive mode. "Think of this as a second birth. When you were first born, a violent mark was placed upon you—here." She drew her fingers across the faded scar at my temple. "This was done in ignorance by a man who presumed to call himself a doctor. This time you shall be born in the care of women, and it will be a time for rejoicing and celebration. There will be no scars and no bad dreams."

I had told the Baroness of my nightmare, soon after I arrived in the household. One night, when I awoke screaming, she insisted that I tell her what had disrupted my sleep. When I told her of the cruel bird-man who haunted my mind at night, for the first time I thought I saw the colour of anger come into her quiet face. "You have been wounded not only in your flesh, but deeper still," she said and then did her best to comfort me. "There was no such creature. It is a fantasy and in time it will fade from your mind." Now, when she spoke of celebration, I could not contain my curiosity. I wished to know *when, when!* and asked with an almost impertinent eagerness. "Soon," she said. "The time must be carefully chosen."

I was told I must wait for the first full moon of the summer, still two months away. Twice more until then I experienced the bleeding, and dealt with it as I had been shown. My fears passed, but not my disquiet. I was quickly reconciled to the fact that I must accept this vexing predicament, but I could not see why Lady Caroline believed there was pride to be taken in it. Despite her assurances, I found this so unnatural a thing that I was certain I must be visibly marked by it. Surely others knew of my condition and found it unclean. I waited, therefore, with rising anticipation for the event I had been promised, hoping it would bring me something more than the shame I felt. As June ran its course, I watched each night at my window as the moon waxed in the heavens from a fragile crescent to a great glowing pearl. At last, it was the eve of its fullness; and on the next morning, Anna Greta woke me with the words, "Tonight, little one. Be ready."

That afternoon, Mme. Eloise broke off my lessons early and led me away to my bedchamber, insisting I must have a nap. This was not my usual way. "Attend me," she said. "The Baroness says that you will be up late tonight. You must be rested." Since I had not seen Lady Caroline all that day, I asked where she might be. Mme. Eloise shook her head. "Away, my dear, making preparations."

I tried to sleep as I was instructed, but not successfully. An air of high anticipation surrounded me. This was no ordinary day, though I could never have said in what way it was extraordinary.

That evening I was served no supper, but was instructed by Mme. Eloise to go to my room, bathe, and put on the new dress she would give me; then I was to wait until I was summoned. The dress she laid out upon my bed was a flowing white nightgown that came to my ankles. Was I being prepared for sleep? I wondered. Nevertheless, though puzzled, I did as I was told, and I spent the waiting hours at the window, gazing at the rising moon which covered the garden and the fields beyond with a veil of shadowed silver. I had not noticed until then the strangeness of this light, which is both frigid and molten, how it pours a mercurial sheen over all it touches. Things are blanched of their colours and take on uncanny shapes, as if they were the ghosts of themselves. How long I waited I cannot say, for in spite of myself I finally dozed where I sat. I woke with a hand upon my shoulder; it was Mme. Eloise, there to lead me away.

We stole through the sleeping house as silently as thieves and made our way out the kitchen door. There we met Anna Greta, who, like Mme. Eloise, was dressed in a bulky cloak and hood. Asking no questions, I followed where they led. Though the way was circuitous, I recognised this route. It led to the little glade where Victor and I had spied upon the Baroness and Francine. Along our path, I was startled to see a robed and hooded figure step out upon the path—then another and another. I judged that they were women, though I saw no faces clearly. One held a lanthorn, the others long, forked sticks. Mme. Eloise stepped boldly over to them as if to identify herself. We passed by, leaving the three figures behind in the woods; but when we had moved several steps farther, one of them sent up an owl-like wail that made my blood chill. Had I not known it came from a woman, I might have thought it was the call of a hunting bird. Twice more this happened; these figures were, I gathered, sentinels waiting along the path for us. Each time they sent us on our way with an eery hoo-hooing. The last group we found stationed just outside the entrance to the glade. This time, when I slipped through the tight passage that concealed it, I discovered the grove was lit with lanthorns on all sides; they hung from trees and were fitted into every crevice of the surrounding rock, creating everywhere a subdued glow that was neither night nor day.

At first, the glade seemed empty. But as Mme. Eloise and Anna Greta led me down the mountain ledge toward the stream below, I became aware of silent and unmoving figures concealed behind the trees. At the centre of the glade where I was instructed to kneel was a rugged table made of standing stones. Upon it sat a chalice, a bell, two crossed knives of a strange shape, upon the knives a circle plaited of flowers, and behind them three tall candles as yet unlit. Mme. Eloise and Anna Greta now removed their cloaks, beneath which they were wearing loose grey gowns with hoods which they drew over their heads; with me they knelt at the stone altar. After a moment during which the only sound was the gurgling of the stream, I heard a high, tremulous wailing in the nearby woods. It was the sound I might have expected an eagle to make as it descended upon its prey, but it emerged, I knew, from a woman's throat. Three times it rose and fell, as if it might be a summoning call. And then the woods all round were alive with sound. Drums, rattles, tambourines initiated a rhythm; and circling high above them the voice of a flute embroidered a sinuous melody. It was music of some other world or of another age far gone; it beat with the rhythm of the blood and breath; the body longed to move with the elemental flowing of it. From the four quarters of the grove, columns of hooded figures emerged, all dressed like my companions at either side. Some carried the instruments I heard; others glided among and between them in a slow, circling dance. My heart raced, not with fear, but with anticipation as the circle slowly wound round me where I knelt. Mme. Eloise, as if to bolster my courage, took my hand and squeezed it firmly.

I could not tell how many women there were both before and behind me, but they numbered at least twoscore. When they had ringed me round, they stopped in place and sat upon the ground, still making their music, and now taking up a chant, the words in a language I could not understand. At last their voices fell silent and the playing ceased. From behind me I heard the rustling of footfalls in the grass. Two figures had made their way through the seated women and now stood across from me on the far side of the altar. They were gowned and hooded like the others. One continued standing, to utter what I took to be a prayer; the other bent to light the candles and then the incense that was heaped in a fretted silver receptacle. When that was done, the two raised their heads and dropped their hoods. I knew them both. One was Lady Caroline, who I had suspected would appear at some point; but the identity of the other left me more surprised than I could ever have expected. It was Celeste, the cook! She stood solemn-faced and austere before me, her curling grey hair undone and falling about her shoulders. To see her here in this setting, wearing this costume and assuming so regal an air— this was a sight that jarred me.

"Rise, Elizabeth!" Celeste ordered in a strong, deep voice. "Thou art here to become a Woman, as Woman is known among Women."

I rose promptly, as I was instructed; I think I should have hastened to obey her no matter what she asked; though I had known her only as a servant in our house, she was now as intimidating a presence as I had ever stood before, and no mere cook commanding me. At a nod from her, Mme. Eloise and Anna Greta busied themselves to my left and right, working at my ties and buttons. I realised that they were removing my clothing. Though my heart was racing, I stood staring bravely into Celeste's face, determined to show no misgiving. When at last I stood naked, all the women in the circle rose and stepped closer to the little stone altar; there they briskly shook their loose garments from them to stand as naked as myself. Stealing a glance at those I could see closest to me, I now recognised several faces. I spied three more of our chambermaids, and Germaine the game-keeper's wife; she was carrying the largest of all the drums. There was Mme. Laplanche our bailiff's wife and beside her Mme. Perroud the magistrate's wife, who was often a guest at the Baron's *soirées*. On my other side I saw Mme. Jussieu the boatman's wife, and Mme. Grimaldi with her two daughters, who tended our vineyard with their husbands. I caught sight of women I had seen at work in the fields as our carriage passed along the roads, and of women from La Belotte, whose husbands caught the fish we ate. How far they had walked to come to the glade this night! All the way up from the lake, finding their way by moonlight. And how odd it was to see them here this way, unclothed, their hair undone, standing shamelessly in the lanthorn light. Without their dresses and adornments to mark them off from one another, they became a society of equals, where one could not tell which was a woman of quality and which a woman of the meaner orders. How brave it was to remove one's clothes, I thought. For one must leave behind all distinction with them. I noticed, too, that here and there were women who wore the sort of waistcloth I had been lately given to staunch the blood; both high and low, they shared that condition, and in this company wore nothing to conceal it, displaying no sign of unease to be so revealed. Some I now realised for the first time were thin and sunken of build, some strong and lean, some portly, some wizened, some strikingly handsome. And there among the ranks of women was someone I was startled to see, even though I had been secretly seeking her: Solange, who stood proudly beside her mother. She was every bit as voluptuously endowed as I had enviously imagined. But how well she performed her rôle this night, moving to the music, when it played, with the elegance of a courtly dancer.

Glancing this way and that, I saw the bodies of women as bent with age as the grandmother of Jacques the stable-boy, and others as brightly flowering as Marianne the tax-collector's daughter, a girl not much older than myself. Some bore upon their persons the marks of injury— scars and bruises, a crooked limb, a hunched shoulder. How much of what we are is written in our bone and flesh, but hidden by our habiliments from the eye of the world. Celeste, in her nakedness, was of particular interest to me. I had always known her to be a buxom woman;

now I saw how truly corpulent she was. Her breasts, which I had seen only trussed up like a great loaf of bread across her chest, now depended heavily down her torso, resting on a barrel-sized stomach that folded like an apron over her private parts and hid them from view. Her stubby legs were as thick round as my entire body. I should have found it impossible to think of a woman so encumbered by her size as a figure of authority. But so she was—and unmistakeably so. She stood proud and stern beside Lady Caroline, sharing the leadership of this flock.

The Baroness picked up the crown of flowers from the altar; turning, she brought it to me and held it above my head. She smiled down at me and said, "We welcome Elizabeth, wearer of the blossom and the thorn. Who speaks for her in this company?"

A voice spoke from behind me. "I do" was all it said, but I recognised at once whose it was. I turned to see Francine standing just behind me. She too was naked, except for a bright silver disk she wore on a chain round her neck. She stepped forward, smiling broadly, and gave my nose a playful tweak. Then, positioning herself behind me she placed her hands on my shoulders. At that, the Baroness settled the flowered circlet upon my head and stepped back. Two women approached from either side of the altar, holding forth dishes; on one rested a single apple; on the other, a metal flagon. Celeste took first the apple and held it high over her head. At her side, Lady Caroline lightly stroked the bell as Celeste concentrated her thoughts on the uplifted fruit; she then handed it to Francine, saying, "Eat this in memory of Mother Eve, blameless for our sorrows."

Francine took a small bite from the apple, then held it out to me. When I had bitten, it was returned to Celeste, who shared the remainder with Lady Caroline. Celeste then took up the flagon and from it filled the crystal chalice upon the altar. She raised the cup above her head, and again the bell was rung. To Francine she said, "Drink this in the memory of Mother Lilith, who suffered first at the hands of Man."

The flagon was passed to Francine, who shared with me the wine it held. Then at my ear Francine whispered, "Come!" I stood and followed where she led. A low drumbeat reverberated through the glade like thunder rising from the ground.

Now at the centre of the circle of women, I stood with Francine directly behind me, her body pressed so tight against my own that I could feel her breasts rise and fall against my back. Celeste stepped forward, holding a great scroll of yellowed parchment as thick round as her arm. It was tied with a tasseled leather thong. She did not open it, but hugged it tight against her bosom while, with eyes closed, she intoned what I took to be a prayer in a language I did not know. She went on for many minutes, her brow frowning with the effort, her face glowing with emotion; all the while the drum sounded lowly, its rhythm steadily intensifying. As her incantation grew more impassioned, Celeste passed into a stupor, swaying from side to side, her body shining with perspiration. Her prayer seemed to have become a recitation of names, at first strange and ancient, then names I could recognise as those of women, first name and last, names French, Italian, German, English, Spanish . . . Then abruptly she finished; the drum beat a rapid, forceful tattoo and stopped. Celeste held the scroll out first to Francine to kiss, then to me to do the same.

The Baroness came forward; in her hands were the two knives I had seen lying on the altar. These she handed to me, the white knife in my right hand pointed skyward, the black knife in my left pointed to the ground. From behind, Francine prompted me to spread my arms wide to either side. Another woman—it was Mme. Kleist—stepped forth from the circle; she held out an earthenware bowl to Lady Caroline, who reached in and brought her hand away stained a deep crimson. Turning back to me, she drew her fingers across my brow, making an odd sort of scribble, then, dipping again into the bowl each time, she did the same at my lips, my breast, my abdomen, between my legs just above the sexual cleft, and upon each foot. I knew, from the moment she touched my lips, that this was blood, and I winced at the taste. I looked down to see the mark she had made upon me; it was a six-pointed star composed of a doubled triangle.

Francine turned me round to face her and let Lady Caroline hold me against her body. Again I spread my arms, holding the two knives wide apart. The flute began a dark, mournful melody as Francine removed the necklace she wore—the silver disk on a chain—and, holding it high overhead as if she wished to touch the glowing moon, she spoke in a tongue I at last understood. Each phrase she uttered was echoed by all the voices in the glade.

> Lady of Pearl,
> Look down, look down.
> Queen of all Stars,
> Draw down, draw down.
> Ship of Silver,
> Sail far, sail near.
> Jewel of Night,
> Bless us here.
> Dove of Darkness,
> Descend, descend.
> Blade of Hathor,
> Defend, defend.

Francine then slowly lowered the disk she held and with its edge, touched my brow lightly where the blood had been painted. "She blesses you here for the purity of all you shall think," she said, and then pressed her lips against my flesh where the disk had been. This she repeated at every point where the Baroness had drawn the emblem in blood.

At my lips: "She blesses you here for the purity of all you shall speak."

At my breast: "She blesses you here for the purity of all you shall love."

Passing over my belly—which I had thought she would next touch— she pressed the disk between my thighs: "She blesses you here for the purity of all that brings you pleasure." And then bending, she pressed a kiss firmly upon me. I think I would surely have flinched at the boldness of her act, if Lady Caroline were not holding me fast.

Francine then returned to my belly: "She blesses you here for the purity of children you would willingly bear."

And then, bowing before me to touch and kiss each foot: "She blesses you here for the purity of every path you tread."

When she had finished, the drum roared out, building to a boisterous crescendo and the women raised their voices in a joyous wailing. Francine stood to place the disk round my neck, and kissed me warmly on the lips. "Welcome, sister," she said. And all the group echoed her words. There was much laughter now round the circle, as each woman freely shouted out words of greeting and congratulation.

Several of the women next stepped forward to lead us in a procession. They danced in a stately sarabande before us, scattering the petals of flowers to make a carpet. I was astonished to see how gracefully even the old and ungainly moved to this music, as if it touched them with a special dignity. With Lady Caroline at one side and Francine at the other, I was led into the trees at the far end of the glade. Celeste, carrying the great scroll tight to her breast, and the others formed in a group behind us and followed, the drum and flute and tambourine playing gaily. Through the trees I could see another light: a burning brazier in an open space. In the pool of light it created, I saw a figure seated in a sort of throne roughly made of branches. As we approached I saw she was a woman, naked like ourselves but greatly wasted with age. Her skin was dark-hued and hung loosely from her hunched frame; her hair was snow-white and fell in thin wisps about her face. I did not know this person, but she seemed to be of high importance. When we stood before her I saw she wore several necklaces at her throat and bands of bracelets up each of her emaciated arms. She seemed unimaginably old, yet there was a fiery light in her eyes as she gazed at me.

"Come to me, Elizabeth," she said, summoning me to the foot of the throne she sat on. Her voice was dry and raspy, but kindly in tone. She studied me closely, then stroked my hair. "Fair Elizabeth, golden one," she said. I was amazed to hear the words, for they were spoken in Romany, the language of my childhood. She smiled at my surprise. "Yes, I speak a little of your Gipsy tongue, but, I fear, no longer well enough." Then, in French with an accent that might be Italian, she asked, "Do you know who I am?"

"No, I do not."

"My name is Seraphina. I am as old as you are young. The blood that flows richly from your body long ago dried up in mine. But we are both women—whether at the beginning or the end of our path. And we are sisters. Can you believe that?" I said I could not, at which she laughed, making a dry wheezing sound. When her mouth gaped open there was not a single tooth to be seen in her jaws. "You have more sisters than you know, Elizabeth. This very ground you stand upon has been trodden by sisters—yours and mine—since time out of mind. There are springs here where women came to speak of deep matters so long ago that even these great mountains may not be old enough to remember. The men call the knowledge they find inscribed on stone or written on parchment 'ancient.' But by the reckoning of women, their great ones— Aristotle and Pythagoras—are mere young boys. Before men read from scrolls, our mothers and grandmothers read from the forests and the stars and the stones. This grove is one of our oldest schools; every tree you see here knows more than the greatest natural philosopher. They have been our teachers."

At this point, I was startled by a sudden rush of wings near my ear. A great dark bird had flown down from the trees above and settled on the old woman's wrist. There it sat, cocking its head at me as if it were studying me closely. I had never seen such a bird before; it was as large as a raven, but its colouring was an iridescent purple and its hooked yellow beak was larger than its head. I would have judged by the shabbiness of its feathers that it was quite old. One eye seemed blinded: half-closed and clouded under the squinting and wrinkled lids. I was not sure if I should regard it as menacing, but none about me showed any sign of fear at its intrusive presence. Indeed, Seraphina, to whom the creature seemed to belong, reached to run her finger under its throat— at which the bird chortled, then reached up one of its legs to scratch at its neck.

"Do not be afraid," Seraphina said, opening her mouth in a wide, toothless grin. "This is my particular friend Al Ussa. She has come to meet you. She will make up her own mind about your qualities—but I will see if I can persuade her to think well of you." Seraphina bent to whisper at the bird's ear; I heard my name mentioned in the midst of a language I did not understand. "As old as I am, Alu iś older still. She has been my companion since I was but your age." By this time the old bird seemed to have lost interest in me and had fluttered to Seraphina's shoulder, where it sat watching all that followed, though with a distracted, somewhat bored air.

"All the women who stand beside you," Seraphina explained, "are my sisters as they are yours—yours to call upon in time of joy and fear and sorrow. They have been good and grateful friends to me. None of them would know what they know if I had not taught them. And what is that? I have taught them never to sorrow or to be ashamed that they are women. I have taught them to care for one another's needs. I have taught them that the blood is their strength, for it is the power of the heavens and the Earth within them. Look now and I will show you. Let me see the knives."

I held out the knives I had been given.

"These are yours to keep, Elizabeth. They are to remind you of this night and of all you will learn. Keep them hidden as you would your most precious possession. Here is the silver knife; it binds you to the moon you see above. The moon is the woman's star; it governs the tides of our blood as it does the tides of the sea. Men have nothing like this to tell them of true order. So they think they can make up their own order of things; but they cannot. We must remind them of that.

"And here is the dark knife. This knife binds you to the Earth. The Earth is a woman as we are. She bears children as we do. She makes the trees and crops and beasts out of Her flesh. We know of this power in our very bodies. Men have nothing like this to bind them to the Earth; their ignorance gives rise to strange fantasies. They rend the Earth and reshape Her and dig into Her. They steal the gems and metals She hides in Her womb. They would move the mountains if they could, and turn the rivers round in their natural course. They think they can make what they would of the world. They are wrong. We must remind them of that."

She leaned forward in her seat and reached out an unsteady arm toward me. "Come here, child. Come close. I shall tell you a secret." I inched forward as far as I could toward her throne; she brought her lips beside my ear and spoke in a husky whisper. "Deep, deep under the Earth there are stones buried where no eye will ever see them. And inside these stones, if you were to break them open, you would discover wonders and delights that would make your mind drunk with such beauty. Here, let me show you." And drawing me toward her breast, she stretched out one unsteady arm to display the several bracelets she wore on her wrist. Depending from one was a large, teardrop stone that scintillated gold and purple and green in the glancing rays of the firelight. "What do you think, my dear?" Seraphina asked. "Is it not exquisite?"

"Oh yes . . . it is," I said as I stared with fascination at this tiny fountain of coruscating colours. The gem seemed to be lit from within, so bright was the light it emanated.

"The longer you gaze upon it, the more wondrous it becomes," Seraphina said. "It is a rainbow from far below the Earth. Yet it is as nothing compared to the stones that lie where this stone came from. Now tell me: Why do you think the Earth has placed something so beautiful for the eye to see where no eye can ever behold it?"

"I do not know."

"You shall learn the answer to this and many riddles. The Earth Herself will tell you." She released me and instructed me to stand. "Take your knives now and lay them crossed upon the Earth just there, the white atop the black."

I scrambled down to do as she told me, gently laying the two knives upon the ground at the foot of her throne.

"Did you hear Her speak when you did that?"

"No, I did not."

"But you shall before you return to your bed tonight." She reached out a withered arm to summon Francine to her. Francine knelt beside me at her feet. "All these women are your sisters, Elizabeth, just as I am. But Francine is to be your special sister. She will teach you things no man can teach you, matters you must learn if you are to be your own woman. She will tell you the meaning of all you have witnessed this night. With her you may share secrets that you would share with no one else. You are already marked in all your holy places with blood she has freely given for this celebration. With her you will be linked by blood in your very veins. Are you willing to have this be?"

I said I was, though I felt some trepidation. Seraphina asked for my hand and for Francine's. Holding our hands in hers, she shut her eyes, bowed her head, and muttered words I could not hear. Then Celeste stepped forward with a knife; she wiped the blade with a leaf, then pricked my first finger; she did the same with Francine. Seraphina pressed our fingers together and held them in a tighter grip than I could have imagined possible for one so old. Once again Francine offered me a kiss on the lips, then stood back. "Tonight we have lit this grove with lanthorns," Seraphina explained. "But walk just a little way into these woods and you will come to a place where the light leaves off and darkness begins. So too, words leave off. There is much no one can teach you, many things that must teach themselves, things that will not come out of the darkness into the light. What happens in your body when life begins there is hid in darkness. But the darkness can speak in its own way." As if she were no longer a baroness in this company but Seraphina's servant, Mother knelt at the old woman's side, holding out a small bowl from which Seraphina scooped a mushy substance. She held it at my lips on her quivering fingers. "Here. Take. Eat," she commanded. The odour that arose was pungent but not unpleasant. The taste, however, was exceedingly bitter; my throat all but closed down, at first refusing to swallow. I forced the concoction past my gullet and in a moment felt myself growing dizzy. I tried to steady myself, but my limbs had become weak. Francine and Lady Caroline helped me to make my way back from the throne, and stretched me upon the ground with my head just below the knives I had crossed upon the Earth. Francine stationed herself just beside me, placing one hand flat upon my forehead and the other upon my heart. The dizziness I felt had become a warm, sweet sensation; my entire skin seemed to be glowing. Staring up, I saw the moon as if it were so close I might touch it by merely climbing the highest limbs of the trees; it was fairly dancing among the branches. The women were dancing, too, in intertwining circles round me where I lay. The music of the drum and flute and rattle filled the glade. I heard the joyous harmony come and go, come and go at my ears. It would thunder in my head, then fade far off. Gradually I became aware of a trembling in the ground beneath me; the tremor raced along my veins through my body. It was a tickling of my entire frame and yet at the same time a sort of speaking, as if my body were the tongue that spoke; I think I began to laugh, and everybody about me laughed, a high raucous female laughter. The Earth beneath me also laughed; I could hear it—or feel it. Francine's face looking down wore the moon as a halo. I felt comforted and safe, indeed almost giddy in her embrace.

What transpired that night, I was sworn never to reveal. "We keep our secrets not out of shame or fear," Seraphina instructed me, "but out of respect. What we do here is *ours*. There is little in the world that women can claim to own; but these rites we own. Others would not understand. They would see evil where we see good. They would punish and destroy. You must respect what your sisters wish to keep as their own. Do you promise to keep what you learn locked away in your heart?"

And I promised.

Even now, when I am determined to tell all, it is as if an unseen hand reaches out of the past to seal my lips and remind me of my vow. But in truth there is much I could not tell even though I should wish to, for as the night wore on, things became strangely dream-like and swoonish and my mind drifted. I know there was dancing and great merriment; the women shared food and laughed together with an ease and gaiety I had never previously remarked in women. Before the night was over, all had come to embrace me and pledge their love; many gave me tokens of their sisterhood, simple crafted objects for the most part, but more precious to me than gold or jewels could be. When I was returned to my bedroom, bathed and groomed, I felt light as air—as if, at any moment I pleased, I might fly above the trees to embrace the moon and stars. And what was real and what imagined, I could not surely say.

When I woke the following morning, then and for the next few days, I felt strangely and sweetly elevated, a mood I wished to have nothing disturb. I felt as if I had been cleansed to the bone, or rather *polished* to a gem-like brightness. Crystalline. And there was also a peace in my heart, for which I felt an upwelling of gratitude. It was as if I had stood before a gate I could not see beyond and had been fearful of what might lie waiting there, only to have passed through and found there was nothing whatever to fear. Others—my sisters—were there to welcome me.

And one thing more, this the most precious. For the first time since she had taken me to be her daughter, this woman I had regarded as the remote and regal Baroness became—in my thoughts and not merely in words—my mother. There was still a difference of levels between us that exacted my deference. But underlying this was an equality that I knew would grow to be our greater bond. I knew that she wished this to be, as much as I. We had become blood of one another's blood, not as mother and daughter, but as women together.

I was "of age."

The Two Streams

There is a place at the heights of the Bois de Bâtie, no more than half a league outside the ramparts of Geneva, where one can observe the rivers Arve and Rhône as they flow together. One day, Father took me to see this remarkable confluence. For several hundreds of yards after they have met, the waters of the two streams—the pensive grey of the Arve, the regal blue of the Rhône—run side by side, as if they might forever remain separate in their common channel. But then, subtly, gracefully, they blend to become a single river, the greater Rhône that will roll forth to water the rich farmlands of the South.

After I had been admitted to the mysteries of women, this was how I came to see Belrive in its spiritual nature. More than a stately mansion, the estate was a crux in time where two great currents of life converged. The one was embodied in the Baron's works and hopes, a mighty stream that flashed into the future, carrying the thrusting aspirations of all humanity. Father was mind, science, invention: the force of revolutionary endeavour. The lightning bolt he had boldly chosen for our family crest spoke of his fiery vision in which there lay a power that might set the world alight—or perhaps aflame. Though he spoke of this power as "Reason," it was no matter of cool geometrical precision. It was a passion of the soul that might righteously sweep all that stood against it.

Outwardly, in the world's eye, Belrive was Father's house. His were the grand *soirées* and matters of state where lords and ladies and men of letters assembled. This was what one saw of Belrive if one stood on its velvet lawn on some grand occasion to observe the chandeliers burning in every window and all the rooms thronging with people. But now I knew my home was much more than this. Even when the château was lit from top to bottom with its lustres all ablaze, it was still but a tiny point of light vastly enclosed by night and silence. Surrounding Father's island of Enlightenment were the dark forests and secret glades that had been there from the beginning, older even than the bones of those barbarian kings who lay sleeping at our foundations. That encompassing darkness was the second Belrive—Mother's Belrive, a stream that issued from deep in the Earth, bearing memories of primordial ways. Father's was the forward course, driving the ship of civilisation toward unknown continents. Mother was the defender of ancient springs. Only these two taken together, the questing current and the river of remembrance, made the true Belrive.

I was at times tempted to call the one current all male, the other all female. But they were not so. For again and again I saw Father's tenderness of heart revealed in acts of kindness. Even more so, I saw flashes of masculine wit in Mother. Intellect existed in her as a talent of the mind; but it was balanced against that other current that existed in her as a loyalty of the heart. As I was soon to learn, she wished to see this balance instilled in me, and even more so in Victor, who often seemed wholly driven by the questing current. We were intended to wed the two rivers in graceful union. This design she set in motion almost immediately following my night of initiation.

To begin with, the Baron became conveniently preoccupied in urgent commercial ventures that kept him away from home for months at a stretch. Since he worked mainly out of his quarters in the city, which was more than two hours distant by barque in a favourable wind, his activities remained largely mysterious to me. I knew little more than that his trade was principally in gold, which he transported in great shipments to trading centres round Europe and far beyond. But I had no idea *how* far beyond until one day, shortly before he was to depart for an extended journey, he took Victor and me to visit his banking offices on the Grand Rue. Frankenstein Fils was a snug set of chambers where some dozen fiercely concentrated men bustled about exchanging documents and comparing ledgers. Its main feature, to my uninitiated eye, was the enormous map that stretched across one wall and on which numbers were plotted and lines drawn to record the Baron's business ventures. Now, for the first time, I saw how distantly our family's name had travelled in the world. For wherever the demands of commerce might take the Baron, that place was marked with a tiny flag that bore the Frankenstein arms. "In June, I shall be here . . . and in September, here . . . and in December, here," the Baron said as he pinned each new marker to a city. By now there were flags scattered across the map of Europe from the Kingdom of Portugal to the plains of Muscovy. One journey had posted the Frankenstein arms as far up the Nile as the Great Pyramids and another as deep into the land of the Grand Turk as the fabulous cities of Baghdad and Samarra.

"Is it permitted to trade with the Mussulmen?" I asked, recalling the many lectures he had delivered on the Great Crusades.

"And why not?" he retorted. "The heathen's gold is as good as any man's. And," he added in a sly whisper, "I assure you, the Sultan has far more to be relieved of than any Christian banker . . . including myself."

But lately his interests had shifted in a new direction: across the Atlantic to the distant West, where the American colonies had of late been in rebellion against King George of England. As he described the journey that lay before him, he fastened flags upon towns called New York and Boston. "And beyond these outposts," he declared, sweeping his hand across the remainder of the continent, "wilderness, nothing but wilderness. Deserts, mountains, savages with painted faces. It will be the work of centuries to bring civilisation to this God-forsaken land."

"And must you travel to so wild a place?" I asked.

"This time, child, I do not travel for reasons of commerce. The gold I have sent to the New World I do not expect to see again, nor would I wish to have it returned. It has been expended to do M. Voltaire's work, and that is reward enough for any Enlightened mind."

I understood this reference. Just as Mother had given me Rousseau to read, the Baron had insisted I study the works of Voltaire, who was his particular hero. I was all but assigned the *Essai sur l'histoire générale* to read and quizzed upon it at dinner every evening. The Baron had many times engaged with the famous sage of Ferney, whom he called "the foremost social regenerator of our time." And when, just a few years before my coming, word had arrived of Voltaire's death, the Baron, who could not hold back his tears, had vowed forthwith to become the great thinker's loyal disciple. As I understood, the brave colonials who clung to the forested shores of America had rebelled against the British in behalf of their liberties; in the Baron's eyes this was a blow against tyranny that Voltaire would have approved. Victor had told me what part the Baron played in securing the independence of the rebels; he had sent them shiploads of gold to buy their armaments, thereby becoming a champion of revolution. Now that the insurrection had ended, he was invited to visit the nation in whose birth he had assisted in order to be honoured for his services.

"And right here," he continued as he attached a flag to a town called Philadelphia, "at the very edge of the Indian frontier, if you will believe it, lives the most brilliant mind of our time—save for M. Voltaire himself."

Victor already knew who this was. "Dr. Franklin," he said.

"Correct. Have you heard of Dr. Benjamin Franklin, my dear?" he asked me.

I had not.

"Victor can tell you more. He is especially well-versed in Dr. Franklin's electrical studies. This man has captured the living fires of the heavens for us, like some modern Prometheus. One day, we will use the electrical fluid he has investigated to create a new civilisation. For this is a prodigious power. Who can say? Perhaps we shall be able to spark our little friends to life. Think! A whole new race of humans— perhaps superior to ourselves." Then, rolling his eyes in Victor's direction, he added, "And what would you say, my boy, if I told you that I am promised the honour of meeting Dr. Franklin?"

Victor's mouth gaped with amazement. "Truly?"

"Truly. He has arranged for me to become his honorary fellow citizen. I shall bring you back a souvenir of the occasion. Perhaps one of Dr. Franklin's remarkable inventions."

"Tell me about electricity," I said to Victor after dinner that evening.

"It is a dangerous study," he answered, knitting his brows self-importantly. "One must be quite fearless to pursue it. Dr. Franklin might have been killed in tempting the lightning as he did."

"Is lightning made of electricity, then?"

"Of course. It is the selfsame element. Dr. Franklin has proved that. Soon we may treat lightning as our plaything; we shall use it to cook our meals and warm our homes. Men shall tame it as they have tamed the wild horses and make it work for us like a slave."

"But how can a thing as wild as lightning ever be tamed?"

"First it must be captured out of the ether in a Leyden jar."

"Do you have such a device?"

"The finest in Geneva. Father bought it for me. It can store the substanceless essence of electricity so that one may study it."

"Will you show me the jar?"

"Better than that, my dear. One day when you are old enough to understand I shall perform an experiment for you and you will witness this great power with your own eyes."

❧

Not long after the Baron departed on his travels, there was another change I welcomed even less. With Mother, Victor and Ernest were to take an extended sojourn; I would remain at home. They would stay for several weeks at Thonon-les-Bains. I had once been there with the family to take the waters, as did visitors from all parts of Europe. It was said to be a salubrious place, but I was not fond of it. I disliked the dank sweatiness of the baths and the odour of infirmity that hung in the air. I had found it more interesting to visit the many Romantic ruins that decorated the lakeside mountains. Some of these were said to be haunted by restless spirits; it was rumoured that a living skeleton had been seen walking the parapets of the ducal palace where we had stayed. But surely Mother was not going to Thonon for so long simply to bathe or to scout for haunted castles. Even Victor had no idea why he was wanted on the journey; Mother insisted and he complied. It would be the first time we had been parted since I came to Belrive.

Francine Becomes
My Tutor

I consoled myself that, during Victor's absence, I was to be left in
Francine's care. It was Mother's wish that, in the days immediately
following my acquaintance with the mysteries, I should as often as
possible be alone with Francine. "She will be your special tutor," I was
told. "She will teach you what others cannot."

Francine began now to visit the château for the first time on her own;
she came when the curate was abroad and stayed sometimes for several
days in succession. Most often when we wished to talk together she
would take me to the glade where our rites had been played out. Were
there questions, she asked, that I wished to have answered? Were there
indeed! So many I could not think which to ask first, and all came tum-
bling out at once. Where had all the women come from? Did they
gather often in the glade? Who had summoned them thither? Why had
we gone unclothed? What was the meaning of the silver disk? And of
the two knives? And what had come over me at the end of that remarkable night, when I was certain I had flown above the trees?

Francine laughed to hear this flood of queries burst from me. "One
question at a time!" she insisted. "And you must ponder each answer I
give you closely and not race on to the next. For these will not be such
lessons as you are familiar with—no, not even like the catechism you
learn from the pastor. Knowledge of the craft is knowledge of another
kind. The women you have met are wise women whose teachings can-

not be writ in books and taught in sermons. Yet theirs is simple knowl-edge of ordinary things; if all were well with the world, you would have no need of special instruction to learn it, nor would we have to hide ourselves away to speak of it. But as things are, if women did not teach the girls, you might never know what lies as close to you as your own skin."

"Is Seraphina a wise woman?" I asked. I wanted to know a great deal about this mysterious lady.

"Oh, yes. The oldest and wisest amongst us, wiser even than your mother, who was my teacher."

"I have never seen such a bird as she keeps with her."

"Alu! Nobody has ever seen such a bird. Seraphina says she comes from the islands of the southern seas, where such birds are honoured as oracles."

"And is she truly as old as Seraphina says?"

"She may well be. She is surely a witty animal. Seraphina converses with her constantly—but in a language none can understand. I have heard that Seraphina sends the bird to scout her way when she travels and to warn her of dangers. A cunning woman who travels abroad runs great risks."

"How has she become so wise?"

"Her people are said to be Gipsies from the isle of Sicily, but she has studied the craft in many lands—as did her mother before her. The women who taught her reach years and years into the past; Seraphina believes they go back to ancient times, to the time of Pharaoh and the Great Pyramids. You would not have learnt their names in your books; women, you see, have no history—except what we remember for our-selves. That is why the names of our great ones are always read when we meet at the first full moon of the summer. You saw the great scroll Celeste held? It must be the oldest writing in the world, the whole of it writ by women and in many languages. The names of the wise women are entered there; Celeste has learnt them all by heart. After her, another among us will do the same. Many of those who are named have suffered greatly for the craft; they have died like the martyrs of the Christian church. Above the names of some you will see a jagged line like this;

these were burnt alive at the stake. Beneath the names of others, you will see a wavy line like this; these were drowned. The names of others are circled; these were hanged. And all were tortured and violated before they were allowed to find their peace. Do you know what I mean by 'violated'?"

I said I did not.

"It means their sexual organ, this place that ought to be respected as the door of life, was forced open against their will and thrust into by men. This is a way men have invented to employ their sex—not for the sake of pleasure, but to humiliate and hurt, as if their organ were a weapon. The world does not honour the women who suffered this way, but we do. For we are blood of their blood, and proudly so. What these women have given mankind, no one will ever be able to calculate. All the arts of life stem from them, so Seraphina teaches: what we know of planting and weaving and cooking and feeding. Did you know that the great Paracelsus once said that if you would know how to heal, go among the women and learn from them? He was himself the student of a sorceress whose name is among the unknown."

"But why then have the wisewomen been made to suffer?"

Francine gave a sardonic little laugh. "This is a great puzzle. Among the Christians, it is because the fathers of the church would scrub the world clean of superstition; but the worst superstitions are of their own making—lies and follies they attribute to others. They believe we can fly like bats in the night and summon pigs out of the Earth, can you imagine! They make up this nonsense and then charge us with devilry."

Even when Francine explained as carefully as she could how she had used the silver disk that night to draw down the moon that it might bless me, or how the knives were the two voices of the world—the voice of the heavens and of the Earth—I did not understand all that she tried to teach me. "Nor do I myself," she admitted with a laugh. "Not *here*," she said, pointing to her forehead. "But *here* I think I have a kind of understanding." She passed her hand over her breast. "There is a knowledge of the upper world, which is bright and clear; that is the knowledge of the white knife. And a second knowledge, which prefers the darkness and the silence. That is the knowledge of the black knife. Each alone is a half-truth; but together, the one makes the other fertile." She held out her hands with the two first fingers crossed. "Sometimes, this is how we greet one another. When we are in the company of strangers, we make this sign. If another is our sister, she will return it. See? Like the two knives crossed. This is a token that darkness has its part to play; so we must find a way to trust it as much as we trust the light. What happens inside a woman—here—when a child forms, that happens in darkness. Our bodies need no words to know what they do."

And what of the silver disk? What did it mean that she had touched me and kissed me as she had?

"This was to teach you that you must not be ashamed to be a woman, nor ashamed of any part of yourself. All parts are to be honoured equally: the mind, the heart, the flesh . . . all."

"But you kissed me *here*," I told her, pointing.

"Yes, that too. That part is also holy. No man will tell you so, but it is true. In the church, the Christians taught me my sex was unclean, not to be touched or seen or spoken of, not even when it might need to be healed. My body was to be covered as if it were a shameful thing. Men taught my mother this, and her mother before her. Those who lust for our bodies—for they do, every one—shame us into keeping covered as if we were wily temptresses. That is why we go unclothed when we meet together as women: to show that we will no longer be shamed by what men believe of us. And to remember that we are all equal in our womanhood, burdened by the same tribulation. Nature made nothing to be ashamed of. Nature is, after all, herself a woman; some have called her a goddess."

This was a startling thing to hear. I had never seen this word except in books that spoke of ancient times. "Is she?"

"Do you not think so?"

"God is a man . . . I have learnt. Is there another god besides Him?"

Francine rubbed at her brow. "Lord! Your mother could tell you better about this. Or perhaps Seraphina. I have no mind for these matters." She laughed. "Remember, I am the pastor's wife. My poor head is still brim full of my husband's chattering catechism—and of his endless, wordy sermons. Talk and talk and talk about God, God, God! For myself, I feel there are powers like that of God all about us, in the trees . . . and the mountains . . . and the noble animals. I cannot tell where God stops, nor what in all the world is *other* than God, to be treated like some base and cast-off thing. Seraphina has taught us that even the distasteful things—things that rot and stink—should be honoured, for they breed life out of the Earth. But not many people would understand this. This much I know and will warn you of: it is unwise to speak of any god besides the one the Christians blather on about. Christians are pleased to believe that the world needed no mother to be born, only a father. So be careful of your words. In some parts of the world—not Geneva, thank goodness!—you would be condemned to death by fire or water for doubting the Father God."

When we talked like this of the world and God, my head would fairly swim with confusion. But there were other subjects that were very much clearer in my understanding. Only now, under Francine's instruction, did I realise how little I knew about the workings of my body! Though each day when I looked in the mirror I could see changes coming over me more visibly, I had no idea why this might be happening. *Why* does a woman change like this? I asked, at the same time blushing to admit my ignorance. "But you are not so ignorant as other girls," Francine assured me, amused by my embarrassment. "Your former Gipsy mother took you to see how babies come into the world. You do not realise how privileged you have been. Can you believe that there are women who have never been permitted to witness such a thing—for fear they are too delicate? They must wait until childbirth is thrust upon them."

"Truly?"

"Indeed. I was one such woman. At your age, my mother would tell me nothing. I was not permitted to bathe without wearing my petticoat. My very body was a stranger to me."

"You have never been present when a baby was born?"

"Not until but a few years ago—when Seraphina arranged that I should watch one of her women deliver."

Seraphina, I had by then learnt, was a midwife like my foster mother Rosina; she had attended the births of many ladies in the region; she had delivered Victor and Ernest. Now too frail for the work, she sent out midwives she had trained, and often allowed women in the craft to observe.

"Worse still," Francine continued, "girls are not permitted to know how these babies get into them—for fear they will be shocked."

"But how do they?" I asked, for of this even Rosina had never spoken.

"Such a simple thing!" Francine laughed. "Yet we are raised in life to think of it as if it were the secret of secrets." Then, quite blithely, she proceeded to tell me; but when she came to the father's rôle in this, I could not, despite the promise I had made to keep silence, refrain from letting her hear about Victor. "But I have seen a boy like that," I blurted out almost smugly. "I have even . . . touched him."

"Ah! Of this we must talk more," Francine said, assuming a more serious air. For she knew I spoke of Victor. "Tell me, my dear, how would you feel if you woke one morning soon to discover there was a baby *here*, inside this girl's body?" She placed her hand upon my stomach.

I was shocked at the thought. "In *me*? How could that be?"

"Think of what I have told you. Everything that is now happening to your body makes you ready for such a thing, young as you are. You are often alone with Victor, are you not? In the château; here, in the woods? Is that not so?"

"Yes."

"Victor could be the father of that child—if you permitted it. It might seem like a game. Mere child's play. But it would be more than that in consequence. Many girls your age in all the villages round about find themselves with child; some have no idea what has happened to them until the baby is nearly born. I know this from the visits I make with Charles. These poor girls have not chosen to be mothers; but suddenly that is their fate—and some not even strong enough to undergo the strain. What a price women pay for their ignorance! You must never trust a man to control himself. There is something of the beast in all of them; and the more they deny it and pretend to piety, the less they are to be trusted. It is a favourite device of such canting men to show their baser self only to women, whom they can then squelch."

What she suggested filled me with distaste and with fear. It was the furthest thing from my desires. Though I thought I had been listening carefully to all that Francine told me, this single thought—that *I* could become a mother!—at last gave what she said a terrific meaning. "But what am I to do?" I asked, as if I were under immediate threat.

Francine reached out to take me in her arms. "It is what you must *not* do that matters, child!" she answered merrily.

"But what if I cannot make Victor understand?"

"Oh, but he does. Be assured: Victor has been told all that you know. And he is an intelligent lad."

What was in my mind had little to do with intelligence. It had to do with the wildness I had discovered in Victor, which I doubted I could tame. He was too agile and daring. Francine could see that I was fretting. "To be sure, in these matters, knowledge is not in itself enough. That is why you and Victor must help one another to be mindful."

After that day, the prospect of being a grown woman made me for the first time fearful. It left me wanting to avoid Victor, whose high spirits now suddenly seemed to me a menace. When, on another visit to the glade, I confessed this turn of mind to Francine, she showed the greatest concern. "Oh, but it is not my intention that you should be frightened. On the contrary. There is so much to take joy in." Then pausing to look me deeply in the eyes, she asked, "Do you trust me to be your true friend, Elizabeth?"

"Yes," I answered without hesitation.

"Then understand what I do as an act of friendship, nothing more. Sometimes we must let our body speak; I think it is our best teacher. Come now, and I will show you."

She stood and began to remove her clothes. "Come, come," she insisted. "You must join me." And I did. "What I have to teach you," Francine told me, "is so very easy—no more than knowing the lineaments of your body. But who else will tell you?" When we were both naked, I could not help but gaze at Francine's physique with envious admiration; she was as fairly framed as the goddesses I had seen in paintings. I could not help but compare her full and rounded body with my own lean form.

"You are so very beautiful, Francine," I said. "I hope I may one day look like you."

At this she laughed somewhat bitterly. "Women are so often flattered for their appearance—as if it were an accomplishment. This is done, as I hope you will learn, to make us vain and to divide us one from another, the fair from the plain. In time, all women, even the fairest, lose these beauties of the flesh. Are we to live in dread of that? But I thank you for your words, my dear. Now attend me." She searched through her purse and brought out a tiny mirror. "Now think of me as your nurse, instructing you in the care of your body." She had me open my thighs wide apart, and held the mirror so that I could see my sex as I had not seen it before. Together we explored this labyrinthine place with its velvet-red folds and rippling recesses. Francine, laying her finger here and here, taught me names for all the parts of me; I might have been hideously embarrassed to be investigated this way, but she assumed so very teacherly an air that we might have been having a lesson in geography! Yet this was my own body I was surveying as if it were some exotic land. "Do you know this part here?" she asked.

She had placed her finger upon a delicate swelling at the front. She stroked me gently there for a moment until I felt a familiar quiver run along my thighs. "Yes," I admitted. "I have sometimes touched that."

"Did you not find it pleasant?"

"Yes . . . but I thought perhaps I should not."

"Oh? Who has told you that?"

"My former mother, Rosina . . . before I came here. Once she saw me touch there while I was bathing. She drew my hand away and said I must not."

"Did she give you no reason why?"

"She said touching there would mark my face with spots, and that no one would think me pretty. She said men would find me disgusting if they knew I did this, and none would court me."

Francine burst out laughing. "Nonsense! That there should be women who believe such things! Let me show you what this is for." And, using both her body and my own, she taught me several ways to caress that part, which she liked to call the pearl because it was indeed hidden away like a pearl within the folds of an oyster. That day was the first time I fully took pleasure of my body, feeling neither shame nor fear. I learnt of postures I could assume and ways to breathe that sent the sensation deeper, and of ways in which it might be prolonged almost without limit. There was an oil Francine gave me to use that seemed to heighten the stimulation, and a bitter liqueur she gave me to drink, a few drops of which sent me into a long, dreamy state that lasted . . . I cannot say how long. The pleasure then was less vivid, but the fancies that were set adrift in my mind brought an elation all their own. "What are you thinking of?" Francine wished to know after my head had somewhat cleared.

I hesitated to tell her. "Of Victor . . . I think of him doing this for me."

"And so he may one day, if you teach him."

"Would that be all right—for a man to touch me as you have?"

Francine smiled, but her smile was veiled with a kind of sorrow. "It is more than right; it is a wonderful and loving thing. But some men will not be bothered. They have strange, sad notions about women, even about their own wives. They think we have these organs but for bearing children, and that we take no pleasure in love—or they would not have us do so. That is why . . . sometimes, women will provide for one another—as I have for you today."

"It is not wrong for women to do this?"

"Do you think it was wrong, what we did?"

"No . . ."

"I was sure you would not, else I should have refrained. I believe that what women do out of love and kindness to comfort one another cannot be bad. But, once more, I warn you: there are those who would not approve of such a thing. They would call it unnatural. Yet for a woman to live lovelessly, in shame and despair, and never to know what delight she can take in her body—that they accept as 'natural.' "

"May I teach Victor what you have taught me about my body?"

"Ah! This is not for me to say. You must ask Lady Caroline. She has certain designs she will make known to you in her own time. But pray, until she speaks with you, be cautious, my dear."

Francine instructed me in many more things during the days that followed. She taught me the full cycle of the women's year, each season celebrated on its first new moon. She taught me many of the rituals and chants of the craft and the meanings of the symbols and implements I would see used in our rites; she taught me about the wise women who had gone before, many of them hounded and persecuted for their beliefs; and she showed me the secrets of herbs I might use to heal myself and to ease the pain that came with the bleeding. But again and again she warned that I must be cautious what I said and to whom. "We keep our secrets not out of shame, but prudence," she told me. Least of all was I to mention the craft to men, few of whom could be trusted to understand our ways.

"Does the Baron know what we do in this glade?" I asked.

"The Baron is a perceptive man. I cannot think he is ignorant of his wife's activities. He surely knows of her paintings, though he will not say so."

"Does he approve, then, of what my mother does?"

Francine smiled gently. "The Baron is a man of the New Age. Like M. Voltaire, he will defend the freedom even of those whose beliefs he despises. Moreover, he loves Lady Caroline with all his heart. She is the one woman he has known in his life; he fairly worships her. I believe she could have any indulgence of him she wanted. You have heard of turning a blind eye? That is what he has chosen to do. As do many of the men of the district, who know what their women do. There are, of course, men from whom the craft must be kept a secret. That is my case. Charles could never tolerate such blasphemy. Therefore, be warned! You are not a child any longer, Elizabeth. I trust you know how to mind your tongue."

Her order left me troubled; for there was one man who knew a great deal about us. Each time we met to talk, I felt the guiltier for not telling Francine of this. At last, when I could hold it back no longer, I announced, "Victor knows of this place. He has brought me here to spy . . . on you. Perhaps he has spied on other things."

Francine pondered this intelligence, but displayed neither surprise nor chagrin at what I told her. Finally, with a certain air of deep puzzlement, she admitted, "I know of this. It is Lady Caroline's wish that Victor should sometimes witness what we do here. She has told him of this glade." She hastened to add, "But that is a secret even from our sisters. You must respect it as such."

I was astonished to hear of this. "But why does she let Victor watch?"

Francine now spoke as if she were feeling her way forward with the greatest circumspection; I saw that she was troubled by what she told me. "She wants Victor to know the mysteries of women; this is meant, she says, as an instruction to him. You must understand, my dear, Victor is quite precious to her. Much that she does, she does for his sake. I would not exaggerate if I said that he is her whole life."

"And you do not care that he watches what you do here?"

She fretted over her answer. "I care. Not because I think what we do in this place is shameful—understand that. Nevertheless, I do not altogether welcome knowing that Victor watches. I can only say that I trust Lady Caroline. She has her reasons for what she does. As you know, she is a disciple of M. Rousseau, who teaches that the curiosity of the young should not be thwarted."

Francine had seen me struggling to study the book Mother gave me. I had not managed to read as much as half of *Emile*, but I surely had not yet discovered in him the genius Mother promised I would find. I had, in fact, found foolish things. Rousseau believed that girls were not made to run and that they must never try! I certainly knew that to be false, for I was an excellent runner. "Lady Caroline says Victor *is* Emile," I told Francine.

"She would have it so. She has sought to raise him in accordance with Nature, as M. Rousseau recommends."

"But what does that mean?"

She burst into a bewildered laughter, but the tone of it was more fretful than gay. "That he is allowed to do as he pleases!"

"Do you not approve of what Rousseau teaches?"

She put her fingers to her temples as if her head ached. " *'Teaches.'* He *teaches.* More words, you see. Words, poor words! Sometimes I believe that is the great trouble. Is there no way to teach but with words? M. Rousseau's head must have been filled to the brim with words. But he abandoned his children to a foundling hospital. I do not think words can ever touch our true nature."

"Do you not like Victor?" I asked after a long silence.

She answered with obvious caution. "I will tell you something that Lady Caroline might prefer that I kept secret. Before you came into her family, it was her hope that I might become Victor's special friend, a sort of sister to him. I do not quite know what she intended by this. I have told you there is a design Lady Caroline has in mind; I was meant to be some part of it. But now that he has a real sister, I have been excused from her plans. I confess that I am grateful. Victor is of course a gifted young man, and so unutterably beautiful." For a moment she turned away with a blush. "I have dreamt of him as he will be in just a few years' time, the handsomest of men. I have imagined him coming to me as a lover and using me as his lover. There! You have that from me as a sisterly secret. But I find him unruly. Unruly . . . and yet strangely cold. *Ideas* seem so very real to him." With a quizzical smile she added, "I almost believe he lusts for them the way other men lust for a woman. This puzzles me. I know Lady Caroline would have you love Victor as your true brother. And so you must—but carefully. Do nothing premature. This may be difficult, but promise me."

And I did.

Under Francine's guidance, I learnt all that an apprentice might and was as surely a member of the craft as any girl of my age. Still, I never came to think of myself as a "witch." In my thoughts, witchery has always seemed an identity for which I was not yet prepared—a wise old woman's identity. And so I never took the name. I thought of myself, quite simply, as the child-sister of the women who stood beside me at our rites, nothing more. It was the joy of their company that made me one of their number; their song and dance and merriment were my delight. And the strength I felt in being among them when our rites were at their most exuberant might soar to the point of intoxication.

What I was less aware of, in my still-childish trust, was the stigma that this company might place upon me in the eyes of others. For as tolerant a community as Geneva is, there is no friendship to be found here (and surely not among the men of the church) for unruly women who make up their own faith and keep their own counsel.

Was it wrong, I sometimes wonder now, for my mother to have drawn me into the coven before I knew the risks to which my belonging might expose me? I know she meant me well; she intended the craft to bring me courage and pride. And so it did. But that was not her only purpose. There was another, far darker motive that held her in its tow like a running tide. This had to do with Victor—and for that reason, because her duty to him overrode all other scruples, I think she would have been quite heedless of my safety if she needed to be.

EDITOR'S NOTE
Traces of Women's Fertility Mysteries in Rural Europe

Elizabeth Frankenstein's report regarding clandestine rites performed by women in the woodlands round Geneva provided some of this document's most unexpected passages. At first reading, I could not help but wonder if these might not be the fabrications of an overwrought imagination. Most of what the author offers in her report is, after all, wildly incoherent, if not wholly hallucinatory. In search of further enlightenment, I turned to Sir Henry Monmouth's recent volume *Popular Superstitions of Europe in Later Seventeenth-Century Rustic Society*. There we find numerous records of just such atavistic practices continuing into modern times, some of which Sir Henry was able to verify with his own eye. In his view, we deal here with the last, decayed remnants of fertility ceremonies that date to the pre-Christian era. In those distant times, when even the keenest minds lacked any appreciation of the workings of natural law, it was commonly assumed that the abundance of crops and the fecundity of livestock depended upon the iteration of certain rites offered up to fabulous nature deities. Where civilisation has penetrated least effectively in the modern world, such practices have sometimes managed to survive into recent times. No doubt the practices Elizabeth Frankenstein describes have long been identified as trafficking with the Devil, and, in less enlightened times, persecuted as such. But what the more discriminating modern mind finds here is simply a regrettable reminder of the fragility of human reason, a fact that is more tragic than criminal.

Observations like those of Sir Henry have invariably been limited to rural areas and mainly to the peasant populations of southern and eastern Europe. This narrative is unique in raising the possibility that women of all social stations, including well-born and educated ladies, may have dabbled in these arcane practices. The rôle attributed here to Baroness Frankenstein is particularly astonishing, for she would seem to have been a priestess of the cult and in that capacity responsible for recruiting—one might literally say "seducing"—young women of the town, including her own adopted daughter, into the cult. But here one fact is significant. In settings well removed from the remote farming areas of Europe, what remains of the element of "fertility," which was formerly the social function of these rites? Only one thing—and that a gross caricature of the original intention: namely, female sexual abandonment.

By her own admission, erotic fantasies played constantly upon Elizabeth Frankenstein's mind; but can we reasonably believe that women in groups that number in the scores shared her pathological condition? Had I not seen the evidence of the Baroness Frankenstein's paintings to attest to her unwholesome predilections, I might have believed that Elizabeth used these tales to slander her mother for reasons unknown. But even if we should conclude that Lady Caroline shared Elizabeth's mania—and was perhaps its instigator—how far beyond this single household may we extend the pruriency of these two women?

As I worked upon the memoir, this question continued to haunt me. So in the summer of 1834, though not in the best of health, I undertook the most strenuous episode of my research. I determined to visit Geneva to see if any trace of the customs Elizabeth Frankenstein reports might still be found. I could think of no better place to begin than with the religious authorities of the region. The pastor of St. Pierre, M. Antoine

Lavater, proved unexpectedly willing to discuss the question. He possessed an almost scholarly curiosity about the period in question, and extended his hospitality warmly.

Though I took care to keep my enquiries as purely academic and nonspecific as possible—I did not allude to Elizabeth Frankenstein, or name this memoir as the source of my information—the pastor recognised at once the practices I described. He told me of a cult that had been exposed in the time of his predecessor. In fact, the wife of one of the young pastors of the congregation—Charles Dupin—had been convicted of belonging to the coven. He did not recall the woman's name, but Mme. Lavater, who attended our meeting and joined in freely on the discussion, recalled that it was Francine. Did either know what had become of Francine? Only that she had been disowned by her husband, who had succeeded in having their marriage annulled.

Pastor Lavater, being a singularly enlightened man, did not subscribe to any diabolical interpretation of these activities. "Witchcraft," he owned, "is a remnant of ancient superstition. Thank God we no longer attach diabolical motivations to such matters!" But he was gravely concerned by the evidence of sexual licence that had attended these cults; this, he felt was unquestionably a corrupting influence. Especially as it affected the women of the community, such misconduct struck at the very heart of family life and must for that reason be rooted out. Had he, I asked, any reason to believe such practices survived to the present day? Almost indignantly he replied that he could confirm beyond question that the covens had been driven from the Vaud, which, he reminded me, belonged to the French cultural sphere of Switzerland. As for the remainder of the cantons . . . well, that was another matter.

"The Germans, as you know, weaken toward the Gothic. And the Italians," he added with a wise chuckle, "are quite hopeless when it comes to controlling their women. I think it is the exception to find an Italian female who is *not* a witch. They are born possessed of the *malocchio*."

In contrast to the vicar's openness, the head syndic of the city, one François Rebuffat, proved highly impatient and abrupt. I had written ahead to announce my visit and request a meeting; but had his wife not answered the bell and escorted me into their home, I think I should have been turned away at the door when I came calling. I had not progressed more than a short way into my questions about the Baroness Frankenstein and Francine Dupin when I realised that something like a wall of ice had descended between the syndic and myself. At first I concluded that his attitude was political; his family, I learnt, had suffered greatly in the upheavals of the previous generation; to some degree he seemed to hold the Frankenstein family responsible for what had befallen his ancestors. Their historical Savoyard connections had, he felt, seriously compromised the Frankensteins' municipal allegiance. The affectation of retaining the title of "Baron" particularly galled the syndic: "Only a Savoyard foreigner would flaunt such a title." He now viewed the turmoil of that era from an understandably reactionary stance. Was I, I wondered, asking him to call to mind events that were too painful? But I soon detected something more, a certain personal edge to his irritation. He at last revealed the reason for this.

"I hope, sir, that it is not the purpose of your current research to further blacken the reputation of our city."

"I, sir? But I would never do such a thing."

"Indeed, you have already done so. Your published conversations with Victor Frankenstein have not been welcomed by many Genevans. We should have preferred to see this unnatural aberration in the history of our city forgotten by one and all. Instead, you have commemorated this man's name and embedded it in our history. Mad doctors! Monsters! These are not creditable associations for a God-fearing, respectable people to bear."

Even though I sincerely asked pardon for any damage I might have caused, and explained that it was wholly unintended, the syndic was not to be appeased.

"You should know, Sir Robert, that many of us regard the entire tale you have published as the fabrication of a deranged imagination. As to whether that imagination belonged to *you* or to Dr. Frankenstein, I could not until this instant clearly determine. But now when you come enquiring about witches . . . *witches!*" At that, the indignant man dismissed me and departed the room, leaving his disconcerted wife to

extend whatever final courtesies she could. The good woman was sincerely apologetic for her husband's conduct, explaining that there had
been bad blood between the Frankensteins and the Rebuffats for many
generations.

"Baron Frankenstein, despite the title he chose to bear, was a liberal
who encouraged many political causes that cost my husband's family
dearly in the time of troubles. The recollection still rankles."

Could she, I asked at the door, help me with any part of my
enquiries? She assured me she could not. "The women you seek to find
have long since been driven from our city. There are few who will talk
with you—for understandable reasons, I believe. I suggest that you give
up your mission before you attract more critical attention."

Despite Mme. Rebuffat's advice, I made further enquiries, especially
among the women of the town: two teachers, a nurse, a prominent *grande
dame* . . . I even loitered to talk with women I met tending the vineyards.
Drawing upon what I now knew about bucolic culture, I claimed to be
a married man whose wife was expecting a child; I pretended to come
seeking the services of a midwife, an occupation that I found to be still
actively practised in the area. The women to whom I was directed were
a melancholy crew, very much the sort of rural hag I would have imagined. I asked the same question of each one I met: Had she ever heard
of a Francine Dupin or of the woman Seraphina? I hoped the names
might open up some avenue of discourse. Everywhere I met with pro-
fessions of ignorance.

It was not until I had made my arrangements to depart from the
town that I was approached with a curious offer of assistance. The afternoon before I was scheduled to board the Swiss *diligence* for Basle, the
inn-keeper knocked at my door to tell me I had a visitor. I proceeded to
the foyer to find a girl of perhaps fifteen years waiting for me. The
maiden, fresh-faced and well-formed, with a particularly haughty
demeanour, did not speak but handed me a note. It contained a single
sentence: "Follow the girl if you would learn more about Francine
Dupin." There was no signature, but the hand was distinctly feminine;
no doubt the message was from one of the Genevan ladies I had lately
approached. I believed I knew which, but I nevertheless asked the girl if

she might tell me who had sent her. As I expected, she would not say. She simply wagged her head no, then turned and headed for the door as if she did not care whether I followed or not. Outside the inn, she had left two mules waiting. These we mounted, and I followed where she led.

Our journey was a steep ride into the forested uplands of Mont Salève. The girl was friendly, but for all she said along the way, she might as well have been mute. She had clearly been sworn to secrecy by whomever had sent her to me. Our ride ended about an hour later, in a glade that presented a wide vista of the lake and the city. To the east, the unmistakeable pinnacle of the Dent d'Enfer loomed against the sky, and beyond, just visible through its eternal veil of cloud, Mont Blanc. From my earlier visits, I was familiar with the area as a viewing point; but I had never wandered so far into the woods as the girl now took me. The day was well advanced toward evening and a chill mist had descended upon the forest round us, covering the ground beneath us like a carpet of cloud. After we had ridden another quarter-hour, I was startled to see a wraith-like form moving among the trees to our left. The girl turned her mule in that direction and approached what I now saw was a woman wrapped in a grey hood and cloak, waiting for us at the foot of a towering walnut. The girl reined in and indicated that we should dismount and proceed on foot. When we reached the woman, she remained with her face turned from me, one hand holding the hood of her cloak across her cheek. I could not see her features, but I knew the voice at once.

"You will not ask me to identify myself," the woman said. "I expect you understand." I answered that I did.

At which she dropped to her knees beside a grassy mound that lay close by the tree. I would not have noticed the stone that marked the place if she had not pointed it out; nor would I have been aware of the incisions it bore had she not pressed my fingers against them. "You have come seeking to know about Francine Dupin. What remains of her Earthly self is here."

In the waning light, I could scarcely read the marks I felt there, but using my sense of touch as well as sight, I was able to make out enough of the inscription to know that it had originally read "Soeur Francine."

"Poor, gentle soul! She suffered greatly at the hands of men and of the church. She was forced to flee Geneva, lest she be stoned in the streets. Oh yes, that might well have been her fate; even in our land there are those who would not suffer a witch to live. For many years she lived an outcast's life in these woods, surviving only because her sisters fed and sheltered her. At length she became one of our wise women. She was laid to rest here in the year 1819 after many hard years."

"Did you know Elizabeth Lavenza?"

"I was a child when she met her death. I knew of it only by rumour. Among the women it is said she was killed by an evil spirit. Others say she was murdered by her husband."

"I can assure you that Victor Frankenstein did not take his wife's life. Did you know him?"

"He departed the city soon after his wife's death. He never returned. The family met a bad end. Cursed, some have said."

Grateful as I was, I had to ask, "Why have you met me here to tell me this much?"

"I took you at your word that your intentions are those of a scholar, one who seeks truth, not slanderous lies. Francine Dupin was my teacher. I would have her honourably remembered. The secrets we keep are not kept out of shame."

With that she removed a parcel from beneath her cloak and handed it to me. It was a square, weighty package wrapped in chamois-skin and tied tightly with thongs. "This was entrusted to me by Francine, as it was entrusted to her by Elizabeth Lavenza before she married. Elizabeth's instruction was that this parcel should be held until it could be placed in the keeping of one whose only interest was to publish the truth about her life to the world. Know that I have never inspected this parcel; nor did Francine. I only ask that you respect the wishes of these women who suffered so greatly." When I swore that I should do so, she added, "Then I am relieved to be free of this responsibility."

She rose to leave, asking me one more time to promise I would keep her confidence. Then she moved off deeper into the woods—where, I assumed, a mule or a carriage awaited her. At my side, the girl, still kneeling at the graveside, reached into the pocket of her cloak, took out a small folded cloth, and opened it. It contained flower petals and a few herbs. These she carefully scattered over the mound, then bent her head for a meditative moment. After a brief silence during which only the wind in the trees spoke, she raised her head, stretched out her two hands, crossed the first fingers in a sign of salutation, and touched them to the stone. I of course recognised the gesture from the memoirs. When she was finished, she gazed into my eyes with a directness that quite unsettled me. Up to that point she had seemed a shy, young thing, unable even to look me once in the face. But of a sudden her expression was so confiding that it seemed to issue a challenge. I saw this was not a mere girl at all, but a mature young woman who had carried out a mission of some daring. And I recognised this expression; I had seen it before, that same bold, candid look. But where?

And then I realised: it was as if I were looking into the face of Elizabeth Frankenstein herself, as I knew her from the miniature portrait that had stood upon my desk these many years. The girl's eyes were asking the question I had always seen in Elizabeth's eyes: *Can I trust you?*

Was this, then, what the women found in their woodland rites, this forthright manner, this candour? In that moment, in the presence of that gaze, I believe I came as close as my reluctant temperament would permit to understanding some small part of what the craft brought to its women—not enough to overcome my deep moral scruples, but possibly enough to introduce a note of mercy into my judgement. I can only say that I hoped my young guide found in my eyes the answer I wished to give, which was yes.

We rose and remounted our mules. On the way back to the inn the young woman and myself exchanged not a word.

That was the year 1834. Since that time, I have faithfully honoured my promise to keep the confidence of the mysterious informant I met on Mont Salève that day; but having learnt only last year of the lady's death, I feel released from my vow. Since it may bear upon the credibility of my account, I will note here that it was the syndic's wife, Mme.

Rebuffat, whom I met that afternoon. Though I never saw her face, I had identified her voice at once. As for the girl, I have felt bound to temper my curiosity regarding her identity. To this day, I have no idea who she might have been.

That evening when I arrived back at my room in the inn, no sooner had the door closed behind me than I fairly tore the wrappings from the parcel I had been given. And what was then my experience?

Now, reader, hear an illustration.

Imagine a scholar of the early years of this century who has devoted his life to the study of Egyptian antiquities. Imagine that one day a captain in the service of the Grand Army brings him a chipped and weathered slab of basalt and lays it before him, having recognised exotic markings upon it. The captain has won the stone at cards from one of his colleagues. Perhaps it is of some interest . . . ?

Now imagine that the scholar is Champollion. And imagine that the artifact that has been placed upon his desk is the Rosetta Stone.

This will perhaps give token of how my heart leapt to see the treasure that lay before me. Two antique books bound in leather: one a pale crimson in colour, bearing an embossed rose upon its cover; the other without marking, dyed a dull purple. As the next section of this memoir will make clear, these volumes—the Rose Book and the Lavender Book—were nothing less than the key to the hieroglyphic secrets of Elizabeth Frankenstein's life.

I Am Given
the Rose Book

When Victor returned from Thonon, I did my best to keep Francine's warning foremost in my mind. I determined to behave as coolly as I could toward him, intending to excuse myself as often as possible from his company. When he entered the château, I did not run to welcome him with a warm embrace; I demurred and held my distance, as if we had only just been introduced. What would he think of my conduct? I wondered. I need not have troubled my thoughts. To my surprise, the Victor who returned from Thonon proved to be even more elusive than I could ever have managed to be. A curious veil had been drawn between us. I was left mystified by this abrupt change until Mother called me to her one morning.

She spoke to me now more gravely and more abstractedly than ever before. She seemed constantly to be listening to a voice I could not hear, taking guidance from it as we spoke.

"What I say to you now, I have said already to Victor," she began. "This is why I took him away with me. I have his sworn oath that he will keep my words before his mind at all times. Now I shall require the same of you. You and Victor are not as other children; and, indeed, you are no longer children. A special destiny hovers over you both. I have sometimes hinted of this in the past; now I will try to make myself as clear as I can. Do you see that book on the chiffonnier? Pray bring it here." I retrieved the tome she asked for, a ponderous antique leather volume whose pages were trimmed in gold. "I shall from time to time ask you to study this work. I do not expect you to understand all that you read, but I shall instruct you as best I can. In time you shall have another teacher whose knowledge goes beyond my own."

I turned the book in my hands. There was a beautiful crimson rose embossed on its cover. I opened to the title page. There my eye was at once arrested by a brilliantly-coloured picture. It showed two cherubic figures: a boy, whose skin was ruddy and whose hair was flaming red; and a glowingly fair girl, her blond tresses worn loose and reaching to her ankles. Little older than babies, the pair lay naked and warmly embracing, the boy atop the girl, his erected organ nestled well into her body. They floated in a vessel of blue water; below them was a green-sward from which the head of a sort of lizard peered out. Above the vessel hovered a splendid, many-coloured bird with wings outspread, and from behind the bird, bright rays of gold fanned out to the edges of the page. "Read here," Mother said, drawing her finger across the words above the picture. They were Latin, but not beyond my powers in the language.

" '*De Coniunctibus Chymicae,*' " I read.

"Can you make out the meaning?" she asked.

" 'Concerning the Chymical . . . Marriage,' I believe."

"Yes; 'marriage' would be the usual translation," Mother said. "But I prefer 'union.' "

Whether "marriage" or "union," I had no idea what this phrase might mean. "Will it all be in Latin?" I asked with some concern, for my proficiency in the language was modest.

"That would be an ordeal, wouldn't it!" She laughed. "I have prepared a translation for you. You will be able to read page by page in our own tongue." She took several folded sheets of paper from the back of the book and opened them for me. They were French, written in her hand.

"You have done this?" I asked.

"With the help of visiting scholars."

"And will it tell me what the chymical marriage is?"

"The picture you see is a symbol of that marriage. The boy and girl are betrothed. The picture shows their union; but you must understand this correctly. Their union is chaste; that is why they are portrayed as mere children. Do you understand the meaning of the word 'chaste'?"

I said that I did.

"Chastity is a demanding discipline for the young—especially for the young and comely. I shall tell you a secret. Chastity is a great magic, but only if you desire it as strongly as others desire the lower pleasures. I realise what I shall ask of you is difficult; but it is necessary." She paused a long while, as if the words she wanted were arriving from a great distance. "I know that it has been your habit—yours and Victor's—to bathe together at the pond. Tell me, have you missed doing that during the last few months while Victor was away? Tell me honestly."

"Yes, a little . . . sometimes."

"You enjoy being naked with Victor?"

"Yes . . . a little . . ."

She smiled wisely. "I imagine more than a little. Come, you can tell me."

"Yes, very much."

"Have you never had cause to feel apprehensive when you are alone with Victor like this?"

As had been my habit since childhood, I answered impulsively. "No!" I said, blurting out the word before I might begin to blush or stammer. This was my way of lying.

"You will not be surprised to know that Victor has also missed your playtime. This feeling that makes you want to be together naked—it has a name. Do you know what it is called?"

I could not think what she was asking. I sorted through the words that came to mind, but found none suitable.

"We will need to find the correct names for many things. This feeling, for instance: some might call it desire, others lust. Pastor Dupin would surely call it lust. And can you not just see the sour, dour face he would make! But would he know *why* we have been made capable of such a feeling? He might say it is the work of the Devil. Christians are quick to attribute what they fear to the Devil. But why do they fear the pleasures of the body, do you think? As Rousseau has shown, the answer is transparent to simple reason: they fear the body because they have been improperly reared. They have ceased to believe in the innocence of children. But in this as in all else, we must 'follow the mind of Nature.' So the great *philosophe* tells us. Suppose, then, we spoke of this desire as a hunger, a *sort* of hunger. For hunger is a natural thing. But for what? Pleasure, yes. But what kind of pleasure? The pleasure of seeing? Of touching? When our stomachs hunger we choose from among many things that will satisfy; and no matter how strong the hunger, we avoid eating anything poisonous. But *this* hunger that we call lust, what does it truly want? Can we be sure we know? There are many who know only one kind of meat to satisfy this craving. You and Victor will learn that there is other food it prefers to feed upon. The Devil is not in the appetite, but in its misdirection. Meanwhile, however, I fear you must hunger a little for one another. For a time I wish your relations with Victor to become chaste, rigorously so. I may even ask you to be like strangers to one another—friendly, of course, but somewhat aloof. And not only physically. I would have you at a distance from one another even in your thoughts. You will have to trust me when I say there is a purpose in this. You are to become Earth to his sky." She studied me quizzically after making the remark. "You do not understand, I realise. But do you trust me?"

I averred that I did. "Has Victor read this book?" I asked.

"That was the reason for our journey to Thonon. There he read it from first to last at my direction, and with the greatest care. And not this book only, but others we have brought back. I wished him to study with the utmost concentration; that is why we took this retreat. In time he will share what he has learnt. What I have taught him, he will teach you. Your union begins with these books, and goes far beyond.

"My dearest Elizabeth, I have already told you something of my girl-hood. Now I will tell you more. When I was just your age, the nurse to an ailing father and as poor as a beggar, it was my good fortune to find a benefactor. No, I do not mean the Baron. Before he came into my life, there was another, a woman. She had heard of my plight. She was her-self poor, and so unable to give me more than a pittance on which to keep myself and my hapless father alive. But in other ways she was infinitely rich, far more so than the Baron. She brought me treasures of the mind. Wretched child though I was, she saw in me what I would later see in you: a pilgrim soul. She taught me what I have now been able to teach Victor, the wisdom of the spagyric arts, or at least some part of it. This word is unfamiliar to you, as it is to many. It refers to the wisdom of the alchymical masters, which you will begin to read in this book. So, too, my benefactor gave me books—this book among others. I tell you, I would have traded food for what she brought into my life: the vastness of the world. Through the years I have carried forward the studies she set before me as far as I could with my poor powers. But at a point one needs another—a companion. We were created male and female. There is a deep reason for this that few are ever privileged to learn. My rôle, she taught me, would be to pass on what I had learnt to a son and a daughter who would bring these teachings to fruition. You and Victor are that son and daughter. I am ready to deliver over to you. Can you guess who this benefactor was?"

I owned that I could not.

"But you have met her! A sage lady who has already turned her attention to your education. She is now supremely old, but her mind is still afire with knowledge."

"Do you mean Seraphina?"

"Yes, my dear. You have known her as the mother of our coven. But she is more than that. She is a remarkable philosopher. She has travelled far beyond the boundaries of Christendom to places where no other woman has ever travelled on her own. She has had the courage to seek the truth among men of other faiths and customs, some who do not welcome women into their secrets; she has had to prove herself their equal, sometimes at great risk. From her adventures she has brought back teachings that could shake the universities of Europe to their foundations. But of course she is a *mere* woman, and a wretchedly poor woman at that. Who would pay her any heed? All that she has taught me, I now will seek to teach Victor. It is my dearest hope that he will bring Seraphina's wisdom to perfection. Only a man can do this in a way the world will heed. But he will need your help."

I had seen Seraphina but a few times more since our first meeting in the glade. She sometimes attended the women's gatherings, but only to watch from a distance, and always with her familiar near by, perhaps in the trees above her, perhaps perched on her shoulder. She had not spoken to me again, though I had many times felt her eyes upon me. "I am not easy in Seraphina's company," I confessed.

"She is a formidable woman, I admit. But she means you only well; and she greatly admires you. How shall I put it? She sees the gold in you, as I did when we first met. From time to time she will ask things of you—unusual things. I pray you to respect her wishes. Her ways may seem strange, but she is a powerful teacher. You will not know how powerful until you have followed her the full length of the path, and that you must do on trust. This is a paradox."

In the days that followed, I was permitted to read several times from what we called the Rose Book, for the emblem on its cover. "What you read and see here you will find bewildering," Mother told me. "Remember only one thing. Nothing in these pages means what it may at first seem to mean, just as in the world at large, nothing is *only* what it seems. Everything is itself and something more: the image within the image, the word within the word. What comes first to view is useful to know; but what comes later—with that the mind takes wing. Though the language you read is French, think of it as a foreign tongue that you will have to learn word by word as a child learns its parents' language. So too the pictures. What you see depicted here summons the eye to rise above its normal powers. You will learn to see *through* the pictures as if they were drawn on glass. You will need careful instruction to do this. And other kinds of assistance."

On a few occasions, I was allowed to take the volume to my room, where I perused it late into the night. As I had been warned, I understood next to nothing of what I read; the language on the page was a thicket of strange allusions. It spoke of fabulous beasts and birds and times and places I had never heard of. All the planets of the heavens were mentioned, and the seraphic beings that ride upon them. Above all I loitered over the pictures, the fantastic, mind-swirling pictures! Not all were beautiful; most were grotesquely strange; some were monstrous to the point of nightmare. Yet I was engrossed by them, and especially by the boy and girl whose images were the theme of the volume. They floated through these pages in a story that faded into total enigma for me and yet haunted my revery.

Here is the tale as I remember it.

The two children lived in a mythic kingdom. It was surrounded by an impenetrable forest inhabited by fantastic beasts. The boy and girl had been betrothed since birth. Their wedding day arrived and festivities were planned. But because the bride and groom had committed a sin (which was not named) they were condemned to everlasting confinement in a tightly sealed prison whose walls were hewn from crystal. There they were stripped naked and placed on display so that all the world might see them in their shame and suffering. On a tiny straw bed they huddled together seeking to comfort one another, but their torment was almost too great to bear. In time, because the prison had been left unattended, the air grew chill and the boy fell sick. His bride, endeavouring to warm him, succeeded in arousing his ardour, and they soon fell to copulating. Or at least attempting to do so; but before their love-making could reach completion, the bridegroom grew so hot that he fairly melted away into his beloved's arms.

Overcome by grief, the abandoned bride drowned the body of her lost beloved in tears. She wept until she had filled the prison to its ceiling. Beneath the waters, she expired clinging to her lover. Rapidly the two turned black and foul and evil-smelling as their Earthly parts rotted away. But then the sun, which was pictured as being carried in the jaws of a gigantic lion, grew supremely warm, and finally hot enough to turn the waters in the prison to mist. And after forty days and nights of evaporating and condensing, the vapours produced a glowing rainbow inside the prison; the waters receded and lo! the corpses of the bride and bridegroom were bathed in a merciful rain that restored them to life. At which point the crystal prison opened its doors and the boy and girl, more beautiful than ever before and resplendent in cloth-of-gold and gleaming carbuncles, were at last permitted to consummate their wedding.

In the final picture, the two seemed to have melted into a single body with a double face, a haunting shape that had the organs of each sex. Behind their coupled form rose a gigantic double-headed raven with its wings outspread; but the children were not afraid. Each now held a sword, the black sword and the white, pointed toward heaven and toward Earth.

The last words in the volume were:

> Sister-Brother, two in one,
> Male and female, moon and sun,
> Sound and silence, light and dark,
> Seed and branch and singing lark.
> Great begetter, time unfurled,
> Center, maker, root of world,
> In joyous song the numbers fall
> Into the ordered dance of All.

Were these two babes, the brother-sister, meant to represent Victor and myself? I wondered. Then what adventures must await me! I was frankly more fearful than eager.

"They are twins," Victor explained to me when I brought the book to him to read. "Royal twins. The Great Work is the story of their marriage."

"The Great Work?"

"The finding of the philosophical stone, that which changes base matter to gold. This is what the marriage means. But this is not to be understood grossly. Nothing about the Great Work is what it seems on the surface. The crystal prison, for example. Do you know what that is?"

"No."

"It is meant to be the retort, the vessel where the substances are mixed. Sometimes it is called the egg, or the sepulchre, or the nuptial chamber. Everything has many names. The retort must be closed so tightly that no air can pass into it. This is called a Hermetic seal, after Hermes, who was the greatest alchymical sage. The vessel becomes then a tiny world of its own where you can watch the elements reacting. That is what I want most to see; in the story, it is called 'suffering.' This is a metaphor, of course, for these lifeless elements have no sentience and feel nothing. The boy, you see, is red; he is the sulphur; the fair maiden is mercury. This is how the substances mingle and make up the universe."

I could not follow his explanation at all. "Why must everything be so disguised?"

"Because it is a secret art. The adepts did not wish to have a vulgar sort of people intruding upon the Work. What they saw was not for everybody's eye."

"What did they see?"

"Great visions. Visions that would drive some men mad. What the adepts do is like the work of God. But if it is not done with pure intentions, it will produce an evil result."

"Mother says you studied the book while you were at Thonon."

"It was the most wonderful thing! I never imagined the world could be so vastly mysterious. Elizabeth, my mind has been in such rapture! As if I were on the point of penetrating the furthest recesses of Nature. Do you realise what these books contain? Secrets within secrets within secrets. All the hidden workings of the cosmos. One must only learn to read the true meanings of these pictures."

At that moment I saw in him the same vaulting passion I had seen when he stood watching the lightning in the mountain passes. But now the lightning seemed to be flashing in his own mind, and that made me all the more apprehensive. "Can you teach me to see what you have seen?" I asked.

"Indeed I *must!* You must be at my side throughout, like the female twin. What I wish to know you must help me to know. We are sister and brother in this adventure. We shall learn together."

At these words, as if by the touch of a magician's wand, all the disquiet I was harbouring within me vanished. In its place came exuberance and high expectation. I no longer feared what lay ahead; above all, I no longer feared the zealousness I saw in Victor. Only one thing filled my thoughts: *Victor wanted me to share his passion!* The adventure would belong to the two of us! Oh then, I would be brave for him; I would dare whatever he wished me to undertake. I wanted so very much to take him in my arms—and not as a sister embraces a brother. But I remembered my promise to Mother. And suddenly I realised that the invisible barrier she had placed between us only served to increase the longing I felt sweep through me. Pretending to be ice on the surface made the fire within me burn all the hotter, as if the flame fed on abstinence. Though I had not realised it, I had begun my lessons in a new kind of love.

On the night Mother showed me the Rose Book I began my diary, knowing that an adventure lay before me, which I must take care to chronicle.

These were the first words I entered in its pages.

I have entered a dark wood where few have walked before. Mother leads me by a silken thread; there are no clear paths; I can only follow where she guides. We wander far into a land where the sun seems never to have shone. I can scarcely discern Mother's form moving ahead of me among the trees. If I should lose hold of the thread!

I am afraid. . . .

I am afraid. . . .

Part Two

EDITOR'S NOTE

I confess to approaching this section of the memoir with considerable trepidation. Nothing requires more judicious attention than the fateful incident of the chemical marriage, for this is the misadventure that precipitated Elizabeth Frankenstein's tragedy. For this reason, I have devoted great time and study to this extraordinary rite in an effort to understand its significance and the practices that led to it. At the same time, nothing could be more offensive to common decency than the rôle Elizabeth Frankenstein played in this episode of her life and which she describes in these pages. Perhaps it will somewhat excuse the frankness of her account if we recall that this memoir was, after all, intended for the eyes of one reader only, and that the man who, as the woman's husband-to-be, was present at the rites. In any case, I ask the reader's forbearance if at this point I indulge in a more candid presentation of particulars than I have permitted myself elsewhere as part of my editorial duties.

The murky and amorphous body of thought we inherit under the label of "alchemy" is in no respect more jarring to the civilised sensibilities than in its erotic symbolism. The pictures that illustrate its texts are frequently blatant in their display of sexual subject matter. This is nowhere more vividly in evidence than in the two volumes I acquired from Mme. Rebuffat at the gravesite of Francine Dupin. Without the benefit of the volumes known as the Rose Book and the Lavender Book, it would have proven impossible for me to explore many shadowed corners of this narrative. What Elizabeth Frankenstein refers to only darkly and in passing in her memoir, or by way of arcane symbols known to her and to her fiancé, is brought fully to light in these works. The precise meaning of her oblique references to such rituals as "the sleeping emperor" or "the feeding of the lions" would have escaped me entirely but for the explanation I found in these pages.

Both books are Latin translations of much older and long-lost works. What the provenance of those texts may have been is impossible to tell; one cannot be certain even of their original language. There is, therefore, no way to evaluate the accuracy of the Latin translation; in general, the narrative is rendered in a stilted, academic style that gives little confidence in its sensitivity to fine points. (I might add that I found no trace of the French translation that Lady Caroline prepared for Elizabeth; only those portions survive that Elizabeth elected to copy into her memoir.) Discovering some hint of the history of the books was in itself the labour of years, for the volumes came attached to no identity, no reliable authorship, no time or place. Their obscurity was unquestionably deliberate, a bulwark of secrecy carefully erected round them to defend their readers from accusations of heresy. Antiquarian bibliophiles I consulted were quickly able to date the publication of the books to Italy of the late fifteenth century, making these among the oldest printed texts in our literary history; but to have established that much was merely to scratch the surface of the enigma. For what the newly invented printing press placed on paper at some point in the 1480s were texts of a much older origin. Here I will but briefly summarise the conclusions of a study that might make for a book in its own right.

At the height of the Italian Renaissance, a school was founded in the city of Florence by the Italian scholar Marsilio Ficino for the purpose of studying certain arcane works of ancient philosophy. These works were rumoured at the time to contain the oldest wisdom of the world, in comparison to which the collected *opera* of Plato, Aristotle, Epictetus, and perhaps the whole of Scripture were the prattling of children.

Among the works we must thank Ficino and his Florentine Academy for preserving is the curious collection of documents now known as the Corpus Hermeticum. This single work contains almost all that we know of the ancient alchemical tradition. At that same time, again thanks to the Academy's scholars, two other books were translated and put into print. One of these was the very Rose Book that Elizabeth Frankenstein was given to peruse by Lady Caroline. This handsome volume might easily have found as large a reading public in its time as the Corpus Hermeticum, and might have become as famous. Vividly illustrated with the rich symbolic imagery one expects in alchemical literature, the book also includes actual formulae and procedures for performing the Great Work step by step. One can only surmise that its absence from the historical record results from a premeditated effort to keep these contents esoteric.

As for its companion volume, the Lavender Book, so called for the colour of its binding, its suppression can be accounted for much more easily. One grasps the reason as soon as one lays eyes upon the first of its many illustrations. The book is frankly obscene. Like those in the Rose Book, the pictures comprise hand-coloured wood-cuts of an exotic origin, either Arabian or Hindoo, but the intention is clearly more hedonistic. In the Lavender Book, the settings are mainly regal: palaces, pleasure gardens, or seraglios where kings, queens, and courtesans disport themselves. Though its anonymous author insists that it is an alchemical treatise, the book is so relentlessly and graphically erotic that it might as well be a catalogue of the sexual perversions.

The Lavender Book posed a moral dilemma for me from the time it came into my possession. While I stood prepared from the outset to place the Rose Book in the public domain once my editorial labours were complete, I remained uncertain of how to dispose of its companion volume. Over the years, as word of the book filtered out through my circle of acquaintances, I was approached several times by collectors willing to pay handsomely to purchase it. But I frankly could not trust the intentions of those who proffered the money. Fearing that the work might all too easily slip into the pornographic *demi-monde*, where it would surely be valued at a premium, I at last elected to make arrangements for the Lavender Book to be deposited in the Vatican library, whose extensive collection of erotica has been carefully guarded against indiscriminate public access for several generations. I refer those who wish to pursue research in this volume to the curator of the Lambruschini Collection in the Giardino della Pigna in Rome.

I will call the reader's attention to one new feature of this memoir. At the outset of her alchemical training, Elizabeth Frankenstein began a diary; it represents the most immediate record of the studies she undertook with Victor. In the last year of her life, as she composed these memoirs, she included excerpts from her diary, along with a series of poems dealing with various phases of the Great Work. These selections came to my hand as so many loose pages affixed to the journal in which the memoirs were written; many are roughly torn so that words have been lost at the edges of the page. The sections published here were chosen for inclusion by the author's own hand. I have been unable to locate more of the original diary than the reader finds herein contained.

Seraphina Begins
Our Instruction

Nature Rejoice! Eden returns!
Beside the Tree, the river burns.
Golden the apple our Mother stole,
Hardship our way, heaven our goal.

In season of shadow, the sun rides low,
The Earth is ruled by carrion crow,
A winter too deep for spring to thaw
Sunk in the grip of unnatural law.

The Work begins in bleak despair
When no bird sings in branches bare.
The Work begins in dead of night
When flowering Nature hides from sight.

Find the blossom in the bone
Find the fire in the stone.
Beneath the darkling season's blight
Find the resurrected Light.

November ——, 178——

 "We must have blood and seed," Seraphina announces. "The blood first, for that is more difficult than taking the seed. To take the blood, we shall have to be patient. For the blood has its seasons even as great Nature does."

Since the summer, each time I meet with Seraphina, she asks about my monthly bleeding. She carefully places her hands here and there about my body, feeling for heat at my brow, my breast. She presses her ear to my belly; she lays her fingers lightly to a vein in my throat and another just inside my upper thigh. At bedtime Mother brings me a tonic Seraphina has brewed for me to drink; then she gently rubs my back and stomach with sweet-smelling oils. Mother tells me that Seraphina is seeking to influence the rhythm of my body. For the Work can go no further until the menses can be made to coincide with the coming of the full moon. This must be done gently and may take several months.

At Mother's invitation, Seraphina has come to live at Belrive. She has been given one of the gardeners' cottages near the arboretum. There she prepares her own meals and takes them privately. She spends her days in study, rarely emerging to mingle with the rest of the household, who clearly regard her with some disquiet, for she does cut a forbidding figure as she walks the grounds. Painfully hunched and slow of step, she makes her way effortfully with the aid of a long forked stick. Her costume is a patchwork gown with jangling Gipsy trinkets at her throat and wrists and ankles. If she appears at all during the day, it is to hunt for herbs, which she deposits in a woven sack. Alu is with her always, either perched on her shoulder, or sometimes smartly walking the path ahead of her. Our servants seem to find the bird even more sinister than her mistress; for sometimes, when Alu goes strolling on her own, clucking and cawing as she waddles over the grounds, the servants hasten out of her way as if an ogre were approaching. Victor and I find this comic to watch, for Alu is a gentle old bird and not at all menacing. But despite her years, she is quite fearless; one morning when the bailiff's great mastiff rushed barking at Seraphina, Alu flew screeching in his face as if she might pluck out his eyes. The poor hound ran yelping for cover.

Mother has told the servants that Seraphina is with us as her personal apothecary. Once, while the Baron was briefly at home between travels, she told him the same. Though the Baron clearly views Seraphina with disapproval, he asks no further questions, except to be solicitous for Mother's health. "This is nothing serious, I trust," is all he says. I know he would prefer that she consult an Enlightened physician.

Seraphina does in truth minister to Mother; she makes broths and potions for her, and with good reason. Mother, who has suffered from consumption since her girlhood, is sometimes faint and pale of late; she takes sick easily and keeps to her room for days at a time. I believe that Seraphina's medications help her greatly; but that is not the main reason for her residence. She is here for our instruction, which happens for the most part at night, sometimes in Seraphina's cottage, sometimes in the glade.

It is not by chance, Seraphina tells us, that we have begun our studies in the month of November, when the dead season of the year creeps in upon us. For a time, at the outset, our study will be sombre, a dark meditation. We must pass through the Valley of the Shadow, taking the dying of the Earth into our innermost thoughts, the better to understand the wondrous fertility of Nature. "We study the foundations of life," Seraphina tells us. "Life and the higher life that hides all about us in the world. But to learn the causes of life, we must first have recourse to death." Victor is well advanced in learning the many chymical correspondences of things. Autumn, he teaches me, is the time of Saturn and the withered rose-bush and the leaden sepulchre and the carrion crow and the King on his bed of pain. In the Rose Book he shows me pictures that symbolise the season of death; there are so many to remember.

There is another name he uses that fills the mind with the most dolorous images of all: the *nigredo.* The black of blacks. The darkness darker than darkness. The *nigredo* is a brooding, melancholy condition of the soul that must be found within; but to help us think upon it as the chymical masters do, Seraphina has us take the Rose Book to the churchyard at Vandoeuvres and there study the pictures that bespeak this morose season. "You must walk among the dead," she instructs us. "You must be among them as if they, even underground, were our companions in life, those who have passed into a destined phase without which life could not continue. You must try to sense all about you the fertility of death, which is not an ending, but a beginning. Time is properly this circle, like the image I have shown you in the book. Remember the snake that bites its own tail. We forget the circle of time when we pay too much attention to events as the history books record them, marching straight into the future on and on and on. We forget that all things return."

Today in the churchyard Victor and I come upon the grave-digger preparing for a fresh burial; he has uncovered old bones that were interred, he says, centuries before. They have become hard as rock, and, as Victor observes, strangely clean. Scoured by decay, free of every memory of life. Finally at peace.

But, I tell Victor, I want no part of such "peace." I would find it a prison of silence and numbness.

November ——, 178——

We begin always with a time of contemplation. Seraphina seeks out a picture in one of her books and sets it up for us to ponder. Her favourite shows the hand of God reaching down to send forth the Holy Spirit in the guise of a fiery dove. "Like Noah sending out the bird to explore the watery waste," Seraphina says. "But here the waste is all the world; and indeed there is no world, but only waste." She draws her gnarled witch's finger over the picture to trace the path of the dove, showing how it descends to hollow out the nothingness that once was everywhere.

Alu watches all we do as if she understood each word, though after a time she often tucks her head under her wing and sleeps. Tonight she comes close to squint at the picture Seraphina shows us. This amuses Seraphina. She asks, "Tell us, Alu: Do you perhaps know this bird? Is this a friend of yours? Come now, you are not that old!"

At which the frazzled old bird clacks her great beak, emits a loud croak, and returns to her perch atop the hearth.

"See how the fiery Spirit burns away the darkness, making a great space," Seraphina explains. "And what is this hole it leaves behind, this nothingness within the greater Nothingness, this void within the Void? That is the great mystery, my children. Take this dark space into your minds; let your thought feed upon it. Empty your mind until it contains nothing. And then empty your mind even of that nothing. For this Nothingness we speak of was not the emptiness of space; it was the nothing that is not even space. Imagine this Nothingness that is beyond all emptiness, imagine a time when there is not even time passing, nor any mind to remember that time has passed or look ahead to see what will come. Imagine this silence that came before there was anything to breathe a word or emit a sound. Nothing, nothing, nothing at all. This void might have endured forever. But it did not. Instead, out of this hole which was burnt from the blackness, the world arises like a seed that flowers in the womb. *But why should this be?* Why should there be anything at all? Why should the sleeping darkness have been awakened? What was there in that Emptiness from which a world might be made? This is too great a secret for words to speak. This is that Moment before there were moments, Time before there was time, when Highest Love reached into the Abyss to make First Matter. You see how humbling it is to hold this great Emptiness in our tiny mind? But this is where all true knowledge begins."

I try to do as Seraphina asks, but find it is impossible to make my mind so empty. Still, after several sessions, just for the most fleeting instant now and again, I discover a vastness within myself that makes me giddy. I seem to hover where there is no place to fall. And I say to myself: *There is a world in here!* Then, in a quiet voice, asking us to fix our gazes upon the dark hole at the centre of the picture, Seraphina drums as lightly as the falling dew upon her tambourine and croons an invocation:

> Virgin Matter
> Seed Divine
> Whose blood and body
> Give bread and wine
>
> Blest the fruit
> That fills Thy womb

Gold and silver
Sun and moon

Primal waters
Bring to birth
The hidden riches
Under Earth

Thy wisdom falls
Like gentle rain
To glorify
Our Mother's name

December —— , *178*——

Our work is meant to be chaste, but we meet together unclothed, Victor and myself, just as the women do when they gather in the glade. Seraphina too. She sits cross-legged beside us, wearing only her Gipsy bangles at the throat and wrists.

I have become used to being naked among the women; I understand the meaning this has in the craft. But I do not find it comfortable to be naked with Victor. My mind wanders from the task before us. I think vain thoughts. I wonder if he finds me beautiful, as beautiful as he found Francine when he spied upon her in the glade. I want him to look at me as he looked at her, though my body is still slight and girlish.

Each time we gather for our lessons with Seraphina, we begin with ablutions. Victor and I assist one another in the cleansing. We bathe with water steeped in chamomile and rub one another with sweet oil of camphor. It is a sign, Seraphina tells us, that we are washing away the dust of mortality. "We are not fallen creatures, as the priests teach," she says, "but emissaries of light whose rôle it is to perfect Earthly creation." But when Victor passes his hands over my body, I have no such elevated thoughts in mind. I think only of the sensation that whips across my skin like little ribbons of fire. I want his hands everywhere. I want him to stretch me upon the grass as he did that day in the meadow and force himself upon me. And I would open wide to him and hold him inside me. I would tease him until he grew wildly excited. I would let him violate me.

I fear my imagination is too lively and perverse.

But that is not my greatest source of unease. Strange to say, I find Seraphina's nakedness more unsettling than Victor's. For she is so very *old.* Her body is withered in the extreme; her wizened flesh hangs loose at every joint. Why would she not prefer to keep it hidden from the eyes of others? I wonder. How can a woman of her years be so shameless, even brazen, as to go unclothed with Victor present? I worry for Victor's misgivings; I see how he seeks to keep his face averted, not wanting to lay eyes upon her unless he must. At last, Seraphina asks after our feelings. Old as she is, she is a perceptive and commanding woman. Nothing escapes her. She seems to read our very thoughts. She watches, she questions. She never holds back her words.

"I see that you often look away from me when we speak, Victor." Her voice rasps like the wind in dry grass. Often she mixes her French with other languages that come more naturally to her, Italian or Greek. "Does my nakedness vex you?" she asks, with a certain amusement in her tone. "Yes, I think it does. Why? Because it is an old crone's nakedness? An unsightly nakedness?" Victor struggles to be courteous, but she will not be put off. "Come now, speak truthfully to me. We keep no secrets from one another here. Do you find me too ugly to gaze upon?"

"It seems improper. . . ." Victor explains, seeking to spare her any hurt.

Seraphina laughs. Her laughter is a sort of breathless cackle. She takes hold of her breast, which is flat and shapeless as an empty sack. She flaps it at Victor. "You do not find that pleasant to behold, eh? Can you believe that lovers have sucked at that dry nipple? No? Ah, but look here!" And reaching across, she boldly chucks me beneath my left breast. I flinch at the gesture and cross my arms over my bosom. "No, no, my dear! Uncover! Let our young gentleman see. Let him compare." Reluctantly, I lower my defending arms. Seraphina again reaches to touch me, this time gently tracing the roundness of my breast. "Do not hold yourself so squashed in, my girl. Reveal! Be proud, as you have been taught to be proud. Let Victor admire you, let him enjoy the sight." At her bidding, I square my shoulders and thrust my bosom forward that I might be fully displayed. I feel audacious, and enjoy the feeling. Until our lessons with Seraphina began, it has been many months since Victor last saw me unclothed; I realise that I have been eager for him to see how my woman's body has grown. "See how sweetly shaped she is," Seraphina says, "how fresh and rounded. But I see you also find yourself uneasy when you gaze upon Elizabeth. Do you not?"

"Yes . . ." Victor answers in some confusion.

"For a very different reason, I wager. Not so? Her nakedness makes you uneasy because of its youth and fruitfulness. Mine because I am so worn and depleted. Odd, is it not, that both beauty and its opposite should distress you—as if you did not know what you expected of woman. Which distresses you more, I wonder, the presence or the absence of desire? Which seems more 'proper'? Now let me tell you something that will amaze you, Victor. Before we are finished, you will be able to gaze upon us both, Elizabeth and myself, with an equal eye. You will see her beauty in me. For it is there, buried beneath the grey weight of years. You will lust for the crone—oh yes, you will! And you will see my age in her, for it is also there, the decay that works within all flesh. But if you learn well, you will see what lies beyond this exterior, the thing that makes us both women. You will find a new way to look at us both that is neither craving nor rejecting."

I have no clear understanding of what Seraphina means. So often she speaks in riddles. This much I know: I surely do not wish Victor to see me as a shrivelled hag! I want his desire, and the full force of it!

Mother Paints Me

December ——, 178——

Mother also studies my body, quite as closely as Seraphina—but with a different intention. She is painting me, as she once promised to do. She began soon after my initiation. She now admits me regularly to her studio, and there I pose while she sketches me. She becomes supremely concentrated while she works; she rarely says a word and pretends not to hear if I speak. At first I felt all the more "of age" to think that Mother should wish to draw me as she once drew Francine and frequently draws her woman-friends. But sometimes our sessions together leave me feeling quite uneasy. There is a way Mother's eye surveys my body when I am uncovered that makes me feel *deeply* naked. Not as I feel when I am among the women, nor as I would feel if Victor were gazing upon me. I believe Mother sees what no one else would see, some more interior part of myself that even I may not know exists. Her eye pries into secret places that I am not sure I wish to have revealed. "I wish to see how you grow into womanhood," she tells me. "I want to capture the essence of this change—not just the shaping of your outward self, but of your soul as well."

Sensing my disquiet, Mother burns a special incense during our *séance*. It has a pungent, herbal fragrance; the odour soon makes me light-headed and then I find no trouble relaxing into our work. I wholly lose awareness of the time. Mother says the leaf she burns comes from Peru and was discovered by the high Incas. Seraphina has given it to her; the midwives use it for difficult deliveries.

Mother each time shows me the sketches she has made; they are not likenesses of me. My face melts away into cloud; but my body is drawn with great care to show every shape and shadow—and every blemish: the small dark spots along my shoulder that I was born with; the all-but-wholly-faded scar at my temple; even the fine hairs that circle my nipples and curl beneath my arms. Often she asks me to place myself in revealing postures, my thighs spread and open to her eye so that she can sketch every strand of hair and fold of the inner flesh. Her depictions are graphic in the extreme, though often decorated with flowering shapes and coiling tendrils that twine across my breasts and sex. She asks what I think of her work. I let a small note of disapproval sound in my voice. "It is too frank, I think."

"How so?"

"I would not want strangers to see these pictures if they knew I had been the model. They show too much."

Mother is amused. "I think you mean the hair."

"Yes."

"You have a young woman's body still beautiful in all its naturalness, with an inner beauty emerging as fresh as the spring that will be with you all your years. Your eye has been too much influenced by the pictures men paint of us. They delight in having women pose for them in the flesh; but so often they prefer to give us angelic little-girls' bodies: waxen and hairless, with tiny geometrical breasts that might have been carved from marble. Unless, that is, they paint us as bacchantes. Oh, how fascinated they are with bacchantes! Women wild with passion—who, of course, lived long, long ago and can no longer be found. Men cannot make up their minds whether they would have us be voluptuous or virginal. Judging by the result of their work, Mssrs. David and Fragonard hardly needed to have naked ladies before them at all; in truth, they were but painting their own fancies. Of course, we know why the ladies were there, do we not?"

"I could never bring myself to model for a man; to lie naked under his gaze for hours at a time! I cannot tell whether I should be more ashamed or bored."

"You are quite naïve if you think those are the only possibilities. In ancient Greece, it was a coveted honour for the most beautiful married women of the city to pose nude for the great Praxiteles. 'Sculpture,' the artist contended, 'is the true school of womanly modesty.' And why should he not say so? He maintained that nothing more attested to the virtue of Athenian womanhood than that every model who had played the part of Aphrodite for him returned to her husband as chaste as she had arrived. Of course, we have only the artist's word for that. I suspect his models left him each day quite unashamed and not the least bit bored."

Mother's sketches are part of a large canvas she has worked upon for many months: a strange painting that I find it discomfiting to see. She tells me it is the most ambitious work she has attempted and wonders if she will ever be able to finish. For it, she has made innumerable studies of Seraphina as well as me; woman young and woman old, these she combines in the canvas. I am shown sitting on Mother's knee, and she in turn is shown sitting on Seraphina's knee. The three of us are naked; and behind Seraphina, supporting her, stretches a line of naked women, each holding the next on her knee. Their faces are obscure. The line winds back and back into the picture and out of sight, but each has a hand on the next woman's breast. Overhead, the moon is shown in all its phases at once. The three of us—Seraphina, Mother, and myself— are oddly entwined in one another's arms. Seraphina's hand reaches round to touch Mother's breast, and Mother's hand reaches to touch mine. Seraphina's eyes gaze upon Mother with an unearthly intensity that I find almost predatory. Mother's gaze is more tender and focussed on me; I am shown looking down into the palm of my hand, which I hold open directly before my nipple. But the hand is empty. I ask what is meant to be there, for this space has an arresting quality. "You shall see, my dear," Mother answers. "I keep that for a surprise."

I ask Mother to tell me more about Seraphina. "She has spoken to me in the Romany tongue. Is she a Gipsy like Rosina and Toma?"

Mother smiles at my words. "Seraphina has lived among the Gipsies, as she has among many other people. If I told you that she is of a tribe called Tamil, I daresay that would mean as little to you as it does to me. It would mean little to the Baron, for all his distant travels. Seraphina's home lies beyond even the realm of the Grand Turk."

"Is that where she has gained her great wisdom?"

"There and in many more places. Seraphina is part of something very old. There is a chain of thought; it stretches far back into time, like the line of cunning women in my canvas. It cannot be found in the chronicles of men, but it exists nonetheless." Mother closes her eyes as if in her mind she is gazing back across the centuries. "The chain is fine as gossamer, but tenacious as bronze; it binds teacher to pupil across the ages. The links of this chain are teachings that cannot be written on the page, but only spoken face to face. In the chymical philosophy, women are numbered among the most respected teachers; they are thought to bring a certain quality to the science. Once, in ancient times, in the great city of Alexandria there was a teacher whose name was Kleopatra. Not the queen, but a woman quite as famous in her time for being among the great adepts. Seraphina has made a particular study of her work and will herself one day be numbered among such women."

I confess to Mother that I do not always grasp what Seraphina teaches me.

"She has a subtle mind. Attend her closely, and not merely her words. Seraphina does not teach only by words. As you will see, she has other devices." She pauses to study my expression. "Is there something more?" she asks. She has discerned the note of worry in my voice. Yes, I admit . . . something I am reluctant to tell. "Come now! We have no more secrets between us."

"When we do the exercises . . . I am left feeling so unsatisfied."

"How so?"

"Victor and I never touch, except when Seraphina directs us to. Will this be so always?"

"Not at all. In time, you shall become the most intimate of companions."

"It is difficult to be patient. You told me I would experience lust. I do. But it goes unfed." My voice falls to a whisper as I confess to her: "I dream of Victor violating me. I let him; I want him to."

A tender, searching look comes into Mother's eyes. "Of course, of course. Poor child!" She moves to a cabinet beside her easel and from there fetches out a small velvet pouch. "You have heard people say that cunning women can fly. Have you never wondered how they do this remarkable thing?"

"Can they truly do so?"

"As truly as the birds, but not in the same way."

Now I become exceedingly curious. "Then how?"

There is a merry look in her eyes as she hands me the pouch to examine. "Here is the broomstick we use."

What I find inside is nothing like a broomstick. It is a small, slender rod only slightly longer than my hand and tightly wrapped in a gleaming silken sheath. From below the sheath protrudes a finely-wrought ivory handle, carved with vines and flowers. There is also a small flask in the pouch, which Mother takes from me and opens. "And here you see the wings on which we soar." She swirls the flask and then carefully dabs two drops of a colourless, acrid fluid upon the silken covering.

"One must be cautious with this potion. It is a powerful mixture. It must never be drunk."

"What is in it?"

"That is Seraphina's secret. But she has told us that it contains belladonna, a deadly poison. One uses it by placing a few drops on the skin and only in a certain place where the body can best feel the power even of the smallest measure. Shall I show you where?"

"Yes," I answer.

"Lie back, then, and make your mind empty. Let your body grow limp. You must open your legs." I stretch myself back upon the blanket and let my breath carry away the tautness of my muscles. Then I let my thighs fall open. Mother hands me the rod and shows me where to position it. It is to be fitted just at the entrance to my cleft and pressed lightly there against the most sensitive part of my sex. She tells me to make the rod quiver lightly and rapidly "like the wings of a humming-bird" so that I feel a sort of teasing pressure. No sooner has the silken surface grazed my flesh than all my lower body begins to glow. A searing blush sweeps over me, followed by waves of softly convulsive pleasure. This pulsing delirium radiates out and back, each time in widening circles. Within seconds, my mind clouds over as if a veil had been placed across my eyes, and I feel as if I am lifting from the ground like a leaf blown in the breeze. I might have grown afraid, but my body seems to have lost all gravity; it is feather-light. I know I am in no danger of falling. Moreover, the feeling that suffuses my body is a sweet ecstasy that quiets my fears. It is indeed as if I am the companion of the birds sailing through the sky. Down below me on the Earth, I hear someone laughing with the delight of the moment; I look down and see that it is *I!* And then I fall into a dark, warm sleep that lasts I cannot say how long.

When my eyes open, Mother is at my side stroking my brow. My entire body is tingling like a bell that has been sounded and still vibrates. Between my legs there is a slight burning sensation. Mother hands me a lotion that I am to spread there, and in moments the irritation is gone.

"Tell me truthfully," Mother asks, "can you imagine anything you might do with a man that would be more desirable than what you have just experienced?"

"But I do not know enough to say."

"A clever answer. And of course you must not accept my word for it. But I assure you, there is no enjoyment any man will be able to offer you greater than what you have known today. That is why Seraphina's tincture must remain our secret. The men wish to believe we have great need of them. They believe that only their *grands bâtons* can give us the pleasure of flying! We must not wound their pride. To be sure, there are other reasons to seek the company of men; there are things you will discover with Victor, ecstasies of another kind. These will take time and study." She adds with a soft laugh: "For these simpler diversions, you have your magic wand."

But she does not let me take the pouch away with me. The potion, she warns, needs to be handled delicately. For if it should be used excessively, it becomes a sort of tyrant that never leaves the mind in peace.

The Toad at
the Damsel's Breast

I still recall the countless hours I spent poring over the Rose Book with its wealth of enigmatic pictures and poems. Especially during the winter nights, after the rest of the household was long asleep, I would sit in my room gazing at its pages, struggling to match the text with the images. The pictures I studied had an inner life; they possessed a thirst that seemed determined to drink deep of the eye until all its powers of vision had been drained. At times I could have sworn I saw the figures move upon the page as if they might step forth into the room. And often, when sleep overcame me where I sat huddled in my blanket before the dwindling fire, unwilling to lay the book aside until my eyes could no longer stay open, the pictures would fuse with dreams that carried me to unearthly scenes where I was the princess or the sage or the mythic hero on his imperilled quest. I remembered what Mother had told me of Seraphina's gift of knowledge to her when she was a young girl: that it had thrown open the doors of imagination and let her mind wander the great world of thought that has been locked shut against women. Now she had bestowed the same gift on me, and the effect was pure intoxication! Though I had not yet been permitted to do more than sip wine at table, I could think of no other word to describe the sensation. This, I felt certain, was how the mind reeled when overcome with drink, in a sort of delicious dizziness that loosened the tongue and turned it rhapsodic.

That this was a tainted knowledge I studied—tainted with a melancholy history of charlatanry, tainted too by the blood of its many persecuted disciples—did not diminish my fascination. I was perfectly aware of the unsavoury reputation alchymists had acquired over the centuries. For had I not heard the Baron himself reproach their practices at our own dinner table, calling the chymical philosophy the blackest of superstitions?

This had happened in the course of a visit from a certain M. Cazotte, a Parisian occultist who had recently arrived at the château from Palermo, fresh from an audience with the notorious Count Cagliostro. I would have remembered M. Cazotte well enough simply because of the many astonishing tales he brought with him; but I remember him now particularly after having recently learnt that it was this fantastical man's sad fate to become one of the victims of the Terror and to die beneath the guillotine.

On the occasion of his visit to Geneva, M. Cazotte reported that Count Cagliostro had taken from him a plug of his ear-wax and had—before his very eyes—turned it into the purest gold. As so often happened with our guests, there followed a heated exchange with the Baron, who, in a fit of exasperation, at last asked: Did this not prove beyond all doubt that the spagyric philosophy was the work of dissembling puffers and Nature-fakers? "If gold, sir, were as easy to come by as reaching into your unwashed ear for it," the Baron proclaimed, "Count Cagliostro would be a richer man than I, and so would every beggar in the streets of Europe. But they are not. To my personal knowledge, sir, your rogue Count is a wretched debtor and defaulter and clipper of coins, as are all his lot." No sooner had he uttered the words than, glancing down the table at Mother, he reddened and hid his face in his wineglass; for he was quite aware of Mother's interests. Afterwards I asked her what accounted for Father's hostility. I could not believe that he counted her and Seraphina among the hoaxers he was so quick to condemn. Sighing wearily, she explained, "Like so many sceptical minds of our age, the Baron knows the ancient teachings only at their most debased value—where one will always find charlatans at work, no less so in his own natural philosophy than in the occult arts. In Strasbourg last summer, there was a mechanistical physicist who claimed he had invented a perpetual-motion machine based upon strict Newtonian principles. And what did the man who bought it find inside? A starved rat running in a wheel! That Cagliostro is a scoundrel goes without question. But that he is universally known to be such by all true adepts, the Baron will not learn."

In my innocence, I took Mother at her word when she assured me that the Baron must be forgiven his "limitations," and especially so when she added with a note of wifely pity, "He is, after all, a man." For nothing had been so strongly emphasised in my studies as the fact that I was learning a *woman's* wisdom. Yet as enchanting as I found the images of the Rose Book, its text was so obscure that my woman's brain grew numb with pondering its meaning. I read:

> Torture the Eagle till she weeps and the Lion be weakened and bleed to death. The blood of the Lion, mixed with the tears of the Eagle, is the treasure of the Earth.

But even when I understood that the eagle was the emblem of supreme virtue and of the chymical process called sublimation, and that the lion was the emblem of the philosophical stone, and of gold, and of the sun . . . I could not make head or tail of such teaching.

"You must persevere, my dear," Mother insisted. "Though these are deep matters, our Higher Reason was made to take them in. Remember the times you have wandered in the mountains with Victor and stood upon the brink of the precipice gazing down? Imagine you stand now at the edge of a great gulf; trust that if you cast yourself out upon it, you will sail like a great hawk on the rising wind. Trust that your mind also has wings."

With a young girl's impassioned curiosity, I was far more drawn to all that the Rose Book said of marriage (and especially of what follows in the bedchamber) than to what it said of symbolical lions and wolves and dragons.

Behold! [I read] There came forward the most beautiful of all maidens, arrayed in damask and silk, with the most beautiful of the youths, dressed in scarlet robes. They walked arm in arm to the rose garden, carrying fragrant roses in their hands. There, finding the wedding guests waiting, the maiden said, "This is my beloved bridegroom. And now we must leave this pleasant garden and hasten to our bedchamber to satisfy our passion."

And here were pictured the loving pair on the bridal bed, their fine garments cast aside, ardently entwined in one another's embrace.

And in another place I read:

This day, this day, this day, the nuptials of the King take place. If thou art born to share in them, go unto the mountain heights, the three-templed mountain and witness there the rites.

And here were pictured the King and his fair consort reclining upon a bower, he pressed well into her vulva and emitting a rich fountain of seed. And I wished, I wished . . .

But not all the images of courtship and marriage were so charming. Another told a repulsive tale. A handsome prince approaches a lovely damsel to whom he is betrothed. He reaches out his hand to caress her, but instead thrusts a poisonous toad into her bosom. The damsel gazes in horror as the reptile seizes upon her nipple and begins to suck fiercely. Below the picture, the words say: "Place a venomous toad at the female's breast that it may nurse there. The woman will die, and the toad grow fat upon her milk. From this you may mix a noble drug that drives poison from the heart and saves all from destruction."

I had no idea what this might mean; indeed, I found the picture so repellent that I formed the habit of turning past it without looking whenever I scanned the book. What a surprise it was, then, to encounter this same grotesque image in a place where I least expected it: in Mother's painting! For that is what she placed in my empty hand—this ugly little beast. She showed me gazing down almost fondly upon the thing, pressing my nipple to its thin green lips as if it were a suckling babe.

What could this mean? Mother had many times told me to think of myself as the females in the pictures; the queen, the sister, the consort. But here the lady was made to suckle an ugly toad, and it killed her. Did this mean that women were at risk in studying the chymical philosophy? "On the contrary," Mother answered with some concern, and went at once to her bookshelf to draw out a fat scroll. This she unrolled on the table to reveal a marvellously intricate drawing of the entire cosmos, circle within circle within circle, world within world within world. "See here," she explained, "this is an image of the Great Universe as no natural philosopher will ever see it in its whole and perfected form. Think of this as a narrow view into the mind of God. And here, linking all the levels of existence, is a golden chain that spans all time and all distance from highest to lowest. The labour of Reason is to climb that chain and ascend to the Divine source from which all things spring so that we may see as God sees. The toad at the damsel's breast is the symbol of the base matter that you see here at the very nethermost point of the cosmos. But as far removed as that point is from God, it too can be made holy. The woman's milk spoken of in the Rose Book is the Philosopher's Stone, which can purify matter and transmute dross into gold. This means that women can also play the part of redeemers, as much so as Christ or Zoroaster or Thrice-Great Hermes."

She returned to her bookshelf and took down a leather-bound volume, which she placed in my hands. "This book, many men believe, holds the future in its pages. I ask you to study it along with the other works I have given you. It is the writing of a great alchymical philosopher, though in this book he has strayed into other, lesser fields of interest. It is, I find, one of his minor works, though highly regarded by many. Where you have difficulty understanding, Victor can help you. Read with care; learn from this how men are sifting the secrets of Nature."

I understood little of what Mother said on these heads, yet when she spoke to me like this, I knew myself to be part of a great design she held in her mind. I saw why she had painted me as she had in her great canvas, a woman taking her place in a stream of women that wound back and back in time toward a knowledge as old as the Earth itself. But I also felt myself carried *forward* on that stream by the force of all the women who had gone before me. Mother viewed the age we lived in as a crossroads in time. Sometimes when she spoke of these things, she assumed an almost prophetical tone, like one who gazed across ages and distances: like a seer—though she was too modest to make such elevated claims. Nevertheless, there was in all she said about our work an urgency that made our least act supremely important, so much so that I might easily have shrunk from the task as if unworthy of it. But this she would not allow.

When I returned to my room, I eagerly leafed through the volume Mother had given me. Here I found no pictures, but only numbers and diagrams that proved even more daunting than the images of the Great Work. Some of the numbers I could construe; I recognised in them many of the geometrical shapes and theorems I had learnt from Signor Giordani, but they went well beyond my comprehension. When I asked Victor to help me understand, he laughed with surprise. "Mother has given you *this* to read?"

"Mother said you would help me to understand."

His amusement deepened. "You see how mathematical it is. It may look like geometry, but it is calculus, which few can read."

"Mother has read it."

"Yes, but she an extraordinary woman."

"And I am not?"

"Not in the same way, my dear. And in any case, you are not yet a woman." Then dropping his voice as if Mother might be listening, he added. "I will tell you a story about Mother. Once when Father was at dinner at Ferney, M. Voltaire spoke of his former companion, the remarkable Mme. du Châtelet. You perhaps know of her?" I said I did not. "She wrote on Newton's science, which she understood surprisingly well. She was fully Voltaire's equal in every respect. This led Voltaire to say that Mme. du Châtelet was 'a great man whose only fault was in being born a woman.' Father believes that if Voltaire had known Mother, he would have said the same of her. You must not tell Mother I said this."

Despite Victor's discouragement, I made what effort I could to peruse the book Mother had lent me, though what I understood I found dry as dust, lacking colour and vitality. I soon laid it aside.

Its title was *Philosophiae Naturalis Principia Mathematica*. The author was Sir Isaac Newton.

I Become Victor's
Mystic Sister

I cling to Earth, he climbs the air.
I seek the deep, he rides on high.
I joy to know the dark and rare
He measures out the open sky.

I stood below and watched him soar
Until he trod among the stars.
I feared he knew my love no more
When he had flown from me so far.

When he returned, the world seemed small
He found it of a lesser worth.
But roots and wellsprings teach me all
And bind my heart to blessed Earth.

When I told mother that I found Newton's great book a lifeless bore, she smiled with satisfaction. "My judgement exactly! This tragic man has given us a strange way to understand the world; neither as the eye sees it, nor as the hand feels it, nor as the heart loves it, but only as numbers measure it. Has he not stripped our lives of colour and substance, without which there can be no Humanity? He appeals to the power of abstraction, a sort of mathematic holiness much prized among the natural philosophers. And the result of that . . . ? Alas! I fear that we shall have a demonstration of this tomorrow evening."

The event to which Mother referred was to be one of Belrive's grand *soirées*. It would also be the occasion of the fiercest argument she and the Baron were ever to have.

The purpose of the evening was to introduce an eminent visitor from Paris, one Dr. Du Puy of the Royal Academy. His particular study was pneumatics, the science of the atmosphere. This he travelled to teach at all the universities. The doctor was passing through Geneva on his way home from Italy, where the clever Venetian glassmakers had manufactured a remarkable new instrument for him: a huge glass dome that I was told stood almost as tall as myself. This delicate contrivance required the most careful transportation with frequent stops along the way. *En route* to Paris, the doctor stayed several days at our château, where, at the Baron's urging, he agreed to offer a demonstration.

On the evening in question, following a sumptuous banquet, the dome was mounted on a pedestal at the centre of the salon; in it Dr. Du Puy placed a canary bird, which proceeded to fly furiously at the walls of this strange glass prison. He then attached a leather hose to an outlet at the top of the cylinder so that it was sealed off tightly. This done, he brought forth the device that many regarded as a wonder of the world: his atmospheric pump, a machine that can suck up the air from any contained space and so create a vacuum. This pump, which he attached to the glass dome, was his special pride; he dilated upon its excellence at great length. Within seconds after the pump began to function, the fluttering canary bird was unable to fly; it could only struggle about on the floor of the chamber. The poor thing was left with no air to fly upon; Dr. Du Puy had drawn it all off. While the poor bird struggled on the floor of the dome, Dr. Du Puy explained why this was a wonderful thing we were privileged to watch. For among the pneumatic scientists the creation of so pure a vacuum was regarded as a prodigious feat. As far as I could tell, his vacuum was simply a great nothingness. And of course the canary bird who inhabited that nothingness was left with nothing to breathe. After several moments of futile agony, therefore, it had little choice but to die, and for no better reason than to prove Dr.

Du Puy's genius. The killing of the bird was, however, greeted by abundant applause from the doctor's audience—except, that is, from me and from Mother, who I saw looking on stony-faced across the room.

Such enthusiastic praise inspired Dr. Du Puy to perform an encore; he placed a finch under the dome and repeated his experiment, with the same result. The finch fluttered, fell to the floor, and was smothered by the magnificent void. Even greater approval followed; and so Dr. Du Puy replaced the finch with a raven, and the raven with an owlet. The result was always the same. One and all the creatures expired in the vacuum. Then, with the blessing of his audience, Dr. Du Puy introduced a rabbit under the dome, and then a mouse, and then a kitten, as if there might be no end to proving the deadly efficiency of the omnipotent void. All expired after several moments of anguish. Death beneath the dome was wholly democratic; it would have claimed any man put there. Soon, the floor at Dr. Du Puy's feet was littered with the lifeless bodies of his specimens.

At this juncture, Mother was no longer able to restrain herself. Calling out across the room to Dr. Du Puy, she asked, "And what, sir, do you believe you have proven by this remarkable demonstration?"

For a moment the doctor was taken aback by the question. Then, seeing it had come from the lady of the house, he answered with the utmost courtesy, "It proves, milady, the capacity of a well-manufactured pump to create a perfect vacuum."

"You are wrong, sir," Mother made bold to say. "It demonstrates the cruelty of your science and what a danger it is to our Humanity. For look, sir, at your feet. You stand overshoes in death." And she implored him to desist. This outburst proved highly irritating to the Baron's guests, who, it would seem, stood prepared to see the entire animal kingdom massacred by this diabolical pump. The Baron was very embarrassed; later that evening, this became the one time he deigned to scold Mother for her discourtesy. But she was unrepentant; she told him plainly that no creature's death was justified by Dr. Du Puy's obsession with well-manufactured pumps.

But, as much as Mother grieved for the poor creatures, they were not her main concern. Her chief anxiety was for Victor, at whose side I had stood throughout the evening. Like Mother, I had observed the avid interest he took in the demonstration. His face was aglow with astonishment. Mother could not refrain from letting him know the strength of her feelings. But her influence was not to prevail. The next day, Victor was closeted with Dr. Du Puy, learning how to make specimens for study. Father eagerly promised to equip him with a vacuum pump of his own, the better to strangle animals by the score.

"I could not stand by in silence," Mother told me when next we met in her chambers. "I wished him to know of my disapproval. But perhaps I should have held my tongue."

"I am grateful that you spoke," I said. "I do not think I could bring myself to speak as boldly as you did in so august a gathering."

Mother laughed. "Dr. Du Puy was courteously forbearing. He apologised afterwards, saying that his demonstration was quite unsuitable for ladies. At which I dared to say that our world seemed then to be in the hands of the wrong sex. Nature would surely rejoice if ladies were to inherit the Earth, for they would care for the animals more than for the machines."

"Did that not anger him?"

"Not in the least! What did it matter, after all, what a mere woman might believe? I am sure Dr. Du Puy attributed all I said to the uterine vapours that supposedly cloud the Reason of woman."

Dr. Du Puy's *soirée* was to have far-reaching consequences. In Mother's eyes, that evening's demonstration of the murderous vacuum represented an unwholesome fascination, and but one of many such fascinations she saw acting upon Victor. "Presumption is the great vice of our age," she told me one night when she had come to my bedside. "It is a corrupting temptation, especially so in gifted minds. Where it takes root, it is hard to pluck up." So saying, she brought forth a book and laid it in my hands. It was not as large as the Rose Book nor so elegantly bound; but Mother presented it with an air of great importance—and with a certain apprehension. "You remember how I told you that nothing connected with the Great Work is what it seems to the untutored eye to be? Everything is itself, *and* something more. Let us hope you have studied well enough to apply that lesson elsewhere. For here you will find an even greater challenge to see what is not plainly shown." Then, leaning to place a kiss on my brow, she left me with the book. "You are still so young, my dear," she remarked in her usual distracted air. "I had not thought to begin so soon, but I think we have no choice."

The Lavender Book, so named because of the colour of its vellum cover, bore no title, nor any author's name. Here too the language was Latin, but the text was slender. Even without the translation Mother gave me with the book, I should have had no difficulty following most of what the work said, which amounted to little more than captions for the many pictures that filled the volume. These were not so handsome as those in the Rose Book, but they were far more arresting. They were presented as so many series, picture following picture as if the sequence might be telling a story. As I soon discovered, the stories were also meant as instructions.

A year earlier, I would have found myself bewildered by Mother's intentions in presenting me with what all the world might think an unseemly work. Now I was far more astonished at my own nonchalance in studying a book that showed, on page after page, man and woman meeting for the purpose of performing acts of love—and in far more unusual ways than I had found depicted in the Rose Book. Instead, the couple disported themselves in strangely oblique, sometimes acrobatic ways that left me more curious than embarrassed. Was this, I wondered, how people of another race made love? The man and woman were, after all, an exotic pair—he an Indian prince, she but one of his several courtesans. I was especially struck by the brazenness of these women. They behaved without shame or scruple, often in ways that betokened unbridled appetites. The book showed in detail how they were to adorn and paint and perfume their bodies, how they might make themselves as seductive as possible, and above all how they might delight men by complying with their every whim. Postures were described that I doubted I could ever assume; indeed, even if I could, I was certain I would find them comic. If this book were to be believed, there was no part of the woman's person that might not be used to please the man who was her master. As I perused the pages, I realised how meagrely limited were the sexual practices of the good Christian people I lived among. If they spoke of these matters at all, it was tersely; and what they did, insofar as I knew at all, was but a single hurried act that I imagined few women found gratifying. But then, the women I saw in the book were harlots, women of the lowest character, who were all but the slaves of men. Was I being encouraged to learn from their example?

When I asked Mother to help me understand, she complimented me on my solicitude. "Your questions are astute. I should not have given you the book if I did not trust that you were woman enough to view it with a critical eye. You are, unfortunately, quite right. The women you see here were trained as concubines; they were treated as less than human precisely because they sold themselves to men. The men, of course, suffered no reproach for their part in the transaction. No, Elizabeth, it is not the harlotry of these women that I would have you learn. These are pictures from another world and another time, when a royal master could subjugate any number of women to his desires. In that world, only by becoming a strumpet and trading upon her favours could a woman fully enjoy the pleasures of her body. It is sadly the case that the Great Work has become entangled with that time of shame. In taking up these books, we must be careful to exercise our women's judgement; it is necessary for us to find our own understanding of the teachings. There is a paradox here, my dear. Until the physical is respected in woman, her spiritual nature will never be truly honoured. As long as we are deemed too 'pure' to have something of the animal in us, we will be treated as childish innocents and disregarded."

"But does that mean I am to imitate what I see in the pictures?"

"You are to perform a rôle in the Great Work. This rôle is that of the *Soror Mystica*. The Mystic Sister. It is not easy to explain this rôle, since it has no counterpart in our world. It may be that Seraphina will ask you to imitate certain things you see in these pictures, though she will take care that this is done in the proper spirit. Do you trust her?"

"I do. But I think Victor would take me for a harlot if I behaved as these women do."

"Victor has been carefully taught to think differently about women than do other men. He knows that what you find in the books has an *ulterior* meaning. Here, let me give you a small lesson. You see the man and woman in the picture? As they are coupling, we think of them as two, brought together for physical pleasure. But now think of the picture as being that of a *single* soul divided between the two. Then these two lovers are not separate beings but parts of ourselves seeking perfect union. The great Plato taught that each of us is but half of a complete being. What we call love is our hunger to find completion in another. You see, then, even the harlot's lust can betoken a higher passion. By the time you have accomplished the Work, you will know many of these things better than I, for I had no male to be my companion."

EDITOR'S NOTE

The Function of the Soror Mystica *in the Chemical Marriage*

In studying the pages of the Lavender Book, Elizabeth Frankenstein was being carefully tutored for her rôle as the Mystic Sister of the alchemical Work. This strange female office, which finds no correspondence in the religious teachings of our society, became my special study during the several years I worked on this memoir. It proved to be among the most elusive problems I would confront.

In alchemical treatises, female images appear prominently in the illustrations, usually in the form of mythic beings, perhaps nature deities, queens, or astrological signs. But in the written text that accompanies such illustrations, the female appears, as it were, only through a glass, darkly. The written word is all but wholly dominated by the sage, who is universally understood to be male. Invariably, he is a learned man who works alone in his laboratory. As early as the third century after Christ, however, we notice a subtle change. We come upon passing allusions to *"femina"* or, more rarely, *"puella."* These designations refer to a female assistant who clearly possesses intimate knowledge of the workshop and its activities. For example, in Zosimus' *Manipulationes*, we find the direction "Have the woman place the implements at the north side of the furnace and there intone the requisite chant." Or, "Have the woman now prepare the tincture and heat it to the first degree." The same casual references can be found in Arabic texts of the seventh and eighth centuries, where again the otherwise obscure female is credited with considerable skill. In illustrations of a later period, a female may appear in the workshop, waiting in attendance upon the adept. Both Arnaldus Villanovanus and Raymundus Lullius refer to this figure as *"soror"* and clearly assume that the adept is dependent upon her presence and her duties. The illustrations are invariably of a demure woman, usually fair and young, her body modestly covered, sometimes shown in a prayerful attitude at her master's side. In at least one case, that of the eminent Dutch alchemist Helvetius, the rôle of the *soror* was performed by his faithful wife, who was said to be as studied in the lore as he. In all this, we may find reason for some curiosity about the exact function of the female; but there is nothing to arouse moral concern.

How unsettling, then, it was for me to learn that the salacious alchemical illustrations, in which one finds acts of sexual congress and perversion flagrantly presented, were not intended as mere symbols! Rather, they were the literal depiction of practices to be undertaken by the alchemical student. It is now clear to me that at every stage of his occult practice, the alchemical sage was to be assisted by a female whose contribution to the Work, while undertaken in a subservient rôle, was understood to be essential. As we plainly see from Elizabeth Franken-stein's own account, the use of vaginal fluid and menstrual blood in the alchemical workshop was commonplace. The female was to permit these substances to be gathered fresh by the sage from her very person. If a compliant woman were not available to provide what was needed, the sage might resort to the services of a common whore. Indeed, according to some texts, the lower the moral status of the woman, the more suitable she was taken to be for her function, thus to emphasise the base level from which the Great Work takes its beginning. At times, the Philosopher's Stone itself was even compared to a harlot's men-struum! Nor was this reference intended to be merely metaphorical. In the writings of Philalethes of Alexandria, the shadowy *Soror Mystica* is likened to the temple prostitutes of the Chaldees; and what he refers to as "the celestial ruby" is not the Stone, but the sexual organ of that prostitute in its sanguinolent state, which then enters directly and phys-

ically into his practice. At points, one fairly blushes at the lyrical extrav-
agance with which Philalethes praises the vagina, treating it as little
short of a cult object. That these passages imply cunnilingual adoration
and hematophagia is beyond question. The acts are all but fully
described; one need only understand where the line is to be drawn in
such texts between the literal and figurative.

The rôle of the female, however, went far beyond merely providing
bodily effluvia. As the Lavender Book makes clear, at the culmination of
the alchemical Work, the woman, after entering into extravagant displays of physical enticement, was expected to engage in sexual congress
with her male master in ways so numerous and irregular as to be startling. A special erotic function is assigned to every finger of the courtesan's hands; entire chapters are devoted to forms of intercourse by way
of the breasts and buttocks. Others dilate upon varieties of oral intercourse that involve the practiced use of the lips and tongue and throat.
The goal seems nothing less than a total eroticisation of the female
anatomy. These rites were, of course, shrouded in religious rhetoric, but
the practices were clearly orgiastic. Some of these acts are alluded to in
these memoirs; others are graphically shown in the Lavender Book. It
was these depictions that led me, in my search for reliable knowledge,
toward the Orient, whence European scholars and missionaries have of
late begun to transmit a wealth of antiquarian materials. Among these
are works associated with a nebulous school of Hindooism called "the
left-handed Tantra," which encourages perverted forms of sexual
licence, supposedly as a means of liberating the adept from the last fet-
ters of social constraint. It is assumed that union with the divine can
only be achieved by those who have attained a condition of antinomian
liberty. One finds the same practices flourishing in certain Chinese
schools of physiological mysticism that date to a time before Konfucius.
In works taken from both these traditions, one finds illustrations of sexual acts that exactly replicate those in the Lavender Book.

By what route practices of this kind, so radically at variance with
Christian morality, might have made their way into the European
alchemical schools remains a matter of speculation; through the mists of
antiquity, no clear links can be discerned. We can, however, say for cer-

tain that the cities of the Near East were the cradle of the first alchemical adepts, and it is there that we find the first references to the *Soror Mystica*. In the Christian period, of course, such sexual practices had of necessity to remain clandestine and must have been communicated only by word of mouth; this no doubt accounts for the extreme obscurity of the texts.

We may conclude, therefore, that the woman Seraphina, whose lineage traces to the Carnatic coast of India where the left-handed Tantra once flourished, was responsible for impressing that unwholesome influence upon the lore she transmitted to her female disciples. Had she and the Baroness Frankenstein succeeded in their purpose, I believe the result would have been nothing less than the root-and-branch subversion of Christian sexual *mores*. The most intimate relations between man and woman were to be turned upside-down; acts long regarded as perversions and obscenities were to be brought into common practice; a tradition which attributed transcendent virtue to these acts was to be elevated to prominence. And why? Because there existed in the eyes of these wilful and clearly unbalanced women some deep connection between the erotic and the spiritual that utterly escapes the categories of European religious and philosophical thought.

How far that influence might actually have spread beyond the Frankenstein household, it is impossible to say; one can but hope that the cultural climate of Europe, so long permeated by cleansing Christian airs, would ultimately prove inhospitable to such an exotic transplant. Surely, the prospect of Western womanhood pursuing the perverse forms of sexual gratification encouraged by these doctrines is not a pretty one.

The Blood
and the Seed

January ——, 178——

> Man not a man
> I lust for thee,
> Woman not woman
> I long to be,
> Stone not a stone
> I covet thee,
> Death not death
> O come to me!

The Work goes on. I dream, I dream, I dream such dreams!

I dream of the deep Earth ablaze with interior light, I dream the mineral fires She hides in her womb. The metals are not what men think, unfeeling matter to be brutally torn from the ground, fired and hammered. They are the living substance of the stars; they are gold of the sun, silver of the moon; they are copper and iron, the hidden signatures of Venus and Mars; they are lead and tin, precious to Saturn and great Jupiter. How brightly they sing! And in their chorus the gem-stones join; opal and amethyst, ruby and turquoise, carnelian and sapphire, jasper and jade, lustrous crystal and lordly diamond. All Earth sings.

Seraphina asks: "Why is such beauty hidden from the eye?" Because it teaches the world's abundance of wonders, teaches us we shall never have done with wonders. As far as our Reason can reach, beyond there waits yet more to amaze us. Beneath our feet, at every step we take, we tread upon a carpet of wonders.

"I have something special to ask of you this evening," Seraphina announces when we meet that night in the cottage. "It is a practice that will help us progress more rapidly. Lady Caroline and I have decided it is time to advance your studies."

At Seraphina's bidding, we disrobe and perform our familiar ablutions. Then she asks me to lie before the fire while she lights the incense that makes the mind seem to float. She brings forth two small Earthen bowls; these she places on the floor beside me. "I will trace a form upon your body, Elizabeth," she tells me. From about her neck she removes a pouch and takes from it what looks like the fang-tooth of a beast. Dipping it into one bowl and then the other, she uses it as a stylus to draw a figure upon my abdomen surrounding the *mons veneris*. She does this with the greatest delicacy, all the while intoning a chant. The two bowls hold coloured substances, one white, one red. These she uses to draw a circle composed of two intertwined serpents, one of each colour. "Red and white, sulphur and mercury, male and female, Victor and Elizabeth. I wish now to have Victor concentrate his thoughts upon this image; and, Elizabeth, I would have you fasten your gaze upon Victor, as if you might see the image through his eyes. Let your minds settle into deep peace. I will remind you, my children, that the chymical wedding is an act of love that makes bride and bridegroom one nature. Gross matter can be the mirror of this union; but what we seek in the Great Work is not the reflection, but its original, which is a thing of the spirit. I ask you to think of this thing as if it were a child that grows in Elizabeth's body, the fruit of your love." She instructs Victor to place his hands so that they hover just slightly above the double serpent, his thumbs together where my thighs join. Thus, his fingers form a triangle that frames the triangular patch of my sex. "Now think that you are brother and sister, lover and lover, man and wife. Think of the union you seek as a child that your love will one day bring into the world. This is the true gold that we seek."

She then takes up the little drum she sometimes uses to accompany our meditations. She beats upon it gently, making a sound that might be the heartbeat of a child inside me. I stare into Victor's face. Watching his eyes fixed upon my sex, I become more and more inflamed; it is as if I know his desire from inside his own thoughts. Our minds have become a circle: the seer and the seen fusing into one. The nearness of his fingers above my sex becomes intolerably tempting; I want him to touch me. *Touch me!* I hear myself calling out in my thought, but I know he will not. Gradually, I perceive an eery warmth rising from my flesh, a sweet fever that I know would vanish if Victor did more than gaze upon me. I feel my body glowing goldenly; and in that ethereal heat, our two minds melt into one. I see myself transformed into a strange, beautiful being: a woman, is it? Or a young boy . . . a boy with the breasts of a girl who hovers weightless above us. I know I am he, I am she, I am a figure of light. Just for a moment—but how long does this moment last?—there is no Victor, no Elizabeth; there is only Another who is the two of us.

"I was some other manner of being," Victor tells me afterwards. "I was both you and myself, boy and girl. I seemed to float upon the air like a spirit."

I tell him that I have known the same feeling, but could not hold to it. It had slipped from my mind. "But I knew your desire for me, Victor. I have lived it. I shall never doubt how much you want me."

February ——, 178——

At last, the rhythm of my bleeding has come to match the waxing and waning moon. Seraphina has sought to prepare me for this occasion. "You have learned to be private about the bleeding," she tells me. "That is as it should be; it is a woman's matter. But now I will ask you to do something you will not find easy. You must let one man see the bleeding. I wish you to uncover for Victor. Are you willing to do this?"

I am not at all willing, but I remember that I have promised Mother to trust and comply with all that the Great Work requires of me. "Yes," I say, but Seraphina hears the hesitation in my voice.

"Only think that this is meant as an instruction for Victor. Our Work cannot continue unless he knows something of our mysteries, and not merely what he can learn from words."

That night we meet in the glade under a clear, chill sky strewn with stars. While we wait for the moon to reach its zenith, Seraphina directs Victor to gather branches and lay four fires to drive off the cold. She spreads an embroidered cloth for me to lie upon; it is of her own making and woven with signs I do not understand. When the fires are crackling, Seraphina and Victor undress; I disrobe no further than to my waistcloth. Seraphina asks me to scatter dry leaves and petals, each of a different blossom, over the fires. These substances, she tells us, correspond to the vital organs of the body, and burn with the second degree of heat. The fire that will be at my head I feed with horehound, the fire at my left with gentian, the fire at my right with pennyroyal, and the fire at my feet with calamus. The flames fill the glade with the sweet, mingled fragrance of flowers. When the moon is at last glowing directly above us, Seraphina pronounces a brief incantation over each fire in her mother tongue. Then she takes a crystal phial from her purse and hands it to Victor. "I have a task for you, child," she announces. "I wish to have you gather the blood we need. Elizabeth will uncover and open herself to you. This is an act of love and trust on her part. You must act in return with love and trust in what you do."

Seraphina seats herself behind me and holds my head upon her lap. She strokes my brow and intones a low, lilting song to relax me; but this strange rite leaves my thoughts sorely divided. I am not shy to have Victor see me; indeed, I would like him to know that, small and slight as I may seem when I stand beside him, I am a woman fully grown. But I fear he will find what Seraphina has asked him to do distasteful; and I fear he will find me sluttish in revealing myself this way. Yet I know he is as eager as I to pursue the Work and to learn what Seraphina teaches. At last I find the courage to open myself to his eyes, at first a little, then fully; I let my soft inner flesh blossom before his eyes. I can almost feel his gaze upon me. At Seraphina's direction, Victor kneels between my yielding thighs; but I see he cannot bring himself to touch me. I feel for his embarrassment; I turn to Seraphina, asking with my eyes if we must continue. She smiles reassuringly, but she is adamant.

"Blood and seed. We must have them both. It is essential for Victor to learn about this, as every adept before him has. He wishes to be a student of Nature, does he not? Here is Nature right before him, a sight he might even say he finds desirable. Ah, but he does not! I can see as well as you. Do you find what I ask of you repugnant, Victor? Be truthful."

"Yes, I do."

"You find Elizabeth's body offensive when she comes to these days in her cycle, is that not so?"

"Somewhat."

"Only 'somewhat'? Perhaps a great deal. But why?"

"It is the blood."

"Ah, yes, the blood! But have you not spilled the blood of animals in your studies? Mice, birds—have you not cut their tender bodies open? Have you not divided their hearts and felt their blood run over your hands?"

Victor frowns at her question. "Yes."

"And did you find that disgusting?"

"No . . ."

"Why not?"

"I did not allow myself—"

"How did you feel? Did you feel that you were learning the secrets of Nature?"

"Yes."

"How, then, is this different? It is your chance to learn the mysteries of the woman's body."

I see that her questions are vexing him. "No!" Victor answers. "It is different."

"Indeed it is! *This* blood is not like any other blood. It is not the blood of sickness or of injury. It is not the blood of something dying. This is the wound that heals itself. The blood issues forth of its own accord; it has its own cycle, like the moon there above us. This blood is a sign of the fertility women share with the Earth. This blood is a miracle, Victor, and yet, at the same time—attend what I say—it is *only* blood, a harmless fluid, as every woman knows." Suddenly Seraphina reaches across my body to run her fingers along my cloven flesh. An image appears in my mind: a ripe red fruit being opened, its juices pressed out. Her hand comes back, a crimson film upon it. "I see you cringe. Yet how simple a thing it is to do! It will not defile you. Or do you wish, when Elizabeth is like this, that she might keep to herself, as if she had reason to hide away?"

"Perhaps . . . yes."

"Do you hear, Elizabeth? Does this show you why women have been shamed? Do you remember when you yourself found the bleeding to be shameful?"

I remember. And I feel a twinge of anger that Victor has brought this thought back to me.

"Elizabeth has learnt—from other women—that there is no evil to be found in our bodies," Seraphina tells Victor. "Every man must father his young upon a woman's body; yet that body is treated with contempt, and especially so when it most reminds of its fruitfulness. Judge for yourself. Here is the Elizabeth you love like a sister, and perhaps more than a sister. But when there is blood, you do not wish to see. When there is blood, you do not wish to touch. The blood is the substance of life, as much as your own seed. What will you know of life if you find the woman's blood unclean? Or do you perhaps know of some better, 'cleaner' kind of life, that does not come of blood and seed?"

"No."

"The woman must touch blood to care for her body. Are you not willing to do as much, not once in your life?"

Victor tries again to do as Seraphina asks. I watch how he falters at the task. I speak wordlessly to him, hoping he will hear: *It is called "vagina." That is a lovely word, a soft, flowering word. Think of my vagina as ripe and warm. It opens deep into me, the passage to a dark, fertile place. I am yielding to you, Victor. Please do not fear me! Do not scorn me!* But again he fails; he cannot put his hand forth to touch me. I almost pity the mortification he is evincing; but my anger is stronger. At first, I had felt shy to open myself to

Victor. Now I find myself feeling quite the opposite. *Let him see! Let him know! I will be no loving friend of his if he finds me unclean!*

At last Seraphina relents and takes the phial from him. "It would be best if you could do this alone, Victor. But we must not lose the occasion. We must take the blood tonight. I will only ask you to help me. Here, place your hand on mine." Victor does as she asks; Seraphina passes her hand once again along the lips of my sex, gently drawing off some of the blood she finds there. This she allows to slide from her fingers into the phial.

"I have no wish to cause you discomfort, Victor," Seraphina explains gently. "Only to teach you. Search your true feelings. Ponder why you could not do as I asked. This blood you could not bring yourself to touch—why does it seem so offensive? Because it is unsightly? No, I think not. It is *fear* that stays your hand. Fear of the woman's power, the one power that cannot be taken from her. Though you say you love Elizabeth, there is fear mingled with that love—as there is in every man's love for woman. We will not progress far with our lessons until that fear has left you and only true affection remains."

Later Victor comes to me to apologise, knowing I have been hurt by him. "Seraphina is right," I tell him. "You make too much of it . . . and yet not enough. This blood is no fouler than the blood you touch when you cut the animal. Why do turn from it as you do?"

"It *is* different, as Seraphina says. I fear to touch it. I feel I have no right to be so close to these things."

"But I give you permission. I do not wish to have you stand off or turn away. You should know my body; otherwise you make me feel ashamed, Victor—as if I must hide away."

I find I have not the wit to make Victor understand. He apologises again, insisting he acted out of deep regard for me; but I do not believe his apology. I think this is a trick men play with women. They pretend great respect; but then this respect becomes a cage to keep us in.

The Sleeping Emperor

Breast to breast we cling each night
Touched, untouching, in chaste delight.
We burn but not with mean desire
This flame is of a hotter fire.

Passion reigns but brings no shame
Friendship is its other name.
I trust my virtue to your will
And yet remain a virgin still.

There is a sanctity of mind
That only truest lovers find.
There is a marriage of the soul
That makes the heart's division whole.

We are in Seraphina's cottage. Outside, snow falls heavily through the dark sky, covering the world with a white shroud. Seraphina stacks several more faggots upon the fire to warm us for the evening ahead. We know why we have gathered tonight; it is time to take the seed. *"Pure* seed," Seraphina calls it, "freely sacrificed and untainted by animal appetite. Will you give us what we require, Victor?"

Victor manfully says that he will. He has been preparing for what is expected of him, following Seraphina's instructions with the utmost care. For several nights in succession, he has taken a broth in which Seraphina has steeped a tiny crimson pellet. She says the pellet is compounded from a measure of purified cinnabar so minute that no scale could measure it. This, she says, will strengthen his fluid and make it more fertile.

She asks Victor to lie on his back beside the hearth, his head between her knees. His lean, straight body stretches full out, revealing his limp member. Seraphina places her gnarled fingers at his temples and begins to stroke him gently. Bending over him, she places her lips beside his ear and chants to him in so low a voice that I cannot perceive a word. Alu, watching all that happens in the room, becomes intensely interested, alert and erect on her perch, stretching her neck to see. Deep in her throat she echoes Seraphina's chant. The ordinary sound she makes is a harsh cackle; but I have discovered that there is another sound she sometimes calls upon when she and Seraphina converse: a soft murmur that seems to be their secret whisper. Alu invokes this dreamy tone to sing along with Seraphina, whose grey tresses have fallen across Victor's face like a veil that screens out all watching eyes. It is as if she has taken Victor away with her into a private place. After she has whispered to him for several minutes, Victor seems to pass into a waking dream; I see the muscles of his body, which have been tautly defined, turn soft. His breath assumes a deep, steady rhythm. Seraphina continues to murmur at his ear. Sometimes her voice takes on strange qualities, a husky resonance that make it sound as if she is discoursing from deep within a cave. When she chants like this, my head grows cloudy; I seem to be travelling far off; shadowy half-pictures float across my mind. They are images of the women in the books, but now I am among them doing as they do, making myself attractive to my lord, attending to his pleasure. I watch myself as if I were an actress upon a stage of the mind, wondering how I have learnt these skills. My body has become voluptuously ripe; I have the breasts of the women in the Lavender Book, and the marvellous haunches. I imagine I have become as beautiful as Francine. I can twist myself like a snake round my waiting lover. Seraphina bends to whisper at Victor's ear again; this time she croons an exotic lullaby, a nasal, sensuous music I have come to recognise as the music of her distant people. Gradually, her voice alters; it grows lighter, more fluid, almost mellifluous. A certain sly gaiety enters her tone, a coaxing laughter. I shake off my drowsiness to look and see: Is this still Seraphina I hear? The voice has assumed a seductive lilt, as if this were another, younger woman whispering fondly to her lover. I wish I could see her face now; would it be the same person? But the veil of her hair, which seems darker, glossier, almost like black silk, once again hides her from me.

After several moments, I see Victor's male organ take on life and begin to stir. A moment more and he is fully aroused. Inside, in the depth of my belly, I feel a sweet, answering spasm. This is a mute language of the body that more and more transpires between Victor and me.

That night, for the first time, I perform the Rite of the Sleeping Emperor as I have learnt it from the Lavender Book.

How long I am occupied at what I do, I cannot say. I lose all sense of time as I perform the stages of the rite. I seem to float upon an ecstatic wave, until Seraphina brings me back to the present. I hear her call to me under her breath: "Elizabeth . . ." I come to myself and discover I am hovering over Victor, holding his member fast in my hands just at my lips. I look up to see Seraphina holding out the crystal phial. "Victor is ready. Place this under him just here, then watch carefully. We must not waste so much as a drop."

I do as I am told, taking the phial in my free hand and holding it ready to receive. Victor's breath catches in his throat; there is the slightest tremor in his limbs; I feel him pulse in my hand—and suddenly a silken fluid issues from his organ. "Quickly!" I hear Seraphina say in an urgent whisper, calling me back to my task. It is time for the Dragon to swim the Nile; I appease the beast as Seraphina has taught me to do until the kingdom is abundantly flooded. How it excites me to see Victor empty his seed in this way! It is a secret thing to watch, a mystery of the man's body meant to happen in darkness and out of sight. Sera-phina, murmuring one of her chants, lifts the phial above her head and slowly swirls the seed and the clotted blood together until the two are mingled.

For several moments, Victor does not stir from his trance-like calm. When he does, he sees Seraphina bending over him. "Did I not tell you?" she asks with a wry smile. "That you would lust for the crone?" He blinks with surprise and, sitting up quickly, gazes at her in fierce bewilderment. She reaches out to stroke his brow. "This blood and seed will not conceive," Seraphina tells us. "Not as they would in the woman's womb. For they are dead matter in the flask. But they have another potency, my children. They will allow you to stare into the very womb of Nature Herself. But you must be patient. You do not yet pos-sess the eye to see the depths of the world. This will come in its own time."

Meanwhile, Seraphina transfers the mixture to a crystal vase—the vase of Hermes, sometimes called the philosopher's egg—where it is to be kept tightly sealed. This she puts away in a closet for our later study.

Can Victor be aware of what has happened? Later, when I tell him, he labours to piece together his memory of the event. All he can recall is a disturbing dream not easily retold. He remembers a veiled woman. Though he could not see her face, he knew she was supremely beautiful. She told him, "Many have perished in our Work; but trust in me and you will find your way safely." Then she brought him close to her breast and embraced him like a lover.

"At first," Victor confesses in a fretful whisper, "I thought it was *Mother!* This made me feel so agitated that I nearly woke. But the woman seemed to govern my sleep and held me back from waking. 'I shall have to lift the veil if I am to kiss you,' she said. At that, I pled with her to keep her face covered, for I was afraid to find out who she might be. 'Then you must kiss me *here* instead,' she insisted, 'for we must have your seed.' And she opened her gown and uncovered herself." He passes his hand across my breast to show me where. "She was so very pleasing to see. . . . I could not help but do as she wanted." By now, Victor's voice has descended into a tense murmur. "But when I took the tip of her breast in my mouth, I was able to see just a little beneath the veil. And I saw that it was *Seraphina!* Not Seraphina as we know her now, but as she might once have been, young and darkly beautiful. No, that is not right. Not young. Beyond age. Someone who could be girl and mother, both. She held me so tightly to her breasts I could scarce take a breath. And then, I remember, she made my entire body feel as if it were tingling with the taste of honey. It was the most wonderful sensation! Afterwards there came a great calm, and I did not care if I might be alive or dead."

"Do you mind that I have taken your seed in this way?"

He coloured briefly. "If the Work requires it . . . But I should have preferred to be awake. I should have preferred to have you hold me waking as Seraphina held me in my dream."

EDITOR'S NOTE

The Rite of the Sleeping Emperor

Elizabeth Frankenstein's reference is to a ritual described in the Lavender Book. There, we find the tale of a legendary emperor who has fallen seriously ill. The symbol of the sick King is a familiar one in alchemical lore; it is interpreted in various ways. In alchemical terms, this is that stage of the Work referred to as "solution," or the "black" stage, when matter has supposedly fallen into its most unregenerate state. Not even the mighty "powder of projection" (powdered mercury) can redeem material so debased: hence the use of symbols that invoke death, putrefaction, morbidity, etc. Theologically, this phase is sometimes understood as the fall of man through original sin.

Because of his infirm condition, the Emperor is unable to perform his duties; his kingdom languishes and misfortune ensues. A drought strikes and lasts for ten years, followed by pestilence lasting another ten years. The land turns sterile; the people famish. At last, the desperate Empress is forced to act. She realises that only the royal semen has the power to return the kingdom to fertility. The Emperor has, however, been rendered impotent by his illness; he cannot procreate. But the Empress, who has studied with cunning women, knows a solution. Over many nights, she places the Emperor in an ever-deeper sleep, until his breathing becomes as calm as that of a fetus. She then brings the youngest and fairest of the Emperor's concubines to the royal bedchamber to assist in her plan. The concubine, who is still a virgin, having not yet been initiated by the disabled Emperor, is placed between her royal master's legs and instructed to venerate his sexual organ. She bathes it, anoints it with perfume, caresses it, and offers it oral stimulation. The Emperor at last shows signs of arousal. The concubine is then shown how to massage her master's testes in a subtle and coaxing way. The text gives explicit instructions in this act, specifying that the pressure of the girl's index finger is to be applied to the urethra at a point just below the scrotum. The purpose is to inhibit emission for as long as possible. Meanwhile, the Empress cradles her sleeping husband in her arms and whispers to him of transcendent pleasures. In his dreams, the Emperor experiences an endless succession of orgasmic climaxes, but without being permitted to ejaculate. At length, after a protracted period of careful stimulation, the Emperor's testes have become swollen with seed. The concubine is at last instructed to permit emission; the result is a veritable river of royal semen that is shown flowing forth to bring fertility to the stricken land. The long-delayed release of the seed is referred to as "the Dragon swimming the Nile," the Dragon taken here as the alchemical symbol of virility. "Appeasing the beast" refers to a technique, described at length in the treatise, for stroking the erected member to prolong emission.

The story of the Sleeping Emperor vaguely resembles later Medieval tales of the Fisher King, whose unhealing wound brings calamity to his realm; the alchemical version, of course, takes on a far more erotic aspect. In Victor's case, the part of the Empress was taken by Seraphina, and that of the virginal concubine by Elizabeth. We must assume from what she relates of the episode that Victor, in his somnolent state, was brought to ejaculation by similar means so that Seraphina might collect all the seed she required.

As demanding as the Rite of the Sleeping Emperor might seem, there was a still-higher stage in the discipline of the alchemical adepts. This involved the total renunciation of seminal emission, even under the most provocative conditions.

The adept might, for example, copulate with a series of females whose freshness guaranteed unlimited arousal, but never allow himself to achieve climax. "In commerce with Woman," says the revered Chinese sage Ko Tsu Chung, "refrain as often as possible from emission so that the sperm may return via the spinal channel to nourish the brain." Retained in this way, semen became the legendary Elixir Vitae.

It is now clear that there has long existed a subterranean alchemical tradition in which these grotesque disciplines survived. For example, a late Alexandrine text credited to Olympiodorus of Thebes and closely based upon a Tantric source encourages the closest examination of the female anatomy. Every fold and crevice of the female's person, every pore and hair, every odour and texture is to be scrutinised and offered loving devotion. The least physical blemish is to be sought out and exploited as an erotic stimulus. A typical passage instructs the adept to

> seek the divine in the Beloved's imperfection, for there it will shine brightest by contrast. Seek the high in the low, the pure in the vile. Count each hair of the Beloved as the occasion of Enlightenment. Induce the Beloved by your most fervent entreaties to open herself to your adoring eye that she may be fathomed and admired in her most secret places. Teach the Beloved the true purpose of her carnal charms, which are the Gateway of the Nameless.

It was only after I had spent years studying texts like this, and the ritual practices associated with them, that I fully grasped what the Baroness Frankenstein hoped to achieve through the revival of the chemical marriage. It was something even more insidious than the subversion of Christian sexual morality. I believe she hoped to bring about *the unmanning of European science.* Recall how often the woman confessed the hostility she felt toward scientific progress and the envy she harboured for the men who guided its course. Clearly she intended to do more than complain and curse. She meant to invade the scientific workplace with forms of erotic dalliance that would undermine its essentially, and necessarily, masculine rigour. The Rose and Lavender books are, then, best seen as a siren song whose purpose was to lure natural philosophy into a chamber of enervating delights.

I am prepared to concede that, in her own eyes at least, Lady Caroline's motives were sincere; she may have wished to exert some salutary influence upon her times. The kindness she expressed for the lower animals is touching. But it is a measure of how rudimentary her grasp of natural philosophy was that she should think the discredited lore of the alchemical adepts might any longer play a part in our society's ongoing conquest of ignorance and superstition. There is such a hodge-podge here! Fantasy and fact, symbol and substance, whimsy and truth . . . all flow together without any rational demarcation. The alchemical universe was the realm of hallucination, not of certain knowledge. I have not the least doubt that if anything like Lady Caroline's bizarre project had succeeded in taking root in our culture, it would have spread like a noxious weed, poisoning the sources of our moral strength.

The Salamander

The rose rules by its beauty
The heart commands by love.
In willing subjugation
Below obeys Above.

I walk among the lions
The golden and the green.
I wander deep in forests
No mortal eye has seen.

The lions' jaws are crimson
They flow with crimson gore.
I walk in trust between them
And laugh to hear them roar.

The law that binds the worlds
Is sweetest harmony.
The stars are chained together
By tender tyranny.

March ——, *178*——

Seraphina teaches us the Feeding of the Lions.

Victor and I have loitered over the depiction of this practice in the

Lavender Book. I have wondered many times if we would ever be expected to perform these rôles.

"Your attention must remain sharp through the long night," Seraphina tells Victor. "This will help keep your mind bright as crystal." She brews him a cup of strong tea laced with succory. The first night, Seraphina herself takes the woman's part; I am asked only to look on. "Remember," she cautions us both, "you are learning to see beyond what the eye first sees. If you have the conviction that there is more, you will find more." By now, Victor knows better than to regard Seraphina as the crone she looks to be; he knows her womanly potency. Within an hour's time, he is lost in his contemplation, his gaze as absorbed as if his eyes were fixed upon the loveliest of women. And so too Seraphina. She seems also to have passed into a somnambulant state while she plays her rôle. I wonder as I observe if I will be able to remain as still and patient as she. When I ask about this, she smiles assuringly.

"Never fear, child. I will give you something to help you maintain your composure. Later, you will require nothing external to steady your mind. Victor's thought will become your thought; you will be united in a way I cannot explain. The night will pass for both of you in an instant. Only think that Victor is offering you the devotion of the true bridegroom, a love that exalts the beloved."

Three more times during that fortnight, Victor and I return to Feed the Lions while Seraphina keeps watch. The cordial she gives me to drink makes me feel I am floating above the Earth; it also makes me inordinately sensitive. I can *feel* Victor's eyes upon me as if he were caressing my flesh, and not always as gently as I might wish. He is sometimes too eager, too forceful. Once again, I realise how defenceless it makes a woman that her body *opens*. But trusting Victor, I yield to the vulnerability, and find the feeling not threatening but exhilarating. There is expectation in the air, born of the strange chastity of what we do: that his eyes should be so intensely upon me and yet we never touch. At first, I would have said my rôle is that of a shameless temptress; I find nothing but lewdness in what I am called upon to do. But with time, as the nights pass, I begin to have another sense of the matter: that the lewdness may be a narrow door we pass through; beyond, there is a wider realm, a pleasure that is calmer, finer, ennobling.

June ——, 178——

Each time, after we Feed the Lions, Seraphina asks what was in our thoughts. At first I am unwilling to tell her—and Victor is, too. Our minds are so often filled with salacious images that we are loath to confess. She does not press us to answer, but she returns to the question each night. At last Victor is bold enough to answer. "I imagine touching her," he says. "I want to touch her."

"Where do you wish to touch?" Seraphina asks, a mischievous note in her voice. Victor is too shy to say. "Here?" Seraphina asks, reaching across to pass her hand slowly along my body from my breasts to my sex. "Or here? You would like to do what I do now?"

"Yes," he admits, blushing in spite of himself.

"And why?" Seraphina asks.

Victor is taken aback by the question. "It seems unnatural not to. The sight . . . inflames me."

A note of honest pity enters Seraphina's voice. "Yes, I am making you burn for her. It is 'natural' that you should burn, as young and eager as you are. And you, Elizabeth? What is in your thoughts?"

What Victor has said inspires me to speak. "I want Victor to hold me like a true lover."

"Only to hold you?"

"No! To *enter* me. Each time I wish it more. I imagine that, I dote on it, I dream of it." These words fly from me edged with shameless anger. I am protesting this hard thing she asks of us. But until I speak the anger, I do not realise how hot it is, or how great my lust has become.

"You think me unkind, I know," she answers, her tone sad but not apologetic. "Yet there is a reason for what I do. I am teaching you the hunger, my dear. I am making it grow inside you. When man and woman rush to gratify the hunger all at once, they will never know how strong it can grow and what greater appetite it is meant to feed. They will not discover what their union means. The delight soon passes, and they never know there is another pleasure that waits behind the first. In time you will see that this second pleasure I speak of lies in the burning; the burning will become your wings and carry you skyward. Now let us see how close you are to that time."

At this she sends me to fetch the vase that holds the blood and seed; she places it before us on the floor. We have studied the vessel many times; we have been told that what we see in this vessel is the black season of the *nigredo*. She has mingled other substances into the mixture— herbs, the shavings of pearl, sweet oil of antimony—and warmed all in the dung of a pregnant mare. These fester and brew in the sealed container, growing rank with the drama of putrefaction.

This time as we sit to contemplate the vase, Seraphina gives us a mixture to drink; it has the bitter taste of the motherwort I have drunk at the women's rites, but more potently brewed. This will bring new powers to the eye, she tells us. Then, waiting for the potion to have its effect, she croons softly to herself, a shadowy song of the night. "Take up the bottle in your hands," she instructs us after a time, holding the vase between Victor and me for us to gaze upon. "Turn it, swirl it, then look closely."

At first and for a long while I see nothing but the slimy black broth that lies at the bottom. "Ah, but watch!" Seraphina whispers.

And then, and then . . . I think I see a flicker of coloured light. Another, and another. The inside of the vessel has caught fire! The light leaps from the dead matter and careers about the inner walls of the jar. I see the flames seep from the bottle and twist themselves like coiling serpents round Seraphina's arms and shoulders. I am so taken by surprise that I flinch as if the flames might leap at me.

"Tell me!" she demands in a rumbling voice, almost a growl.

"I see *fire*."

"What colour?" Seraphina asks eagerly, the blazing braid of light still swirling round her.

"Blue," I answer. "A blue fire . . ."

"This is precious, my dearest. Feed on this fire. Feel it deep within you. Let it warm you from head to toe. Do not be afraid to see!"

Suddenly, the words leap from me: "Oh God! *Something moves there!*"

Seraphina leans forward eagerly, holding the vase still closer to my face. "Look closely! Tell what you see."

"I see— I see—" But my eyes fail me. The light is too dazzling; the scene blurs.

"Very well," Seraphina says. "That is enough for one night. And you, Victor—what did you see?"

"But I saw nothing," he answers in bewilderment.

Seraphina nods judiciously. "In time, in time. Each night we will enter a little further into this mystery."

So we do. Each time we finish with the Feeding of the Lions, she brings out the vase. Each time I see the same brilliant blue flame burst forth inside, always with something stirring slowly inside it—a living thing, I think. But what could live in so fierce a fire? Then, after several nights, my eye remains steady; it does not flinch or blur. And I plainly see: "*A creature!* A lizard." For that is indeed what is there, a reptilian shape with quick, questing tongue and lashing tail, its lithe, gleaming body bathed in the flame.

"What colour?" Seraphina asks. I lose sight of the creature; it melts into the brightness. I stare until my eyes become dry and warm. "Easy, child," Seraphina cautions me. "Let your eyes be soft and welcoming. Ask this thing to show itself."

I do as I am told. Instead of reaching out to seize the sight, I make a small prayer, inviting the thing in the jar to let itself be seen. Slowly, the lizard returns, its scaly hide now ablaze; it wears the fire like a garment. "It is all colours," I say. "Red, silver, orange."

"And what else?"

"It walks in the fire, but it does not burn."

"Can you tell if it likes the flame?"

"Yes. It rolls and frolics in it."

Seraphina holds the vase closer to Victor. "And now, Victor. Do you also see this creature?"

But Victor's eye is not as astute as mine. Though he stares fiercely into the vase, he sees only the dark residue that moulders at the bottom. "I see nothing!" he snaps impatiently. "There is nothing to see but the scum you have put there."

"No matter, child," Seraphina assures him. "In time you will see. This beast is a special sign; it is the salamander arising from the dross. Fierce as the beast may look, it is our faithful guide. It comes as a signal that the *nigredo* is approaching its end. Regeneration is beginning, as much within you as in the vase. Remember: All that you see in the world must first of all exist in you. You will never see the Great Work accomplished outside until it is accomplished inside. Above all, see how the lizard revels in the flames. The fire is its element. It relishes the burning as you will come to do. Remember what I have said: that all things are signatures of something that lies beyond them. What does it mean that there is man and woman? What does it mean that the man enters the woman? That he *enters* her? Why are we created as two who then burn to become one? It is the *oneness* that matters. For this it is worth burning a lifetime."

"Your eye is quicker than mine," Victor tells me later. "I can see nothing in the egg. Are you pretending?" he asks suspiciously. It is the first time he has spoken to me distrustfully.

"I would not do such a thing! I would not try to deceive Seraphina; I could not."

"Perhaps the two of you are deceiving me."

I am astonished by what he says. "Why would we do that?"

He shrugs his shoulders and makes a resentful face. "Because you are women, and you wish to make these things *yours*."

"Not so!" I insist indignantly. "I would share whatever I had with you."

"Then why am I unable to see the lizard? I stare so hard I might see through a wall of stone."

"Perhaps because you try too hard; you are too eager. Let your eyes be calm. Trust that you will see."

But the next night and the next when Seraphina presents the vase, Victor sees nothing, and each time grows more restless. Finally, he breaks off, protesting, "I have no eye for this!" and refuses to continue our *séance*.

"Patience, Victor," Seraphina tells him. "It will come for you in another way. Often it is the *Soror* who sees these signs first; in that way, she helps to exercise prudence."

But I see that Victor is discontented. The next night, in order to spare his feelings, I pretend that I also see nothing. Seraphina is puzzled at this. "Are you sure, child?" she asks.

"Nothing . . . I see nothing. I have lost sight of the creature; I truly have."

"How curious." I see that Seraphina is fretting over my answer. I think she knows what is in my mind. I think she knows I lie. But I lie out of my love for Victor. I would not leave him behind.

EDITOR'S NOTE

The Feeding of the Lions and the Influence of the
Left-handed Tantra on European Alchemy

The erotic devotion cryptically referred to as Feeding the Lions may have been more frequently practised by Victor and Elizabeth than any other alchemical exercise. I would not hesitate to call it the most formative, and very possibly the most corrosive, of the influences that shaped their relationship. The practice is pictorially presented in the Lavender Book as follows: An aged alchemist is shown kneeling prayerfully before a female laborant. She reclines upon a divan, her form well-lit by a double circle of lamps, her thighs brazenly spread to display herself as fully as possible. In the pictures that follow, the sun and moon are shown in transit overhead, indicating the passage of an entire night during which the alchemist never takes his eyes from his consort. His gaze searches every part of the woman's anatomy, fixed for long periods upon her most private of parts.

At some point in the course of the night, the sage begins to hallucinate. The laborant's frame is transformed in his eyes into a luxuriant moonlit forest, its trees richly in flower. Eyes appear among the trees; a pair and then another. Two lions, one golden, one green, emerge from the shadowed hollow of the woman's vagina. Their mouths drip gore. They approach the alchemist, who is rapt in contemplation. Even when the lions take him in their jaws, his concentration remains unshaken. Bite by bite, the lions devour him, leaving not so much as a bone behind.

They return to the woman's body, passing easily into the deep crevices of her vulva. Each carries a bloody remnant of the alchemist in its jaws. There is a picture that shows the lions inside the woman's abdomen, where they lie down to sleep. Toward morning, as the sunrise lights the sky above, the lions vanish; the remains of the alchemist, deposited in the woman's womb, assume the shape of a fetus. In the final picture, the woman gives birth to the alchemist, who emerges from her fully-grown, glowing, and manly. He turns and kneels between her knees, and places a kiss upon her organ.

Images of the adept being dismembered or eaten alive appear frequently in the alchemical texts. They are clearly symbols of some ordeal that leads via suffering to illumination. Among the alchemical philosophers, this experience was frequently portrayed as a *regressus ad uterum:* a return to the womb. Hence in Paracelsus we find: "He who would enter the kingdom of God must first enter with his body into his mother and die." In the texts of the left-handed Tantra, this ritual death is often associated with a blatant display of female eroticism. Oddly enough, there is, as Elizabeth observes, a certain almost perverse "chastity" to these practices, since they involve no direct physical contact between the lovers. Also, if we can believe the accounts as presented, the objective of the practices was to transcend carnality. The result of such constant, exaggerated titillation was finally a numbing of desire, a cessation of craving. As we shall see later in this narrative when we deal with the so-called "Flight of the Griffin," the dangers involved in these practices, all of which required the utmost self-discipline, were great.

The Cockatrice

October ——, 178——

A distressing turn of events . . .

Three evenings ago: we are once again gathered in Seraphina's cottage to perform the Rite of the Lions. From the outset, the *séance* does not go well; there is an impediment. Victor seems irascible, unable to calm his thoughts. At such times, Seraphina has told us to imagine that a candle burns at the centre of our mind; all round it the winds may whirl. We must think that we are cupping our hands about the flame to keep it steady, unwavering, a bright point of light.

But this night Victor's mind is like a windswept fire scattering sparks in all directions. Even the anodyne that Seraphina prepares for him has no effect. When he is so agitated, I find I cannot lie trustingly beneath his gaze. I feel his eyes grasping at me impatiently, urgently. Our minds are now so intimately blended in our exercises that I can detect the least tremor of his mood. On this evening, as on others, he makes me feel whorish to lie naked before him. After some passage of time (how long I cannot say; it is difficult to determine how long our periods of meditation last) I feel so ashamed I am almost on the point of asking that we stop so that I might cover myself. But then I feel his mood change, his thoughts darken. He looks on me no longer lustfully, but with a pathos that makes me want to weep. Waves of sorrow wash over me.

What is happening?

Seraphina, who seems to read our thoughts as if they are her own, also senses Victor's unease. When I clear my mind and look about, I see that she has gone to Victor's side; she is cradling him in her arms, comforting him. She asks if he will tell why he is so distraught, but he will say nothing—only that he wishes to leave.

That night he retires to his room without bidding me good-night. The next day, he is gone before breakfast to go roaming near Mont Salève. I do not see him again for two days; when he returns, he is in the most melancholic of humours and will say nothing.

Then it is last night. I am awakened by the sound of someone moving in my room. "Who is there?" I call out in the dark, but there is no answer, only a rustling at the foot of my bed. I stare into the darkness and listen closely. "Who is there?" I ask again and hear in answer what makes my blood run cold through my veins. There is someone in my room weeping. With trembling hand, I hurriedly strike a flint to light a candle and find Victor standing naked at the side of my bed. He is murmuring something under his breath, speaking urgently, but he sobs so hard that I cannot distinguish his words. When I call to him, he does not hear. *Is this truly Victor,* I wonder, *or some phantom double?* I lean closer and see that his eyes are shut; *he is asleep!* I take hold of his hand and gently settle him beside me on the bed. Even in the unsteady candlelight I can see how blanched he is, and how the tears roll down his cheeks. He is sobbing convulsively. I take him in my arms and seek to comfort him.

After a short while, he wakes and is amazed to discover where he is. "I have had a dream," he tells me in a hushed and quavering voice. "I am afraid to close my eyes lest it return."

I take him into bed with me and hold him close until he regains his composure. He clings to me, burying his face in my bosom the way a frightened child might. I beg him to tell me what he has dreamt. For a long while he will not say; but upon my continued urging, at last he speaks.

"I dreamt that you were with child, *our* child. You were so very proud. You ran to tell me that our union was at last consummated; we had brought the Great Work to its conclusion. Oh, you were lovely to see, Elizabeth; the air round you kindled with a golden light. Your body had grown to be beautifully rounded: full and ripe. I knew that at last you had become a true woman. We rushed to tell Mother the news; but she was not pleased. 'Elizabeth is too young to have this child,' she declared. 'I shall bear it for her.' And at once, by some magic, the baby was removed from your body and taken into hers. She saw how bewildered and hurt we were by what she had done, but this made no difference. 'It was always my intention that the child should be mine,' she explained. 'Elizabeth is not fit to consummate the marriage.'

"After that, things went badly. Mother grew ill; her confinement became a torment to her. She swelled with the child until she looked hideously bloated. Something terrible was happening. 'It is poisoning me!' she cried, and appealed to me to deliver her of the baby. I was horrified. I said I could not do that. I said, 'Let Elizabeth help. She knows how to midwife babies.' But Mother insisted that only I could help her. She would not let you approach her. 'This is your doing!' she screamed at you. 'You are jealous of me, Gipsy bastard that you are!' And she ordered you from the room. I felt fiercely angry, but I could not bring myself to speak out against her. I did what I could to make her ready to give birth. I surrounded her with pillows and began to uncover her, but I was too laggardly at the task. 'Hurry,' she commanded, and tore at her clothes until she stood naked before me and grossly swollen with the child she carried. This seemed so unnatural a thing that I could not keep myself from trembling with shame as I stood over her. We waited and waited. The time was at hand, but the baby did not emerge. I pleaded with Mother to make it come quickly, but she could not. She cried for help. 'Take it from me!' she commanded, and opened herself enormously. I reached into her body to take hold of the child; it was as if my hands had been swallowed into the mouth of a great sucking beast; but what I felt there was a rough, scaly object that squirmed away, farther into her womb. Mother began to scream with the pain of the delivery; I knew I must bring this thing out of her or she would surely die. And at last, drawing upon all my strength, I thrust my hands deep into her and succeeded in pulling out the thing she had inside. But what I held in my hands was no human child; it was a sort of evil-looking bird that glared round in anger. It had a murderous beak and fiery eyes and a long snake-like tail that whipped this way and that. It turned its glance fiercely upon Mother and made as if to fly at her; but I held fast to it and would not let it free. Finally it tore itself from my grasp and flew screeching into the sky. When I turned back to Mother, I was struck dumb with horror. She lay upon the bed cold and grey and still. I touched her . . . and found that she had turned to stone."

And once again he begins to shudder.

I recall that this is the only time Victor has ever told me of his dreams. Once he boasted that he never dreamt at all, and that if he ever should, he would teach himself to wipe what he dreamt from his memory as a foolish fantasy. But I do not believe he will succeed in wiping this dream away. For what remains of that night, I hold him close to me. Victor and I have not shared a bed in many years, not since we were children. I would feel so pleased to have him here with me, if he were not like this, so distressed and fearful. Toward dawn, he falls into a fit-ful sleep; the next morning he wakes feeling deeply ashamed and departs in haste.

※

This was the beginning of a great change in Victor. Or rather, it was the occasion on which I first marked that change. Later, looking back, I could plainly see that for many weeks, Victor's enthusiasm for the Work had been cooling. The impatience I had noticed whenever he found our studies growing tedious was the sign of deeper currents mov-ing in him. For a while, he sought to shrug off his annoyance and main-tain his application; but he was struggling against a discontent he could not easily put aside. Something in his nature was rebelling against the Work—and, I think, against me. There was a time, at the outset of our studies, when a day did not pass but Victor and I found ourselves talk-ing eagerly about Seraphina's lessons. We could hardly wait to be alone with one another so that we might discover what each of us had learnt. But as the months passed, we talked less and less. When our studies were finished or suspended for a day, Victor would withdraw into his own company; he would take to the mountains, never asking me to accompany him. Or he would ensconce himself in his room, claiming to be fatigued by our exercises.

Seraphina was quick to recognise Victor's restiveness. Each time we met, she was at great pains to spare his feelings. For his sake, she spent more time with the gross substances, showing how they mix and mingle and magically transform their nature. This she called the lesser work, a pursuit of a distinctly more vulgar character; but it interested Victor greatly. He at once set about furnishing a small workshop in one of the outbuildings. He built a rough brick furnace and began collecting all manner of alembics and retorts, together with strange substances to cook in them. M. Oudard, an apothecary from Lausanne, himself an ardent spagyrist (though of the grossly materialist kind), lent him numerous supplies, including an ancient athanor he had purchased in Alexandria. Victor's laboratory soon became so foul-smelling and grimy a place that I hated to enter and spend time there. But Seraphina, out of concern for Victor's interest, insisted that we must, and indeed advised him carefully about the implements he would need. Though she regarded experimenting with substances as a lower form of the Great Work, she was nevertheless surprisingly knowledgeable about the processes Victor wished to investigate, a fact that commanded his great respect.

For three entire cycles of the moon—time she had intended to use otherwise—Seraphina loitered over teaching us the secrets of the chymical flame. "Every fire has its own soul," she told us, "and must be addressed with proper reverence. For the fire is a wilful spirit and not easily tamed." Under Victor's insistent prodding, she showed us the use of the dry fire and the wet, and how to pacify the elusive fire of effusion. She taught us how to heat with the black coal and the blue, with camphor oil and with sal ammoniac, with charcoal and with peat. We learnt that each substance takes combustion in a different mode. The yew burns hot and quick and is used when the adept must make haste; the oak is a moody fellow and must be coaxed into burning, but once alight, will kindle obediently to one's need like a Roman soldier under orders, giving a warmth that heats the mixture evenly through the longest night. The birch is impish and often mischievous; he is therefore useless for anything more delicate than crude distillation; the larch is the fire of Gemini, a lively dancer best employed for delicate warming; as for the cedar, his is a priestly flame reserved by the adept for solemn ritual. Seraphina also taught us the use of mare's dung, which gives the most delicate heat of all, capable of warming the subtlest substance for as long as prescribed. Finally, with painstaking caution, Seraphina demonstrated the ways of the vehement saltpetre, whose explosive temper has cost many an experimenter his life and limb. And for each chymical process she taught us the prayers and incantations that guide the elements through their Odyssey of change.

I listened with patience to all she taught, but found little to interest me in these pursuits; they seemed . . . remote. They had nothing to do with the images and correspondences of things that kindled my imagination. There was no heart to them. Yet this was what Victor most enjoyed; he relished observing the minutest fluctuation of the base matter, how it glows and sweats and alters its form under duress. Even when one had to tend the fire night and day and sleep only in snatches so that the flame might be kept steady beneath the simmering concoction, he was willing to do all that was required; he would sit through the long "philosopher's night" fixedly observing the elements as they altered their hues and consistency. He was as delighted as a child to see how the cinnabar, carefully heated, turns to flowing mercury; then how the mercury, combined with antimony, the "fierce grey wolf," congeals into a black lump; and how, at last, when this blackened dross has been blended many times over with quicklime, it will suddenly burst forth into the hundred splendid colours that are called the peacock's tail.

So eager was Victor to discover these wonders that he grew impulsive, wanting more from the substances than they would show forth. Seraphina was careful to tell him that there was more to the Work than mere cookery. "These are spiritual arts," she reminded him more than once. "The alterations you see in the Earthly matter are but the signatures of their philosophic meaning. You must know that in these vigils, we keep watch over time from eternity." Victor was outwardly respectful of all she said, but in his heart he paid ever less attention to her instruction. "My mind runs in other channels," he confessed to me. "I find Seraphina's ways wearisome. These things she calls by name and takes such trouble to invoke with incantations—I mean the metals and the stones—they have no ears; they do not hear her speak to them. I think this is nothing but witchery." When I protested at his impatience, he readily apologised, explaining, "I fear I have no skill at 'women's mysteries.' " But when I pressed him to grant Seraphina more trust, he flashed out at me. "I do not think Seraphina understands the true import of the Great Work. If it is possible to change base metal into gold, I want to master this skill."

"But why? Is the gold so important to you?"

"Not at all! The gold is of no importance whatever. For my part, I would just as soon change gold into lead as the other way round. But to understand the *force* that brings forth this alteration, do you not see? *That* is the heart of the matter. This would mean that all substance is *one thing* in its invisible nature. Master that, and we can remake the world with our own hands. We might turn the sands of the desert into fertile soil and stones into bread to feed the hungry. We might banish disease from the human frame and make men invulnerable to death. We might call up undiscovered powers and drive them to plough and delve and build for us. We might never again need to toil in the sweat of our brow. Perhaps this is the work God has left for us to do: to create a race of happy and excellent men."

I kept Victor's discontent a secret; but before that summer was out, a curious turn of events interrupted our studies.

Victor had made me swear I would tell no one of his dream. I promised; but the secret nonetheless revealed itself. The way Mother had behaved in Victor's dream—so grasping and tyrannical, and so harsh in what she said to me—haunted my thoughts. Again and again I had to remind myself that this was only a figment of Victor's sleeping imagination. Even so, I sometimes felt myself becoming colder, more distant with Mother. Perceptive as she was, she could not help but to discern this shadow of mistrust in me; but she did not ask about it until several weeks after Victor had come to me in the night.

I had met Mother in her studio for one of our painting sessions. She had done no more than dab a few times at the canvas, when, quite deliberately, she laid her brushes aside. "Cover yourself, Elizabeth," she said, "and come sit here beside me."

For some time, she sat pensively plaiting her hair while she gathered her thoughts. "Tell me," she said at last, "have you felt disquieted in your studies of late?"

"In what way?"

"I am thinking of Victor. Has he talked with you about his feelings?"

"Yes. We often talk."

"Has he expressed objections?"

I was reluctant to answer this, but I knew I must be truthful. "He is sometimes unhappy with how slowly we move forward. He is impatient."

"Is he hasty with you—when you summon the lions? Is he unfeeling?"

"Sometimes. He means no disrespect, I'm sure."

"Does he hurt you?"

"I know that he means me no harm."

"Do you find it difficult to merge with him in your thoughts?"

Here I felt my way forward carefully. It was, in fact, true that each time Victor and I returned to the Feeding of the Lions, I felt less comfortable beneath his gaze. As Seraphina had predicted, our thoughts were growing ever more inseparable; I was coming to feel tightly bound up in Victor's revery. But this union of minds was not what I had expected. The lustfulness we were to leave behind clung to Victor's thoughts, more and more forcing itself upon me with an insistence I found unsettling. "I am sure Victor does not always see me as I think he is supposed to."

"And how is that?"

"He is meant to see me as a sister."

"And he does not?"

"No. He sees me that other way."

"Does this disturb you?"

Here I was embarrassed to answer. "No. For I do not always want him to think of me as his sister."

She allowed a long pause to ensue. "Seraphina is troubled. She feels Victor is drifting away from us. She fears he may be . . . unsuited to our work. Do you believe that might be so?"

All at once it was as if the air about us had turned brittle; one ill-advised word might shatter it. I studied Mother carefully before I spoke. Though she sought to ask her question casually, the worry in her voice was unmistakeable. I realised that this was a weighty matter for her to raise, one that I must address with the utmost tact. It would be the cause of great distress if I were to say that I, too, felt that Victor was incapable of continuing our studies. "Victor has said he feels that the Work is more suited to women than to men. I cannot say why he feels this way. I have sometimes tried to hold back in our lessons so that he will not feel I am outdistancing him."

She sat for a long while pondering what I had said. Finally, more to herself than to me, she said, "That is not good." And then, repeating this twice more under her breath, she rose and paced slowly across the room to the window and stood looking out, her brow deeply furrowed. A veil of sorrow fell across her face. I knew I was watching the passage of a hard moment in her life. For a long while she did not speak—for so long a time that I wondered if I should excuse myself and leave her to her thoughts. But there was a question I felt I must ask; I had held it inside for weeks. I took a stick of charcoal from the table and made a sketch on a pad of paper. It was a fierce bird with a snake's tail. "Mother . . . what is this beast?" I asked.

She came to look and recognised it at once. "It is the cockatrice, or as some call it, the basilisk."

"What does it signify?"

"It is a dark sign. A warning. It means that the Work has taken a wrong turning. Why do you ask? Have you seen such a thing?"

"No. I came across it in one of the books."

"Oh? I wonder which. The cockatrice is so evil a sign that it is rarely drawn."

⊱✦⊰

After that, a full month passed before Seraphina met with us again. This time we gathered at dawn in the glade. The morning was cool and cloudless, the beginning of a lovely day. Both Victor and I knew that Seraphina and Mother had spoken together many times; I knew their conversations had to do with Victor, but I was loath to tell him. For his part, Victor was too absorbed in his workshop to think of anything besides "the trials and sufferings of Nature," as he called his studies. But when Seraphina summoned us again to join her, he knew it would be to bid us farewell. "She has been unhappy with my progress," Victor said. "She no longer wants me for her pupil."

This was the very thing Seraphina did most to assure him was not so. When we gathered that morning, she said, more to Victor than myself, "You must not think I am displeased with you. Think rather that I would have you take more time to ponder our studies. Ours is a subtle art, for some the work of a life-time." Though she sought to appear cheerful, she was clearly a different woman than we had known before. As old as she was, she now looked even older—sombre and humbled. "Lady Caroline believes we must have a respite. I believe she is correct in this. You have studied hard, and you are so very young. There will be time later to return to our lessons. Moreover, your old teacher needs rest."

Above us, on the branch of an aged larch, Alu sat watching all we did with a keen eye. I could not recall having seen the bird watch so intently, as if she too knew this was a special occasion and would not miss a word.

Seraphina told us there were women who honoured her in all parts of the world and waited for her coming each year; she would dwell with them for a time. It was her custom in the winters to travel among these friends as she made her way south to her homeland of Sicily. She preferred for a time, to live closer to Nature, in the open fields and by the sea. "I am sometimes more at home among the wild things than among people. I find it cleansing to live with the beasts. And then next spring, I shall return and we shall resume." But what were we to do while she was away? we asked. "You will have your books to study. Lady Caroline will read with you. She is my most gifted student and will teach you well. And you, Victor, will want to continue your experiments, is that not so? I shall leave you treatises that will be of particular interest. The great Van Helmont has set down several accounts of making the powder of projection. You will want to exercise your curiosity upon these writings, for such adventures with the *prima materia* are also a part of the Work. But always remember that ours is above all a philosophic quest. The great change must come in *here*; and then all the powers follow. Think of the Work, if you can, not as something that must be done or made or found, but as something that wants to be born out of your soul, yes?"

Then she turned to her sack and took from it several things, which she carefully arranged before us on the ground. She first spread an ornate covering on which were embroidered many occult signs and words in a coiling alphabet we did not recognise. Upon the cloth she laid her two knives; ancient blades they were, but carefully polished, one with a handle of black horn and the other with a handle of white bone. "Elizabeth," she said, "have you brought your knives, as I asked? Then place them here, the points touching mine." I did as she wished, thus creating a square where the tips of the blades rested against one another. In this space, Seraphina placed a small earthenware bowl, and in its hollow a sprinkling of herbal substances. Turning to Victor, she said, "This is a rite of blessing that is performed among the women when they must part from one another. Men are not privy to it; but you are special, Victor. We wish you to know of our teachings and our ceremonies."

She struck a flint and set the herbs to smouldering. They created a pleasant, honeyed scent. Then, using a hawk's feather, she wafted the smoke toward each of us and toward her own breast. "Now all take hands," she said, and began intoning a quiet song. Overhead in the tree,

Alu spread her wings wide and made a soft, crooning sound in her throat as if she might know this chant. It was as melancholy a note as one could imagine a bird sounding.

> *Bless and let pass, the sorrow of leaving*
> *Bless and let pass, the season of grieving*
> *Bless and let pass, the days spent apart*
> *Bless and let pass, the cheerless heart*
> *Bless and let pass, till love surrounds*
> *Bless and let pass, till joy abounds*
> *Hathor protect*
> *And bind this spell.*

For a long while we sat silently in one another's presence. When at last she released our hands, Victor drew from his pocket a trinket that I at once recognised. It was a small prism about the size of the palm of his hand. I had seen Victor employ it many times in his experiments, but that was not what made it precious to him. On his tenth birthday, he had been given it as a gift from M. Saussure, who had taught him how to use it for the deep study of light. Victor had attached it to a silver chain and now wished to make it his farewell gift to Seraphina. She examined the token a long while, turning it this way and that to catch the rainbow reflections. "The crystal is one of the ancient spirits of light. She is the mother of rainbows. See how she gives birth to colours; they are her loving children. I see it amuses you that I speak this way, Victor. But I hope you have learnt this much from our studies: that *things* have souls within them even as we have, can hurt and weep and make beauty. That is what the Great Work teaches: that all the world moves with will and spirit. *Nothing* is dead, not even Death itself. All speaks." She held the prism out to him. "This is a fine gift. I will treasure it. Will you place it round my neck?"

And he did. Then, raising herself with the aid of her stick, Seraphina offered her last farewell to us. "Until the spring," she said, and shuffled into the woods to the south; she moved so slowly that it was difficult to believe she would ever travel as far as a league from us. Alu followed overhead, gracefully flapping the great sails of her wings as she floated from branch to branch; and at last both were lost among the trees. But later that day, gazing toward the Voirons with my spyglass, I was certain I saw Alu in the distant sky, a tiny black speck slowly circling above her mistress.

For days afterwards, Victor and I were desolate. As much as he had complained of her ways, Victor felt Seraphina's absence as keenly as I. There had been a certain bracing tension between them that Victor found to be an enjoyable testing. Above all, I think he had, almost in spite of himself, admired the uncanniness that enveloped her. For she was a magical spirit.

As Seraphina told us, Mother now assumed the place of our teacher, promising to read with us and explain the inner meaning of the books. Together, she and Victor and I read the sage writings of the alchymical masters. We examined the towering visions of Paracelsus and Robert Fludd and Basil Valentine, loitering over every image and symbol on the page, for there was always more to be found if we looked with care.

⋈

With the return of spring, I could sense Mother's rising expectation as she waited for Seraphina's return. She had confessed to me that whenever they parted, she feared it might be for the last time. "She is old and fragile, and not as watchful as she was. I fear for her safety." Once each month, she summoned me to her room at bedtime to join in a small ritual that prayed for Seraphina's safe return. Then one morning, I woke to a familiar sound. It was Alu's harsh caw-cawing. I rushed to the window, looking this way and that, but could see nothing on that side of the château. At once I raced to the stairs and down to the breakfast room. There, I spied Mother outside the window, kneeling on the lawn, her face buried in her hands. I had never seen her in such a posture, and ran to her at once. She was weeping, her body shaking powerfully; Alu was just above her in one of the elms. The bird was crying out as if a knife were in her, a rasping stream of shrieks and chortles.

"Where is Seraphina?" I asked.

"Alu has come alone," Mother murmured through her tears.

Almost furiously I called up at the jabbering bird, "Where is Seraphina? Where? *Where?*" Then I noticed that Alu wore something looped around her neck. I looked more closely and saw it was one of Seraphina's bangles. After a while, as if she had delivered her message, the bird ceased her clamour and fluttered down to stand at Mother's side where she sat upon the lawn. Asking for no invitation, Alu finally took her place on Mother's arm as she always had on Seraphina's. She chortled at Mother's ear, but Mother gave no response; she sat cold and silent as a statue and spoke not a word for the remainder of that day.

The cunning women lived as if within some invisible, living tissue of knowledge. Intelligence of their adventures might travel over hundreds of miles, conveyed from village to village as if their words were written on the wind. Some said the birds carried messages for them; others that the women could converse through the roots of trees from one end of a kingdom to the next. In this way they might learn of dangers and disasters more rapidly than any royal court. So famous a teacher as Seraphina, whose students numbered hundreds from one end of Europe to the other, could not go long without report; so it was that in early spring, at one of the gatherings in the glade, we discovered what had happened to her. A month before, she had been taken for a witch not far from her home in Sicily. Inquisitors who were despatched to investigate in the island had questioned her about a potion she gave to one of the local women. She had been put through the ordeal by water, condemned, and burnt. Four women of good family in the community had sought to save her, but they had also been taken under arrest and confined. Several more women had been burnt as Seraphina's disciples. Women everywhere in the South of France and Italy were to be warned.

Could this hideous report be true? Mother accepted it immediately as proven. For her, Alu was all the evidence she required. "The bird would not leave Seraphina if she were still alive," she said. "She has come to me as Seraphina told me she would—to be mine after our teacher's passing. I had hoped never to see that day."

A few weeks later, at the full moon, the women gathered in greater agitation than I had ever seen. The air in the glade fairly crisped with fear and anger and bewildered grief. Celeste once again recited the roll of names, her voice growing more choked with tears as she approached its conclusion. She could hardly finish. After a struggling pause she spoke the final name: "Seraphina of Sicily." There followed a long interval of wailing and keening among the women that grew steadily more frenzied. Some hurled themselves to the Earth, where they rolled and twisted, howling with woe. Mother, with Alu at her shoulder, sat silent and stone-like amid this whirlwind of raging grief; all her tears had long since been cried out of her. At her side I sought to control the storm of feeling inside me, but in vain. Surrounded by so much wild lamentation, I at last let all restraint slip away and sent forth my voice to wail with the others into the night. I fell to my knees and beat upon the ground until I was exhausted with the effort. There was grief in my mourning, yes; but the greater part of what I felt was the fury of help-lessness. What good woman could ever stand before such terrible, unfeeling power and make herself understood? Had no one looked into my teacher's heart and seen the wisdom and gentleness there? Had they tortured her for their absurd beliefs—that she flew in the air on a broomstick or turned mother's milk to vinegar? Had they burnt her so that they could continue to speak of God as *He, He, He?* I thought of myself cast into the flames and shuddered with terror.

Victor was no less furious than I. With a cold, fixed anger he said, "Father is right. They must all perish, these tyrants of God. They are the enemies of truth. Is this not odd? That the witches and the men of sci-ence have a common enemy?"

In the days that followed, Mother lost all heart for our studies. Her vitality faded, her constitution began to weaken. The consumption she had held at bay for years returned; she was often confined to her room with fever and a racking cough. Victor blamed himself for her distress, for he knew she was despondent over his failure to complete the Work. He laid all our books before her and all but begged her to read with us again; but it was clear that the light had gone out of these writings for her. She seemed almost in pain, reading of mysteries that she felt she would never see unfold. Now that she was burdened by disease, her tone in all we did became one of darkening despair.

"I expected too much of him," she confessed to me one night while I sat up with her waiting for the fever to abate. The consumption had wasted her severely, and her mind wandered. "Perhaps his intuition is right; perhaps the Great Work *is* a woman's mystery. Yet the mystic union cannot be achieved by the woman alone." She rubbed her brow in bewilderment, like one who has seen the great design of her life collapse into impossibility. "What is to become of us? In the New Age, are women once again to be made mere cyphers, leaving the world in the hands of soulless arithmeticians?"

With each passing month, she grew more withdrawn. She would not participate in the women's rites, where her presence was sorely missed. A still more telling sign of her dejection: she no longer made use of her studio. There her canvases lay like so many relics of an earlier life. Often I would visit that lonely sanctum, whose disorderliness I had once found so odious; now I saw the room as the outward expression of my mother's soul, a place of exotic fascinations and unearthly glamour. Even the rancid odours that filled the air, the dust motes that floated thickly in the sunlight, possessed a charm I treasured. Through the door to this room I had entered some higher realm of experience. Here I had first learnt of another science, whose language was that of dreams and fancies, and which was best set down in the sort of grand, glowing symbols that filled Mother's paintings. Though she had given me no permission to study her pictures, each time I entered the studio I explored another stack of sketches and canvases. How strange was the world of my mother's imagination! It brimmed with intimate studies of women's anatomy and of the carnal pleasures that women are said not to desire. I discovered a shelf of paintings that showed the caves and ravines and grottoes of the nearby mountains, and these too had been transmuted into the female form: all were curiously shaped to resemble the generative organs of women. But then there were also many visions of inner worlds, heavens and hells of the mind. Foremost among these was the great canvas on which she had worked so long and in which I was the principal figure; it stood unfinished on the easel. I could never lay eyes upon it without suffering a vivid sense of loss. There I saw myself frozen in time, the girl-woman balanced between childhood and maturity, held lovingly in the embrace of her mother, of Seraphina, and of all the women who had come before us, back and back in time to the earliest days when, as Mother believed, man and woman had lived together in harmony. It had been her supreme hope that the Great Work would show how we might regain that lost paradise. I had for a time been part of this great adventure. Abandoned now! I could but wonder what delights of the mind and spirit had awaited me just a little farther along the road.

And there was one morose canvas I recall loitering over many times. Surely some prophetic instinct was at work in the curiosity that drew me so often to the picture Mother had painted of our tragic sister, the lady in chains whose fate I was soon to share.

Each time we visited Mother, Victor came away feeling the more chagrined that he had failed to serve her as she most wanted. "I have lost her love," Victor told me. "The Work is what she cares for most of all in life, and I have fallen short. I have been selfish and blind; I have made her sick to death." It was futile for me to try to dissuade him of this conviction, for even more certainly than he, I knew it to be true. At last, in his desperation to make amends, Victor proposed a daring course. "We have stopped within reach of the goal. Let us resume the Work on our own."

The idea astonished me. "But we have not the skill," I protested.

"Nonsense! We have been well taught. And we have the books. What a gift it would be for Mother if we achieved the chymical marriage."

He proposed this with an ardour I well remembered; it was the same passion I had first heard him voice when the two of us, still children, had watched the storm clouds sweep down from the mountains. He had said—I recollected the words vividly—"I would wear this lightning like my crown." I secretly adored the defiant fervour that arose in him at such moments. Though the danger was clear, there was the thrill of temptation in his words. Much as I feared what Victor wanted, I would not for an instant have held back. More than anything in the world I wished him to know I was his equal in this enterprise.

That night for the first time we performed the Rite of the Lions with no one present to guide us. The exercise had never been more deliciously enticing; nor had we known such triumph as came of overcoming that enticement. *Then Victor is right*, I thought. *We can go forward without fear.*

The Griffin

From that night, a new exhilaration attended the Great Work. Victor and I were clothed in a deeper secrecy than we had ever known. While Seraphina had been our mentor, our lessons had been discreet, but hardly furtive; we found neither guilt nor fear in what we did. Seraphina had made everything seem a matter of innocent curiosity. Sheltered by Mother's authority, we had no concern for prying eyes. Even the Baron, when he was at home, trusted his wife's judgement and let our work continue. But now, we kept our studies concealed even from Mother, who, as we knew, would not have found us ready to strike out for ourselves. This very air of stealth made us seem truer practitioners of the Work, for we had entered the clandestine state in which alchymist adepts had laboured for centuries, fearing the persecution of authorities who regarded them as evil sorcerers. I do not think the true strangeness of the Work grew vivid to us until we ceased to be pupils in a teacher's care. Our secrets became *guilty* secrets, and our studies an act of daring, if not defiance.

Thrilling as our adventure had become, I found it difficult to free my mind of reservations. How could we be sure that we were on the proper course? The books were so very cryptic; one could not take firm guidance from them; they could not teach us the subtle signs and markers that Seraphina had watched for. Still, Victor was supremely confident, so much so that I found it impossible to challenge his certitude openly.

He was too forceful; where I hesitated and hung back, he would plunge forward, convinced that he knew the true goal of the chymical philosophy—and even better than Seraphina or Mother. He spoke of it as "the innermost knowledge of the world."

As we studied the books together, Victor became steadily more engrossed by the curious figure of the homunculus that appeared in so many alchymical texts. "This," he eagerly declared, "is where the Great Work becomes most God-like." The homunculus, or "little man," was a living simulacrum of our own human frame, able to speak and read and learn, but no larger than the span of one's hand. He was always pictured inside the Hermetic flask which was his entire world. The books said that this tiny being had actually been created by adepts in ages past. Paracelsus, the surpassing genius of medicinal chymistry, claimed to have conjured him out of well-rotted dung and spirit of mercury compounded under the impression of the proper stars. "At this I many times failed," the great doctor reported in his treatise on the alchymical compositions, "until at last I discovered a way to maintain the athanor at the exact heat of a mare's womb for forty days." Victor was dubious of this account, as indeed he tended to be of much that the masters said. "Paracelsus, I think, was a great prevaricator. For if he had created the homunculus, why did he not grow him larger so that he might become useful? Why did he not turn him out into the world to live and work amongst us? If he had done so, we might by now have a race of slaves to do our bidding." Did Victor believe, then, that the quest for the homunculus was futile? Not at all. "I am certain the homunculus can be created," he told me, "but it shall be possible only with the use of electricity. This is surely the true vivifying agent, and better able to generate life than the heat of any womb, which is but a frail, fleshly organ. With the aid of the celestial fire we shall one day be able to create a new species of man, one that lives uncaring of disease or pain or death." But this great project required that the electrical fluid be captured and tamed, which was no easy matter.

Victor's fascination with electricity had a particular origin. One day in the year before Mother brought me to live at the château, Victor had witnessed a most violent and terrible storm. It had advanced in an instant from behind the Jura and swept across the lake, overtaking him out of doors; the thunder had burst at once with frightful loudness from various quarters of the heavens. While others ran for cover, Victor had stood watching the progress of the tempest with curiosity and delight. On a sudden, he beheld a stream of fire issue from an old and beautiful oak tree which stood about twenty yards from the château; and so soon as the dazzling light vanished the oak had disappeared; nothing remained but a blasted stump. Visiting the site the next day, Victor confessed he had never seen anything so utterly destroyed.

From that day forward, the laws of electricity became his constant study. This lent an aura of danger to his research, for it required the use of the giant Leyden bottle that Father had brought home with him from London when Victor was still a boy. This device was fearful to me; I saw in it a formidable and occult power, as if there were some wild, invisible jinni trapped under the glass. I had read reports of electrical experimenters who had generated shocks of such power that an entire battalion of the Pope's Swiss Guard, holding to an electrified wire, was sent into convulsions. In Ireland, a physical scientist seeking to strengthen the spark thrown by the jar had been crippled, and in Frankfort, a team of oxen had been killed by electrical infusion. Victor chided me for my fears, calling them womanish. But my distrust was not entirely a matter of fear; there was also revulsion. I hated the experiments in which Victor would electrify living creatures. He claimed that the electrical effluvium would rejuvenate the plant or animal that received it. He had electrified trees and seen them produce more fruit; in an electrified solution, zoophytes proliferated marvellously. But applied to animals—to cats or cattle or birds—the shock seemed obviously painful. Once, Victor invited me to watch while he passed a current into one of Father's hunting beagles; when I exclaimed at the cruelty of treating the poor, confused beast as he did, he relented, but only with a scowl of resentment. "One day, electrical fluid will cure every disease we know and restore the entire world to health. A small measure of pain is not much to pay for that."

A few days after that occasion, he came to me with a sly look. "I have devised an electrical experiment that I think you will find rewarding. Come and see!"

When we reached his workshop, he had us stand upon a flat glass sheet beside the Leyden phial. "Hold this," he said, handing me a wire and taking another himself. With some trepidation, I took what he gave me in my hand. Then, standing close, he leaned forward as if to kiss me. But just before his lips touched mine a sharp spark flew between us and nicked my upper lip. Startled, I leapt back, nearly falling off my feet, at which Victor burst out laughing. I found this not at all amusing, and let him see my temper. "It is called the electric kiss," he explained, without the least hint of an apology. "It is all the rage in the salons of Paris. See!" And he opened to an illustration in a journal he held. The picture showed a man and woman standing beside an electrical machine where an operative sat turning a wheel. They were kissing as we had just done; a tiny spark was shown flying between them. "Parisian ladies are said to find this an admirable application of electrical science," Victor said with a teasing grin. I knew he was making sport of me; Victor enjoyed pretending that women can only understand science in trivial ways. But before I could display my displeasure, he became intensely serious in a manner that never failed to catch me up in his fascinations. He opened the magazine to another page. "Here in the same journal it tells of a Bolognese physician named Galvani who has done the most remarkable thing. He has restored animation to dead matter by electrification! He can shock the limbs of dead creatures back to life. See here the drawing of the frog's legs? And this is the instrument he has invented, a sort of discharging wheel that can deliver a calibrated cascade of shocks. Is it not marvellous that a man should be able to invent such a device? Think what this portends! Soon we shall be able to endow the morbid parts of a corpse with vital warmth and salvage them for the living. We will be able to replace a stricken organ and continue our lives. No one need ever die! This is the true elixir of immortality that we have seen written of in Seraphina's books. I would give all my fortune to study with Galvani; the man is storming the last citadel of Nature."

As drawn as Victor was to electrical experimentation, this did not encumber his pursuit of the chymical philosophy. On the contrary. His course was set upon becoming both metaphysician and mechanistical theorist. For he remained convinced that everything the chymical adepts had ever sought since the time of Thrice-Great Hermes lay within the reach of man, if only it were pursued by the correct system; and that system, he was certain, now lay at hand. In his mind a grand new philosophic edifice was taking shape, one that artfully blended past and future, the piety of the ancient adepts and the cunning of the Galvanists. "Was not Newton the greatest alchymist of all?" he often asked. "I but tread in his footsteps. Had he known of the full power of electrical matter, I am sure he would have introduced it into his alchymical researches. But that has been left for me to do—or rather, for *us* to do. For I will not leave you behind, Elizabeth. I believe all that Seraphina and my mother have taught us is so: that the marriage of our souls will open the secret of the gold."

Victor and I had many times studied the pictures in the Lavender Book that described the Rite of the Griffin, wondering if Seraphina would ever call upon us to attempt so daring an exercise. It was among the last matters we had spoken of before she departed. The conversation was not an easy one, but marked by contention. Seraphina would not talk willingly of the Griffin; it was necessary for Victor to press her. What was the meaning of this exercise? he wished to know. Seraphina answered that Riding the Griffin came so close to achieving the chymical wedding itself, that we must be patient. The Griffin's flight, she cautioned, was greatly misunderstood even by the most learned adepts. "You see, children, the books I bring you for study are great treasures— but only if they are approached judiciously. Used improperly, they will occasion great harm. Always remember: we deal here with a borrowed wisdom—in kindness I say 'borrowed' rather than stolen. It has been borrowed from those who understand the true meaning of the Work and of the woman's part in it. There was a time when woman was honoured for her power to bring forth life. This was seen as a great mystery. It is a mystery still; but now there are men who think otherwise, and so the proper reverence is absent. I have been told there are schools where the men cut open the bodies of women to see how life grows there. They take out the womb and gaze at it through lenses—"

Victor, hearing me draw my breath in horror at what Seraphina said, hastened to correct her. "These women are dead. They are cadavers. Dead bodies feel no pain."

"Yes. And where were they found, these dead bodies?"

"They are poor wretches who fell dead in the streets or in the infirmary."

"Or whose graves were robbed in the night, perhaps? You do not know that the doctors do this?"

"Well, and if they do, what of that? These bodies would have rotted in the ground otherwise, and served no good purpose."

"It makes no difference to you, that the bodies may have been stolen from hallowed ground?" Seraphina asked.

"But why should they not be dissected? I have done this with my specimens."

"You see no reason why the body of man or woman should not be treated with greater respect than to become a specimen?"

"Not at all," Victor protested. "How else can we learn what is inside the body and how it is made?"

"And after they have looked inside to see how the woman's body is made," Seraphina continued, "do you know what these learned men conclude? They think the life that grows there comes from their seed and their seed alone. They think the woman is but a vessel to carry the life men have put into her. They say there is a whole tiny person hiding in the man's seed waiting to be deposited in the womb." Here she burst out in a dry cackle that made Victor wince. "Can you imagine! Men who have never seen a baby born make up these things and write them in books for other men to read. And so it becomes 'knowledge'! It is men like this, in their overweening pride, who have rewritten women's books as if these too were *their* creation. That is why, as Elizabeth has already seen, the women who appear in these pages are lowly courtesans and slaves, people of no consequence. Here in the Lavender Book, the *Soror* is merely the great lord's concubine. She has no name, no position, no soul.

She might be any female, a stranger who comes and goes in the same night after doing her master's will, as any harlot might. But this is very wrong. The Work will only be well-performed by a man and woman who know each other deeply; they must meet in love and make a pledge to one another. They must rise above the fleshly desire that first brought them together, so that they can see its greater purpose. You are not ready for this, Victor. It would be a great danger to teach you the Griffin before your time. You will one day know what I mean when I say that the man and woman must share the reins of the beast or all goes wrong—to the great detriment of the *Soror*, who has much to lose."

"I would never let that happen," Victor protested, allowing his anger to show.

"So you say now, my boy. But the Griffin is not easily tamed. In the moment of desire, O! he will fly with you! He is fierce as the hunting eagle, bold as the lion. He can be the most savage of beasts. He will rend and tear and devour those who cannot tame him. We deal here with fiery passions, Victor. To the one side love, to the other side lust; to the one side wisdom, to the other, wanton appetite. It is not easy for men to tell one from the other. Even you, Victor, could weaken in this way. It is something in the twist of your man's nature. That is why I take so long to teach you; there is much in you that must be *unlearnt*." Then, as if to spare his wounded feelings, she added, "Nor is Elizabeth ready to attempt this rite. Though for a different reason. I shall tell you why.

"In the lands where the Griffin is practised, women learn a form of dancing that makes the stomach as strong as iron, yet supple and dextrous. This dancing is as ancient as the temples of Babylon. Those who master it can move their bodies with the grace and vigour of the snake. By this means, they strengthen muscles here, deep within their sex, so that they are both powerful and gentle. This is a skill few women attain, for it requires long study. In many lands, only harlots still know these things; but once they were common knowledge taught to all women. Here, I will show you."

She took hold of Victor's hand and placed it against her stomach, the tips of his fingers resting on skin. "Now press," she said. "Press as hard as you can. See how far into my flesh you can force your fingers."

Victor gazed at her in bewilderment. Only after she made the same request again did he do as he was asked. At first he pressed lightly, then with greater force. At last he placed all his strength behind the effort, but with no result. Seraphina's belly was firm as a wall.

"You see," she said. "I am an old woman; but these muscles are so well trained, no man's hand can force its way forward. And *inside*, Victor: I could still hold a man's organ as if it were in a vice. Or stroke it as gently as a mother strokes her baby's cheeks. I can coax a man to do whatever I wish. Elizabeth has no such capacity. She has not yet the power to govern the man. She and I have discussed this; she understands better than you, Victor, the dangers of the Griffin."

I saw how stung Victor was by Seraphina's chastisement. Afterwards he lamented her ignorance, as he saw it. "The woman knows nothing of science; she is a superstitious old crone. She maligns the anatomists who have taught us all we know about the human frame. And how can she be so certain that the male seed does not contain the complete child? Van Leeuwenhoek believed so; does she pretend to know better? It is, in any case, not a midwife's place to question physicians as if she knew better in such matters."

As long as Seraphina continued with us, Victor reluctantly promised to await her guidance in preparing for the rite. But now, after her departure, he felt released from his promise. "Why should we wait longer?" he asked. "We are more than learned enough for so simple a practice."

I protested that the practice did not seem "simple" at all. But, as always, Victor was eager to rush forward onto unexplored ground. I recall that once he told me how ignorance *hurt* him like a burning pain he must eliminate; whereas knowledge worked on him like laudanum, a soothing drug that drove away the pain. I confessed to him that the very image of the Griffin, let alone the ritual that bore its name, was fearful to me. I could see no relationship between a loving act and this monstrous creature with its predatory claws and fangs. Was this not clearly a warning that the rite was hazardous in ways we did not know? Else why were there pictures of the Griffin devouring the lovers?

"This is only to drive off the faint-hearted," Victor insisted. "The adepts wish to keep their knowledge secret. So they surround it with hobgoblins and witchery. One must be bold to learn new things."

Still this rite remained frightful to me for reasons Victor could not understand. It would change my body; afterwards I would no longer be a virgin. I had not thought on this until Victor began to press me so insistently to join him in the exercise. Now I realised there was a barrier that I was loath to cross in haste and out of mere curiosity. I needed a woman to assure me of my decision, and there was no one I could turn to. I knew that Victor would think me foolish to hold back for this reason; he would say that I was being "womanish," the word he used for everything he wished to dismiss. And I knew that in time I would surrender to his wishes.

EDITOR'S NOTE
To Fly with the Griffin

In alchemical lore, the Griffin is a dual symbol. As the legendary guardian of the Golden Hoard, it represents secrecy and so emphasises the necessarily occult nature of the alchemical Work. The Griffin also represents carnality, seen as an uncontrolled animal passion. Taken together, the two faces of this fabulous beast are a warning that the sexual exercises employed by the adepts are a deep secret that must be well-guarded, lest they be improperly used.

The practice here referred to as "Flying with the Griffin" is presented in graphic detail in the Lavender Book; it takes the form of a series of elaborate sexual postures which guide the male and female partners into a state of suspended genital congress that may last for as long as an entire night. The man and woman progress through several stages of coupling that supposedly parallel the reaction of the chemical substances sulphur (hot/dry/male) and mercury (cool/wet/female) in the retort as these elements evolve toward becoming the Philosopher's Stone.

The scene depicted in the pictures is a lush pleasure garden, the fruited trees fully in bloom and crowded with songbirds; in the back-

ground of the series, one sees the setting of the sun, the passage of the
moon, the rising of the sun, indicating that the ritual is intended to last
through a full night, or at least for a term of some hours. The male is,
as usual in the book, a handsome, swarthy figure who approaches the
garden dressed in regal attire under a many-coloured canopy and followed by an entourage of odalisques. The female who awaits his coming is a typical Oriental concubine; voluptuous of form, richly costumed
and bejewelled, she waits beneath a magnificently flowering tree at the
centre of the garden. She and her princely consort greet one another
affectionately and are disrobed by the concubines; the harem remains in
attendance while the partners perform the prescribed ceremony, at times
bringing them nourishment as the long night passes. Their intercourse is
described as an exacting, highly ritualised discipline. The man is to
remain fully aroused and inserted in the woman for several hours; his
rôle is to remain largely immobile, more acted upon than acting. The
female's rôle, symbolising the specially active character of quicksilver in
the alchemical process, is particularly onerous. She is required to arrange
her torso and limbs in a variety of provocative poses, allowing her partner neither to lose his tumescence nor to attain climax. By the time the
night has passed, if the female has performed well, the male's desire is
meant to subside; a superior state of non-carnal bliss ensues. The male
is then permitted to remain in a trance-like condition for several hours
longer. The illustrations suggest that his mind has become as vast and
formless as an ocean of light. He communes with the divine; the women
bathe and perfume the courtesan; she dutifully waits at her master's side
for his return from his ethereal travels.

While there can be no doubt that these illustrations were used for
guidance by generations of alchemists who understood their cyphered
meaning, the relations between Victor and Elizabeth deviated signifi-
cantly from the conventional pattern. In consequence of their mentor's
idiosyncratic influence, there is no hint of the female subservience one
finds in the courtesans who fill the Lavender Book. No doubt this is the
meaning that lies behind the phrase "sharing the reins." In Tantric texts
that have only recently been translated one does find references to a
practice called "serving the goddess." These passages describe tech-

niques for the arousal and protracted gratification of the female; but surely the women who would submit to such practices would, once again, be prostitutes. The demands imposed by Seraphina upon her pupils, therefore, have some other origin, which deviates from the alchemical tradition as it survives in any document I have been able to examine.

As Seraphina would have it, the rites she taught descended from an early period of matriarchy in which the procreative powers of women were surrounded with an aura of magic. This fanciful historical construction bears all the earmarks of an old wives' tale. It should be noted, however, that travellers to certain remote areas of the South Seas and the African interior have reported the discovery of tribes in which reproduction is to this day shrouded in such ignorance that men are understood to play no part in the process. Whether a source of this kind can be identified for the alchemical tradition, and how far back in time it reaches, only future scholarship will be able to say.

How Things
Went Awry

April ———, 178———

I worry that Victor is so forceful with me; his impetuosity quite unsettles my confidence. So much depends upon his powers of control. Yet he presses me constantly to undertake the Griffin. He tells me he has used the cinnabar mixture that Seraphina left with us and that this can be relied upon to govern his emissions. But I believe the risk is too great. I plead with him to wait until the bleeding is near, when it will be safer to try the rite. He agrees—but he is impatient.

April ———, 178———

I ask Victor if he will love me less when I cease to be a virgin. He returns my question. "Will you love me the less when I have given up my virginity?"

"It is not the same for the man," I tell him.

"Only because men are not so quick to be fearful."

"Men take; women are taken from. So every girl is taught."

"I shall not 'take' from you. I am not some vile seducer—or is that how you regard me?"

He assures me that he finds in me a purity that can never be sullied, a virtue greater than the state of my body. I ask if he will take care not to hurt me. I want him to know my fears. He promises to be careful in the extreme; I believe him, but I shudder at his eagerness.

April ———, 178———

This night all seemed exactly right . . . but I am reluctant to proceed. I feel a sickly kind of panic rising in me . . . I break off the exercise and plead with Victor to wait another day. He agrees—but sullenly.

April ———, 178———

Again I draw back.

May ———, 178———

Victor is cross with me because I delay so long. He withdraws to his workshop for the entire day and works alone. "You think I am impelled by lust," he tells me later. "You do not trust my love." I protest this is not true; I would gamble my life upon his love—but love is no protection from the danger I fear.

May ———, 178———

My evil dream has returned. I wake in the night to find myself crying out in my sleep. I see myself once again struggling to be born . . . I cannot draw breath. I see the bird-man stretching out his claw. When I wake, I dash to the window and throw it open as if there were no air left in my room.

"Think of the Great Work," Seraphina said, "as something that wants to be born out of your soul."

May ———, 178———

Again I refuse. Victor says I have no daring. "This is why the Work takes so long to reach its goal," he tells me. "It must wait upon the whims of the woman. Mother says the woman must take part; but what if she will not? What if she fears too much? Then how is the Work to go forward?"

He is unjust, but I know it is his disappointment that makes him so. He longs to learn what the Griffin has to teach us, and I, in my caution, hold him back from that knowledge. Victor asks correctly then: How can the chymical marriage be accomplished?

I cannot say.

Once Francine told me that Mother had selected her to be Victor's *Soror.* What would she do now? Would she ride the Griffin? Would she trust Victor? If only I might ask her! But Victor and I have agreed to study in secret.

May ———, *178*———

I visit Mother's studio and loiter over the picture of the chained maiden. Was she pressed by the man the way Victor presses me? Did she finally give way out of love or out of exhaustion? Did she fear to be seen a coward—as I do?

If only I might talk to Mother . . . but Victor is right. If I went to her, she would forbid us to continue. Victor would say I had betrayed him.

He does not know how hard it is for me to choose. He means me no harm. He asks me to be his companion. I must be as brave as he would have me be.[1]

⟡

But did I say the words? Or only intend to say them? And did he hear? Or did he not wish to hear? I cannot remember. I recall only the animal panic that swept over me. And the cruel pain. And the astonishment that was even crueller. And after a moment of merciful confusion, the knowledge that all had gone awry.

This I remember of that night, now weeks away in time.

For hours we lay together sweetly curled into each other's embrace. I let him pass his hand over my nakedness again and again so that he might soften me; I let him touch me everywhere. He explored me eagerly, making me ready to be entered. I became all water, silvery yielding water; and he all fire, crimson consuming fire. He was so magnificently aroused, taut to bursting; I took pleasure in his excitement. I wanted to taste it on my lips. I wanted to clothe myself in his excitement and make it my own. Did he feel the same? Did he also want to feed on

---

[1]Following this entry, two pages have been torn from the book. The next entry has no date assigned. —R.W.

my passion? Now I saw how effortless it was to do as the women do in the pictures, guiding the man along the very edge of desire. How delicious it was to stand with him so close to that edge, to tempt falling! A moment more and we would mount and soar, sharing the reins of the beast.

I sat myself as the instruction showed, our eyes gazing directly at one another. I let one leg stretch to the ground, the other I drew round him at the waist to hold him tight against me. My breasts were placed so that the tips might lightly brush against his chest. We waited until we could feel one another's heartbeat, until the cadence of his breath joined with mine. He reached to spread me and make me ready. Then he waited as the pictures show, only just touching where I open. He waited while I made him moist. The heat between us was as fierce as the alchymical furnace. I pressed closer; my breasts spread against him. He entered.

We were that close. . . . There was mounting hunger, and mounting fear, the two wildly mingled. I relished both. I wanted this again, this moment of freedom before the irrevocable moment. I wanted and did not want.

And at last when it seemed there was no time left to turn back, I said at his ear, *Not yet, my love. Wait with me, one night longer. Let me cling to this virgin's body one night more.*

EDITOR'S NOTE
The Fate of the Lady in Chains

For love she unwisely wildly gave,
For love past all that flesh could bear,
She wept by waters that would be her grave,
Lady in chains whose fate I share.

At no point in my editorial labours did I find it more necessary to play the literary detective than in solving the mystery of the nameless lady in chains. The poem I quote above, in which she anonymously appears, came to hand as a loose page that lay unbound in Elizabeth Frankenstein's memoir; I was left with no way of knowing where it might belong or when it might have been written. For years I kept it gummed to the inside cover of the memoir, waiting to find its proper place in the chronicle. It was only when I recovered the paintings of Caroline Frankenstein from M. de Rollinat in 1816 that the riddle began to unfold.

I have already mentioned the fourth and smallest of the paintings I bought from M. de Rollinat: I will remind the reader that this was the picture of a drowning woman wrapped in chains. No sooner did I lay eyes on this, than Elizabeth's enigmatic poem reverberated in my mind. The lady in chains, then, was named Rosalba, the word I found scrawled on the back of the canvas.

But who was Rosalba and in what sense did Elizabeth Frankenstein claim to "share her fate"?

The answer to this question I found by the sheerest good luck, as so frequently happens in the course of the scholar's quest. In the winter of 1831, while pursuing my investigations into the alchemical tradition, I chanced upon a paper in the current *Transactions of the Ashmolean Society* by Sir Almroth Crosland. Titled *"Mysterium Coniunctionis:* Alchemical Allusions in the Later Writings of Sir Isaac Newton," Sir Almroth's paper hinted discreetly at the same conclusion I had by then independently reached: namely, that alchemical rites frequently masked an underlying erotic intention. In his study, Sir Almroth focussed upon the possibility (unlikely, in my judgement) that Isaac Newton had dabbled in certain forms of sodomy as part of his alchemical experiments. This, Sir Almroth believed, accounted for the severe bouts of guilty depression the great scientist suffered in his later years. In passing, Sir Almroth noted: "What risk these practices carry for the mind and soul is well attested by the case of the unfortunate Rosalba di Gozzi, which may serve as a stern warning to the uninitiated. The full story can be found in Mme. Louise Isabeau de Damville's *Mémoires historiques 1647."* How could I doubt that this Rosalba, mentioned by Sir Almroth in connection with alchemical research, was the very woman in the painting I saw each time I lifted my head to peer across my study?

Sir Almroth's authority, however, proved to be an elusive document. I spent no less than three years tracing Mme. de Damville's memoirs. In the meanwhile I discovered that its author, a learned mistress of the French Dauphin, was herself rumoured to be something of an alchemical adept. When at last I was able to locate one of the few surviving copies of her work, I realised at once that the search had been worthwhile. The lady's history made everything brilliantly clear, though the truth it revealed was perturbing in the extreme.

Rosalba di Gozzi, the subject of Lady Caroline's enigmatic painting, was the youngest daughter of Alessandro di Gozzi, Doge of Venice during the early seventeenth century and head of the notorious Council of Ten. Serving as confessor to the Gozzi family was a young Dominican friar named Lorenzo Querini, also the scion of a highly-placed Venetian family. Querini was a practitioner of the alchemical arts, who had begun his studies under Sendivogius in Byzantium; his reputation included rumours that he had found the Philosopher's Stone itself and had publicly transformed the metals. His alchemical training brought him to the notice of Signora di Gozzi, who was an avid student of the spagyric arts. The true moral character of Querini is difficult to assess; Mme. de Damville suggests that the friar may have become the paramour of the Doge's wife. This ambiguity makes it impossible to evaluate his intentions toward Rosalba, who, though only fifteen years of age, joined her mother in becoming the friar's pupil. The result was both scandalous and tragic.

One morning in the fall of 1647, the Gozzi household awoke to discover that Querini and Rosalba were gone. Signora di Gozzi gave out the report that the two had eloped. Agents of the Council of Ten were hot on their heels, but only Querini was found. Within a fortnight of his flight, he was hunted down—half-starved, hiding in a cave in the south of Italy. What followed was the sort of primitive vengeance that was typical of Italians of that era. He was given no trial; instead he was mutilated and emasculated by the Doge's henchmen before being subjected to judicial strangulation. Only moments before his death, the conscience-stricken Querini confessed that he was guilty of a crime far blacker than elopement; he had violated the young virgin placed in his charge. But where Rosalba might be found he could not say; not even the most expert torture could wring an answer from him. He claimed he had fled Venice in shame, leaving her behind. The only defence the man made for himself was to claim that he had been tempted beyond all endurance by certain alchemical rites and that, in a fit of madness, he had been driven to his crime. Needless to say, his appeal did not succeed in saving him from the garotte. It was not until two months later that the full tale was known.

The remains of Rosalba were found one morning by a gondolier; she was dragged from the depths of the canals, wrapped in chains. At first it was suspected that Querini had murdered her; but a message in a locket found on her otherwise nude body made clear she had taken her own life. The message confessed that she had indeed been violently dishonoured by Querini and that she could not live with the shame of that act. But she sought to absolve her lover from all guilt by insisting that "the Griffin" was to blame. Only the most learned of alchemical adepts could understand what this confession meant. By the time I came upon it, the full particulars of the rite that is associated with the Griffin's flight had become known to me from other sources, mainly those dealing in the left-handed Tantra. The Griffin, I had learned, was the most demanding of all the sexual yogas, rarely attempted and more rarely carried to a successful conclusion. The rite failed so frequently that it was dismissed by some as little better than a seductive deception without any spiritual efficacy. Mme. de Damville gives no details on the matter, but she offers this cryptic warning:

> Let women who would become pupils of the Work take heed. All their sisters who have sojourned in the shadowy terrain of the spagyric arts know full well that the faithful *Soror* makes her person available for the chymical marriage at the risk of her honour— and, indeed, of her life. The fact that these perils are not frankly recorded in the literature is a treachery against all laborants. Be it known that I speak from onerous personal knowledge. Particularly in this rite, the rôle of the woman is supremely hazardous even when the male consort is a trusted intimate. For we deal here with passions over which even the most virtuous of men exercise uncertain governance. I firmly recommend that no woman undertake

the Flight of the Griffin (or even other rites that are less extreme) except under the attentive supervision of a female companion.

The events that led to Rosalba's death explained the lurid way in which Lady Caroline had painted her in her canvas, which doubtless she intended as a warning to all women who would undertake the journey to the chemical marriage. The vaginal blood that turns the seas to crimson was the sign of the trusting young virgin's violation. The winged beast that appears in the sky of Lady Caroline's painting is obviously the Griffin; there can be no doubt that the limp body the beast holds in its mouth is the condemned friar. Thus, piece by piece, I had assembled the full story. After so many years of searching, I had learnt the historical parallel Elizabeth Frankenstein drew between herself and the lady in chains. And at last I understood the full measure of Victor Frankenstein's depravity.

Part Three

The Letter

I shall make no comment on your conduct or any appeal to the world. Let my wrongs sleep with me! Soon, very soon, I shall be at peace. When you receive this, my burning head will be cold. You will never . . . . again.

I would encounter a thousand deaths, rather than a night like the last. Your treatment has thrown my mind into a state of chaos; yet I am serene. I go to find comfort in the one . . . .

Had I experienced this horror at the hands of a stranger who sought nothing more than the pleasure a man may steal from a woman, I should have sunk to the very depths of shame. But to have been used thus in a solemn rite by one I have loved so well shatters all . . . .

God bless you! May you never know by experience what you have made me . . . . Should your sensibility ever awake, remorse will find its way to your heart; and, in the midst of . . . . and sensual pleasures, I shall appear before you, *the victim of your . . . . and deviation from rectitude.*[1]

[1]Elizabeth Frankenstein elected not to rewrite this letter, but to preserve it in her memoir in a deteriorated condition that leaves several passages all but illegible. The writing was done in obvious haste. The paper, a roughly torn sheet, is creased many times over, suggesting that it was at some point crumpled; the ink is water-stained and in places wholly washed away. Given its significance, there is no question but that the letter must be reproduced here; even so, I have reconstructed only those portions whose meaning was reasonably certain. —R.W.

The writing of this letter, begun over and again, occupied me through most of the night that followed. Outside my window as I wrote, a steady downpour drove in from the lake, hammering incessantly at the pane; it did not abate until dawn was almost arrived. When I could write no more, I folded the page into a wallet and left the house, having slept not at all. The morning was storm-tossed, frequently crossed with showers; lightning danced a mad jig upon the rain-swept mountains to the east. By the time I reached the quay my dress was streaming and I shook with chill. The fishermen had not yet set out for their day's work. Untying a battered skiff I found tethered at the dock, I cast off upon the lake. Would the boat stay afloat even long enough to carry me beyond the shallows? An hour later, lulled by the gently rocking rhythm of the lake, I found I had drifted as far as Hermance and had fallen into a sort of stupor. By then the sky had cleared; in the distance, Mont Blanc, which so often hides its lordly face in cloud like the God of the Hebrews, stood suddenly revealed, still, snowy, and serene, a roseate pyramid burning in the morning light. O, consoling beauty! "See," a voice within me whispered, "there is still such grandeur to behold."

And my heart answered yes!

An hour later, I had managed to guide my boat back to shore and begun the long walk home. A wagon heading to Belrive to load hay stopped for me at the turning and delivered me to the château. Celeste was just laying out breakfast; bewildered to see me in my distraught condition, she hurried me off to the kitchen, brought me a blanket, and served me steaming coffee. She besieged me with questions, but I answered nothing. I warmed myself at the fire and then, returning to my room, laid aside my drenched clothing. Not until weeks later did I discover the wallet that held this letter. By then, what I read seemed to me the words of someone else—a girl I had once known. I preserved the missive as if it might have been written by another person.

An Unchronicled
Time

How odd a work a diary is, a register of experience more than a calendar of days. It is the record of time's mental dimension. A fleeting instant of hope, joy, or fear may unleash a torrent of words; whole books may not suffice to write down what one gleans from a single moment's amazement. But there might follow uneventful weeks or months that reduce to a few poor lines, a dead time when nothing of import happens. And then there are the pages that matter most of all, those where silence governs: the chapters that shall never be set down because the will to write—perhaps the very will to live—evaporates. History breaks off when experience surpasses words, when grief, suffering, or shame runs so deep that one despairs of the future. Yet in these unrecorded passages of life there can occur changes that shape the soul for the rest of one's days.

If the importance of such unchronicled times were to be measured out in pages, there would now follow in my diary entire volumes—all blank. For months I wrote nothing—cared not to write, could not bring myself to write as much as a word; the pen weighed in my hand like a mountain that I had no hope of moving. In truth, my mind was as void as the sheet before me; I had been rendered witless, shocked into mute incomprehension like a soldier who, struck by the cannon's blast, wanders from the field of battle no longer knowing where he stands.

After that night, nothing could be the same. We were not enemies,

Victor and I. Our condition was worse than that. We were fragments of a loving union that had been shattered by the worst of treacheries. There was no hate between us; hatred is at least a bond of passionate warmth between antagonists. But for us there was only the cold of absolute mistrust and immeasurable despair. We met, we spoke—guardedly, minimally—across an Arctic waste of remorse. Both knew that what had been broken was beyond mending; Victor could not even bring himself to beg for forgiveness. No doubt he took my reticence to mean that anger had closed my mind against any appeal he might make; but in truth my condition could best be called one of *surprise*, stupefying surprise that left my faculties in suspension. I lived in stunned bewilderment. If we spoke, I found I was not listening; a single burning question occupied my thoughts: *What did it mean that Victor had used me so?*

And having asked that, I brooded on the terrible possibility that he had never harboured true affection for me, had never seen me as anything more than a sluttish amusement. Could it be that, for all these years while he pretended to be my affectionate brother, he had been plotting this assault upon my virtue? Or was this something worse than one man's villainy revealing itself? I arrived at the blackest thought of all: What if his love had been real as he professed; and what if love, even when real, is so fragile a thing that none can trust to it? Is our nature so perverse that a moment's evil impulse can shred even the truest bond? The compunction I saw etched in Victor's expression told me that this must indeed be the case. He cared; he sorrowed; he would give his life to make amends. He was a victim of the same horror that had touched me; a frenzied, unfeeling passion greater than he could withstand. Even so, I could offer him no forgiveness. Pity, perhaps . . . but not forgiveness.

As I chased these doubts round in circles in my mind, the vitality ebbed from me; I lost all appetite, grew listless, and wandered the house wraith-like in a haze of distraction. Some days I kept to my room from morning to night. Everyone took anxious note of my decline; they assumed I had fallen ill, which in truth was soon to be the case. For this was a plague year. The scarlet fever, advancing inexorably westward from the Levant, reached Lyons that spring, then moved like a phantom marauder through the villages of the Rhône. When word went out that the conquering contagion had extended its deadly perimeter to the environs of Geneva, I went to bed each night praying it would soon claim me. *I did not want to be with him! I did not wish to be reminded!* Yet all the while I knew there was no way to keep from being reminded. Each night when I undressed, I saw the marks he had left upon me in his frenzy. In time these would heal and fade; but there were other, deeper wounds I bore inside me. These I would see every time I gazed into a mirror and saw the sullen shade that had fallen across my eyes.

Others might attribute my melancholy to illness, but there was one who could not be deceived; Mother's astute intuition told her there was more to my sorrowing mood than I had yet revealed. She took me aside and asked what troubled me. Did it have to do with Victor? she wondered, knowing full well that it must. She pleaded with me to say; I kept my silence, but her persistence made evasion difficult. For this reason too I wished the fever might take me. I would then be locked away and given permission to become a recluse—and perhaps finally . . .

Lady in chains whose fate I share . . .

I had never understood how one so young could cast her life away. But now the bleakness to which I woke each morning taught me how burdensome existence can become. When the fever did at last seize upon me, I gave thanks, hoping its invisible hand might bring me the peace I would never find the courage to grasp for myself. As I lay near death, secretly I hoped the fire raging in my blood would become my chains, my drowning pool, my deliverance. But Mother would not let that be. Weak as she was herself, she insisted on being my nurse. Many arguments were urged to persuade her from attending upon me; Father all but placed himself on guard outside my door to bar her access. But when she heard that the life of her favourite was menaced, she could not still her anxiety. She insisted upon being at my sickbed by day and night, cooling my brow and feeding me with her own hand. Her watchful attentions at last triumphed over the distemper; I was saved, but the consequences were fatal to my preserver. A week after my fever broke, Mother sickened. Her illness was accompanied by the most alarming symptoms; soon enough the physicians whom Father summoned for her were prognosticating the worst event. "We shall lose her," Father announced after the doctors had been with her, and unabashedly broke into tears.

In her last days, the fortitude of this best of women did not desert her. Even though the fever had seemingly depleted the last ounce of her energy, she asked if she might sketch me to pass the heavy hours. I of course agreed and sat at her bedside while she made a miniature drawing of me, carefully bending over the task until her stamina failed or the light of day faded at the window. This diverting project momentarily buoyed her spirits. "How distressed you are, my dear," she said as she searched my face with her keen artist's eye. "Not all the concern I see there can be for me. I see anger and hurt; I will not ask you why, for I hope these are transient humours that will soon pass. You will understand if I omit them from my sketch. I want to draw you in your pride and strength, as the woman I would have you be when I am gone, one who shall be her own master."

And so she did, making as fine a work as any she had ever done. I gazed upon the result as if I might be looking into a magic mirror that showed the ideal identity lying behind the afflictions of life. But when she had finished, Mother did not give the miniature to me but to Victor, asking that he see in it the sister-bride she had meant to be her best gift to him. "My children," she said, joining our hands at the last, "my firmest hopes of future happiness were placed upon the prospect of your union. This expectation will now have to be your father's consolation; for my sake, please do not cheat him of this one blessing. Elizabeth, my love, you must supply my place in the household. I regret especially to be taken from you, my dear. For you are that bright spirit on whom my fondest hopes were set. Your destiny in this dark world remains unfulfilled. Yet how golden you look to me still! Happy and beloved as I have been, is it not hard to quit you all?" She fell into a deep calm. At her side, I bent to listen if she had more to say, for I saw her lips moving. Her final words, repeated again and again were, "A little patience and all will be over."

She died peacefully; her countenance expressed affection even in death. To the last she held tight to the sprig of green that was ever with her; even in death she would not release it until I had pried open her fingers. I could not imagine suffering a greater loss in all the rest of my days; yet I confess that some coward part of me found welcome relief in her death. She was now beyond knowing the truth about Victor and myself. I would never be called upon to tell her that the union she died still urging upon us could never be, that it had been torn out of our lives by the roots.

Less than a fortnight after Mother was buried, Victor, waiting no longer than minimal propriety demanded, announced that he would be leaving for Ingolstadt to begin his university education. With one swift stroke, this resolved a question about Victor's future that had long divided the family. Father had never approved of seeing Victor become Seraphina's pupil; he regarded the alchymical Work as an intolerable waste of time. I had several times heard him press Victor to turn his attention to "the modern system of science," as he called it. "The Newtonian philosophy," he contended, "possesses far greater power than the ancients who were sadly burdened by wild fancies. Agrippa, Paracelsus, Albertus Magnus . . . these have become, with the progress of time, intellectual refuse. They do not merit your genius." Perhaps if Father had been at home more often, he might have taken greater issue regarding Victor's studies with Seraphina. But in his absence, Mother's wishes prevailed and the alchymical adepts remained for a time the lords of Victor's imagination. Now at last, with Mother gone, Father would have his way. Victor agreed—nay, more than agreed, *insisted*—that he be sent away. His reasons, as I well knew, were not wholly academic. The university would be his escape, a chance to be out of my sight, removed from my hostile eye and the condemnation he found there each day. Only my illness and Mother's death had delayed his departure as long as this.

In less than a week, Victor was gone, leaving me with a curt farewell, frankly too ashamed to raise his eyes to mine for more than an instant—and yet resentful that I would offer no hint of forgiveness. From that resentment I saw a small flame of defiance leap forth, as if to serve notice that he would not let one vicious act crush his hopes in life. We did not kiss; we did not embrace. My hand in his at the door was limp, my gaze cold. I was not alone in bidding him a chill farewell; Alu flapped to my shoulder and sat staring sullenly at Victor. Glancing once at the bird, he seemed to grow visibly more ashamed under her scrutiny than under mine, and turned quickly to leave. I sent him on his way cruelly judged, no longer my brother, my lover, my friend. He would surely not be back until Christmas, and made no promise even of that. All that night I wept convulsively for my stubborn harshness. But I could not, *could not* forgive!

The following week, Father, still nursing the deep melancholy of his loss, was making ready to travel again. He had no wish to go and apologised profusely for leaving me so soon after Mother's death. But he felt his private sorrow overtaken by the affairs of the greater world. This time he would be bound for Paris, where fateful events were taking shape. King Louis's financial condition had reached the very climax of desperation. Even while Mother lay dying, a succession of couriers had arrived from Versailles to deliver pleading messages to Geneva's leading money-lender; at last a minister of the Crown had travelled apace across the Alps to beg Father's assistance. Father was given to understand that, if he did not come immediately to compound for a loan, the King would be forced to summon the Estates-General and beg for subvention, the which he dare not; for what might happen then, none could say. Father grumbled with reluctance, even while he made arrangements to answer the summons. "It would serve the royal dunce right if his entire decrepit house came crashing down about his ears. Save for M. Necker who tends his empty treasury, he is surrounded by knaves and fools. Anything I lend him now will be good money thrown after bad; but what choice have I? When a King becomes your debtor to the tune of four hundred thousand *livres*, you may as well regard him as your blood brother."

As I watched Father's chaise disappear along the road to Geneva, I realised that, for the first time since I had come to the château, I was without family. Once again I was an orphan. Only the slow-witted and painfully diffident Ernest was left behind with me; but no one could be less cheering company than he. With each passing year, he did less to mask how much he despised me for diverting our mother's favour. And now, with Mother gone, he felt free to express his loathing of "the Gipsy bastard" openly. We thus took pains to stay out of each other's way. I would have all the solitude I needed to think upon the bleak turn my life had taken.

I hoped Francine might visit and stay; I feared that my evil dream would return, as it often did when my mind was unsettled, and there would be no one to turn to for solace. But more and more Francine was compelled to play the pastor's wife and travel where Charles's ever-widening responsibilities took him. His work in the world took him to convocations far afield; he and Francine might be absent for months at a time. Once when she found an occasion to spend the day, I tried to unburden myself to her, but discovered I could not rehearse my grief. She saw at once that I was distressed, but when I could tell her nothing of the reason why, she set my melancholy down to mourning and assured me that my despondency would pass. *Why,* I asked myself, *can I not open my heart even to my closest friend in the world?*—and realised I was shamed speechless for Victor. When, upon his departure, he had raised his eyes to glance briefly into mine, I had read there the mute message: *Please never tell!* And I would never do so; I could not separate myself from his disgrace. This much, a slender bond of shared humiliation, survived between us.

Alone much of each day, I told myself I must concentrate my thoughts and make the days pass productively; but I found myself at sixes and sevens, unable to take up any task that required application. With Alu following through the trees—for she had elected to become my companion—I wandered the grounds, often straying for whole days into the high meadows. Or if the weather grew foul, I turned to my poetry or practised the harpsichord. I took book after book from the library, but my attention invariably wandered from the page. I gathered my clothes for mending, but found my fingers too nervous for the work and finally laid all aside as too tedious. Nothing held my interest more than transiently. Yet my mind seemed strangely alert with an expectant restlessness, as if I might be waiting to hear some signal . . . something, but what it might be, I could not guess.

One morning in the second week after Father left, I woke to find myself deathly ill. My bedclothes were sweated through and nausea gripped me fiercely as if an ogre's hand were trying to tear the insides out of me. A relapse, I thought at once, and feared the fever had been fanned back into flame. I kept to my room most of that day, taking no food, hardly any water; even so, when there was nothing left inside me, I retched up spit and empty air until the muscles of my belly ached. The next morning brought no relief, nor the next; I was unable to lift myself from bed, so depleted had I become. At last Joseph the major-domo sent for Dr. Montreaux, who arrived late in the afternoon of a stormy day. He was a stiffly formal man whom I found intimidating. He had attended me on several occasions in the past, mainly for childhood diseases that had required him to do little more than touch my pulse and look down my throat; but this time he examined me with much greater care, asking me to disrobe. I did so, obliging him passively in all he asked. As he lit candles on the bureau to provide more light in the darkening room, I arranged myself upon my bed and, at his request, opened myself. As he leaned above me, he covered my face with a linen kerchief, as doctors do when they examine the woman's lower parts. I thought, *What foolishness this is, to cover my face while all the rest of me is stripped bare! This way our eyes cannot meet; but is that to spare me the embarrassment of revealing my blushes, or Dr. Montreaux the discomfort of seeing me blush?* His manner was suitably detached, but his touch disagreeably rough as he explored well inside me. All the while he worked over me, I peered out from under one corner of the kerchief at the dismal counterpane above my bed where the rain trickled down in crooked streams like tears from a weeping sky. Stray thoughts ran in my feverish head: How odd that a man might be licenced to see women so fully revealed when no woman is similarly licenced to look upon men. Why was this permitted? Of course, because this was a man of science who explored my body with a cold, anatomical eye. He did not find the sight of me in the least stimulating—or so I must believe. I recalled telling Mother how I would blush to pose naked for a man who wished to paint me. Yet a painter would not touch or probe me as the doctor did. I remembered how Victor had gazed upon me when we Fed the Lions, deliberately allowing my body to arouse his voluptuary nature. But he had not touched me either, not then. How many ways a man might gaze upon a woman—as artist, as physician, as lover. Strange to say, I found the safest of these to be the physician; for I was nothing more to him than a lifeless automaton he might take apart and put together. Physicians learn the body by studying the dead; perhaps Dr. Montreaux has learnt to view the female form as if it were a corpse laid out before him. But, in truth, he was scrutinising more than my physique. An examination as thorough as this allowed him to see right through to my moral character. A woman's honour is stamped upon her body. He would surely discover that I was no longer a virgin; he might finish by believing I was a common slut. And how was I to exculpate myself? Would he understand if I told him about the Rite of the Griffin? Would he condone what is expected of the Mystic Sister? Would he—

And then he was finished. He drew the coverlet over me and said, gravely but gently, "It is not the fever, my dear. You are with child."

The doctor stayed the night at the château as my fever mounted and my pains grew worse. He did not wish to ride back to Geneva along the dark, rain-swept roads and have to ring at the gates of the city. The next morning he departed, promising to look in each day until the crisis was resolved. When he called on the morrow, he found Celeste at my side. She had guessed what my condition might be even before Dr. Montreaux made his examination, and now stayed to cool my brow and hold me close when I began to shudder. I soon lost track of time, but knew vaguely, whenever Celeste came to feed me some broth and bread, that another day was passing. Nothing I ate stayed down; I was racked with convulsive vomiting. My pains were often more than I could bear without swooning, and then my mind would pass in and out of lucidity, sometimes leaving me lost among cruel hallucinations. The bird-man, who now resembled Dr. Montreaux, came to me in my dreams each time I shut my eyes, making me afraid to rest. When I woke, I pleaded with Celeste: "You will not let him use the claw!"

She, knowing my fears as well as Mother once had, was quick to assure me, "Never, never, child! I have sent for Christina. She is on her way and will tend you as long as need be."

"The doctor will permit her to be here?"

"He is a good man and will understand. Be assured, I shall *make* him understand what you want."

Christina was the most trusted midwife among the local women; she had learnt her craft directly from Seraphina many years before. Despite my pains, I was comforted just to know she would soon be in the room. But as the spasms came and went with ever greater ferocity, I felt my courage draining away. "I am with child, Celeste," I said sinking my face into her great aproned breast and letting tears of self-pity flow. Though she was permeated by the pungent aromas of the kitchen, the Celeste I clung to in my need was not the cook but the cunning woman who could recite ten centuries of martyred names when the women met in the glade. Gentle, wise, and courageous Celeste! How good it felt to be in her embrace. I knew my condition was bad; the child inside me would likely not survive to be properly born; the fever had made my body inhospitable. In my weakened condition, I feared I might suffer my mother's fate: to die giving birth, though my child was yet a half-formed life.

I had no way of knowing how long I suffered like this before the baby was ejected. Several times I woke to find Christina standing over me, patiently waiting. Once she bent to whisper at my ear, "When *he* is gone, I will give you something for the pain." And so she did, an herbal mixture that made me dizzy and numb and soon lulled my raging mind into a dreamless sleep. Other times, Dr. Montreaux was there, looking ever more grave. "The worst will soon be past" was the most consolation he could offer. On one occasion, as he prepared to leave, I heard him in my half-sleep instructing Celeste to send word to Victor and the Baron. That jolted me sharply awake. When he was gone, I called out to Celeste anxiously and pleaded with her not to send to either. "Promise me!" I insisted.

"But they must know sometime, my dear."

"Why must they ever know?"

"Because Victor is the father. He must do what is honourable."

"You are wrong. Victor is not the father. You are presumptuous to say so."

"What are you saying, child? Who else could be the father?"

"That is for me to know, not my servants." I said this trying to sound as haughty as Mother had sounded when she wished to have her way.

"You have no reason to fear," Celeste continued. "Victor will marry you, as is proper."

"Never! I have no desire to marry Victor." In my desperation I began to babble feverishly. "I have no wish to see him at all. He is not the father, he is not! Many men come and go in this house. Vile seducers they are, as you well know, Celeste. Have I not heard you warn the serving girls about the Baron's guests? You tell them to tie their skirts at the ankle when they are sent out among the gentlemen. *Gentlemen!* Alley cats, that is what Father calls them. He says they would not be respected as betters by the barnyard animals. Do you not recall that the Marquis de Chastelneuf came calling in . . . June—yes, June it was. He is known to keep at least four mistresses my age—and younger. Perhaps he . . . or Pietro della Valle the poet, who was with us before that; is he not an infamous roué? Maybe *he* is the father. . . . But how shall I tell which, which, *which?* There have been so many, how can you expect me to know? When the Countess Landseer visits, she leaves her bedroom door open—with her husband's knowledge. She was visited by three lovers in one night when last she was here. Why should I be expected to name the father of my baby when it is said the Countess cannot vouch for the father of any of her children? Why do you look shocked? You think of me as an angel; but you do not truly know me. Remember I was raised a Gipsy. I live by another law. All Gipsy girls are whores. My sister Tamara was a whore, with her own father—"

"Child, child, you are raving," she said, rocking me in her arms. "Be guided by what I say. We must tell Victor. . . ."

Whereupon, infirm as I was, I raised my voice to cut her cruelly short. "I am mistress of this house. You will do as I say. I do not wish to have Victor here. You are not to send for him. Nor for the Baron; he has important work before him. It would be folly to distract him for a matter that must run its course no matter what he wishes. I beg you! Do you wish to see me disgraced in Father's eyes? I will never forgive you for that! You will be my enemy." I was by now melting away into convulsive sobs, clinging to Celeste for comfort and at the same time pummelling her with weak-as-water blows as I vowed to hate her forever if she defied my wishes. "Promise me you will do as I say! Oh, as you are my *sister*, swear it as you would upon your knives!"

And she did. But there was no need to exact the oath. The next morning at dawn I was jolted awake and knew the climax was at hand. I hurt as if a fiery spear had been plunged into my sex. There was blood everywhere: the sheets, the covers—all blood. I screamed, and suddenly a great dark form was hovering over me. *The bird-man*, I thought at once. But no; it was Dr. Montreaux reaching out to take hold of me and pin me against the bed lest I hurl myself to the floor. "You must lie still," he commanded. "We must be certain it has all come out." Freeing one hand, Dr. Montreaux reached into his pocket and took out an instrument, a sort of pincers. With this he raked through the bloody heap that lay between my legs, quickly inspecting what he found there. "I think there will be more," he said. "We must wait."

I cried, "Give me the potion!" I meant Christina's calming mixture, which stood on the table beside me. I wanted to reach for it, but the doctor was holding my arms fixed.

"Nonsense," he said. "It has no efficacy."

"Yes, it helps . . . it makes the pain less."

"It cannot. It is not a proper physic. It is an old wives' brew." So saying he swept the bottle from the table and again took hold of me. "Be strong, Elizabeth," he commanded. "There is nothing anyone can do. You must bear the suffering as all women have."

For the rest of that day, I lay in a torment of pain; then, toward evening, the spasms ebbed away and I had a few hours' peace. When Dr. Montreaux left the room, Christina stole furtively to my bedside, bringing a draught of her potion. I drank it eagerly and at last felt lightheaded enough to sleep. But in the night, the racking contractions returned, and again there was a gush of blood forceful enough to make me swoon. In the time that followed, I knew day and night were passing, but had no exact sense of the hours. Several more times my wearied body sought to rid itself of what my womb jealously held fast. At last, when I had convulsed still again, Dr. Montreaux decided he could delay no longer. I heard him say, "She will bleed to death if we do not clean her out." Then bending over me and telling me I must be brave, he threw up my bloodied nightdress and forced his hand into my sex, spreading it wide. Using his pincered instrument, he worked about inside me, scraping and tugging. My head whirled with the anguish. "There, I think we have it all," he declared. Looking down, I saw my spread legs divided by a swatch of blood and between them a clotted mass of crimson tissue, a sight fit to turn one's stomach. Yet I knew that the shapeless remnant of my baby, Victor's child and mine, lay somewhere there. Then, roughly tugging the bedsheet out from under me, the doctor used it to wrap the gore. He turned and shouted an order. "Old woman! Take this away! Bury it where the animals will not find it."

For the first time I realised that Christina and Celeste were in the room standing well off and watching closely. Dr. Montreaux threw the bedsheet on the floor at their feet; dutifully, Christina stepped forward to retrieve it. To Celeste he said, "You may clean her up now. It is over. She is fortunate to have survived. Bring her beef tea when she can hold down food; we must restore her blood." He bent to stroke the hair back from my blazing brow. "It is better thus, my dear. The child would surely have been malformed; it could never have lived. We shall tell no one of this, I promise you. There is no need. I believe you have learnt a hard lesson this day. Pray, do not err again."

I was unconscious before he had finished speaking.

When I woke, I found the room filled with a bright, sweet odour. In a dish beside me, some herbs were smouldering, sending up a fine white curl of smoke. But once I was fully awake, I felt as if I had lost half my body. I had hardly a trace of sensation from my breasts to my feet. Looking down, I saw I had been washed and dressed; Christina was there, still gently spreading an oil over my wearied limbs, carefully massaging my legs. The oil dimmed awareness to a minimum, which was a great mercy. "I am sorry I could not help you," she murmured. "He would not let me close to the bed. He has no knowledge of how to take away the pain; it is so simple to do, but he does not know. Nor did he clean you. He left you with a wound that would surely fester. But I have washed you with a balm that takes away corruption; it will let your flesh mend. Come now, we must also use the steam."

Gently, she helped me onto a stool beside the bed and had me lift my bedclothes to the waist. When she took away the bandage that covered me, all between my thighs looked raw and hideously engorged; there were still a trickle of blood oozing from me. Christina brought a bubbling kettle from the hearth and placed it between my spread legs. An acrid odour, familiar wherever the midwives came to deliver, emerged from the spout: horehound and vinegar. As the healing steam flowed over my thighs, Christina fanned it into my body with a hawk's feather and smoothed her hands over my stomach and loins.

"I have lost the baby," I moaned.

"Yes. But in this he was right—the man. The babe could not have lived. Likely it was dead inside you and spreading its decay. The fever killed it."

"Was it malformed, as he said?"

"No one would be able to see. It was little more than a white patch. But it is a kindness that it died; you are little more than a child yourself, not ready to be a mother."

"It is not right that one should suffer so for nothing."

She smiled wisely. "When you are strong again, you shall have the chance to say farewell."

My Life in
the Forest Begins

There were ten of us gathered in the glade that early morning, most of us mothers who had lost their babies. The sky was overcast, threatening rain. It was a month after I had lost the child; I was still skin and bones, but strong enough to make my way out into the world again. Because this ceremony was held in daylight—it was one of the very few prescribed for that time of day—we kept our numbers small and dispersed quickly, lest we be noticed. Christina had brought the remnant of my unborn child preserved in chamois-skin and tied in vines. It made a package smaller than her hand; yet it was the beginning of a life and its passage needed to be honoured.

I had been part of this ceremony several times before, for many children die without seeing the light of the world; cruel Nature gives us many babies to bury, and often their mothers with them. The midwives may be gentler and more competent at birthing than the physicians; yet even they lose many babes. But unlike the men, they mark the occasion solemnly; they carefully preserve the unborn that the mother may mourn over it before it goes under the Earth. Even if the baby has died as an abortion, its death is marked. In this way the child is sent away in dignity and the mother may relieve her grief.

This morning again there were the slow drumbeat, the cymbal, and the flute making a sweet, mournful dirge. And again, as in the past, Christina intoned the simple chant, signalling all the others to join her. But this time it was my part to add the mother's sorrowing refrain.

Christina said:

No birth is harder for woman to bear
Than the birth that ends in death.
Mother, speak this last time to your unborn.

And I said:

My little one
My nameless one
I return you, I return you

And the women said: *Whose eyes never opened on light of sun or moon*
I: *I return you, I return you*
THEY: *Whose lips tasted neither the sweetness nor the bitterness of life.*
I: *I return you, I return you*
THEY: *Whose ears never heard the calling of birds*
I: *I return you, I return you*
THEY: *Spared the pain, denied the joy*
I: *I return you, I return you*
THEY: *Life unlived*
I: *I return you, I return you*
THEY: *Name unspoken*
I: *A piece of my heart goes with you*
THEY: *A piece of our heart goes with you*

Then the tiny, wrapped form was handed to me. Each woman gave me a sisterly embrace and stepped back. I knew that now I would be left to myself, and so I gave them thanks and bade them go. I had brought what I needed to spend the day out of doors: a blanket and some simple provisions. If the weather turned bad, there was a hut, which the women had built, where I might shelter. I was to be alone with my dead little one for the remainder of the morning and then to bury it. Only Alu accompanied me; but even she attended me this day at a respectful distance, staying high overhead in the trees and only occasionally casting a glance my way, so I might mourn as long as I wished: briefly, or well into the night.

I walked off along a familiar trail until it ended on rocky soil, then walked deeper into the woods. There could be danger here, I knew, so I must take care. Wolves wandered in certain parts of the upland forest, and bears too. But I felt strangely unconcerned, as if I knew that none would harm me. At the edge of a high meadow, beside a shining pond I stopped to rest and here said my farewell to the nameless babe I held in my hand. I could not resist unfolding the chamois-skin to study what it held. Inside were odiferous cedar and camphor leaves, and within them a smear of dried blood. I found a tiny nodule of whitish tissue and realised that this was the way a life begins, so small and indistinct that no eye could make it out. Nothing more. Yet from this seeming nothing a whole human being is destined to grow and make its way into the world. Was the baby, I wondered, truly malformed as the doctor said? Or might it have lived to be as beautiful as Victor, angelically shaped and bright of eye? I stared as closely as I could at the little, featureless patch until it swam before my eyes—and suddenly thought I saw a blurred form, a face that might be staring up at me from beneath the surface of a pool: eyes, a nose, a jaw. I squinted harder and the face took definition. And then I nearly cast the thing from my hand—for the face I saw was a twisted horror. This was not the face of a baby; it was the visage, rather, of some leering monstrosity that looked more corpse-like than alive. But its eyes were open and staring out at me. Was *this* what my child might have become had it lived? Then far better it never drew breath.

I hurried to complete the ceremony. I wrapped the leaves together once more and sought out a place where I might lay my unborn child to rest. I chose the foot of an ancient spruce; having brought my two knives with me, I used the black one to hollow out a deep space among the roots beneath the spruce and bury the chamois packet as deep as to my elbow. The odour of camphor and cedar would protect it there from animals until the Earth reclaimed it. I covered the opening and over it spread blossoms from a packet the women had given me.

As I had been instructed, I sat at the secret grave and chanted, "I return you, I return you," waiting for the words to entrance my mind so that I might rise from my task with my heart unburdened. But after a long spell of chanting, I felt no ease. Instead, my bosom was roiling with emotion. I longed to be free of grieving for my dead child, but I could not. I remained as agitated and distraught as before the ceremony began. Why? I asked of myself. What held me so closed and troubled?

After a time, I walked to the nearby pond and dipped my hands in the cool water to wash them. The sun had emerged bright and warm in the sky and now glinted on the surface of the pond, throwing up waves of light that held my eye. For a long while I sat at the water's edge as if spellbound by the shimmering light. In time the water stilled and became clear as a mirror wherein I could see my face gazing down. How strange I looked! This was no longer a young girl's countenance, but that of a grown woman. I seemed so very worn and shadowed. And why should I not be? I had lived many years of life in the space of a little time. Twice in the past few months, death had brushed against me. And I had become a mother—or almost one, suffering more pain to deliver the dead piece of a baby than many women suffer to produce a whole, healthy child. I saw care and sorrow in the face that looked back at me from the water; but still more I saw anger. I saw the face I wear when anger burns inside me. The set of the mouth, the hard stare of the eyes. I was an angry woman. Anger choked my breast and would not let me mourn my baby properly. *Victor*—was the source of that anger. He had inflicted a grievous wound upon me, had humiliated me, had betrayed me—all by a single blind act. He had held me and forced me the way I imagined captive women being forced by conquering soldiers. Nor would he set me free until he had taken his pleasure and left me burdened with a child I did not want.

Without thinking, I raised and beat my hands down upon the Earth, again and again; then threw my head far back and opened my throat. A long wailing cry emerged, so powerful a cry that I was amazed it could be my voice. *No,* not a cry—a howl of rage that would reverberate for leagues across the mountains. Alu, taking fright at the sound, flapped skyward from her perch in a lofty pine, croaking worriedly. How good it felt to emit this cry. It said all. The howl was more an expression of myself than I had ever uttered between walls or among people. I waited eagerly to hear the echo as it volleyed through the valleys and ravines. And listening, I thought that for the first time I heard myself. This was *Elizabeth* speaking. And the echo was transformed into an invitation that called back to me: *Come! Come!*

For the remainder of the day, I walked deep in thought along the edges of the pond until a broken disk of the moon, silken-white and transparent, emerged in the evening sky. Then, reluctantly, I made my way home with a clear resolution in mind. *I could not stay for long in the world of men.* I must go where I could let my soul cry out as fiercely and freely as I pleased, asking no one's permission, practising no one's decorum, fearing no one's judgement. I would return and sojourn in this wild land where I could live as a wild thing, no more governed by man's laws than the elk or the eagle, the running brook or the crashing glacier. *This* would be my new home, for how long I could not say—a week, a month, longer. I would live as Seraphina lived—or as I had come to imagine her living, a cunning woman wandering where she pleased, holding more discourse with the streams and the stars than with humankind. Mother had bade me be my own master. And where else could a woman be her own master, save in the wilderness that men did not govern?

Over the next several days I laid plans carefully for what I wished to do. I chose what I needed and laid by each item: warm clothes, good boots, a blanket, flints and iron to strike a fire, candles, a lanthorn, some ceremonial possessions, my two knives, my diary. But for all my planning one thing eluded me and delayed my departure: I could not find a lie that would set me free of the concern of others. For I knew my plan would be resisted. Any who thought they had authority over me would say I must put this mad scheme out of my mind. A woman, they would tell me, has no right and no capacity to roam free. What any man might do—what Victor had often done—I would be told I must not do. If Father had been at home to say this, I might have yielded. But there were only the servants to resist me.

At last I simply and boldly spoke the truth, not caring what anyone might say, and felt the stronger woman for having been so candid. I summoned up my courage and informed one and all that I intended to take a walking trip into the mountains, as if indeed this were the most ordinary thing in the world. But of course it was not; it was a startling announcement. Joseph was especially distressed; in the Baron's absence the poor old man felt he stood *in loco parentis* to the entire household, and especially the women. "Perhaps a fortnight," I answered casually when he asked how long I intended to be away, "perhaps longer." And in my mind I thought, *Perhaps forever!* He knitted his brows disapprovingly and warned against the enterprise. But when he threatened to forbid me, I chided him gently, reminding him I was not his child, but the mistress of the house. If he intended to prevent me leaving, he must place me under lock and key, for I would go my way at the first opportunity. Seeing that I was unmoved by his threats, he next insisted I take one of the manservants with me. And this too I refused, to his consternation.

I understood his fear; it had less to do with the dangers of the wilderness than with the people who now encamped there. The countryside roundabout thronged with distressed folk, many of them driven to the extreme edge for their survival: bootless soldiers left behind by the wars, *émigrés* escaping from the troubles in France. These days one might see entire dispossessed families travelling the roads with their few remaining belongings on their backs, seeking a new home safe from the revolutionary upheaval of the time. Many had taken to the woods to live like wild men; others in their desperation turned to brigandage. The Age of Reason and of Natural Law had brought us a time of unparalleled lawlessness and savagery.

But I feared none of this; I knew the nearby woodlands well; I had sojourned and made camp there with Victor and with Father. I knew where I might sleep safely and take shelter from the elements or any human danger. Moreover, I had great confidence in my cunning and agility for my health was fast returning. Besides, I would not be alone in the forest. I would have the most trusted of companions with me. Alu would be there, the guide who had served Seraphina throughout her life. Beneath her watchful eye I felt safer than if I had a mastiff with me. And one final precaution: I intended to disguise myself to appear as penniless as the poorest beggar I might meet. Who would trouble to molest me then?

Celeste was not persuaded by my plan. "No matter how poor a woman may be," she warned me darkly, "she has that which a man will tarry to steal."

I shrugged off her fears. "Then I shall dress as a boy as well as a beggar. And carry a stout stick with me, which I know well how to use— and a flask of rancid civet with which to dowse myself should I be accosted."

⊱✳⊰

It was an early morning in August when I struck out upon my adventure. I was well-packed the night before, and stole from the château before the moon had vanished from the sky. I set my course unhesitatingly: east into the high Voirons, then along the ravine of the Arve toward the vale of Chamonix. And then . . . as fancy might direct my feet.

The journey was not easy to undertake on foot, especially if one wandered from the bridle paths. My first day of walking left me still well short of Belrive's ragged eastern boundary; the next day's hike exhausted me before I had reached the Menoge. Clearly, my strength was not what I had estimated. But the towering peaks and precipices that overhung on every side, the sound of the river raging among the rocks, and the dashing of the waterfalls soon elevated my spirits. Nowhere on Earth might I expect to see the elements displayed in so terrific a guise. As I ascended higher into the pinewood, the valleys assumed a more magnificent character. Ruined castles hanging to the sides of piney cliffs, the impetuous Arve below, the jagged glaciers steaming beneath the sun formed scenes of astounding power. And all this was augmented and rendered sublime by the mighty Alps, whose blazing white pyramids towered above all as if belonging to another Earth.

Having no clear destination, I wandered circuitously over the land, tending generally south at a leisurely pace. For the first several days of my journey, I was never out of sight of the cottages and cowsheds that dot the mountain landscape. Each day I had occasion to watch the herders driving their beasts along the paths; the air for miles round resounded through the day with the clangour of their heavy bells. The rugged folk who tend these animals readily extended their hospitality, making food and drink generously available. When the weather turned and the rains descended, they took me in to share their hearths. The *pâtres* accepted me trustingly as the vagrant lad I had disguised myself to seem. My costume spoke for me; their taciturn habits spared me the need to prevaricate further. Indeed, it was not likely they could imagine that a well-bred woman would play the rôle I had assumed: that of a wayfaring youth alone upon the road. They let me rest for the night in their cabins and outhouses and sent me on my way with warm drink and fresh provisions in the morning. Invariably I left some lesser coin behind to compensate them, but concealed a florin in a place where they were sure to find it after my departure. I had no desire to give myself out for anything but the mendicant wanderer I appeared to be.

Eventually, my roaming took me beyond these peasant outposts and then, for days at a time, I might not see a single human being. Alu, the clambering ibex, and the lordly eagle who kept watch over his empire of the air were my only companions. I felt as if I were walking over the ruins of the world, the only human being to survive the wreck; I could scarce persuade myself that I was not left alone upon the globe. I welcomed the solitude that the clear, chill heights brought me; but I knew I was now at risk as a lone traveller. Outlaws and contrabandists roamed these mountains. Each night, I chose my shelter carefully, taking pains to shield my campfire beneath the overhang of a *couvercle* and to keep it alight no longer than I needed to prepare a hasty repast and scratch down some notes in my diary. I trusted to Alu to keep watch; on those occasions when she gave warning of approaching travellers, I extin-guished my fire and took shelter in the rocks. I ate sparingly from the provisions I carried, feeding whenever I could on berries and nuts along the way. My frugal dinner finished, I made my bed with a view to con-cealing myself from discovery whether by lynx or wolf or man; which of these I feared most, I cannot say. I sought out ledges in the hillsides where I might curl myself away from sight, often collecting branches with which to cover myself.

A fortnight out upon my unhurried trek, I found myself wandering in the vale of Servox; three days further along and I passed the bridge of Pélissier, where the ravine opened out before me and my course began to ascend the mountain that overhangs it. There I entered the valley of Chamonix. The high and snow-clad mountains were the vale's immedi-ate boundaries; here I saw no more fertile fields. All was bare, wild, and sublime. Immense glaciers, vast glaring seas of ice, encroached upon the edges of the paths where I walked. Distantly the roaring thunder of the avalanche, the white smoke of its passage, the echo of rocks falling from their aerial summits, punctuated the day. At the far horizon, Mont Blanc rose above the sharp and naked *aiguilles*, its tremendous dome over-looking the valley like a giant's head. I had not viewed the mountain this closely in many years and had forgotten its dreadful splendour. I did not strike out across the valley that day but summoned Alu to idle with me through still another night before attempting to thread my way across the Mer de Glace.

I had by now taken to conversing with my bird as if she understood every word I spoke. How I regretted that I did not know her language! For I was certain of her intelligence and would not have been surprised had she begun to give me articulate counsel when I asked. "Does the beauty of this place speak to you, Alu?" I asked. "Or are you and all your animal kin a part of that beauty, so sunk within it that you have no capacity to reflect on what is you and not-you? It is perhaps the human rôle to muse on our separate fantasy."

I sheltered for hours that day in a stand of firs, marvelling at the sight before me, allowing it to elevate me above all petty apprehensions.

What comfort I found in the gruff impersonality of Nature and in its lofty disinterest in the transient cares of men! That evening, with no clear idea of the date—neither the day nor the month—I resumed my diary.[1]

---

[1] The diary entries that follow appear in the memoirs as smudged and tattered pages, roughly written, clearly under less-than-ideal circumstances. Many passages were illegible and so have been omitted. —R.W.

I Become a
Feral Woman

A fine warm day. I roam east of Chamonix across a windswept *col*. Beyond is a dark region of mist and cloud.

I brood constantly upon the Great Work. It is in my thoughts every night when I lie down to sleep. The burning bright moments of joyous discovery and the dark moments of disappointment jostle in my memory. Above all I think of Mother. She had bestowed so much hope on this enterprise. "Great things are stirring all about us in the world," she had told me. I recalled her words so vividly. "Men are challenging the eternal laws of heaven. But women also have a part to play in this, we who share Nature's sex and rhythm and who carry the Earth's fertility in our body."

Mother had groomed her son to be the alchymical Isaac Newton, a mind that would raise this revolutionary age to new spiritual heights. So wise and deep a woman, could she have been mistaken? Consider: no man had ever been more carefully schooled for the Work than Victor, nor had any been more impassioned in his pursuit of the chymical marriage; yet he, *even he*, could not stand against the temptation of the Griffin. And did I not do all that could be expected of the *Soror*? Still Victor overstepped, as other men have overstepped. For I know I am not the first sister to have been misused by her consort. Can it be that Mother was wrong, and that the woman's part in the Work must forever be that of the harlot who asks no respect, no love, no friendship, but who bears all for the man's sake? Have the adepts required of men what no man can give—a true desire for the union of equals? There was such a fierceness in Victor for knowledge; it closed his mind to my distress. When I pleaded with him to hear my will, he was deaf to my appeal. But it was not carnal lust that drove him on to the climax of our intercourse; of this I feel certain. It was rather his overriding desire *to know:* to know what lay waiting at the end of the Griffin's flight, and to know at all costs. I have heard that the Cartesian philosophers perform dissections upon live specimens, dismissing their cries of anguish as a merely "mechanical" twinge. "Clocks," they call the animals. I have heard they nail cats and dogs to the boards and cut them and beat them to study their response. I know how these poor creatures suffer; I have tasted their humiliation. I have been that beast nailed to the wall.

✠

I no longer see the world and its works as they formerly appeared to me. Before, I looked upon the accounts of vice and injustice that I read in books or heard from others as tales of ancient days; at least they were remote and more familiar to Reason than to imagination; but now misery has come home and men appear to me as monsters. I feel as if I were walking on the edge of a precipice toward which thousands are crowding and endeavouring to plunge me into the abyss.

✠

Woke to a fresh breeze. Rain, threatening all morning, at last breaks in the afternoon. I shelter in a crystal mine.

The world is a teaching written in cipher; the Great Work is the reading of that cipher. This is what Seraphina taught me. Today, while I bathed naked in a spring, I sought to apply this teaching to my own person. Say, then, that these organs of generation that divide us into men and women are also a cipher. What is their proper reading? What do I see when I study this tender vaginal cleft? It is a passage, a tunnel, an open window, an unbarred gate . . . it is a basket, a chalice, a vessel. It is fashioned to open and admit, to hold and protect. Once Victor, in one of the rites, said it reminded him of a devouring mouth; at which both Seraphina and I laughed, for it is surely nothing of the kind. Rather I see there the image of a house, a cave, a shelter. I see the baby's original home. And my breasts, which have grown so much fuller? They remind me of nourishing fruit.

And now consider the man. He is fashioned to thrust and penetrate. The seed shoots from him. Victor called his organ his "pike," a hard thing made for combat. A ram, a spear, a cudgel. Has Nature assigned us, male and female, such different rôles to play? Giver and taker, vanquisher and vanquished. The Work proposes to unite what has been divided, making One of Two. *How if this be wrong?* What if the Two have forever displaced the One? What if time makes this difference and time may not flow back? How if time, which made these bodies, is more real than the adepts have realised?

✻

I begin to lose count of the days, and discover I relish the freedom that comes of this ignorance. I am no longer tied to clocks and calendars. I have adopted Alu's time, having only the moon to track the month for me, and the sun to track the season—these, and the rhythms of my body. But what else is true time than this? The time that is kept by clocks is a fiction of calculating men; no plant or animal respects it, nor any celestial sphere. It is the cage that men would catch the world in. I live more and more like the beasts in the immediacy of my experience, letting necessity determine my schedule. I wake and sleep as fatigue dictates; I lie down wherever I please and eat as appetite decrees; I spend my days gathering food, sampling of leaves, berries, grasses; I watch for signs in the weather. I relieve myself in the brush; I spend the night in caves or nested in the trees; the stars overhead are the last I see of the world before my eyes close. For days at a time, I find no reason to speak; perhaps I shall forget the skill of speech. I give no names to things, to flowers or animals or mountains; none need to be named by me. Adam named the animals in Eden. *Adam.* Not Eve.

I bathe in the stream, enduring the flashing cold. Afterwards I wander for hours unclothed in the wood, carrying only my knife and delighting in my nakedness despite the brisk air. I run among the trees until I am weak with exhaustion. I revel in the wildness of what I do, and have no fear at all. How readily all civilised custom falls away. Underneath the animal faculties wait. I can step soundlessly over the ground; my ear is sharp; I can catch the scent of things on the wind; I move with the stealth and grace of a cat when I must. The chill air toughens me. I have turned nut-brown from lying uncovered in the sun, displaying my body proudly to the sky. My fair, soft skin has been stripped away; I let my hair grow as it pleases, a wind-blown mane.

If I should be observed now, I would be set down for a wild woman and might be hunted. I have read tales that in the New World there are such women in the forests. But these are born savages. Are there any who were raised to be ladies of the salon, who have made their home in palaces and sat at table with people of genteel conversation? Any who *reverted* from the laws of man to return to the primeval wood? I trust I am the only such.

I am drunk with the freedom of my condition. Rousseau was exactly right. Civilisation is an ill-fitting suit of clothes. But even he could not imagine the woman I have become: the feral woman, the beast woman, the female child of Nature.

I shall never return to society!

⊁✳⊰

I am racing among the trees, as fleet as the doe I follow—or so it seems, until my stamina flags and she races far ahead, bounding over a bush and out of sight. I fall to the ground breathless, staring into the endless burning sky until I feel dizzy enough to swoon. I fear none of the beasts; I am their cousin, as wild as any. And now I know that I can kill with innocence as the cat does or the hunting bird.

This morning, wading in a stream, I look for fish. My eye is unaccustomed to the task, but Alu seems to know what I am about and, hopping along the bank, soon calls to tell me she has spotted our quarry—a mountain trout, emerging from beneath a rock. I have seen clever Alu catch fish with a stab of her beak. But this time she waits patiently as if to see whether I can provide for myself. My knife in hand, I strike! The fish comes flailing from the water on my blade. I let its blood flow over my hand as I watch it die. I am so hungry, I eat without waiting to cook the meat, sharing the scraps with Alu, who chortles with satisfaction.

How selfish I am to roam the woods so long! I know there are those at home who worry for me. By now they will think I have fallen victim to brigands or been eaten by the wolves. But I have no wish to return! Not yet. I am not yet my own woman.

❧✳❧

Stormy morning, hail and rain. Afterwards, a warm, sunny day.

Through the night, the peasants try to shield their crops in the high valleys from frost by building a line of fires at the middle of the range and sending out the smoke. This barrier of fires, set like signals all along the ravine, provides a magnificent spectacle in the night. The fires pierce the curtain of silvery mist in which the valley is shrouded with crimson stains and columns of black smoke. Over a few summits swept clear by the wind, great stars shine in a chill sky. These mountain peaks, lifting a dark, compacted horizon up to the skies, make the stars seem brighter. Fierce Aldebaran rises above a dark spire that looks like the crater of a volcano from which this infernal spark has just been shot.

The next morning I find dead birds on the frozen ground, victims of the early frost. I gather them like fallen fruit, pluck them, and cook them at the open fire. Alu watches, expressing no disapproval; but she will not share the meat.

For days, I do not see a human being, or a chalet roof. Two sheer cliff faces covered in evergreens that appear to grow from each other's crests hem me in, pressing close, and with the countless detours seem to push me onward, shutting me into inextricable solitudes. I come upon the remnants of an ancient hermitage and spend the night there; nothing stands to mark it but a few elegant arcades half-buried under landslides over which the turf and the wildflowers have grown again. Here there are no perspectives, no contrasts; only magnificently and uniformly green grassy slopes and depths of forest without issue or the slightest break for either eye or thought. Distantly from every chasm in the rocks, vapours rise and greet the sun like awakened spirits on the Judgement Day. Eternal mists, fir trees everywhere, narrow meadows and forests cut into the invincible bulwark of the mountains. Once again, on waking, I greet Mont Blanc, a snowy fortress, and see beneath me the valley floor, a vast, many-coloured carpet.

Wonders, wonders . . . it is enough to see these beauties. What need I "know" more than this?

Several days have passed since I last took up my diary. My mind has been too unsettled to write. Not by remorse . . . I insist, not by remorse! But by an exuberance that makes me too free and wild to set down my thoughts.

Does the prowling bear trouble to record its deeds, or the hunting eagle? Do they mark their way with monuments?

Reflection is a foolish human habit, the fruit of guilty conscience. Animal freedom is to live in the moment.

I had come to the end of a hard day's wandering. My modest repast finished, I sat to watch the pallid lightnings play above the mountains until lassitude overcame me. In the distant gorge, the rushing of the waterfall acted as a lullaby upon my too-keen sensations; no sooner did my eyelids droop than sweet fatigue crept over me where I sat and I sank down to sleep for the night, not even covering against the cold.

I thought it was the chill that woke me, for I was frozen through to the bone when my eyes next opened to see the frost-ringed moon above me. But it was the sound of voices that had penetrated my sleep: voices of men not far off, their tones strident and surly. Listening closer, I recognised the language I heard as Italian, a vulgar dialect of the region where I had spent my childhood. I counted two voices, then a third; each sounded more drunkenly dissonant than the last. They fouled the night with ugly oaths. Off to my left, the light of a campfire flickered through the trees. I looked for Alu in the trees, but could not see her. Creeping forward to peer into the woods, I discerned three men perhaps twenty paces down the slope; they were roasting game over their fire and passing a flask of spirits from hand to hand. Soldiers, I would have guessed from their dress, but clearly irregulars, whose dishevelled state suggested they were deserters or free lances. Or possibly they were contrabandists preparing to move by night over the frontier. I caught some snatches of their conversation on the breeze; they spoke of a campaign in the region; they had plundered the field after a battle. I wished to hear nothing more and so silently gathered up my pack and made ready to steal away.

Giving their camp a wide berth, I circled round through the undergrowth toward a lower stretch of the bridle path. In my hand I held one of my knives, which I had hurriedly pulled from my pack. I would scarcely have known how to use it to defend myself; still, it gave me the illusion of safety. Feeling my way forward blindly in the dark, I often misstepped, rustling the brush or breaking a stick under foot; the noise I made would stop the men in their conversation while they looked about to see if a bear might be upon them. I was not yet beyond sight of their fire when I saw a second light just ahead through the trees. Another camp lay in my path. Here two more shabbily uniformed men lounged across a fallen tree, laughing drunkenly and exchanging raucous banter; they seemed even more inebriated than those in the first group, their words more slurred, their language coarser. But there were others at the fire who did not speak at all; these cowered in silence. A group of women; I counted three, two of them youngish, the last old enough to be their mother. Their clothes were little better than rags, hardly whole enough to cover them. The women huddled together on the ground in a most unnatural posture. Then I saw that they were tied together at the ankles and staked to the ground. They were the captives of the soldiers, taken perhaps for ransom—or so I thought, until suddenly a third man crashed out of the bushes from beyond the fire dragging a squealing figure behind him: a woman, sobbing fiercely, her eyes wild with fear, her dress torn open at the breast. The man flung her to the ground and proceeded to bind her to the other women, cursing her all the while. When he raised his hand to strike her, she cringed and cried out in a coarse peasant French, imploring him not to hurt her more. His mercy was to spit upon her and stagger off.

Joining his comrades on the other side of the fire, he raised his voice, calling into the night toward the first group. "Ho! Your turn," he shouted. "Are you coming, or should we let the sluts sleep?" A gruff voice roared back from the direction of the other campfire. "On my way, on my way." Before I knew where to turn, a man shambled past me making his way from the one group to the other. He passed no more than a few paces off from where I crouched at the foot of a tree. Stumbling past the fire, he went for the group of women, hovered unsteadily over them, walked once round them, then, stooping, began to untie the same woman who had just been brought back. I saw now she was a young girl, barely older than myself. Across the fire, one of the men shouted, "Leave her be. Choose a fresh one. The wench has been——— a dozen times. Take the old one; in the dark you won't know the difference." His compatriot laughed wickedly. " 'Tisn't made of soap. Won't wear away." Unstaking the girl and pulling her roughly after him, he headed directly toward the place where I sheltered in the darkness beyond the circle of firelight. I had time to shrink back no more than a few steps before he reached the foot of the tree where I had been hiding. Just a few paces beyond, he hurled the girl roughly to the ground and ordered her to uncover as he struggled out of his trousers. Sobbing piteously, the girl drew her skirts above her waist and lay back to endure her fate. In another moment the man had kicked his boots and pants away and stood half-naked over her, rubbing vigorously at his organ until it lay in his hand like a blunt club. At last he spat upon it, then flung himself atop her like a marauding beast, and, deaf to her cries of protest, commenced to thrust wildly at her.

By the distant light of the fire, I saw all that happened; and I watched, not turning away to spare myself the sight. I could hear each laboured breath they drew, and the obscenities he growled into the girl's ear. "Come, little chicken!" he snarled. "You like it, don't you? You like to be taken. You could service a whole battalion, couldn't you? Come let me hear how much you like it!" And he struck her across the flanks again and again. "Beg for it! Let me hear you!" The girl did nothing but moan and whimper. "Bitch! You'll be sloshing inside all night." Had I reached out twice the length of my arm, I might have touched her hand: I was that close. Frightened though I was that I might be discovered, I longed to come to her rescue. But what might I do? Fall upon her attacker and pummel him? Strike him with a rock? I knew that would be useless. Still, I could hardly keep the fury that seethed in me from overwhelming all caution. For I *knew* this thing that was happening to her! I had buried the memory as deep in forgetfulness as I could; I had tried to leave it behind when I came to the woods. But now it returned to me—the time I had lain like her, helpless and pleading, and had endured the same humiliation. My very flesh remembered the tearing violence. But the man who had treated me so had not been a drunken stranger and an enemy of war; there was not so much of an excuse. I could see his face burning with delight above me, feasting on my anguish more than he enjoyed any pleasure I might freely offer. Even through my tears I had seen it was the joy of *taking* that he wanted, not that of accepting.

The anger that rose in me was like a drunkenness that obliterated all better judgement. My ears were filled with one sound only: the pathetic whimpering of the girl—my sister, as I thought—who lay not six paces off from me enduring such degradation. The thought that I must help her flooded my mind, washing away all else. Once again I felt a howl of rage rising within me—a cry that would shake the mountains sufficient to bring down an avalanche. A moment later, I realised there had been no cry. But as if a piece of my life had been cut away, I stood somewhere else in time. My rage was satisfied, but I had uttered nothing, not a sound. Instead, in my fury I had delivered a blow; I had struck blindly, instinctively—as an infuriated beast might strike. But what had I done? I could not say until I saw my knife in the man's neck, driven so deep that had he tried to call out, my blade would have sealed his throat. But he gave no call; only a small, strangled cough. And he made no struggle; only a single shuddering spasm. After which he lay dead upon the girl's body. I had done this thing before any clear intention formed in my mind.

At once I became strangely alert. I rushed to roll him off the girl and free her. "Be still!" I whispered close at her ear. "He is dead. Quickly now! Save yourself! For they will think you have killed him." At first the poor stunned creature had no idea what to think. What was she to make of this strange figure who had leapt upon her out of the darkness? Was I another ravisher who had come to double her misery? But she was not a stupid girl; as soon as she saw the knife buried in her assailant's back, she grasped my meaning and began at once to stumble off into the forest, hugging her torn clothes about her. She had no more idea than I in which direction lay safety; even so the noise she made blundering through the brush actually served to frighten the men, who assumed a stampeding animal might be closing upon them and fled for cover. This provided my chance for escape; but first, bending over the dead man, I sought to tug my knife free. I discovered it was driven into the bone and would not come loose. I stared in amazement; I could not imagine I had delivered so powerful a blow. With no choice but to leave it behind, I gathered up my belongings and stealthily crept into the undergrowth, moving in the opposite direction from the fleeing girl.

Breathless with terror, my stomach roiling, I felt my way forward inch by inch into the night. With no idea which way to turn, I blundered into obstacles on every side, lacerating my face and hands. Behind me, I saw firebrands moving rapidly among the trees and heard the voices of men crying out, calling their dead comrade's name—and then cries of horrified surprise that indicated his discovery. I ran harder in any way that seemed open, only to discover that I had become turned round. The firebrands were suddenly before me! I was running toward them. A man stepped into my path, waving his burning stick at me. "Stop!" he called out. "Who is there?" He fumbled to raise his musket. Panicked, I turned to flee the other way. At once there were men behind me shouting, running hard. I would never outdistance them.

All at once, I heard a familiar sound. It was Alu screeching overhead—but shriller than she had ever cried out before. I heard her wings beating over my head, and the fearful screams of the men. Alu was flying at my pursuers, hurling herself into their faces as I had once seen her fly at dogs. "A demon!" I heard one of the men cry as he and his comrades dispersed for safety into the woods. Gunfire rang out. Long after I was out of earshot of the men, I could hear Alu's rasping shriek sweeping over the trees again and again like some vengeful spirit. She did indeed sound like a voice out of hell.

Though I was now well clear of the area, I continued to run as if I were being pursued. Again and again I stumbled on the rough ground and fell to my knees. What little I could see ahead of me by the moon's light was blurred by tears. But the tears were tears of triumph; I was all but laughing aloud as I raced forward in the dark wood. My heart was high and buoyant to the point of giddiness. *How good it felt to have spilled this blood!* I revelled in the deed I had done, in the killing of this brute who had represented all brutes, all violators of women. I would never regret this act. Even when I was a half-league or more away from that dread scene, I was certain I could still hear the piteous screams of the women, whose ordeal was not yet over. This convinced me even more of the rectitude of my act. *If only I could have killed them all!*

At last, when I could run no longer, I slumped down beneath a tree and buried my face in the Earth. Again and again I repeated to myself, "I have done right! This was no crime," until exhaustion overcame me. And in my slumbers a great mercy was granted me. The horror to which I had been party faded from my thoughts; while my eyes were closed in sleep, sublime scenes were congregating round me. I did not wake until the morning was well advanced. The first sight I saw when I had wiped the grainy residue of tears from my eyes was a scene of elevating wonder offered to me like a medicine for the soul. There across the valley stood mighty Montanvert intersected with terrific chasms and frosted hollows. All about the immense steaming glacier stood the precipitous haughty mountains, the motionless torrents and silent cataracts, an empire of unrelenting ice.

I did not notice until I had surveyed the vista: my hands bore stains, dried and crusted about the nails. Was this not blood? Had I wounded myself? Before I could think further on the matter, a branch of berries fell at my side. Above me in the trees, I heard Alu clacking her beak. "Thank you, Alu," I called, and searched my pack to find what more I might have laid by for my breakfast. There I found but one of my knives: the white one.

Only then did I remember where the blood had come from.

And where was remorse? Nowhere to be found. I was astounded to know how *clean* it had made me feel to kill. Not merely "justified," as one might be judged in a court of law . . . but *cleansed.* This blood had purified me; it had drained the fury and the spite from me as if I had reset the balance of the world. I had done justice with my own hand, a *woman's* hand! How often is that permitted? In the eyes of men, the violation of the woman's body shames the woman; she is not to speak of it; the crime goes unpunished. But I had righted this with a single lethal blow.

Not far from where I woke, I found a chill trickle of water seeping from the rock. I caught enough to wash the blood from my hands. When I had scrubbed the stains away, in a gesture that might have been one of spontaneous prayer, I raised my hands to the sun. The purity I felt was more than a matter of washing. And then almost immediately I turned to find food and fell to eating with great appetite, for I was fairly famishing.

✢

A fine sharp morning. Frost on the hilltops. I find little to eat in my sack: some dried fish and bad cheese. I must forage for nuts and mush-rooms.

In this wilderness are beasts that hunt and kill; there is the avalanche that sweeps all life before it into oblivion. And even so, Nature is *good*. For nothing in Nature is malicious, nothing is bent on evil; nothing deceives, but is content to be simply what it was made to be. All crea-tures live like simple prayers offered to the eternal magnificence of things, honouring its laws. How then, in the presence of this splendour, can man, whose God-like Reason comprehends Nature, alone become so vile? What sane proportion is there between the soaring grandeur of these mountains, which greets me each morning, and the cruelties that man visits upon his fellows?

✢

But why do I say "man," when I mean *men*? Why do I so generously agree that women should share any part of the shame? Who are the sackers of cities and makers of war? Who massacres the innocent and grinds the faces of the poor? Who are the enslavers, pirates, and vandals? Who the witch-hunters, the inquisitors and torturers? I cannot name them one and all; but this much I know: whatever their names, they will not be the names of women. If I walk through a burning village strewn with bodies, I may not know the race or nation of those who committed this crime; but have I any need to enquire after their sex?

⢎⢳⣗

I meditate too much on death and horror; I cannot say why. Here in the presence of these ice-crowned summits is no place for such thoughts. What is worst in man? His pettiness. That he cannot rise above his lesser loyalties to creeds and customs. There is but one code that matters: the law of Nature, which is engraved upon these heights and born into our hearts. Father believed the book of Nature is written in the language of mathematics. I say no. It is written in the language of feeling, known to every unlettered child.

⢎⢳⣗

I wake to hear Alu screeching. Above me I see three vultures sweeping the sky: besides my companion, the only living things I have seen in days. The roads are icy this morning; they slow my travel. Toward noon, a snow-squall blows down from the ridge. I come upon an abandoned shepherd's hut and shelter there for the remainder of the day. My hand is too cold to write more than a little.

⢎⢳⣗

Just before the sun descends today, I spy a column of smoke rising over the next summit. An hour later, after following circuitous paths, I discover a religious hospice, the chimney smoking. I ring at the door. One of the brothers, a portly, good-humoured man, greets me and invites me to enter. It is a Capuchin house, warm and well-kept. While I wait in the foyer, I remove my cap, as I must, but am careful to tuck my hair well down into my raised collar, hoping to be accepted as the young boy I pretend to be. I am shown to the kitchen and given hot onion soup, bread, a plate of boiled vegetables, and red wine, the most filling food I have had in many weeks. That night I attend the evening prayers and then retire to a bed of straw in the loft. I sleep like the dead that night. In the morning, I am sent on my way with my sack well-filled. How distressed these men of God would be to know they have spent the night with a female under their roof, sleeping close enough to hear them snore!

⟫✕⟪

Each day the weather grows cooler. This morning there is keen frost upon the steep hillsides; the ground slippery everywhere I walk. Crisp wind. Where the sun does not reach, the streams form ice. Alu brings me food, though it is not always palatable. I thank her for the grubs and flies she disgorges at my feet, but leave them untouched. I find fewer berries on the bushes; by midday I hunger greatly and make a broth of aspen bark and rhododendron stalks; it hardly fills me. I have not enough nuts left to last another week. I come upon meadow mushrooms growing just below the snow-line. Though they are badly rotted, I gather them; they will make a thin broth. Still, the day is cheerful and bright; I would not be any place else. But will I be able to last the winter?

⟫✕⟪

I wake in the night, my stomach in knots. My head reels. Fiercely ill. I think I see all the glaciers burning in the night, like tapers upon an altar. What god is worshipped in this barren wilderness? I wonder. An owl settles at the entrance to my cave; I hear it speaking to Alu in the common language of the birds, which now I realise I can understand. The owl reports that it has seen machines in the sky, iron wheels and gears. It tells Alu that I must return and give warning. At last, toward morning, I vomit up what poisons me. I am too weak to journey today. Alu brings me what she can find—some chilled berries, some soft bark.

⟫✕⟪

The shapes of cloud slowly moving. Passing over the mountains, they almost seem alive, a grazing herd. Unseen birds singing in the mist. Last night the crystal-cold air circled the moon with a rainbow and trapped two stars within it. Again, too weak to travel. I find nothing but crumbs in my sack. I shall have to visit an outlying farm, or else starve down to my bones.

❧✳❧

I wake to Alu's crying. I listen and hear the distant jingling of bells in the air. Searching through the blowing clouds, I see, well below, a line of men and mules threading the walls of the ravine; they are wending their way toward the same *col* I have in view. Alu follows them overhead, showing me the shortest way forward. Weak as I am, I make haste to intercept the men and beg food from them, playing the pauper lad. They are workmen sent from the villages below to clear the passes for merchants. They prove to be generous and leave me with dried beef, cheese, and bread enough to last three days. I share what I have with Alu, who takes only a few pecks at the bread, leaving all the rest for me.

❧✳❧

I have wandered beyond all the valleys I can name. Mont Blanc is now well west of me, nearly sunk out of sight. I wake in the night to a piercing cold; overhead I see the moon racing through driving clouds. Every tooth and every edge of rock is visible. And there just above me a high out-cropping shaped like a gigantic man looms against the black-silvered sky.

❧✳❧

I wake from a delightful dream, a child's dream, in which I hear Anna Greta calling me to breakfast as she did so often when I was first come to the château; I think I smell the bread and cakes. I rush to the kitchen, and there is Celeste waiting with a tray of chocolate and biscuits. I wake laughing to find my belly playing such tricks on me in my sleep. Poor thing! It wants feeding, and food is growing harder to find. I must return to the valley and find shelter among the *pâtres*.

In the late afternoon, after hours of wandering, I find a pond and stretch out upon my belly to drink. Alu gives a sharp short warning cry. I draw my head back and see the cliffs above me reflected in the water, and on a ledge to my left I catch sight of something moving. Turning slowly I see that it is a lynx, her fire-yellow eyes fixed upon me! She has crept forward and now crouches to spring. I have no time to run. Alu has placed herself above the cat, waiting to see if it will pounce. I lie still where I am and stare the lynx full in the face. The moments crawl by while we study one another. Time freezes. My heart that was racing so fast has slowed; suddenly there is no fear in me. My eyes are telling the beast something I could not say in words, and, yes, she understands. Slowly she rises up, licks once at her lips, turns, and lithely leaps to the ledge above. In another moment she is gone.

I have been acknowledged.

It is time to go home.

❧✻❧

> Lock all doors, bar all gates
> Hide where you will, the wildness waits.
> In open field, in city street
> You and wildness must one day meet.
>
> By holy cross and altar stone
> The wildness waits to claim its own.
> Inside the skull, inside the skin
> Abides the wildness deep within.
>
> Build walls so high and all about
> To hold the roaring wildness out,
> Still wildness owns the greater part
> It rules your own and only heart.

EDITOR'S NOTE
An Assessment of Elizabeth Frankenstein's Feral Period

The several weeks that Elizabeth Frankenstein purports to have spent in the wilderness present an intractable editorial problem. By no stretch of the imagination is it possible to credit all that she reports. We deal here in whimsy and illusion. But where are we to draw the line between fact and fantasy? Certainly the murder she claims to have committed is wholly delusionary; a young woman slight of build, untrained in the use of weapons, and of the greatest gentility possesses neither the physical nor the emotional resources to carry out so vicious an act. The very fact that she could invent such a grisly scene and commit it to writing bespeaks the infirmity of her moral condition. This, like much else she records in this portion of the memoir, must surely be attributed to the nervous strain she suffered following her illness and near-fatal miscarriage. As the pages to follow will make clear, this guilty fantasy came to be associated in her mind with the rancour she quite legitimately bore toward Victor. She herself came to see that this imaginary homicide was born of a vengefulness she found it too painful to admit.

While the factual authenticity of the episode must be set at close to nil, we can find at least this much biographical value in these pages: we have here an unmistakeable indication of the woman's increasing emotional fragility. It is from this point forward in her life that Elizabeth Frankenstein begins to display ever more signs of mental aberration. The image she invents of herself as a "feral woman" is a poignant attempt to recapture the innocence and security of a childhood she had forever left behind. Keener minds than hers have sought out similarly illusory consolations. Rousseau's fictitious state of nature has provided many a poet and philosopher with dreams of a free and happy life in an Arcadian landscape. In Elizabeth Frankenstein's case, that same philosophical yearning clearly became more than an intellectual exercise; in her desperation, she fashioned it into a brief hallucinatory respite from painful reality. Would that the episode had brought her the solace she needed to regain a sure grip on her sanity!

Victor's New Life
at Ingolstadt

And what was there left for me in life after my return from the forest? I offered no apologies or explanations for my long absence; I let all know that I regarded it as my right to do as I had done. Despite my reticence, I was forgiven by Father, by Joseph, by Celeste, all of whom had worried for me night and day. They welcomed me back, making what sense they could of my seemingly mad conduct. "She is her mother's daughter," I overheard Anna Greta saying to one of the other maids. So this was how they saw me: as a woman who had been raised from childhood with a wild streak in her. In a sense they were right; owing to Mother, I was not as other women. I had learnt to live with the wolf and the lynx beyond the laws of men—and took pride in the fact. Perhaps one day I would thank Victor for having driven me to that act of daring independence. Perhaps . . . But for now, the cold rancour that lay between us was undiminished. He was the man who had taught me the treachery of men—and who dared take offence because I would offer his conscience no solace.

"Ingolstadt has opened a New World of the imagination to me. . . ."

So Victor's first letter announced. It had arrived only days after I had departed the château for my wilderness excursion; Father had saved it for me to peruse, as he had all the letters that followed. Indeed, he insisted on sitting over me while I read, even asking me to repeat his son's words again and again. Victor's letters were never addressed to me, though he knew full well that every word he wrote would pass under my eyes. Still he pretended to write exclusively to Father, ignoring my existence as if to widen our separation by a distance of sentiment that was even greater than the distance of miles between Geneva and Ingolstadt. How hard, then, it was for me to read these letters aloud to Father, as he invariably insisted I do! The poor man, now a heart-broken widower, found such joy in every word Victor sent home from university; in his eyes, his wayward son was finally embarked upon his proper course in life. I could not be the one to dim the happiness of one to whom I owed so much. I had no choice but to echo his elation. He could never have guessed that I was the intended audience for these letters in which Victor boasted of his achievements. Nor could he know how it tore my heart to hear what he could not: the undertone of hurt, resentment, and self-pity that underlay all I read. I saw Victor's feigned high spirits as nothing more than a brazen declaration of his guiltlessness. All that he wrote in his letters, in whatever rhetoric it might be garbed, was intended as a stinging riposte to the woman he had shamed. He wished me to know that he had gone out into the greater world to make his mark and that he was not prepared to let his crime against me bar him from success.[1]

Ingolstadt, September ——, 178——
Dear Father:

Ingolstadt has opened a New World of the imagination to me. But unlike the savage American wilderness, this World is the Utopia of Voltaire's dream, the true El Dorado that all mankind is seeking. Here I have discovered the gold of knowledge lying strewn in the streets and the promise of worldly happiness growing on all sides like ripe fruit on the tree.

My first day of classes, I set out to find Professor Waldman, to whom you recommended me. To my great disappointment, I am told he is away, not

[1]The letters that follow were crudely glued to the next several pages of the memoir. I can attest that they are in Victor Frankenstein's hand. A few echo the words Frankenstein himself dictated to me upon his death bed, but these take on a new meaning if, as Elizabeth Frankenstein suggests, they were intended primarily for her eyes. —R.W.

expected to return until the end of term. His place is taken in the curriculum by one Professor Krempe, whose lecture I attend. I find him at first an uncouth fellow: squat and crook-backed in form, with a gruff voice, repulsive countenance, and a mordant habit of conversation. He lectures at a feverish pace, pausing to make no clarification, then mocks his students pitilessly when they answer incorrectly. And his colleagues too: he makes cruel sport of all those he disagrees with, as if they were idiots. There is something of the imp—or, indeed, the malicious troll—about him that makes me certain I have nothing to learn from him. But how wrong I am! In his first lecture this abrasive little man, like some Biblical prophet, shakes the scales from my eyes and opens my sight to thrones and dominions. He speaks of electrical science, hailing it as the advancing wave of natural philosophy. When he poses questions about the subject, I prove to be far ahead of my fellow students. I see that Professor Krempe is impressed; I notice how frequently he studies me while he speaks. Even so I am reluctant to approach him outside of class; but at last I do— on your advice that I must be bold with my teachers and demand proper attention.

Professor Krempe, of course, recognises our family name and is eager to have me visit. He asks several questions concerning my progress in the different branches of science. I carelessly mention the names of the alchymists as the principal authors I have studied. He stares in disbelief. "Have you really spent your time in studying such nonsense?" Somewhat sheepishly I reply in the affirmative. "Every minute," he continues with warmth, "every instant you have spent on these books is utterly wasted. You have burdened your memory with exploded systems. Good God! In what desert land have you lived, where no one was kind enough to inform you that these fancies, which you have so greedily imbibed, are a thousand years old and as musty as they are ancient? I little expected, in this Enlightened age, to find myself discoursing with a disciple of Albertus Magnus. My dear young sir, you must begin your studies entirely anew."

So saying, he steps aside and writes down a list of books treating true natural philosophy, which he desires me to study; and dismisses me, after mentioning that in the following week he intends to commence lecturing upon the nervous influence of animal electricity in all its mysterious connection to the sensations and motions of organic chemistry. The most recent findings of Volta, Galvani, Valli, and Morgan will be covered, together with Herr Krempe's own research on the electrification of opiated muscle tissue. He openly chuckles when he sees my dumbfounded reaction. "Well, young Paracelsus," he chides, "are you ready, then, to come out of the wilderness?"

I have you to thank, Father, for the fact that I am at last breathing the clear air of authentic science. My mind has never been more alive than in this monastery of the intellect where I live by day and night in a bracingly fraternal milieu. Here I trade rough critical blows with my fellows over every meal and continue in learned combat until the last candle has flickered out in the small hours. My bed and board are Spartan, but this assists in sweeping away the nonessential. I go for days without troubling to trim my beard or launder my clothes. I care little for what I eat or the other comforts of the flesh, least of all for the social distractions that come of living in mixed domestic company. I live, indeed, as if I were a disembodied intelligence whose only purpose each day is to force Dame Nature to strip the veil from one more of her precious secrets. I am unutterably happy!

Your grateful son,
Victor

Ingolstadt, November ——, 178——
Dear Father:

For the privilege of studying with Professor Krempe I would have been at a loss to give thanks enough; but I have at last met Professor Waldman, your old schoolboy friend. Suddenly Krempe, for all his genius, becomes in my eyes John the Baptist sent forth to announce the true Messiah. Professor Waldman returned to Ingolstadt just this week, and at once I sought out his lecture. He is very unlike his colleague. Where Krempe is acerbic to a fault, a man who takes keen pleasure in the cut and thrust of debate, Waldman is the very soul of generosity and cultivation. His voice is the sweetest and mildest I have ever heard; his aspect expresses the greatest benevolence. He begins his lecture with a recapitulation of the history of chemistry and the various improvements made by men of learning, especially the most distinguished discoverers. Over the work of Van Helmont, Scheele, and Priestley he loiters with loving care; but upon reaching Lavoisier he soars to the height of rhapsodic praise. "With his analysis of combustion," Waldman announces, "we light every corner where superstition might take refuge; we are done with the regimen of spectral fluids and ethereal hypostases. The epoch of rational philosophy begins." He then took a cursory view of the present state of the sciences, concluding with a panegyric upon modern chemistry, which I have committed to memory:

"The ancient teachers of this science, or rather of its abortive precursor, called alchemy, promised impossibilities and performed nothing. The modern masters promise very little; they know that metals cannot be transmuted and that the elixir of life is a chimera. But these philosophers, whose hands seem made only to dabble in dirt and their eyes to pore over the microscope or crucible, have indeed performed miracles. Standing not upon false ceremony like some timid suitor at the damsel's gate, they boldly open the forbidden recesses of Nature in order to find what she hides in her private places. They have discovered how the blood circulates and the nature of the air we breathe. They have acquired new and almost unlimited powers. They can command the thunders of heaven, mimic the earthquake, and even mock the invisible world with its own shadows. In this great enterprise I invite you, young gentlemen, to join."

I knew at once that this man must become my mentor, and could not wait to seek him out. His manners in private were even more mild and magnetic than in public, for there was a certain formality in his mien during his lecture, which in his own home was replaced by the greatest affability. I recounted my former studies as I had for Professor Krempe. I saw him smile with kindly indulgence at the names of Paracelsus and Valentine; there was none of the contempt that Herr Krempe had exhibited. In fact, there was generosity. "These are men," he said, "to whose zeal modern philosophers are indebted for the foundations of their knowledge. We may honour their names, even though we must lay their systems to rest. But let me ask, Herr Frankenstein, if my lecture has perhaps had some influence in removing your prejudices against modern chemistry?" I hastened to say it had, and at once requested his advice concerning the books I might procure. "Then I am happy," he continued, "to have gained a disciple, for Herr Krempe has already informed me of your high promise. Chemistry is that branch of natural philosophy in which the greatest *improvements have been made; I recommend it to your attention. But if you wish to be a true man of science and not merely a petty experimentalist, I advise you to apply yourself to every branch of natural philosophy, especially mathematics."*

All together, we spoke for less than an hour; but his words have changed my course in life. That night I felt as if my soul were grappling with a palpable enemy; one by one the various keys that form the mechanism of my being were touched, chord after chord was sounded, and soon my mind was filled with one thought, one conception, one purpose. So much has been done, *I heard my soul exclaim;* more, far more will I achieve. Treading in the footsteps already marked, I will pioneer a new way and unfold the deepest mysteries of creation!

I pray you remember me to the rest of the household. I expect you will understand if I am unable to spend the holidays at home. My studies consume my every waking hour; often the stars have disappeared in the light of morning whilst I am yet engaged in the laboratory. Understand, then, if I must delay the pleasure of your company until the spring.

Ever your affectionate son,
Victor

Ingolstadt, January —— *, 178*——
Dear Father:

In Professor Waldman I have found not only a model of scientific intellect but a true friend. His gentleness is never tinged with dogmatism; his instructions are given with an air of frankness and good humour that banishes pedantry. He has permitted me to make use of his private laboratory, which is better stocked for the study of electrochemical fluids than the university. As we work together my vision of electrical energy grows more encompassing. This is no longer the paltry science it was once fancied to be. Though still in its infancy, it proves to be connected intimately with all operations in magnetism, with light and caloric, with biological processes at every level. It is likely a property of all matter, and perhaps ranges through space from sun to sun, and from planet to planet. Not improbably, it ranks as the secondary cause of every change in animal, mineral, vegetable, and gaseous systems. Currently, Professor Waldman is creating electrical discharges in albumen, resulting from which globules of organised matter emerge. It is his theory that the first step toward the creation of life on Earth was a similar operation by which simple germinal vesicles were excited into vitality from shallow sea-water. Is it possible, then, that this is the very secret of life itself?

I have rapidly become Professor Waldman's favourite student; he shares his every conjecture with me. In his presence, by some ineffable force of persuasion, I discover my entire outlook to be changing. I am chagrined to believe that I ever viewed the spagyric theoreticians as more than mere literature. That I tore myself free of these antediluvian absurdities stands as the most welcome event of my life; it has liberated my mind to think at its maximum level of efficiency. Lord Bacon prophetically spoke of an age when we should witness "a masculine birth of Time." In word, thought, and deed I have experienced just such a birth under Professor Waldman's tutelage. How foolish I was to waste my time seeking to coax spirits from inert matter! And even more the fool for believing others had actually succeeded in seeing apparitions in the elements. For what is there to be found in chemical substance but atoms? Learn the atoms, Professor Krempe orders me; they answer to all needs. The elements and forces of Nature are not personages to be placated and invoked; they are constellations of brute matter which we conquer by prediction. Seen in this way, they become our slaves to command and the field of our true dominion.

Your ever faithful son,
Victor

Ingolstadt, May ———, 178———
My dear Father:

I am sorry to say I will not be able to return home for the summer, much as I miss you. I know you will understand when I say that my work with Professor Waldman has reached a crucial pass. The excitement of discovery so fills my life that I cannot tear myself away. None but those who have experienced them can conceive the enticements of science. Discovery is science! It races forward to make war upon the unknown, to sack all cities that rest secure in their ignorance. I would be one of the far-seeing eagles of natural philosophy, ever on the wing and soaring higher. Those who settle for less are beasts of burden, mere plodding mules loaded with musty systems and shopworn certitudes.

My work with Professor Waldman stretches across all conventional philosophical boundaries. It is at once chemical, biological, and medical. To explain briefly: I have learnt that dogs can be kept alive on a severely reduced diet by daily infusions of electricity. Measured charges of electrical fluid can replace all forms of nourishment; the longest term of survival has thus far been twenty-four days. If water is separately supplied in normal amounts, the beast can be kept alive for over two months. This is the clearest indication yet that electrical energy participates in the vis vitae *and can be assimilated into living matter. How far can this process be extended? This is what we seek to establish. It is our intention to complete the experimental series we have begun and then to report our results; Professor Waldman has promised that he will let me stand as the author of our results and recommend my research for publication. You can imagine my elation!*

> *Your ever affectionate son,*
> *Victor*

September ———, 178——
Dear Father:

An astounding day: my first experience assisting Dr. Von Troeltsch with human specimens in the dissection theatre, an honour normally reserved for senior students. I have long since proven my advanced knowledge of animal dissections. Von Troeltsch knows this and asks me to assist with the demonstration; he has recognised me as the best-prepared, despite my young age.

What a contrast we have in this chamber between the Gothic gloom it inherits from the past and the Enlightened use to which it has been put by men of science. The room might be a dungeon: stone walls and floors, a few narrow windows, guttering candles overhead. The air reeks of decay, this ancient stench barely offset by the bracing chemicals we bring to our work. The stones are rarely scrubbed here; it would do no good. The blood and bile of generations has by now soaked these old tiles through. Nevertheless, as dank and foetid as the theatre is, from here we launch voyages of discovery—not out across the open seas, but downward, *into the hidden ocean deeps of the organism. Von*

Troeltsch conducts the class with his unique combination of Prussian discipline and wry wit, insisting upon absolute concentration, absolute silence. He orders the first cadaver to be brought and lifts away the canvas with the flourish of a ring-master to reveal . . . a female, salted for so long in lime and nitre that she has turned blue from head to toe like some alien being. Still, she is young and well-shaped—except for the head. The queer tilt of her neck tells us that she was hanged, following which at some point the skull was crushed and rendered valueless for study. "We begin," Von Troeltsch announces, "by eliminating what we cannot use." At that, without a moment's hesitation, he cuts across the throat and, severing the head from the body, holds it high above the table. "With females it makes no difference. We would find nothing inside anyway." This brings a loud chorus of guffaws from the students. "And who will dispose of this rubbish for me?" Von Troeltsch asks, quickly surveying the room. He picks out a new student, a nervous young man on the far side of the table who is struggling to control his stomach. Without warning, Von Troeltsch boldly pitches the shattered cranium directly at him, a fine spray of its remaining fluids following it across the room. The poor fellow has no choice but to catch it— and then stands horrified to see the thing in his hands. In a moment he is out the door with it and we hear him taking sick in the passageway. The room breaks into laughter as each of us determines he will not display the same frailty. Callous as this jest may seem, it serves a worthy purpose. After one lad has shown cowardice, the rest resolve that they will be all the more manly. In this way, Dr. Von Troeltsch "bloods" his pupils, sorting the stout-hearted from the squeamish.

He turns back to survey his now-decapitated specimen. Placing his blade casually beneath one nipple, he remarks, "Do you agree, Herr Frankenstein? Is this not the perfect model of woman? From the neck down, all the necessary and pleasurable parts remain; the mouse-like brain, the jabbering mouth— gone. The perfect wife for a doctor!" Again the room roars with laughter.

For all his crude humour, when it comes to the dissection, Von Troeltsch is a master; he manages to keep every organ intact. Even the ungainly liver comes out in a piece. Each organ he drops deftly in a jar to "pickle," as he puts it. As he plucks each part from the corpse, he makes some vexatious witticism; all for a purpose. His goal is to undo the inhibiting dread that invariably envelops the *human frame among the new students. Even when the cadaver is that of a criminal or a pauper, many scruple to cut, as if the carcass might feel the blade. Such superstitions die hard. He has told me privately that the teacher's first step is to harden these boys to what their profession demands of them.*

He works rapidly down the anatomy from the throat, naming the parts and delineating the internal structure. Then comes an unexpected dividend. When he removes the uterus, he discovers that the wench was with child. This I have seen before. Often the female cadavers arrive pregnant from the prisons; the gaolers treat these doxies like their private harem. Von Troeltsch at once slits the bag open to show us its contents. The embryo is in its third month. "Stupid girl!" he comments. "She might have pled her belly and saved her neck. But hush! Don't tell the hangman! He will want to be paid double."

I am handed the fetus so that I might show it round the room. I think: How monstrous a being this is I am holding; a thing more like a fish than a human. *How merciful that our loathsome origin is hidden from view. For even the most glorious Adonis begins his existence as a gargoyle.*

We work steadily through the afternoon until the light fades at the windows. When we leave, what a ghoulish troop we are, overshoes in offal, our aprons smeared with blood. As we come again into the light of the open courtyard, we break into the Song of the Worm, the dissector's favourite anthem.

Think how greatly a single session like this moves us forward in history! In these few hours, my fellow students and I have learnt more about our inner workings than was known to Plato or Aristotle or Moses. I frankly cannot understand how mankind lived in such ignorance for so long. Right inside our skin, there has been a world waiting to be discovered. But only when we grew bold enough to apply the knife did we come out of the shadows. Now we see clearly that the inside of the living thing is no different from the inside of one of your automata, Father. Instead of wheels and gears we have muscle and tendon and joint. Still, it is a mathematical order of parts, that is all, and each time we cut we find out one thing more about that order and how to make it superior.

I will make every effort to be home this year for the holidays. If nothing else, the journey will at last give me reason to wash and shave and visit a bar-

ber. You would not guess what a filthy specimen of humanity your son has become. I live like a hermit in a house built of books. When I come home, I shall soak myself three full days in the largest tub in the château, and keep the maids bringing hot water.

Your ever grateful son,
Victor

The _Soirée_

Victor's letters arrived in a running stream, never less than one each month, sometimes as many as three. All reported his scholastic triumphs and his growing enthusiasm for chymical studies. This became the feeble excuse for his continued absence. A year passed, and the greater part of a second before he made his first passing reference to me. "Remember me to my sister," he casually added, seemingly an afterthought at the close of a letter otherwise filled with details of lectures and experiments. _Sister._ He knew full well how chilling that title would sound to me, coming as it did from one who had been my lover, and perhaps the only one I should ever have. Still, this betokened a curious change. I once again existed in his eyes! I, with whom he had practised the high rites of the chymical marriage, was now granted the reality his guilty conscience had formerly sought to deny. Why? Was this some wishful effort at _rapprochement_? Upon reading closer, I thought not. There was something more troubling here: a steeliness of heart that lent the man an unearned innocence, an innocence he claimed as if he no longer cared what his accuser might think. I noted that the letters in which I was so casually named reflected something else: a growing sense, on Victor's part, of restless independence from the teachers who had shaped his mind. In the course of his second year at Ingolstadt, even his relationship with his beloved Professor Waldman was growing remote. He complained of having exhausted all that his professors had to teach him. Accordingly, he pondered moving his residence from the university. Since this was mentioned in connection with his intention of returning to Geneva at the end of term, Father and I assumed he would once again share our home. But not so. As later letters made clear, his plan was simply to sojourn with us briefly, staying at Belrive as any guest in transit might.

"Nonsense!" Father declared, interpreting Victor's behaviour as a display of modesty. "I shall not hide my son's fire under a bushel basket. Write to him. Tell him we shall make a fitting occasion of his homecoming. It is time for Belrive to come to life again."

Dutifully, but with the utmost formality, I wrote to Victor, telling him that Father intended to welcome him home by opening the château for a grand *soirée*. To which Victor replied in a tone so curt that I refrained from showing his letter to Father. "I beg you to do what you can to spare me this agony! Nothing would please me less than an evening of mindless badinage with an uninformed herd of gossip-mongers and triflers. My work is utterly beyond communication to any except men of science, and even then only at the most advanced level. I would agree, if Father insists, to meet with a select group of my peers to make some small demonstration. But you must understand that much of my work is still at an experimental stage; there is much I am not yet ready to reveal."

Far from being disappointed by this response, Father proved even more eager to host the select gathering I told him Victor proposed. "By all means," he agreed with high enthusiasm. "We shall have an assembly of notables for Victor to address. All the schools must be represented."

But who would arrange this illustrious event? It fell to me, as the new mistress of Belrive, to draw up the guest list and issue the invitations. This utterly disagreeable task became my first assignment as lady of the Baron's household. Within a week's time I had sent to the Academy in Geneva and to the universities at Bern and Lausanne, inviting some dozen or so renowned naturalists and physicians of Father's acquaintance to gather at Belrive upon Victor's arrival. Each morning at breakfast, Father would quiz me regarding my preparations for the *soirée*. How many had accepted our invitation? he wished to know. What number would require hospitality at the château? Had I discussed hiring more kitchen hands with Celeste? The pride Father took in presenting his son to such an august assembly restored his ravaged spirits like a healing balm. But for my own part, the thought of Victor's return filled me with trepidation. Weeks ahead I began to prepare myself for—or shall I say *arm* myself against?—the occasion. I all but rehearsed my rôle like an actress waiting in the wings for her cue to go on the stage. I would dress soberly, almost like one in mourning. I would remain aloof, perhaps not even deigning to emerge from my room the first day. I would say little, and that only with polite frigidity. I would ask him nothing about his work or about his plans, and show no interest when he spoke of them. He must know by my every intonation and gesture that he was unforgiven. But I would, if he made the request, agree to speak privately with him and then show my feelings.

Alas! I was preparing myself for an encounter that would never take place because the person for whom my rôle was designed no longer existed. The Victor who stepped from his chaise and swept through our front entrance that summer was not in the least what I had expected. Rather, this was a sort of human tempest who came bounding brusquely up the stairs and into the vestibule, complaining amid a stream of oaths of how ungodly uncomfortable his journey had been. He entered wrapped in a black high-collared cloak that made him seem as ominous as a highwayman: a dark, brooding figure who paced the hall impatiently, waiting to be received. This was clearly no schoolboy come home for the holidays; this was a man of the greater world who troubled himself not at all about anybody's opinion.

I had always found Victor beautiful; so much so that I could not imagine how any man might be more pleasing to a woman's eye. Now, if he was not more handsome than before, he was more powerful—sufficiently so to undermine the mental safeguards I had so carefully erected. There was an unmistakeable forcefulness about him that I could sense from the moment I gazed down from the stair. He had grown a moustache and a dagger-sharp beard that lent him a rakish air. His hair was as wild a mane as ever, if anything, grown thicker and more curled; but his face had become leaner and more intent of expression, bearing the mark of the ascetic. As I approached, he shot a quick, enquiring glance in my direction: a searching eye beneath an arched brow. There was not a hint of apology in his manner. "Well, sister," he called out boldly, "have you arranged to put me on exhibition? I warn you: you may not be pleased by my performance."

He did not wait for a reply, but turned to greet Father, who entered to clap his son in his embrace. That was the last I saw of him until dinner, where his conversation was formal and distant. With respect to the two years past, he talked freely and in grandiose terms about his studies at Ingolstadt. He spoke of the notable figures he had met at school, and of how he had exhausted their intellectual resources. He sounded at times like a conquering general who had vanquished his every foe and appropriated their riches. But when it came to the future, he spoke only glancingly of his plans. He had taken quarters on the outskirts of Ingolstadt where he would continue to have access to the university and the advice of Professor Waldman, but far greater freedom and, above all, privacy. He expected to be wholly absorbed by his new studies for the better part of another year, but as to what these studies might be, he gave no hint. Why then had he bothered to return to Belrive at all? I wondered. This was soon answered. Victor was in great need of money. He had a workshop to furnish and equipment to purchase. "When I am finished, I shall have a finer laboratory than even Professor Waldman," he boasted. "The electrical apparatus will surpass anything outside of the Italian universities." He called what he asked of Father a loan; but of course whatever Father gave him would be his outright. And no one could be more eager to give what he requested.

"You shall have all you want, never fear!" Father said at once, as Victor had very well known he would. "Be bold in what you do and never count the cost."

Victor's last thought upon rising from the table was to ask about the *soirée*, which was scheduled for the following evening. Once again his tone indicated clear displeasure with the event.

"It was Father's wish," I hastened to tell him. "I only acted for him."

"And invited whom?"

"You requested a meeting of peers."

"Ah, yes. Saussure, I hope."

"Yes, Professor Saussure." I quickly mentioned a few of the others.

He shrugged. "A wasted effort. Only Saussure matters. And yourself, sister. I hope you will attend."

"As your peer?"

"As my guest."

Thus I became the only woman in that celebrated company where Victor's work was first revealed. That night, with the Baron presiding proudly over a rich feast, a wealth of scientific experimentation was brought under review. Of particular interest were the experiments of Dr. Erasmus Darwin, whose latest paper reported how he had preserved a piece of vermicelli in a glass case till by some extraordinary means it began to move with voluntary motion. "But not in this way," Victor pronounced with pontifical certainty, "will life be restored to dead tissue." Electricity, he insisted, was the secret of reanimation. At which, the talk turned to his own studies. He told at length of the visit that Galvani had made to Ingolstadt and how he had inspected Victor's experiments. "I was astonished to learn that I had found my way to principles Galvani did not himself know," Victor declared with an undisguised self-satisfaction. "The man has never even dissected an eel to examine how the nerves conduct electrical stimuli!"

Throughout the evening I remained a devout but silent listener. I felt myself swept along by the infectious intensity Victor brought to the conversation. Nor was I alone in my fascination with all that he said; glancing along the table to the right and left, I observed respectful concentration in every face. The room was charged with the thrill of discovery and Victor was at its vibrant centre. No ecstatic saint of former times could have equalled the fervour that burned in Victor when he spoke of his studies. Yet my admiration was mixed with a growing melancholy, for I realised that I had been wholly displaced in his affections by his new vocation. Knowledge had become his sole mistress.

"And what can you show us of your own work, Victor?" Professor Saussure asked at last.

"Too little, I fear," Victor answered with a thin display of modesty. "I am only at the beginning of my research. I can at best show you some trifling token of progress."

As if he were an actor pouncing upon his cue, the Baron rose to say, "Shall we, then, gentlemen—and, of course, my dear Elizabeth— adjourn to the library, where, I believe, my son has prepared a demonstration?" The Baron was fairly glowing with pride in playing the part of Victor's impresario.

All that day, Victor had busied himself in the library, which he had kept locked against the entire household, including the Baron and myself. The luggage he had brought with him from Ingolstadt had been carried in by the footmen soon after his arrival, but none had been permitted to see it unpacked. One great trunk had required the strength of three men to lift it into the house. Observing their struggle, I could not guess what might account for such weight. When on that evening Victor unlocked the doors to the library, we saw that he had transformed the room into a small workshop cluttered with a variety of strange apparatus. On the floor beside the central table were two great ungainly pyramids of metal plates; these had clearly accounted for the gravity of Victor's trunk. The metallic piles were overlaid on all sides by a jungle of wires that ran by way of various metres and gauges to the apparatus on the table; there, surrounded by a circle of candles, rested two mysterious objects draped with cloths as if they might be sacramental articles upon an altar. Between them stood a curious machine consisting of a wheel and glass sphere. Our guests, drawing close to the table, at once became concentrated on this device. Victor used a crank handle to spin the wheel, which was positioned to rub against a circle of amber beads. At once a stream of small blue sparks appeared inside the sphere. He explained that the machine was a new sort of Leyden jar copied from a design by the English electro-physician James Graham. It was capable of generating a moderate electrical current for as long as the wheel remained in steady motion.

"The Voltaic piles you see here," Victor explained, "are zinc and copper, sixty plates of each. The power of the electrical fluid is amplified as it passes through the piles. I cannot tell you what the upper limit of the charge might be. I can only report, speaking from personal experience, that the arcing fire can be potent enough at a four-foot distance to render the experimenter unconscious for a quarter hour—and severely burned." He drew back his sleeve to reveal an ugly welt along his forearm. "So I pray you, gentlemen, stand well back as we proceed."

When the men had satisfied their curiosity about his experimental machinery, Victor uncovered the first and smaller of the two objects that flanked the wheel. Beneath the cloth was a glass container filled with an opaque red fluid that masked its contents. Using a pair of tongs, Victor fished about inside and brought out a limp and wrinkled object that I could not identify until it had been deposited on the table. What lay before us was a human hand. It was positioned on its back with fingers curled like some small dead animal. I believe I was the only person in the room to gasp, but my shock went unnoticed, drowned out by father's exclamation at the head of the table. "My God!" he blurted out as he leaned forward to see more clearly; he was seemingly more taken aback than I. Furtively, I directed an enquiring gaze around the table. Was I alone in experiencing such intense discomfort? If that were so, I must do all I could to hide the feeling.

Ignoring the questions that were raised on all sides, Victor busied himself stretching wires from the generator to several pins protruding from the wrist of the severed hand, finally turning it over so that it rested on its fingers. "As you see," Victor said with a dry chuckle, "my assistant—or what remains of him—was a seaman." He pointed to a ship's anchor that was tattooed on the back of the hand; below the anchor on a furled banner were the words "Mary Rose." "His trade no doubt accounts for the rough texture of the hand. The man was also a drunkard and a brawler who met a bad end. He was arrested for murder. I attended his trial, expecting the sentence. This accounts for my presence on the scene. After the execution I purchased the corpse and delivered it immediately to the dissection theatre. The embalming fluid, I might mention, is a mixture of oil of lavender, nitre, and denatured vermillion. In this respect, as you can see from the evidence before you,

I have made considerable progress." As he spoke, Victor idly stroked his fingers across the knuckles of the lifeless hand. "Now then, please watch closely."

Victor requested Professor Saussure to spin the wheel of the electro-generator; again the sparks produced by the turning wheel formed a ghostly blue bridge of luminescence across the interior of the glass sphere. A hush fell over the room; all eyes were fixed intently upon the shrivelled remnant that rested in a yellow pool of candlelight. After several seconds, there was a slight movement in the thumb, then a twitch in another finger. The flesh on the back of the hand shuddered; suddenly the fingers splayed themselves out upon the table's surface. Then, clenching its fingers again, the hand seemed to be trying to drag itself forward. As it struggled to gain a purchase on the table's surface, its broken, discoloured nails made a hideous scraping sound upon the wood. Taking a small-bladed knife from his pocket, Victor pricked one finger of the hand. It flinched; it had unmistakeably felt the wound. Again Victor jabbed at the hand, and again it drew back, this time raising its fingers as if to ward off the threat. "You see the instinctual reactions," Victor explained as he continued to thrust at the hand, which now bore several small cuts that oozed a purple fluid. "Clearly the hand has retained its life-long memory of pain; it reacts to attack and seeks to protect itself."

Taking up one of the candles that stood around the edges of the table, Victor held the flame to one side of the disembodied hand until the heat had charred the flesh; as if it recognised the danger of fire, the hand scrambled as best it could to escape. But like some blind beast that knew not where to turn for safety, it awkwardly scuttled first this way, then that, dragging behind it the tangled wires to which it was attached like some broken tail. As Victor singed the thing on one side and the other, the sight became too much for me to watch. Turning my eyes away, I whispered across the table to him, "Please stop!"

Victor glanced up in surprise. "Yes; well, the point is proven, is it not?" he asked. "The part comes alive with the memory of the whole— at least at the level of primitive reflex. One last demonstration." Victor took a small piece of rope from his pocket and slipped it under the palm. The hand recoiled at the sensation, then closed upon the rope and held tight. Victor lifted it from the table-top and conveyed it to its container. There he plucked away the wires that were attached at the wrist; the hand loosed its grip on the rope and slid back into its preserving bath.

Dr. Bertholon, a member of the medical faculty at the Academy, was the first to speak. "Surely, Dr. Frankenstein, you are not claiming that the hand actually *feels* these sensations."

"But of course it does," Victor answered. "It has been perfectly preserved and is now revitalised by electrification."

"I would say this is no more than a passive muscular reaction," Dr. Bertholon insisted. "The movement does not betoken life."

"It does!" Victor snapped impatiently. "It *lives!*"

Dr. Bertholon, displaying undisguised scepticism, raised a further question. "If, as you say, the hand is alive, does it not require a blood supply?"

"In time it will," Victor answered, "if the tissue is to be renewed. If the organism were whole, it might replenish its blood by eating and digesting. That is, provided the tissues have been carefully preserved in the interim."

"You have observed this happening?"

"I have. With smaller animals—mice and a variety of birds. After emerging from the embalmed state and feeding, they have regenerated their circulatory system. The organism does not forget its skill for making blood."

"Your findings," Professor Saussure commented, "are indeed impressive. But as to the vitality of the specimen: how can you know this, Victor?" He added with a benign sarcasm, "The hand has no tongue to tell you."

"True," Victor admitted. "But the tongue, though mute, is with us." With these words, he slipped the cover off the second veiled object. Even at the time, what most surprised me was how little disturbed I was by what I saw. Perhaps the sight of the severed hand had taken the edge off my initial revulsion and left me prepared for even more macabre developments. In any case, I flinched not at all to see a human head before me resting in a bowl of greyish fluid that surrounded what remained of the neck. It was held in an upright position by a metal armature that gripped it across the shaven scalp and at the temples and the jaws. At the brows, the cheeks, and the base of the skull, wires had been taped that led through the bowl and then away toward the metal pyramids on the floor. The face belonging to the head was not a handsome one; it was gruff and heavy-browed, with coarse jowls and a flattened nose. Yet, with its eyes shut and its facial muscles in repose, there was a sort of Stoical serenity about this object that I took to be the composure of one who had passed beyond the affronts and indignities of this life. Or perhaps the calm with which I greeted this ghastly display arose from its air of unreality. From the embalming process the flesh of the face had taken on a bluish translucence that lent it the appearance of a porcelain effigy. I did, in fact, hope that this might be some grotesque *objet d'art,* and no human remnant at all. But of this I was soon to be disabused.

Dipping a cloth into the bowl that held the head, Victor proceeded to smear the ashen fluid over the face. This, he told us, was volatile alkali and would heighten the conductivity of the skin. "Hand and head come from the same cadaver. It was my good fortune to be able to remove both, along with other undamaged parts." Then, once again, he turned to his electro-generator and began to spin the wheel. Within seconds, the eyelids of the dead man's face quivered and then suddenly blinked open. At this I was not alone in registering amazement; several around the table sucked in a breath of disbelief. "Professor Saussure," Victor asked, "will you be good enough to move the candle slowly just before the eyes?"

Professor Saussure did as he was requested. He slid the candle back and forth before the impassive face. Now, for the first time, I felt emotion surge within me. It was not disgust I experienced, but a sorrow that brought sobs to my lips. For never had I seen anything more pitiful than the eyes that were now perfectly revealed in the candlelight. Far from expressionless, they presented a look of helpless misery; in their shadowed sockets they swam in the very abyss of despair. Was I, I wondered, alone in seeing the despondency there? I could not shake myself free from the conviction that these were the eyes of one who had been torn unwillingly from the annihilating darkness and now suffered some hideous form of twilight awareness. But Victor had no interest in matters of this kind; instead, he directed one and all to watch the action of the pupils. And indeed in the candle's light one could see the irises dilating and contracting.

"You see," Victor explained with rising giddiness, "the eyes are reacting to the light. They are trying to focus. The visual response to light is only the most primitive of mechanisms; it happens autonomically. Now, if a functioning brain should be attached that could make sense of the sensory signals, even if it were only the brain of a lower animal . . ." Here he broke off in his burst of enthusiasm to give a weary sigh of resignation. "Unfortunately, on this most important front, I confess that my research has been stymied. The human specimens to which I have had immediate post-mortem access have been badly damaged. Hanging, as you can imagine, all but wholly destroys the cervical vertebrae. The specimen before you possesses only the rudiments of the brain stem; the rest I have had to remove lest it spread its deterioration to the adjacent tissues. With animal subjects, however, where the organs can be removed before death, I have made great advances in preserving the brain in nearly perfect condition. Now watch, gentlemen."

Victor threw a switch at the base of the wheel and set to work spinning his generator more vigourously. I guessed that he had directed the current to another area of the head, for now the flesh of the cheeks began to shudder as if with pain; the jaw worked, moving to the left and right; and at last the lips convulsed and drew back to reveal the yellowed and broken teeth that lined the gums behind. Gone was the placidity that had earlier characterised the face. In its place was a bestial grimace; one could almost hear the snarl that was meant to accompany the scowl. For several seconds, as Victor spun the wheel, the muscles of the face laboured and tightened, the eyes protruded until one feared that they might leap from their sockets. Not wishing once again to be the single voice raised in protest, I lowered my gaze and watched no more until the rasping sound of the wheel ceased. When I looked again, the face had reverted to its formerly relaxed state. Victor reached across to draw the lids down over the lightless eyes and then to wipe the brow and cheeks dry with a cloth. Once again the head had become a porcelain bibelot. But, looking more closely after the others had turned away, I was certain that I saw a drop of moisture form at the bottom edge of one eyelid— and then at the other. The drops grew heavy and then streamed down the cheeks. If these were not some remaining beads of moisture, they were surely tears.

His demonstration completed, Victor turned to his peers for their response. Dr. Dupraz, a Genevan physician who often treated Father, was the first to speak. "I commend you on your mastery of embalming chemistry, Victor. You have made a great step forward in the preservation of organs; this will surely benefit our research. But I frankly believe it is premature to interpret the reflexes we have observed as vital signs. More likely these are the same muscular contractions one sees in Galvani's frogs, which I believe we now know are due to the reactivation of residual nerve fluid." There was a murmur of approval on all sides.

Victor was not pleased with this judgement. "I beg to disagree. What you have seen are more than random reflexes. The hand's movement was recognisably caused by pain—and possibly by the fear associated with fire."

"As you say, 'possibly,' " the physician answered. "But how can one know? Both pain and fear are subjective sensations. Now, perhaps if the hand were able to write a note for us reporting its feelings . . ." The remark was made with a gentle facetiousness that inspired polite laughter round the table.

Victor did not share the amusement. "Unfortunately, it is likely that the hand is as illiterate as the man who once owned it," he replied sardonically. "I have perhaps erred in not seeking out the appendage of a more educated specimen."

Sensing Victor's displeasure, Professor Saussure hastened to make an end to the evening. "I believe we can all agree," he sagely commented, "that Victor's work is an extraordinary contribution to our ongoing study of the electrical foundations of life. Much remains to be done; but we have this evening witnessed a notable beginning."

His words were applauded; yet I was certain I had detected signs of both doubt and discomfort in the room, even though one and all had sat through the demonstration in a state of burning curiosity, myself no less than the others. I, too, had sat in attendance as if bound to my chair. The passion with which Victor presented his work had carried me along like a swift stream. So enthralled was I by the force of his conviction that I had fought down my unease. I will also admit to simple cowardice: I would not have the only woman present be the one person to manifest distress. Now that the demonstration was finished, however, I reflected more critically on what I had witnessed. Before me lay the head and hand of a pitiful man who should have been allowed to go to his rest. Yet here were these parts of him, being used to prove a theory in which I could see no possible good. As irrational as the feeling was, I felt ashamed to have seen a fellow being so improperly used.

"But what is the use of this?" I asked quite suddenly. The words were spoken before I could think. I had no desire to detract from Victor's praise, but the query leapt impulsively from me, an expression of honest perplexity. In bursting out, I had interrupted one of the men, who, with exaggerated courtesy, now encouraged Victor to "answer the good lady's question."

"You see no value in the demonstration?" Victor asked with true concern. There was a note of hurt in his voice.

"What value can there be in such a macabre achievement?"

"How if my work—repugnant as it may, regrettably, seem—makes possible the replacement of a man's damaged hand or blinded eye? How if it makes possible the creation of *better* hands and eyes than any man has ever known? In the process of time, we shall be able to bring a new species into being. We shall renew life where death now devotes the body to corruption."

Victor's sincerity was obvious; it fairly blazed in his face and voice. His profession of faith took me quite by surprise. "You believe this will come to be?"

"I am certain of it. My work is not idle curiosity—nor, in heaven's name! some ghoulish diversion. It is certain to be of the greatest benefit."

I waited to see if any would second my objection. None did. I had spoken foolishly, allowing my squeamishness to outweigh my judgement. "Ah, then," I stammered, "if that is the case . . ." At once I felt as if all eyes were turned in my direction; a stifling wave of condescension gathered about me. I realised I had no place in this company. Hurriedly excusing myself, I withdrew and sought out my room. The words that followed me through the door were expressions of gratitude for the event I had arranged; but I heard in them an unmistakeable undertone of relief that I had elected to absent myself.

Looking down from my room into the courtyard, I could see the brightly-lit salon below, where Victor and his guests—the men he was proud to call his peers—talked on. Perhaps it freed them to speak more frankly that the one woman who had been present was gone. My mind swirled with loathing and embarrassment. Had Victor truly discovered the secret of life? I wondered. Surely I was not incapable of appreciating so towering an achievement. I could not deny that it chilled my blood to think that these severed parts of a dead man might truly live and feel and remember; but was I not allowing faint-hearted revulsion to cloud my Reason? What, after all, had Victor done but preserve the physical remnants of a poor wretch—a criminal who had done his kind no good—so that they might be studied for the benefit of others? I wondered, then, if perhaps I had spoken merely out of spite, a woman who could not forget the grudge she bore.

As I stood at my window, my fingers idly traced the design that had been carved into the oaken shutters. I turned to look at the panel where my hand rested. It bore the picture of the dying Tristram cradled in the arms of Queen Iseult. Had I forgotten who first told me this story and awakened my soul to high Romance?

Some two hours later, Victor's *soirée* had ended; our guests had departed or retired to their rooms. Belrive fell silent.

It had become my habit, if the night was clear, to walk in the garden before I retired. My purpose was to search out the stars, and so remind myself of the time I had spent in the wood; that wild, magical time when I lost my way and found myself. In that wilderness, when "day its fervid fires had wasted," the last sight I saw before I slept were these stars above me. They had become my companions . . . Cassiopeia, and

Cepheus, and the seven patient daughters of Atlas. They shone now in the moonless and unclouded sky, patterns of imperious light, and brightest of all among them Venus, like a burning pearl above the Jura. This night of all nights I wished to stand under those figures of cold fire, remembering how I had proven my independence. But tonight they brought back another memory that was as bitter as it was sweet. Victor had taught me these stars when I first came to the château as a mere girl; and when he had taught me all that could be learnt by the unaided eye, he brought me to Father's great telescope that I might see the more distant, newly-discovered heavens. He had shown me the haunting rings of Saturn and the double star in Aldebaran, all more marvellous than I could have imagined. And he had taught me his own impassioned wonder. How much I had admired his intellectual fervour, and wished to be like him! His mind as much as his comely countenance had become my childish standard of manly beauty; I had fallen in love with him before I knew what to call the emotion. Though he may only have been showing off for his new sister, all he told me remained with me as vividly as if the words had been uttered yesterday. He had given me the gift of the stars, the gift that alone remained when he had taken all else from me.

Now that he was again beneath this roof, I was left to ponder the foolish thing my life had become. No woman had more reason to hate any man than I had to hate Victor. Only by hating him could I respect myself for all I ever wished to be: free, proud, and honourable. But to hate him was as impossible as to kill my heart and stay alive. "Each of us is but half of a complete being," Mother had said. "What we call 'love' is our hunger to find completion in another."

I had walked to the foot of the shadowy orchard where the gloaming gathered thickest. A waft of wind came sweeping down the laurel-walk and trembled through the long avenue of beeches that marked the end of the garden. I heard a nightingale warbling distantly, the only voice of the midnight hour. I paused to listen . . . and then, quite suddenly, Victor was beside me; he had stolen across the lawn so that I would not hear his steps upon the walk. At the sound of his voice, a shudder of joyous expectation ran through my blood. *He is here!* my heart said. *The only man you shall ever love stands at your side.*

"Can you still name these stars?" he asked. His voice had lost its forceful edge and grown gentle.

I was of a mind to rush away, but did not. I, who had stared down the lynx, was not to be sent running from my faithless lover. I stood firm and answered. "I remember them as I learnt them—every one."

"There, the three stars just above the mountains . . ."

"The belt of Orion the mighty hunter."

"And the reddish star there just off his right shoulder?"

"Betelgeuse, which the Arabs say is the eye of an evil spirit."

"And there, straight above?"

"Andromeda, bound to the rock as a sacrifice to the monster."

"And there, the bright orange star?"

"Aldebaran in Taurus. Not one star, but two."

"And do you remember why such doubled stars are important?"

"Because their masses can be exactly calculated by Newton's law. That is the importance a man of science would see."

"Is there some other importance?"

"Only that binaries are destined to be companions for all eternity— like lovers who have no choice but to circle forever in obedience to one another's gravity. Aldebaran, I think, means 'follower.' Loving is a kind of following, do you not think? A desire to be with. But neither of the binaries leads. Both follow."

"How like you to find poetry in the calculation of masses."

"I was taught that the world teems with signatures deeper than any man's science knows, messages for our hearts to read."

He did not take his eyes from the stars, but continued to speak while still scanning the heavens. His profile was outlined darkly upon the sky: the high, fine brow and sculptured jaw—all framed in a glowing, unruly nimbus of hair. He was, I thought, more beautiful than ever. "I have wanted many times to write to you," he said.

"But you have. In Father's letters."

"I mean to you directly."

"And I say again: You have—in Father's letters. Are they not, every word of them, written for me? I assume so when I read them. I have read them all, Victor. I know of all your triumphs."

"Come! I am a novice. I have had no triumphs, not yet."

"Modesty does not become you. It rings hollow. You shall be a great man one day. Your name will rank with Newton's. I hope to see that happen."

"But you have not said what you thought of my demonstration tonight."

"Do you care to know?"

"I care more for your opinion, Elizabeth, than for that of any man who was gathered in that room—even Saussure's."

"Why should that be? I am not one of your peers."

"I affect a certain arrogance. I know this. I have found that it helps concentrate my mind to behave as if no man's opinion matters to me except that of my peers—and perhaps not even theirs. But I know I must at last be judged for what I do in a greater world than that of the professors and the doctors. You are the best of that world. I would know what you think."

"I will be frank to tell you that I found your demonstration repugnant."

"And yet you stayed to see it through—and, if I am not mistaken, with as much curiosity as any who were in the room."

"Yes. I admit to curiosity. I wished to know what has occupied your attention so powerfully at Ingolstadt. I see that you still seek to create a race of happy and excellent men."

"How pretentious that sounds!"

"They are your own words."

"Are they? I was so often carried away—as a boy."

"It is the same in your letters. Your ambition is no less. But it is now empowered by knowledge. I pray that you will use that power well."

"As yet I have no more power than to perform the idle parlour tricks you have seen. Which, as I have learnt tonight, do nothing to persuade the sceptical. You saw the condescension. They regard me as little more than a student."

Some time passed before we spoke again. In the interval, I felt myself growing dizzy with the strain of standing in his presence, struggling to overcome, to live, rise, and speak my heart. In the deep silence, I could feel the tug of the turning stars as the night wheeled round toward morning. Did he know the vehemence of emotion that grief and love stirred within me, this man who had taught me so much that I knew of grief and all that I knew of love?

"There are matters on which we should talk," he said at last.

"Talk? What time is there to talk the night before you leave to go I know not where, to do I know not what?"

"That need not be of any concern to you."

"Oh, Victor! Everything you do and feel and dream, everything you suffer and take joy in—*all* is my concern." And there were these words that pressed to be said, balancing on the very brink of speech: *What is there in my life but you?* But, biting my tongue, I held them back, and said instead, "We need the rest of our lives to talk—not these few poor hours that are left after you have come to beg Father for money. That would only be time enough to feign remorse and pretend forgiveness."

"I had no thought of remorse."

"Then perhaps the remorse is mine, and the forgiveness yours to bestow. I worry often that I unsettled the course of your life and burdened you with spite. I think there is much you have done that is meant to vindicate yourself against me."

"I will be back in a few months' time—so I expect. What I have to do will by then have proven to be either a failure or a success. Then you shall know all. I promise this. You will wait until then?"

"What choice have I? Where would I go, a spinster woman? Off to seek my fortune? What other life have I but to wait where I have a roof provided for me? I am my father's daughter or my husband's wife. Or shall I, perhaps, go to live in the woods and lie down with the wild beasts? Can you imagine such a thing? Forgive me; you will think this is self-pity speaking."

"You have reason for self-pity and for anger."

"Yes. But can you believe that I have grown beyond that? You would do me great honour if you listened to hear what is strong and happy in me. I do not live, any longer, waiting for propitiation."

"I can perceive that. You are your own woman, Elizabeth." He extended his hand to touch my arm; I drew back a step beyond his reach.

"Then leave me knowing that. And return when you are ready to meet me as if for the first time, not as sister, or lover, or even long-lost friend, but as a stranger you must pretend you do not know. Assume nothing. Then we shall talk through many nights and days." I drew away with a last request. "Wait here. Let me return to the house alone."

He did so. I passed him with my face turned away, fearing that even in the dark he might catch sight of my dazzled eyes. Hurriedly, I made my way along the laurel-walk, hoping the tears would wait until I reached the château. A small mercy: the wind came up and, rustling along the beeches, covered over the weeping I would not have him hear. For if he had heard, he would never have known that these were tears, not of sorrow, but of pride and triumph. I had shown him nothing but independence!

The next morning, I waited until I heard his post-chaise depart before I left my room.

He said "two months." But two *years* were now to pass, during which Victor's reports grew more obscure and perfunctory, sometimes no more than a few rapidly scrawled lines that offered still another apology for his long absence. Then for the final half-year of that time—the eventful spring and summer of '92—we received not so much as a letter. We assumed it must be because the world had turned upside-down.

EDITOR'S NOTE
Regarding Victor Frankenstein's Research

Many readers of my original history have expressed both puzzlement and consternation at how briefly I enter into the particulars of Frankenstein's research. Questions have been raised especially regarding the cursory way in which I there describe the formation of the creature. This lack of detail has led some to dismiss my account as a patent fabrication. I now stand ready to repair that failure, which I confess was the result of deliberate censorship on my part. Frankenstein offered a great deal more intelligence about his scientific investigations; I, however, elected to limit my report to little more than the general lineaments of his narrative. My justification for this decision is easily stated; it proceeded from a combination of scepticism and moral horror.

The reader must understand that at the time I recorded Frankenstein's words, the man frequently drifted into fits of despair and self-recrimination; he was at points little short of hysterical with remorse as he passed the terrific events of his life under review. I could not easily tell where lucid recollection left off and delusion began; Elizabeth Frankenstein's memoir now makes that line far easier to draw. She attended the single public occasion at which Frankenstein openly discussed his research; her account confirms remarks that were made to me by the man himself as part of his death-bed reminiscence. I am therefore persuaded to lay all doubt aside. Here, then, are the full notes as I took them down from Frankenstein's own lips.

It was soon after his visit to Belrive recounted above that Frankenstein established his laboratory in the wooded outskirts of Ingolstadt. The place, "a workshop of filthy creation" as he described it, was an abandoned watchtower; nearby ran a stream and upon its bank a water-mill that provided the mechanical force his labours sometimes required. Here, within convenient reach of the university and the hospital, he found the privacy his research demanded. And here he set to work disturbing the tremendous secrets of the human frame.

"How hard I laboured at my task!" he recollected. "I seemed to have no soul or sensation but for this one pursuit. In my exuberance, I vowed to make my creation as finely-wrought as the exquisite anatomies of Michaelangelo, whose portrait of Adam waking into life was the model I placed above my table. I was more the artist than the scientist as I crafted flesh to bone and delved into the intricacies of fibres, veins, and muscles. So swiftly was I borne along in the anticipation of success, that I was utterly blinded to the shortcomings of my effort. In the giddy fevers of my toil, I was persuaded that I could in time make good each failure and bring the whole to a magnificent conclusion: a superior being to any that had ever issued from the womb."

But as remarkable as Frankenstein's success had been in preserving and revitalising the anatomical remnants he harvested from his specimens, he soon found himself facing a stubborn obstacle.

"The brain," he averred, "was the greatest problem. I could find no way to preserve this fragile organ long enough to restore it to consciousness within a new body. As you can understand, Walton, there would be no way to prove that I had achieved reanimation—and surely no way to demonstrate that I had restored sentience to a human specimen—unless the nervous stimuli could be passed through a living brain and reported by the specimen itself. Anything less than this might be dismissed as some form of post-mortem muscular reflex.

"No scruple inhibited me from torturing the living animal to animate the lifeless clay. As a result, my experiments below the human level bore swift and encouraging fruit; I soon proved conclusively that the brain of a still-living specimen of as high an order as a cat might be extracted and preserved in such a way that it would regain its function when grafted upon a new nervous system. But in what way could this be demonstrated upon a human subject? Even when I arranged to be in attendance at the moment of death, there was no opportunity of removing the brain until the deceased had been honoured with all the usual burial rites; by the time these were finished and the necessary formalities discharged for obtaining the body—if indeed permission could be gained at all—the cerebral tissues had begun to decay. In consequence, I turned to the prison morgue, where I might be on hand whenever an execution was scheduled. But the hangman's rope invariably did more cerebral damage to these specimens than my research could tolerate. I will confess that, more than once in my impatience, I was sorely tempted to leap the ethical barrier that forbids human vivisection. Suppose I came upon someone fatally-ill and comatose upon his death-bed . . . would conscience permit me to do what the opportunity made possible?

"At last, by a stroke of good fortune, I hit upon another way.

"Occasionally, among the cadavers that were delivered to the medical college from the gallows or the almshouse, one might discover a pregnant female. In one instance, when the woman's body arrived post-haste, I found the embryo, then in its fifth month of gestation, still viable. I removed it and kept it alive long enough to extract the brain. Unfortunately, I could not preserve the tissue more than a few days before decomposition set in. Nevertheless, I had found a method. I at once made enquiries among the midwives of the town, requesting that I be notified if any should be summoned to abort a well-advanced fetus. To my surprise, several of the women I approached greeted my offer with grave suspicion and no little horror; they refused to countenance my request until I explained what my intention might be. This forced me to proceed with caution. These hags believed I might be a ghoul! If a rumour to that effect should be spread abroad, I might find myself accused of practising the black arts. Only when I agreed to pay handsomely did I overcome the scruples of at least a few among them. Within the month I received word that one of the women would be attending a troubled pregnancy that had entered the third trimester. I accompanied the midwife and waited in the alleyway until the deed was done; the fetus was in my hands within minutes of its delivery. I lost no time in undertaking the dissection; it was done in the very carriage that had brought me to the scene. The brain was embalmed at once, and preserved for three weeks before it showed the first signs of decay.

"By that time, I had acquired another specimen in the same manner—and then another, and so pressed my investigations steadily forward. On each occasion I managed to prolong the period of vital survival until, in the second year of my research, after scores of reverses and failures, I discovered a way to use the mother's own uterine waters together with certain chemical nutrients to nourish the isolated brain artificially so that its development might recapitulate the full term of pregnancy. Nay more! This same technique, if it should be supplemented by subtly bathing the brain in an ambient electrical charge, allowed me to accelerate the organ's growth until it corresponded in weight and complexity to the third year of post-natal development.

"You see the significance, man? I had established beyond all question that the brain, the seat of our God-like intelligence, if it might once be freed of its cranial enclosure, develops more rapidly. I had seen this most miraculous of organs blossom before my eyes, and with no trace of the creasing and folding that the imprisoning skull-case imposes upon it. I tell you, Walton, it was almost as if the thing *wanted* to be liberated from the physical confinement to which the human frame condemned it. Perhaps here was the root of Man's age-old conviction that mind and body are uncommensurable substances. And perhaps here was the solution to this seemingly intractable metaphysical conundrum. I had brought the tissues of intellection to the very brink of speech and logicality, keeping them unspoiled, free of idle fantasy and childish misconceptions—free, too, of whatever distortions gestation and birth may entail. Did I, then, have before me the philosopher's true *tabula rasa:* a virgin mind waiting to be rationally formed and perfectly educated—perhaps to evolve new, unimaginable capacities? You see why I was so tempted to believe that it was my destiny to have a new species bless me as its creator and source."

He had been recounting his discoveries with heightening exuberance, reliving the excitement of the original adventure. But suddenly his voice fell silent. I looked up, and only then realised how vividly my expression must have betrayed the misgivings I felt. Yet if the truth be told, the fascination that underlay my aversion was every bit as great as his. Was it possible, I wondered, that this wretched man who lay expiring in my cabin had actually mastered the secrets of life and death? Was it by so gross an assault upon the sanctity of human life that he had achieved this astonishing discovery? His tale was as fantastic as it was grotesque; but there was an ardour in his voice that lent all he said the irresistible force of truth.

"Ah, Walton, I see the repugnance etched in your features," my companion sighed with true disappointment. "You are not yet sufficiently the man of science to view my efforts with a dispassionate eye. Or perhaps I am no longer sufficiently human to look upon my deed with the abhorrence it merits. You are right to be wary of me. How can I expect you to condone the extremes to which I was driven in the first enthusiasm of success? I confess that, in my few moments of moral lucidity, even I shrank from the deeds I had performed. There were times I felt like some druidical priest called upon to sacrifice the infants of the tribe to a cruel god. This much I beg you to believe: I went no further than to use aborted fetuses, life that stood no chance whatever of surviving, that had not so much as drawn a breath outside the mother's body. I am no murderer, my friend! I swear to you that I but salvaged for useful experimentation what would otherwise have gone profitless to the refuse heap. Only in this way, was I able to nurture the organ of Reason into an independent existence."

Here, then, is Frankenstein's entire confession; this was how his unnatural creation was given intelligent life. All that is lacking from this account is the exact formulation of those chemical substances that so perfectly preserved and nourished the isolated organs that made up the creature's frame. This, too, Frankenstein promised to communicate to me, for I pressed him insistently to reveal the minutest details of his discovery. But before that could be done, the man was dead.

I would be less than candid if I did not admit that, despite the moral discomfort Frankenstein's words inspired in me, for many years after our encounter there was also a buried spark of envy. If I could once let myself believe his tale was true, I must accept that this man had gazed into the blackest depths of the unknown; he had unveiled the mystery of mysteries. The project that had brought me to the Arctic wastes—for that matter, every task I had ever imagined setting before myself as a measure of my worth—paled in comparison to that achievement. And even if so daring a goal should ever present itself to my imagination, would I possess the courage to do what he had done?

Time has dulled the secret admiration I once felt for Frankenstein, replacing it, I hope, with sounder judgement. Yet to this day I still find myself torn by conflicting sentiments whenever I look back across the years, uncertain which bespeaks the true scientist in me. Was it the envy I once harboured for Frankenstein's daring—or the shame I now feel for ever having weakened to that feeling?

Restless Nights,
Perturbing Dreams

That summer the Revolution came to Geneva.

The Swiss, ever the most realistic of people, had known since the troubles in France began that even our mountain borders would not long defend us from the political storm that threatened to engulf Europe. All knew it was only a matter of time before the fury that had been unleashed against the *ancien régime* spilled across our frontiers, bringing blood and devastation. No sooner had the Bastille fallen, than revolutionary Swiss *émigrés* ensconced in Paris began plotting their vengeful return from exile. When that day came, the Frankenstein household would be particularly at risk, for the twisted logic of events had made us the enemy of both sides in this Titanic struggle. Despite his wealth and station, the Baron had long been recognised as an outspoken champion of the liberal cause in Europe. The rôle he had played in supporting the American colonial rebellion and the Girondists in France was common knowledge. Noble as his intentions might be—and the Age of Reason had produced no more devoted son than he—his service to the party of Humanity had earned him the hatred of his benighted aristocratic peers. Unable to tell the difference between a constitutional Republican and a sworn regicide, frightened and vindictive Swiss oligarchs denounced him as a traitor to his class. How ironic it was then, that, as the Revolution drifted more and more under the influence of its extreme wing, the very forces of liberty that Father had fostered now turned upon their benefactor as if he were no better than any other hated *aristo*. Accordingly, he became as much a target of rabble-rousing fanatics as the most reactionary feudalist. Both sides were out to have his head.

I never admired Father more than in this critical hour when he stood so valiantly in defying his foes in either camp. Still, he was prudent enough to take precautions. From the summer of '92 on, as France descended into chaos, we lived with carriage and mule-train packed and in readiness to depart from either end of our estate. At a moment's notice, the family might flee—north and east into the Germanies, or south toward the Piedmontese. A household guard was recruited from among the servants and out-workers and hurriedly trained in the use of musket and pike; they would hardly have proved an effective defence against the unruly mobs that crowded the roads, but they might at least give the carriages their chance to escape.

In October, the event we feared most of all took place. We received news that General Montesquiou's forces were advancing upon Geneva. As the home of Rousseau, the city was seen as one of the spiritual capitals of the Revolution. Inspired by the approach of the French legions, demagogues who were pleased to call themselves "Patriots"—disciples of the murderous Robespierre and Saint-Just—rose to overthrow the government of the city and to launch a general attack upon property and privilege. For several weeks we lived in fear of attack by the radical element, whose nightly bonfires we could see on the highways and in the village squares on all sides. Each night bands of incendiaries were despatched throughout the Vaud to loot the homes of the rich and to hang their inhabitants; but before these savages could turn their attention to Collonge and Belrive, the earthquake struck. Word arrived that King Louis had been beheaded. Terror now reigned in Paris, calling itself the Republic of Virtue. With the Jacobins in command, a France gone mad was soon under attack on all fronts by the forces of civilised Europe; war would now become general. Montesquiou's army was called home and the invasion of Geneva abandoned. With that, the Revolution in Switzerland came to an abrupt halt.

I had little difficulty in believing Father when he declared that never before in human affairs had there been such an era of upheaval. The fixed foundations of the world were shaking; no grotesque extreme seemed inconceivable. The century that was ushered in by Newton and Locke like the sunrise of Reason now stood, in its waning years, beneath the shadow of the headsman's scaffold.

It was in these turbulent circumstances, that Victor returned from Ingolstadt.

I had prepared myself to greet him with the same fierce independence I had shown upon his departure two years before. But that intention melted away as soon as he stepped from his chaise. I saw at once that something was desperately amiss. For this was not the Victor to whom I had bade so cold a farewell. Here was a broken soul—thin, sallow, and a-tremble, so obviously the casualty of misfortune that he seemed no longer to care what further misery might be heaped upon him. I was amazed at how spontaneously pity flooded my heart when I saw the sorrow writ upon his person. Where had the distrust gone that had lately been my single feeling for him? It had vanished. I no longer saw Victor as the callous ravisher; instead, I saw him now as the pathetic wreck of all the boyish exuberance I had once loved and admired in him. I could not help but believe that, like the revolutionary ideals I saw turning monstrous all about me, the Promethean fire that once blazed in Victor's mind had turned to ashes. And, in fact, though I could not have known it at the time, another kind of Terror was abroad in the world, something far worse than the fate to which the tumbrils carried their victims through the streets of Paris. The man who stood before me was its prophetic witness; he alone had glimpsed the dark destiny of the laboratory.

Victor testily turned away all enquiries about his condition. He claimed he was suffering from nothing more than the aftermath of a nervous fever; but his infirmity was clearly a condition of the soul more than of the body. Grief and shame mingled in his expression. At every turn he seemed to be in need of forgiveness—and for some greater transgression than I might charge against him. I wished we were once again on loving terms that I might ask him the truth; but there was too little trust between us for that.

And so I must endure the ignorance to which he consigned me, must stand by helplessly day after day as he brooded over his secret grief, fit company for no one. At night, loitering outside his bedchamber, I could hear him pacing the floor. His nights were restless, his dreams perturbed. More than once he woke the house with a cry of strangled terror as if he had been attacked in his bed. All had heard it, but Victor would offer no explanation. On one occasion, rising on a warm night to throw open the casement, I was startled to see the light of a lanthorn moving through the garden. I watched more closely and discerned a cloaked figure darting stealthily over the grounds. Was this some phantom come to haunt our house? No, it was a man armed with a sword, probing among the hedges as if he were hunting out someone who lurked there in the darkness. I knew this must be Victor. I called to him *sotto voce*; he spun round and gazed up at me. His face was a white, twisted mask of fear. "Elizabeth!" he called back, his voice quavering. "As you value your life, lock the windows! Bolt the doors! You are in the gravest danger." Then, backing off rapidly, he disappeared into the night. The next day he would not emerge from his room.

At last, just when I thought I could endure his suffering no longer, Victor broke under the strain of his condition. As he had done once before, he sought me out in the dead of night. He tapped at my door, and when I woke and asked who was there, the only reply was a hoarse whisper: "Please, help me!" I knew the voice and opened the door at once; Victor nearly collapsed into my room. He fell to his knees at my feet and began at once to moan through wrenching sobs. He was so ashamed that he would not lift his eyes to look at me; his hands he kept tightly folded at his chest, never once allowing himself to reach out to me. Even when I bent to help him to his feet, he scuttled away. "I do not trust myself to touch you. Only let me be here with you. I must not be alone!"

"Please," I said, "sit here by my bed."

I recalled the last time we had been together in this room, in this bed.

It was the night Victor walked in his sleep and came to tell me of the cockatrice—that first ominous sign that the Great Work would fail. Still children at the time, we had nevertheless embraced and spent the night in one another's arms. Now, in spite of his resistance, I finally succeeded in drawing him awkwardly to my side, where I sought to comfort him as best I could. With his hands fisted at his temples and his body rigid, he told me of his troubled dreams and mental terrors, yet his revelation was bafflingly veiled; never once did he indicate what the source of these evil presentiments might be. Nor could my most tactful interrogation pierce the shield of secrecy he carried.

"I fear that I am breaking into bits," he confessed. "Here, inside, I seem to be two people struggling for supremacy. Often, my thoughts are not *my* thoughts, but those of another, a dark and savage thing that is born out of me at night. When I walk the corridors, I think I see this Other lurking at every turn; it is myself . . . and not myself. Sometimes I feel that I—Victor—am melting away into a grey, colourless realm, a living tomb; and the Other, the dark one, is taking my place here in this world. This morning, I thought I saw the Other stealing into me just as I woke. It poured itself into my mouth like a fume; it is in me now. I dare not sleep, for fear it will come out and walk the world. Sister, I have done no wrong! Whatever evil the Other does . . . I am not to blame."

These were whirling words. They brought me no understanding. I could but sit close beside this wretched man and take pity. At last he petitioned me with a humility I would never have expected to find in my Victor. "I fear for my sanity, dear sister," he said at last. "For your sake and Father's, I would not inflict the burden of madness upon this house where I have already caused so much misery. Will you help me?"

"But how can I help you, Victor, if I do not know why you suffer as you do? What relief can I offer?"

"I am in need of more skilful care than you or any physician can offer—save one. The one man who can offer that care resides not one week distant from Geneva. I wish to see him."

"And who is this man?" I asked.

"His name is Dr. Mesmer."

Here was an answer I could not have predicted. "You would trust yourself to a man who is regarded as a charlatan?"

"I am convinced he is not! You shall read his papers yourself. The world fears men of such daring and reviles them as madmen or frauds. Mesmer is neither. He has brought 'the mind diseased' within the province of medicine; he treats it as any physical organ might be treated, rather than as a spectral entity. I am prepared to place myself in his hands. But I am too weak in my present condition to travel on my own." He added with a note of shame, "And I am afraid to travel alone. Some one must keep watch while I sleep."

Unhesitatingly, I said that I would help. Whereat Victor, thanking me profusely, wept into my bosom with gratitude. At his touch, so close and impassioned, all my resistance melted away. Had he turned his face to me, I should in an instant have covered him with wild kisses.

⊰✦⊱

It was left to me to prepare the journey. This began with the most difficult step of all: I must persuade Father to agree to our plan. He, as Victor predicted, was undisguisedly hostile. "Mesmer? But the man is a mountebank," he objected at once. "Dr. Franklin has shown this animal magnetism of his to be no better than quackery."

I had prepared myself carefully for this response. Victor had provided me with the very papers that Father now invoked against Mesmer, and I had studied them closely.

"You are right, Father; Dr. Franklin did call the Mesmeric doctrine into question. He did so because it lacked a material cause. In that respect, I understand your scepticism. But I remind you, sir, that Dr. Franklin also hazarded the guess that Mesmerism might nevertheless achieve its curative effects by activating the forces of the imagination. Perhaps there is some new principle of medicine in this. For if a disease be mental, as we agree it is in Victor's case, might not the cure also perforce be mental? Where we deal with derangement of the mind, the application of Mesmer's methods may yield good results even if the cause be mistaken. Surely this is worth a trial."

Father thought hard upon my proposition, and at last reluctantly agreed. Making his best coach and drivers available for our journey, he wished us godspeed, though with the gravest misgivings. Our destination was the tiny village of Frauenfeld near Constance, where Dr. Mesmer now dwelt. With every sign that the spring had thawed the roads leading north to Zurich, we made ready to depart that very week.

EDITOR'S NOTE

Scientific Assessments of Dr. Mesmer's Theory of Animal Magnetism

In the section that follows, we have a rare first-hand account of Dr. Franz Anton Mesmer's work as it was experienced by an observant and articulate patient. Elizabeth Frankenstein's memoir thus serves to shed considerable light upon one of the most perplexing questions in the medical science of our time.

From the late 1770s, when he first announced his discovery of animal magnetism, Dr. Mesmer steadily expanded the province of his system until it grew from a method of medical diagnosis into a grand cosmic scheme. There were, the doctor taught, great magnetic tides that rolled through the universe even as the waves roll through the sea. These effluvia, he claimed, permeate all things including the human frame and are the very breath of their being. If their free flow should be blocked, the body grows ill. But by the skilful therapeutic use of magnetism, the flow might be released and the patient would then recover. Everything, even plant life and minerals, might benefit from being magnetised. Charged from a Leyden bottle, ailing trees could be induced to flower, and the failing springs of the Earth gush forth.

These hypotheses, which were all the rage in the peculiarly eclectic, often wildly speculative scientific climate of the later eighteenth century, have since been effectively exploded. But it was as a physician rather than as a natural philosopher that Dr. Mesmer reached the pinnacle of his fame. In case after case, he displayed an uncanny capacity to heal those abandoned by others as hopelessly diseased. In one celebrated case that blazoned his name across Europe, he even restored sight to the blind. It was later determined, however, that the blindness was merely hysterical blindness and not due to a physical lesion. Discredited and ridiculed, the doctor was forced to leave Vienna.

Sceptics on all sides, especially members of the medical profession, were quick to denounce Mesmer as a charlatan. This only inflated his reputation, which inflamed his enemies the more. In France, at the height of the Mesmer craze, a royal commission was appointed to investigate his claims; its chairman was Dr. Benjamin Franklin, then serving as ambassador from the new American Republic. The commission delivered a devastating blow to Mesmer and his theories. It concluded that Mesmeric cures had been achieved, not by a true physical phenomenon, but merely by the power of suggestion. Overnight, Mesmer fell into disrepute in Paris, as he had done in Vienna some twenty years before. Shortly after the execution of King Louis, who had been his prime benefactor, he wisely decided to remove to his homeland of Switzerland, where scores of people flocked to his clinic to be treated and to witness the wonders of animal magnetism. He continued to practise his healing arts until his death at eighty-one years of age in 1815.

History has not been kind to Dr. Mesmer; indeed it has affirmed his ignominy. Like so many of the mysterious fluids and supernatural effluvia that were hypothesised in his time, animal magnetism has been cast into the dustbin. Even in the practice of medicine, the atomic hypothesis now sweeps all alternatives from the field. Even so, there are those who cling to the possibility that Mesmerism might be of benefit in the treatment of neurasthenia and various forms of emotional debility. The testimony of Elizabeth Frankenstein will be of special interest to those who wish to pursue this line of research. For one thing, she clearly vouches for the fact that the hypnotic state is real; she reports how it was produced and how it affected her behaviour. She makes clear that, once Mesmerised, she was able to follow Mesmer's instructions even when this involved a suspension of physical sensation.

We are left to wonder what mental capacities still remain unexplored in man? What genius and what horror will we find concealed in those dark regions of our nature that Mesmer was the first to investigate? Let us hope that, as this most rational of centuries unfolds, this elusive inner province of reality will at last be liberated from the necromancers and witch-doctors who have been the traditional caretakers of the mind so that it may find its way into the hands of competent medical practitioners.

Our Visit
to Dr. Mesmer

Never have two travellers behaved toward one another so circumspectly as did Victor and I on the road to Frauenfeld. Anyone who chanced to overhear the conversation that occupied us in our carriage might have mistaken us for strangers who had only just met. When we spoke at all, we studiously avoided all personal discourse. Instead, we contented ourselves with the discussion of various philosophical doctrines, among these the nature of the principle of life and whether there was any probability of its ever being discovered and communicated. Above all, we debated Dr. Mesmer's strange new universe of animal magnetism, about which I knew appallingly little. To my surprise, Victor was as well-versed in the field as ever he had been in electrical science. This was, indeed, because he regarded Mesmer's work as an adjunct of that same study.

"How if all forms of electricity and magnetism be fundamentally the same?" he asked, warming to the subject with the intellectual ardour I rejoiced to see in him. "Do not both forces possess the power of attraction and repulsion; and cannot both, as Mesmer has shown, propagate themselves through intermediary bodies? M. Coulomb's thesis has given token that the law of the inverse square may apply to both. Priestley and Cavendish concur in believing this possibility worth investigation. For consider: Mesmer has but hypothesised that the magnetic force acts upon the nervous constitution as well as upon inert Nature. Why may it not, then, be used to heal the mind?"

And, taking out pencil and notebook, he proceeded to explain Coulomb's law in all its mathematical intricacy, a subject that absorbed hours of our time. Though I found no great interest in these calculations, I welcomed the opportunity they offered Victor to apply his attention to some neutral matter that did not touch upon our troubled relations. I listened attentively to all he said about the animal magnetic system, but kept my own counsel. I had heard such fanciful accounts of Dr. Mesmer, whom some mockingly called "the prince of vapours." Others regarded him as a perverted mind, for, reportedly, he filled his chambers with naked supplicants whom he could persuade to behave in unseemly ways. Women especially were warned to consider their virtue when they visisted the Mesmeric clinic.

I took care not to reveal my strong reservations, fearing to diminish Victor's high hopes; for even as we travelled, his need was growing more urgent. Sometimes, dozing in the coach along the way, he grew restive and muttered desperately under his breath. At night, when we stopped, he forced me to promise that I would keep watch over his sleep. So we gave ourselves out to be husband and wife that we might share a single chamber. But this imposed severe demands upon my own stamina; it meant I must watch over Victor until I could no longer keep my eyes from closing. "*He* will not emerge if you are here on guard," Victor said of the Other he was certain lurked inside him. It was to this fancied Other that he spoke in his sleep all the while he tossed upon his bed, calling it "fiend," "wretch," and "devil." At one station along the way, when we halted at an inn outside Lucerne, Victor awakened in the night so filled with anxiety that he rushed from his room into the gallery, crying out and rousing the household. By the time our carriage arrived at Dr. Mesmer's mansion, I was as willing as Victor to believe that the man who lived here could work miracles.

"Welcome! Welcome, Dr. Frankenstein! We are honoured by your presence." So we were met at the front entrance by Dr. Aabye, who identified himself as Dr. Mesmer's chief assistant; he was the tallest man

I had ever met. He towered above Victor and made me feel dwarf-like. His great, thrusting jaw, fully as large as a melon, made up more than half the girth of his abnormally large head. His accent gave it out that he was Danish; his voice possessed a peculiarly oily quality, as if every word were being greased so that it might slide persuasively into one's mind. Chuckling, he introduced himself to us in the foyer as one of Dr. Mesmer's "angels." "It is a name the patients assign to the medical assistants, believing our healing powers to be supernatural. But of course, they are not; they are the quintessence of science, as you, Dr. Frankenstein, would be the first to recognise."

Victor had written ahead to arrange an audience with Dr. Mesmer. Dr. Aabye had been despatched to meet us at the instant of our arrival and to escort us to the rooms prepared for us. Victor was invited to rest before presenting himself for his first *séance* with Dr. Mesmer. That night we were to dine *tête-à-tête* with the doctor and his staff in his private chambers.

"One day we will learn the great lesson of the healing sciences," Dr. Mesmer proclaimed. "Namely, that the mind cures all. '*Mens sana in corpore sano*,' the wise Juvenal has said. But here we reverse that dictum. Here we seek *corpus sanum in mentem sanem*. The sound body is to be found *within* the sound mind. You follow my meaning, Dr. Frankenstein? Here we seek to bring the mind wholly under scientific control. But of course we deal here with more than human health; animal magnetism is a manifestation of the universal force that holds the great cosmos in being."

Dr. Mesmer was a portly man with heavy jowls and a small, flat nose. He was now in his sixtieth year, but still alert and highly animated. At either side his "angels" sat in attendance, eager young men who treated him like a true adept, hanging on every word he spoke. Dr. Aabye was the senior assistant; the others spanned the Continent in nationality from Spain to Greece, and each seemed to make more brilliant conversation than the last. The dinner hour had been taken up with heady discussions of electrical and magnetic theories, in which Victor found a welcome distraction. But before the evening was out, he made a point of emphasising the main purpose of our visit.

"How much I wish I were free to appreciate your research on the purely theoretical plane, Doctor," Victor said. "But as you know from my note, I am here to be your patient, and never did patient need physician more than I."

"You will perform your research upon your own experience, sir," Dr. Mesmer answered. "And what better material can there be?"

That night in my room, I surveyed the bookshelves and happened upon one of Dr. Mesmer's early works. Browsing through the pages, I came upon long autobiographical passages in which he related the exhilaration he found in the pursuit of natural philosophy. In the presence of Nature, he wrote, "a feverish passion overwhelmed my senses"; and then he dilated like a poet upon the beauties and marvels of the universe. I realised that this now-wizened old man, whom so many condemned as a fraud, had spent his life in the grip of a grand vision. Animal magnetism, he had named it: another transcendent system to set beside a score of others that men had invented since the time of Newton. We lived in an age of systems: ethereal media, elastic corpuscles, subtle essences and fluids roiling and bounding across the infinite void, all meant to reveal the One Great Cause whose mastery would make man the equal of God. Dr. Mesmer had lived out his life seeking the key that unlocked the secret of secrets, and had found it—or so he believed. But how brutal that quest can make men, I thought. How the love of truth can warp them, and especially when they think it is just within their grasp. Then let nothing bar their way! They would tear down the gates of heaven to have that secret.

They would betray their beloved.

I read further. I learnt of the doctor's painful sense of estrangement from his fellow scientists. Many cruelly mocked his precious research, for there is nothing in the faculty of scientific Reason that necessitates kindness. And then I came upon touching passages in which he confessed that only when he was roaming in the seclusion of free Nature did he find solace. "O Nature, would I say in my crises, what do you want of me? And I imagined embracing her tenderly, asking her, impatiently, to surrender to my wishes. Fortunately, only the trees could witness the vehemence of my plea, for I must surely have looked like a maniac."

She, she, she. Here was also a man for whom all-nourishing Nature was a woman, a lover, a mother—and yet one whom he would bend to his ambition. Yes, they court Her, but only to conquer Her.

The following day, Victor and I made ready to attend our first *séance chez* Mesmer; it was scheduled for the early afternoon hours. Dr. Aabye was once again to be our chaperon; but this time when he met us in the foyer, he was costumed in a long silken gown beneath which, judging by what one could glimpse with each step he took, he seemed to wear nothing at all. As we made a brief tour of the grounds, he proceeded to explain something of the doctor's methods.

"Dr. Mesmer gathers his patients in groups of up to twenty; the effects of magnetisation are enhanced by the number of participants. While they are under treatment, the patients take rooms at inns nearby, returning to the clinic daily for a fortnight—except for Fridays. On that day, the indigent from Constance are permitted to come for treatment as an act of charity. The groups are carefully balanced between neophytes and the more experienced; we also seek a harmonious blend of the highly susceptible and of those who have proven to be resistant. The objective of the *séance* is to induce a state of convulsion. If this occurs while you are present, you must not be distressed by what you see. It is a sign of health. Those who fall into the convulsive state are admitted to the crisis room, where Dr. Mesmer will give them his personal attention."

After a turn in the garden, we returned to the villa with Dr. Aabye leading the way. At the end of the central hall were two great doors; these he opened upon a room that was tightly shuttered and curtained against the sun; only a few candles burnt in the sconces along the walls, offering hardly enough light to see one's way. When the door closed behind us, the eye needed time to adjust to the obscurity. But even before my eyes could see more than shadows, I knew that I disliked this place. Its atmosphere was foul in ways that were not entirely physical—though in that respect, the air in the room felt unwholesomely clammy upon my skin. It was also heavy with the odour of attar of roses; the carpet and drapery were saturated with the scent, which was more sickly in quality than pleasant, like a fragrance used to cover over some obnoxious odour, in this case, a foetid mixture of burnt candle wax, mould, and sweated bodies. The room was in need of a thorough airing; I longed to rush to the windows and let the sunlight in—either that, or excuse myself and return to the open air outside. But even before my eyes had grown fully accustomed to the dim light, I felt someone take my arm. There was a young man at my side; he smiled pleasantly as he led me forward. As my sight cleared, my gaze followed up his arm, which was bare, to his bare shoulders and chest—until I realised that he was completely unclothed. I turned to remark to Victor about this, only to discover that he was being similarly escorted by a winsome young woman who was quite as naked as the man who was assisting me. Now, as I looked round the darkened chamber, I became aware of more unclothed people both male and female. They had gathered round a large, steaming baquet that dominated the centre of the room. Some were already immersed in the water it held; others were dabbling their limbs over the edge, in the process spilling water on to the floor. At the side of the baquet, the young man stopped and began to undo my dress.

"No, no! I do not wish to participate," I informed him, drawing back from his hand. "I am here only to observe."

The young man, who I now saw was exquisitely handsome, looked across to Dr. Aabye in bewilderment. Having heard my protest, he came to my side. "Ah, that is not possible, dear lady," he said with an oleaginous smile. "Each body in the room exerts a magnetic force. All must be included; otherwise the effluvium is scattered."

"But why must I be undressed?" I asked.

The young man answered, "You would not wish to wear your clothes in the bath."

"You intend to seat me in the bath?" I asked in some astonishment. I saw that one by one the others in the room were taking their places in the baquet, whose water reached just below the women's breasts. A rope was being strung among them by other assistants, and each was tying it loosely about the upper torso. By now Victor had been completely stripped by his assistant and was compliantly allowing her to caress his chest with long, slow strokes.

I appealed to Dr. Aabye. "Do you mean that if I wish to stay, I must join the others? But I am not ill."

"In matters of the mind, one does not always know one's true condition," he informed me politely. "Things may lie buried there. . . ." When he saw I intended to contradict his remark, he continued, "In any case, the baquet can only do you good; even if you are not ill, it refreshes and vitalises. If you join us, I assure you, you shall come away feeling more magnetically balanced."

I saw Victor's eyes pleading with me to stay; reluctantly I agreed, but insisted on undressing myself. Noticing that at least a few of the ladies wore gowns while out of the baquet, I asked if I might have one of these to cover myself. The young man brought one, and I slipped into it hurriedly as the last of my garments fell about my ankles. These I allowed the young man to fold and set aside.

By now my eyes were capable of picking out details round the room. It was a vast chamber with an ornate plaster ceiling; no doubt it had once been a ballroom. Where there were not full-length mirrors, the walls were painted with zodiacal and Masonic signs. Those of the senior assistants who were garbed at all wore silken robes like the priests of an ancient mystery, and each was carrying both a glass and an iron rod. The atmosphere in the room was almost theatrical, as if some spectacle were about to unfold. But who might the audience be? Perhaps the stuffed animals whose heads hovered above us as if they might be watching us with their glassy eyes.

Dr. Aabye, his gown billowing out from him to reveal his muscular limbs, stepped forward to seat himself beside me on a small stool.

"If I may," he said, opening the front of my gown and reaching his hands inside to press them upon my breasts.

I flinched. "Why do you do this?" I asked.

"As you saw with Dr. Frankenstein, it is necessary to stimulate the magnetic fluid within the physique. This region of the body is known as the 'breast pole.' It surrounds the heart; it is the most powerful magnetic centre of the organism. My purpose is to manipulate the area so that it will radiate its maximum energy in the baquet." Seeing my reluctance, he explained further. "Dear lady, let me do what I can to elucidate our methods. Dr. Mesmer has discovered that there is a natural affinity between the sexual impulse and magnetic attraction; the former may be the major organic manifestation of the latter. For this reason, we seek, quite frankly, to produce a heightened state of arousal at the baquet. We minister to our patients in mixed pairs, male *vis-à-vis* female, and encourage them to experience this sensation freely. I assure you all is done in the name of science and sound medicine."

He smiled and offered to resume. For several minutes, he chafed my bosom. His single hand was large enough to cover me from nipple to nipple, but at least his touch was gentle, and more than gentle—soothing. After a time I did indeed feel myself radiating an extraordinary heat, which I did not particularly welcome. "You can feel the effect," he observed. "You will respond very well to the treatment, I feel certain."

As hopeful as he sounded, my feelings were very much to the contrary. I smelt corruption in this room, a moral decadence that could not possibly have the effect of healing. I surveyed the others with whom I was to share these strange ministrations. The male patients (Victor excepted) were physically decrepit: pock-marked and wrinkled, with bodies that were either overly gross or bent. Here and there they coughed or wheezed; one quivering old man who seemed but semi-conscious was audibly flatulent. In contrast, the women, upon whom I noticed the men casting furtive, lascivious glances, were all much younger and quite comely; they did not look in the least diseased—though there were two ladies who seemed distracted to the point of being addle-pated. These sat together in the baquet stroking one another's shoulders and breasts and intoning a vague wandering melody. They might, I supposed, be emotionally deranged. Another woman perched on the edge of the bath was allowing a male assistant to massage her in ways that did not seem at all clinical; in fact, she persisted in giggling salaciously. I began to fear that all the worst I had heard about Mesmerism might be true.

And then the music began.

Suddenly the house reverberated with the most unearthly tones I had ever heard, a hollow, vibrant harmony that penetrated the deepest interiors of the mind and body like spears of sound. At times its tenor was almost that of the human soprano voice on the brink of speech, but then it would soar to heights beyond those a bird could scale. And the melody! it was celestial. Was this the music of the spheres? I wondered.

"It is the glass harmonica," Dr. Aabye answered, as if he might have read my thoughts. "Dr. Mesmer has perfected its use for medicinal purposes. Is it not delicious to hear? This composition was written for Dr. Mesmer by the young Amadeus Mozart. It is played in our sanctum regularly each afternoon. Sometimes the doctor himself performs. Take it into your mind like nectar. Let it carry you away, away, away."

The ghostly tones of the harmonica were having a remarkable effect upon me, as they were upon everybody in the room. My mind soared with a sense of vast dark spaces, as if I were adrift in the infinity of the cosmos. I suddenly felt completely relaxed and free of all care, and when I was asked to take my place in the baquet, I complied without a moment's hesitation. I wanted only to be left in peace to savour the music, which was now as sensuously near to me as a hand stroking my body from the inside. I was given the end of a rope and shown how to tie it across my bosom. And at once I felt a tingling sensation rush through my body, a sweet liquid fire. One of the assistants approached and positioned the two rods he held next to me in the water on either side of my chest. I felt a surging current run between my shoulders and across my breasts, prickling my nipples. On all sides people began to writhe and moan—but with pleasure rather than distress. I realised that I, too, was moaning; I felt my body growing unbearably warm; I broke out in a sweat and began to tremble. The assistant repositioned the rods, now placing the glass rod hard against my back and the iron rod tight between my thighs. The tingling stimulus strengthened, now shifting to the base of my spine, under and round me, radiating up across my stomach. I was breathing as heavily as if I had run a great distance, panting with the sensation I felt engulfing me. To my left, one of the women emitted a groan that grew and grew into a frenzied scream. She began to flail in the water. She was joined in her seizure by the man behind me. At last I, too, began to shake violently as the tingling reached deep into my body. Images began to flood my mind, memories of Victor and me caught up in passionate embrace. I felt my lover pressing into me and blushed with the sensation, knowing full well what this was . . . and it was nothing I wished to experience in so public a place. Seeking to escape, I rose from the water and tried to make my way out of the baquet; but I had no sense of balance. I lurched forward . . . and found myself in the arms of the young man who had assisted me in undressing. Our flesh slapped together as I fell against him; I was in his close embrace, clinging to him and convulsed with sobs. And then my lips were upon his mouth. . . .

I was some place else: a smaller room but even darker than that where the baquet was located. I sat in a chair. Someone—I looked up and saw it was Dr. Aabye—was steadying me so that I would not fall. My gown had been draped loosely about my shoulders. Underneath it I was still wet from the bath. The music was gone, though I thought I still heard distant echoes of it floating near the ceiling. I was breathing in short, uneven gasps, as one does after long, hard weeping. Someone was approaching holding a candle; it was Dr. Mesmer. He placed the candle on a nearby table and seated himself opposite me.

"There, my child . . . calm yourself," I heard him say, his voice sounding soft as velvet and far-off. "Breathe deeply. You feel tired. Let yourself be tired. I am here to help you rest."

He moved his chair closer. My knees were now squeezed tightly between his own. He raised his hand, on which he wore a white glove that glowed in the shadows. I watched as the luminous glove moved slowly up and down, passing several times before my face. "If you feel you wish to sleep, my child, that is perfectly acceptable. Would you like to sleep?"

"Yes," answered a distant voice that I recognised to be mine. A deep peace settled upon me, not sleep but something like it that left me attentive.

"You must feel free to tell me all that is in your thoughts," he said.

The far-off voice answered for me, my own voice but no longer under my control: "Shame, shame, shame!"

"Why do you feel ashamed, dear child? Because you have transgressed here?" His hands inside my gown lay against my stomach, then shifted lower; he rubbed gently with the tips of his fingers.

"No!" I heard the strange voice saying. "Here!" it declared. And involuntarily my right arm reached above my head, making a fist: a fierce and violent gesture.

"What does this mean, child?"

"Like this!" I cried. My hand drove powerfully down against my thigh once, twice, again, striking hard enough to bruise.

Dr. Mesmer interposed his hand to stop me. "You shall hurt yourself, my dear. What is it that you do?"

"Kill! I have killed. I have killed Victor."

"But Victor is here with you. You have come to me together."

"No! Victor lies dead where I killed him—in the forest. I drove the black knife into him. I killed him so that he could not violate any woman again." And suddenly there was a scene as vivid before my eyes as if I were watching it in a theatre. I was in the forest on a dark night. There, little more than an arm's length from me, was the drunken Italian soldier atop the squealing girl, driving himself into her like a crazed bull. I stole up behind him; but when I looked down, over his shoulder I saw that the girl's face was mine! And she, looking up at me, cried out for help. I was both beneath him and behind him. And then I was striking at him with my knife—not once, but again and again until he lay unmoving and rolled from the girl's body to lie beside her on his back. His face, now upturned, was Victor's face. "I have killed him, and I would kill him again!" I heard myself shouting. "All violators should be killed! The women they have humiliated should be given this right."

"This is your fantasy, my dear," Dr. Mesmer said. "I tell you, Victor lives. He is here in this house."

"No, I killed him. I killed him because I hate him! He has torn the heart from me!" I felt myself trembling in the chair; if Dr. Aabye had not been there to hold me, I should have tumbled to the floor.

"You are no killer, child," Dr. Mesmer said. "But you have carried this evil fantasy within you for too long. It is time for it to be gone, for it weighs cruelly upon your mind. Are you willing to let this sorrow leave you?"

"Yes, oh yes," I answered with all my heart.

"Then let it show itself fully and depart."

And at the word, tears rained from my eyes, and my body shook with sobs. I was astonished to know how much grief was locked away within me. I had taken a life, and now I saw I had killed not to save this girl, but to punish Victor. How deeply hidden must this truth have been, and the remorse that grew from it! The weeping went on for what seemed like many minutes. Then I heard Dr. Mesmer's soothing voice ask, "Is that not enough, my child?"

"Yes."

"Then it is time for you to rest. You may let yourself rest. When I touch you here, then you will wake. This sorrow and all that attaches to it will be gone. Do you believe me when I say this?"

"Yes."

"Then let yourself find peace." He reached forward with his gloved hand and passed it several times slowly before my eyes. "Sleep now until I come to you," he said.

And then I remember nothing.

When next I woke, I felt the touch of fingers on my forehead. Dr. Mesmer was beside me. I lay on a chaise in yet another room, covered only by a single sheet. "You may wake now, my dear," he said. I would have guessed I had been dozing for but a few moments; but through the windows I saw a darkening sky. I must have lain for hours in a deeper sleep than any I recalled. One of the assistants stepped forward to drape a gown over my bare shoulders and to guide me to the door. As I walked through the room beside him, I saw other patients stretched on couches as deeply asleep as I had been.

Though I had slept for hours, my body cried out for still more rest, as if I had been through a fearful physical ordeal. Once we were back in my room, the assistant helped me into my bedclothes and extinguished the candle. I slept, not dreaming, and woke to find my mind was whole once more; I acknowledged that I had murdered, and had relished the deed. A woman can also wield the knife, kill, and take joy in killing. I did not know there could be such vengefulness in me until anger brought it forth; nor such cruelty; nor such taste for blood. I had discovered myself through anger. *No!* Not through anger, but through the *act* that anger inspires. To *act!* That is what a woman must do to know herself.

Thus, I, the most critical of Dr. Mesmer's visitors and the one person who had not come to be his patient, proved the most susceptible to his treatment. In the days that followed, there was a lightness in my heart I had never felt since girlhood; now that I had reclaimed my deed, my sleep was sounder, more refreshing than any I ever knew. It was as if a thorn had been removed from my flesh. I spent my days wandering the gardens that surrounded the villa, taking joy in the beauty of the vista.

But Victor, who had brought me to Dr. Mesmer, proved a more difficult patient. His cure required several days more, during which he attended the baquet daily. The magnetisation failed to go rapidly with him; he never reached the convulsive state. He did, however, undergo several hypnotic sessions with Dr. Mesmer, which seemed to quiet his mind and free him of the nightmares he had been suffering. In a fortnight, fragile as I believed him still to be, he claimed he felt well enough to return to Geneva.

On the way home, I longed to unburden my heart to Victor, to speak to him of the child I had lost, *we* had lost. If only I could tell him, my healing would be complete. I was even more eager to know what sickness of the soul he had brought with him to Frauenfeld and how successfully it had been treated. But neither of us could bring ourselves to speak of these matters. At one point Victor asked with the greatest timidity, "Did you experience pleasure in the baquet?"

I answered, "Not pleasure. I would call it release. And you?"

"Neither pleasure nor release. But I believe I have found a measure of peace. I came asking Dr. Mesmer to help me forget; he has shown me how this might be accomplished. When I call to mind his voice and the passage of his hands before my eyes, I can hide the thoughts that trouble me—as if I had put them in a secret room, under lock and key. And then I can sleep."

Beyond this, he would say nothing. Whatever self-knowledge we had gained from Mesmer's strange methods, we had not gained the freedom to share it. Instead our conversation once again reverted to matters of philosophy. Thus, we spent the weary, jostling hours of our homeward journey debating Professor Kant's latest work on practical Reason, which we had read with equal eagerness. Was this, I wondered, perhaps the true purpose of learned conversation—to divert the attention from all we would prefer to keep unspoken? All the while we drew fine distinctions between Dr. Kant's noumenal and phenomenal categories, my thoughts were haunted by what I had learnt at Frauenfeld. The lesson made a mockery of all logic, all metaphysic. At Dr. Mesmer's hands, I had found the courage to call forth the painful past, which I had buried in a comforting oblivion, and to stare at it unflinchingly; Victor, in contrast, had found a way to submerge his disturbing recollections. But where did these memories reside when they were "out of mind"? What was this "secret room" Victor spoke of? It was as if there were a mind within the mind; a dark, second mind, dark as the far side of the moon, where all that was most important in our lives—the fears, the shame, the horror—was kept. If this were so, what did it portend for the power of Reason in which our age believed so passionately? Did this explain why so much had gone wrong with the highest designs of men?

I could not help but reflect: the French commission that had once sat in judgement upon Dr. Mesmer and condemned him as a fraud numbered many notables among its members. These included the great chemist Lavoisier, as well as a certain Dr. Joseph Guillotin. Even as we made our way back to Geneva, the machine that had made Dr. Guillotin's name famous throughout the world was busily at work in the Place de la Concorde, separating Lavoisier's brilliant brain from his body and slaughtering all the fairest flowers of the Enlightenment. Dr. Mesmer himself, had he not fled the Terror, might well have been a victim of that efficient blade. Was it possible that, in his search for animal magnetism, this doctor of the mind had stumbled upon a far greater discovery: the beast that lurks beneath the dreams of Reason?

EDITOR'S NOTE
Rumours of Sexual Licence in the Mesmer Cult:
The Evidence of Elizabeth Frankenstein's Memoirs Considered

From its earliest days, Mesmerism has been haunted by rumours of sexual misconduct. This was among the reasons Dr. Mesmer was forced to leave Vienna in disgrace in 1778; later, in Paris, similarly scandalous reports of libertine excess emerged. These mainly concerned the women who came to Mesmer for treatment. It was a curious fact that all but a few of the females whom he accepted as patients were young and nubile; nothing in his writings explained the theoretical basis for this choice, a fact that could not help but arouse suspicion. Many of these women later hinted that, while they were in the hypnotic state, liberties had been taken with their persons, including outright physical violation. And indeed everything in the typical Mesmer *séance* contributed to such possibilities. The women were invited (though not required) to disrobe in mixed company; they were subjected to the strangely enervating influence of the glass harmonica; they were asked to submit to certain preparations, which included stimulation of the erotically sensitive areas either by Mesmer himself or by his invariably young and handsome male assistants. The "breast pole," in particular, was said to require extensive manipulation in order, supposedly, to increase the readiness for magnetisation. As for the magnetising process itself, we have Elizabeth Frankenstein to thank for a frank disclosure of its nature as it was experienced by the subject. Many of the younger women who resorted to Mesmer for treatment were either incapable of recognising these gentle torments for what they were or, as a matter of natural modesty, were too shy to describe their experience in any detail. But as is obvious from these memoirs, the procedure culminated in an orgasmic release of a particularly forceful kind. Even as self-possessed a woman as Elizabeth Frankenstein succumbed to this erotic convulsion and finished by all but throwing herself upon the nearest assistant. It should hardly be surprising, then, if more-naïve females under the influence of less-principled practitioners should have yielded themselves in these circumstances to seductive overtures. Further, women taken into the private sessions that ensued in the "crisis room"—and which Mesmer never allowed investigators to observe—were subjected to manual stimulation of the hypochondriac region, specifically the ovaries and the vaginal area. Once again the procedure frequently terminated in an experience of sexual climax.

That lascivious practices took place, we now have no reason to doubt. But this leaves open the question of the end toward which these procedures were directed. Was the magnetist's goal a simple, shabby act of seduction? Or was there a deeper purpose in his technique? In its investigation of 1784, the Franklin commission drew the most sceptical conclusions about Mesmer. It called his moral character into question and issued a clear warning that women should not consort with the animal-magnetic movement. The commission, however, was influenced primarily by the fact that it could find no empirical evidence for animal magnetism; this led to the damning judgement that Mesmer's work must be a hoax and, therefore, must be traced to some nefarious motive. Drawing upon the well-established medical facts that woman possesses a more labile nervous system than man, that her imagination is more vivid and excitable, that she is far more sensitive to touch, and that she is in general more emotionally unstable, the commission concluded that Mesmer's main purpose was the abuse of female virtue under the guise of medical ministration.

But Elizabeth Frankenstein's account permits us to entertain another, more charitable interpretation, one that we, living in this more liberal age, may take under serious consideration. In her case, we see that the orgasmic impulse produced an indisputably beneficial emotional result; the woman was able to summon up the contents of an unbearably painful delusionary episode. The recollection was, so to speak, catapulted beyond the inhibitions that are innate to the female character. This permitted Mesmer to identify the murderous deed to which Elizabeth Frankenstein confessed in her hypnotic state as a fantasy that was deeply intertwined with her unhappy sexual history. Is it conceivable, then, that Mesmer, however accidentally, happened upon a significant discovery regarding female psychology? Namely, that there exists in woman, as Elizabeth puts it, "a mind within the mind"? One is prompted to ask: Is the female of the species, born to a modesty from which the male is exempt, able to free herself of certain sexually-related disorders only by resorting to—or being offered the opportunity for—strong, even hysterical erotic release? In such cases, the sense of shame, that would ordinarily protect the respectable woman from disgracing herself, would have to be temporarily suspended, though of course under vigilant professional supervision.

As distasteful as such practices may seem to the layman, the physician can only greet with the utmost interest any procedure that allows emotional infirmity to be brought within the province of therapeutic treatment. It is difficult to imagine a similar technique applicable to males, in whom one normally expects the libidinous impulses to be governed by frank acceptance. Yet if Mesmer has done no more than to open the *terra incognita* of female sexuality to rational investigation, he may yet be credited with a significant contribution to medical history.

Victor's Sudden Departure

During the summer that followed his convalescence, Victor resumed his habit of wandering the mountains. As his stamina returned, he ventured farther out from the château, frequently camping for days at a time under the stars. At first I feared that he might overtax his strength; but my mind was set at rest when I observed the restorative effect these sojourns had upon him. His colour and his vitality returned as his expeditions took him as far as the scarps of Mont Salève or deeper into the ravines of the Arve, where he might sometimes stay for as long as a fortnight. He found much that was consoling to him in these familiar haunts, nostalgic vistas that he associated with the light-hearted gaiety of his boyhood. The very winds, he reported, whispered to him in maternal accents. He once again explored the ruined castles and long-abandoned monasteries whose ghostly poignancy still suffused his thoughts with Romantic fancies. I, too, benefited from his elevated spirits. The exuberance he brought back with him reminded me of those better days when I first came to love the intellectual passion that burnt within him.

The sight of the awful and majestic in Nature had always had the effect of solemnising Victor's mind and causing him to forget the passing cares of life, and now more so than ever—though the explanation he offered for his newfound serenity quite eluded me. "When I am there walking the heights of the world, the heavens themselves speak to me of

Omnipotence," he said. "And I cease to fear. Why should I quake before any being, no matter how inhumanly monstrous, when I realise how far short his power falls beside that which rules the elements?"

Taking to horseback and riding still farther into the craggy passes leading toward Chamonix, he enjoyed especially seeking out the hospitality of the herdsmen whose rough-hewn cottages one finds at every turn of the path, clinging precariously to the glacial slopes. "These simple folk," he said, "might almost be of a different race. They require neither companionship nor commerce, least of all the plaudits of our corrupted kind. How I envy and admire them!" As uncouth as they were, the mountain folk invariably welcomed strangers to their bed and board, for often these travellers brought them the first intelligence they had received in months of the civilised world. Some had heard nothing whatever of the wars and revolutions that convulsed the Continent; the blood that flowed in the streets of Paris, the great issues of Justice and Liberty that stirred our thoughts meant less to them than the recovery of a lamb that had strayed from the flock. Such unworldly innocence worked upon Victor like a tonic. Though I constantly fretted for his safety when he was away for any length of time, I nevertheless welcomed these excursions. It was good to see life once again pulsing through him, like a stream that had unthawed with the coming of spring. And at last there came the moment I waited for most eagerly, when Victor opened his heart and spoke to me of his love—shyly at first, as if he feared I might take offence, but then more boldly when it became apparent how eagerly I greeted his words. At which, he proposed that we marry in the summer. And I, of course, accepted.

For days afterwards the very air about me seemed to sing as I went about my chores. It was not my happiness alone that buoyed my spirits; by his proposal Victor had finally given me the chance to let him know that he had earned my complete forgiveness. I wished him to know that the brutal failure of our youthful liaison now lay far from my thoughts. I rejoiced to see the shadow of guilt fading from his expression. We knew the marriage we now planned would not bring the transcendent bliss we had once sought; it would not be the marriage our mother had wanted for us: an occasion to be celebrated among celestial choirs. But it would be a wedding of human hearts, fulfilling and enduring. And it would be enough.

I wished Francine to be the first beyond our family to know of my happiness; I sent a note imploring her to come to me as soon as she was able. It did not reach her hand until she had returned from travelling with Charles upon his circuit. But between the sending and the receiving of a letter, the world can turn upside-down; and so it was in this case. By the time she could arrange to visit, all my hopes lay shattered at my feet. I had nothing but heartbreak to report to her. There would be no marriage. The blow befell me like some blind act of Nature, a thunderbolt or a gale that destroys but gives no explanation.

Victor had been on an excursion that took him to Montanvert; he had been gone for nearly three weeks, long enough, indeed, that I could not help but be fearful. I could not imagine that his return would bring anything but joy; instead it brought bewilderment and hurt. For Victor returned in the extremity of distress. I could see no sign of harm upon him, but, to judge by his expression, he must have suffered a calamity. His face was haggard, his complexion hectic, his manner distracted. Dismounting at the front entrance, he would speak to no one, but looking neither right nor left rushed unceremoniously to his room and there locked himself away until the next day. When he emerged, I could see he had been weeping, but his demeanour was that of anger more than sorrow. Had he encountered some wild beast, or an avalanche? I asked.

"Yes, yes . . . an avalanche," he answered with a frenzied giggle. "It quite carried me off the mountain. Can you not see? I have been crushed."

But he was clearly not injured. I sought again and again to make him speak, but my solicitude only enraged him the more. For another two days he did little more than wander the grounds in a peevish temper, seeking to avoid conversation. Finally, at the breakfast table on the third morning after his return, he burst out with an announcement: "I must leave!" He flung the words at us as if he expected to be challenged. "I cannot say for how long, nor where I intend to go. But I must leave. It is a matter of the highest urgency." Then seeing Father's bewilderment and my own, he relented. "Please, ask me no questions!" And falling into a fit of tears, he fled from the room.

The next day he began his hurried preparations, sending one of the servants to book his seat on the Swiss *diligence* leaving for Frankfort. I entreated him to tell me at least how long he might be away. "Through the fall," he answered. "Possibly longer. As long as a year." Aware of my obvious astonishment, he turned on me challengingly. "You must trust me when I say I have no choice but to make this journey." Was he truly to leave me like this, without a word of apology or regret about the postponement of our wedding? Or *was* this a postponement? Was he perhaps deserting me? Even if he was not, his state of mind was so deeply agitated I despaired for his safe return.

Again he demanded my trust; but how could I trust a man whose Reason seemed on the brink of disintegration? For days he had neither eaten nor rested; at night, beneath his door I could see the wavering yellow light of the candle burning in his room until far past midnight. Loitering in the dark gallery outside his door, I heard him pacing and at times moaning. It was not the sound of pain but of the profoundest despair. More than once I tapped timidly at his door to ask if he might be unwell, only to find my concern abruptly rebuffed. By the time his arrangements for departure were complete, he was as gaunt as a man who had been marooned in the wilderness. Once more Father and I implored him to delay until he had regained his strength for the trip, but he would hear none of this. It was only when Father pressed him with all his paternal authority for some hint of an explanation that he offered us a few poor words. "I met someone . . . a man . . . at Chamonix, an old acquaintance. It was quite by chance. He has a claim upon me, a long-standing debt. I have agreed to travel with him and do him a service. I can tell you no more."

I was certain this was no better than an improvisation; indeed, I felt a flush of embarrassment at the transparency of his fabrication. But the Baron, taking his son at his word, at once offered to pay any debt Victor might have incurred, no matter how great. Victor waved him off. "It is not that kind of debt, Father. The man needs my help—as a scientist and physician. There is someone who requires my special attention; he can turn to no one else. He will take me to that person. I will do what I can and return."

"But where will you be?" I asked.

Reluctantly he revealed his destination. "I travel to England," he told me. "I cannot say exactly where; possibly to the northern islands. I have research I must do there as part of my journey. I shall endeavour to write."

"But this is quite unreasonable of the man!" the Baron protested in astonishment. "Surely you can find someone in England who can come to this fellow's assistance. Why must it be you?"

"Believe me, Father, I wrangled with the man for days. I did everything in my power! But he would not allow us to break camp until I had given my solemn word. I am uniquely skilled in the medical service he needs."

The next day, he was off at the first light of morning, leaving me with as brief a farewell as if he might return in a few hours' time. Never once had he mentioned that our wedding would not take place.

For the second time Victor had left me behind with no assurance of when he might return. Seven years ago to the month, he had departed for Ingolstadt, there to spend the next four years of his life with only the briefest and most perfunctory visits home. It struck me that the emotional tumult I saw seething in him now at his departure was exactly the state in which he had returned from university: the same turbulent combination of self-pity and desperation—but now mixed with these a certain furtiveness that implied criminality. I could not help but believe that these two moments in Victor's life were in some way linked. But I could not remotely imagine why he should now be on his way to the far north of England. I knew only that I felt cruelly abandoned.

If it had not been for Francine, I would surely have gone mad during the long, desolate winter that followed Victor's departure. Once again my best of friends found herself called upon to save me from despairing to the point of self-destruction. The deed was no easy one for her, for the winter proved particularly harsh that year, and often the roads leading from Geneva to Belrive were snowbound to the point of impassability. When the gloom of the season's isolation settled heavily upon me, dear Celeste did what she could to comfort me; but the poor woman was herself ailing with the stone and I had not the heart to tax her too greatly. Left to my own resources, I resumed my diary, in which I had written nothing since my sojourn in the deep woods so many years before, and so passed the lonely season in conversation, as it were, with my own fears.

EDITOR'S NOTE

Victor Frankenstein's Relations with the Fiend
in the Light of Elizabeth Frankenstein's Memoirs

Readers of my original narrative will recall that Victor Frankenstein was for the first time accosted by the fiend and held conversation with it in the course of the extended Alpine excursions that followed his return from Ingolstadt. In that account as it was dictated to me, Frankenstein compressed the fiend's tale into a continuous, lengthy chronicle, which was, in effect, the story of the monster's brief but eventful life. It was difficult for me to believe at the time that so much of this creature's history could have been conveyed in the course of a single encounter. The clear implication of Elizabeth Frankenstein's memoir is that Victor and his foul creation spent a much longer period of time together, possibly camping for several days in distant reaches of the desolate glaciers surrounding Montanvert.

I will remind the reader that this fateful rendezvous culminated in the fiend's outrageous demand that Frankenstein create for it a mate. If, as I now suspect, doctor and monster spent a much longer period of time together on this occasion, it becomes the more credible that the creature was able to exert its influence over Victor and thus gain his reluctant acquiescence in this mad plan. Elizabeth Frankenstein's account preserves for us the moral horror with which Victor confronted the prospect of creating a second monstrosity; it also provides an accurate chronology for Victor's journey to the Scottish islands, a matter that is left quite confused in the original narrative. His absence from his family estate can now be securely set at a period of ten months, from October 1796 to July of the following year.

To his credit, Frankenstein at last reneged on the promise the fiend had extorted from him and, rather than sending the she-monster forth into the world possibly to multiply its kind, destroyed the unnatural thing before he had brought it to life. By that act, which may have spared Mankind the grim prospect of sharing our world with a new and monstrous species, Elizabeth Frankenstein's fate was tragically sealed.

Part Four

I Encounter a
Mysterious Visitor

March ——, 179——

This morning begins the fifth month since Victor's departure—and the third since I received my last letter from him. I am desperate with apprehension. Until the weather turned wild and precluded all intercourse between neighbours, Francine was ever at my side. Now, through this worst of winters, I have been left without companionship.

I have assigned myself a strict routine to pass the time. In the morning, I am the first in the house to wake, often before dawn. I lay a fire in my room and occupy myself with plaiting straw as Mother did to begin each day. I find it soothes the mind. When I hear the household stirring, I go downstairs to help with the bread and cakes and to prepare Father's breakfast. We take our meal together, speaking of the weather, the state of the grounds, the household duties. We silently conspire to say nothing of the one matter that burdens our thoughts; we pretend that Victor is no farther off than the next room. The pretence is easier for Father than for me; since his last seizure, his sense of time has somewhat dimmed. There are days when I think he quite loses track of how long Victor has been away. I envy him the mercy of his faded memory.

Later in the morning, I read. Nothing demanding, nothing that will weigh upon my mind heavier than a wisp of down. Completed Mrs. Radcliffe's *Udolpho*, a frivolous thing; I find it not the least frightening. Horror, I have learnt, has little to do with haunted castles and graveyards. True horror is compounded of human intentions; it arises from a soul depraved. Rousseau's *Reveries* does nicely to pass the hours when nothing else comes to hand; it was a favourite of Mother's.

In the afternoon, if the weather permits, I work in the garden, preparing for the spring. Seeking to quiet my tempestuous mind, I have set myself a task. I shall transplant the strawberry beds to the sunny hillock at the north side of the vineyard. Felix the gardener cautions me that they may fare no better there than they did last year. In truth the strawberries have never prospered in all the time I have lived here, though the beds have been moved constantly about the estate. Nonetheless, I take up the task. It is heavy work; I must move the beds by the barrowful far across the grounds. The gardeners, appalled to see the lady of the house so unbecomingly employed, repeatedly offer to help, but I have let them know I wish to do the work alone. I am sure I look quite ridiculous in their eyes, for this is likely a futile exercise. Still, it passes the time . . . it passes the time. When I tire, I climb to the top of the knoll to rest beneath the great willow that stands there and allow myself a siesta. From there I can see the rocky knolls in the fairy vale and the mossy streamlet running under the hills to the lake; and beyond, the peasant girls spreading dung to make the fields ready. But mainly I attend to the road that winds away toward the quay, the road Victor is most likely to use upon his return. Twice now I have dozed and dreamt that I awakened to find my beloved standing over me, smiling down. I try to stay outdoors until the chill of evening falls and the vapours rise from the downs. Alu is never far off through the day. She watches over me while I sleep. She rides the barrow when I return from the fields and stays, as if on guard, in the beech tree outside my window at night.

In the evenings after dinner I read to Father. He prefers political fare, though it often has disturbing effects upon him. Since the riots in Geneva, he has grave doubts about the revolutionary cause. I read him Miss Wollstonecraft's remarkable account of events in France, not telling him the author. He is duly impressed by the perceptiveness of her report. When I tell him it is the work of a woman, he is astonished. But when I go on to read from her new pamphlet on the rights of woman, I soon see he does not approve. He has heard of Miss Wollstonecraft's exploits; he complains hotly that "the hussy wishes to be the equal of men—but only in their most debased habits." Poor Father! Freethinker though he fancies himself to be, yet he bridles at the views of an emancipated woman. How amazed he—and all the daring male thinkers of our age—would be to learn that the notorious Miss Wollstonecraft is but the voice of cunning women who have lived for centuries on the margins of their world, meeting by night in the woods and fields to tell their lore and nurse their wounds and worship their deities. How I wish I might tell him this remarkable story, which is the story of the cooks and maids who serve him in his home, and the women who work in his vineyards. The story, too, of his own beloved wife—and of myself in all my truest colours. But how perplexed he would be to hear of this—as would his cherished Voltaire, as would Citizen Robespierre; for the rebellion of the women is a hundred times more an earthquake than the Revolution in France. If the "witches" had their way, they would bring down more than governments. They would bring down the entire clockwork universe of which Enlightened gentlemen are so enamoured; perhaps worst of all, they would turn their marriage beds upside-down!

But this is too much to heap upon a sick old man who is already troubled by the collapse of his revolutionary dream; so instead I soothe his temper by taking up De Volney's *Ruins of Empire*, recently delivered from the city by M. de Lisle the bookseller. Father believes this work richly deserves its fame; the author's sceptical wit cheers him like sweetest music. "This is surely the death knell of superstition," he asserts, clapping his hands warmly. "Not a single knavely priest or canting hypocrite will survive so withering an assault of Reason!" I read until he nods off and the servants lead him away.

I am rarely in bed before midnight, and even so find it impossible to sleep without the aid of laudanum. I fear I take too large a dose, but I must blot out my fears somehow. I wake in the mornings with my head muffled in clouds.

I receive a letter from Francine. She is travelling with Charles, who has been sent on an important mission to the newly liberated Huguenot congregations in France. I pray for the day she returns!

April ———, 179———

Last night slept poorly, waked twice by the frenzied barking of foxes in the woods. Rose by candlelight. Again a mild grey morning with rising vapours. Then brief, warm rain. Saw my first robin at breakfast, a cheeky fellow chasing a scarlet butterfly.

After three weeks, the strawberry beds are not yet half transported; I do what I can to sustain my interest in the project, but my heart is too anxious to give me peace. I frequently bring books and pass the afternoons reading. Count Gramont's memoirs. Goethe's letters from Switzerland. I read idly; my mind takes in nothing. I welcome sleep when it comes over me.

Today, reading the Countess de Genlis, I look up from the page to see a lone figure trudging along the road, advancing upon the estate. It is a traveller, a heavy pack upon his shoulder. *Victor!* I cry to myself, and leap to my feet to see more clearly. But no . . . the man stops far off. Stops and stands, his hat pulled low upon his brow and his hand shielding his eyes; slowly he surveys the grounds. He seems to look in my direction, staring a long while, then passes on into the woods. Alu in the branches above me clacks her beak excitedly; I notice she is watching with particular concentration.

Why do I bother to record this incident?

April ———, 179———

My head bad, I lie long. Doze and wake again to a dullish day that promises rain.

I am determined to finish with the strawberry beds before the month is out. Felix tells me they must be in the ground before the next new moon. By mid-afternoon, I have worked myself into a glow and drop exhausted beneath the willow tree, not even opening my food basket. Despite the onerous labour, I have no appetite. Sleep overwhelms me, but I soon wake feeling eyes upon me. *Victor's eyes*, I feel certain. *He is here!* But there is no one at hand. I look round . . . and see a man standing far off at the stile. I am sure it is the very figure I saw the day before, once again shading his eyes from the sun, studying me. I see now that he is remarkably large; a full head taller than Victor, I would guess. Even at this distance I see that he is dishevelled. A vagrant, no doubt. I grow uneasy and decide to return to the château. The man comes no closer, but stands with one leg perched upon the rail, watching, while I collect my gardening tools and make my way home.

That night I wake hearing Victor's voice beside me in the bed, calling out for help. After that I do not sleep. I stand at the window. A moonlit wettish night; the chill penetrates my blanket, making me shiver. I stand watching the lightning at play upon the western mountains.

April ——, *179*——

Again today he is there, standing as immobile as a statue beside the stile. He watches for several minutes, then turns away and departs. I have thought to approach him. . . . I have some inexplicable intuition that he has come from Victor.

Each time he comes, Alu fixes him with her eye and does not move until he is gone.

April ——, *179*——

Again today . . .

April ——, *179*——

Again today. If he is not there when I arrive, I find myself waiting for him to appear. He comes no closer than the stile. There he stands for as long as a quarter-hour at a time. I know I am the object of his scrutiny. I grow chill to feel his eyes upon me.

If he is there tomorrow, I shall approach him. This thought thrills me as if I had planned an adventure.

To bed late, a restless night. I use my helper for a second time and sleep at last toward morning.

April ——, *179*——

A cold, dry, windy morning. Thick gusty clouds, distant thunder.

I hurry to my work, knowing I shall do nothing but watch for him to appear. I wait until he has been at his usual post for several minutes; then I saunter off across the field toward him. I move at a rapid stride to lend myself assurance. The ever-curious Alu, I note, does not follow me but stays behind in the willow. The man draws off at my approach. I call out, "Sir! Are you seeking someone?"

At my words, he stops, his back turned to me. I see that his physique is of colossal proportions, broad and tightly-muscled as a bull across the back—by far the largest man I have ever encountered. He turns halfway, watching me guardedly from the corner of his eye the way a suspicious cur might gauge my advance. I cannot clearly see his face; he keeps his hand raised at his cheek to fend off my gaze. Several paces off, I stop and call again, "Sir! Whom do you seek?"

He does not speak; I am certain he does not speak—but in my mind, as surely as if he had, there is the one word *Victor*. I am convinced—I cannot say how—that this man brings news of Victor, and this urges me closer despite my trepidation. "Have you come from Victor?" I call out. I am at last positioned so that I can discern something of his features. I see that the hand he holds at his cheek is a tangle of scars and, like the rest of his body, severely misshapen. And then just for an instant I glimpse the face behind the shielding hand. . . . I stop where I stand and go no farther. "Please! Can you tell me about Victor?"

He addresses me over his shoulder in a voice which I can scarcely identify as that of a man, a low rasping murmur that fogs his words. I cannot discern what he says. This gives me an excuse to approach nearer. "I cannot hear you," I call out. "Are you a friend of Victor?"

"I am an acquaintance."

"Can you tell me anything about him?"

"Nothing. I know nothing."

Even as I speak, studying the stranger as closely as the distance between us allows, I feel a sickly ripple of revulsion creep over my flesh. I catch sight of his features for only a few moments before he raises his hand again to cover himself, but that single look is enough to jolt my senses. I cannot tell if this is a face I see or the fleshless skull that should lie beneath it. So tightly drawn is his yellowed skin that it scarcely covers the work of muscles and arteries beneath. I cannot imagine in what world, except the world of the dead, I might gaze upon so cadaverous a visage; yet here before me is a living being with such a face. I wish that Alu were with me, but she has not followed. Only my desperate curiosity to discover what this man knows of Victor keeps me rooted where I stand, willing to endure the sight. "Please," I say as he turns to leave. "Do not go, I beg you."

"You will not want me to come closer," he answers, his face now turned fully away. "I have been injured. I am severely disfigured, as you have seen."

Injured! Of course. Burnt, no doubt, his flesh seared away. Why have I been so cruelly stupid? I am almost moved to apologise. "Sir, will you please stay, if only for a moment? How do you know Victor?"

He does not answer. It would be a kindness to let the poor wretch depart, but with each word that passes between us I succeed in inching my way closer, hoping he will not be frightened off by my advance. I see that his clothes are threadbare and filthy, his boots split at the seams. He has clearly fallen on evil days.

"Are you lodging near by?" I ask.

"I am only passing through. I prefer to make my bivouac in the woods."

I would have extended the hospitality of the château, but how could I explain bringing such a personage into our house? I seat myself upon the stile. Will he sit by me and converse? No, he draws off several paces and stands shifting his weight from foot to foot.

"You have been watching me," I say. "May I ask why?"

"I hoped I might catch sight of Victor," he answers from behind his hand. "I did not wish to perturb you. As you can imagine, I have learnt not to accost strangers. Deformity is always viewed with distrust. Can you tell me when you last heard from Victor?"

"There was a letter at the beginning of the year. It was dated in December."

"Whence did it come?"

"From England."

"Do you know why he has gone abroad?"

"On urgent business. To help a friend."

"A friend? Did he say who this friend is?"

"No. He left hurriedly without explanation."

I can feel his unease as he shuffles his feet in the dust. As large and powerful as he is, his ugliness clearly makes him shy. "I cannot stay," he says at last.

"But you will return? Tomorrow? Please . . ."

"Perhaps," he answers, and withdraws. I watch him as he makes his way down the road. About a furlong off, he veers into the woods and is lost from sight.

May ———, 179———

I am in the fields earlier than ever, praying that the stranger will return. It is well beyond noon before I see him approaching. Once again he stops at the stile. I go to him, trying as best I can to seem trusting. This time Alu flaps across the field to settle in a tree above the man. I see that he has mercifully drawn a handkerchief across his cheeks. Even so I cannot keep myself from wincing as I catch sight of the eyes that show between the brim of his hat and the cloth. The dun white sockets below his massive brow are deeply shadowed; from within these cave-like hollows, the colourless eyes that gaze out—so heavily lidded that he must tilt his head well back to focus on me—have no hint of humanity to them. Rather, they are the eyes of a beast, staring with a blank, predatory curiosity.

"I thank you for coming," I say, and summoning up all my courage I step forward to offer my hand. "My name is Elizabeth Lavenza." He flinches and draws off several steps.

"Please do not come so near!" he asks. "I am not accustomed to that. You are kind to be so forbearing, but it is long since I have touched a woman's hand."

"May we walk together then?" I ask him. Walking, I will not have to look into his face.

He agrees and takes his place beside me. We walk off toward no particular destination, this strange, ominous figure towering over me like a parent walking at the side of a child. He walks with a shambling gait, his heels dragging heavily as he plants each step upon the ground. For all his strength, he seems unsteady, as if he must struggle to hold his balance. Now, standing closer to him than before, I detect a foetid odour about the man, the foetor of decay. I try not to show the disgust it prompts in me.

"Have you travelled far?" I ask.

He: "Yes."

I: "From where?"

He: "The north."

I: "Have you known Victor long?"

He: "We were together at Ingolstadt."

I: "You were at university with Victor?"

He: "Not at school. I assisted him in his work."

I: "What work was that?"

He does not answer.

I: "Why do you come looking for Victor?"

He: "There is a debt he owes me."

I: "Ah! That is easily satisfied. I am certain Victor's father will compound with you."

He does not answer for several paces.

I: "Would that be satisfactory?"

He: "Only Victor can pay."

I press him on the matter of the debt, but he will say nothing more. At last, turning so abruptly on his heel that he nearly loses his uncertain footing, he strides swiftly back the way we came, as if he would prefer to leave me behind. I see he is annoyed to be questioned. I hasten to follow him: "I have told you my name, sir. May I know yours?"

His reply is a long while coming. "I call myself Adam."

"Adam . . ." I wait for a surname but there is none.

When we reach the stile, he continues on his way, hurrying toward the woods beyond our estate. "Adam!" I call out after him. "Adam, will you come tomorrow?"

He walks on, not answering.

That night brings a thunderstorm out of the west. The sky is alive with dancing fire. I cannot sleep. I take a second measure of laudanum and descend into a fitful doze. For the first time in years, the nightmare of my birth returns, more vividly than ever. Again I see my poor mother expire in anguish; again I struggle to free myself of her imprisoning corpse. I wake gasping with fear. *"O God, who is there?"* I cry. For there at the side of my bed, *there!* I see the stranger looming over me, the darkness obscuring his face. In his hand, he holds the claw-like instrument. He bends toward me. . . . My voice freezes in my throat; I cannot call for help. But . . . this is not the waking world; it is a dream within a dream. It shatters like a picture drawn on glass. And suddenly I wake, my body drenched with the sweat of terror.

The storm has passed the Voirons, moving far to the east. My room is empty. That night I sleep no more.

My Conversations
with the Visitor

T hus began an acquaintanceship more astonishing than any I might have imagined. The stranger called Adam came almost every day to meet me where I worked in the fields, always masked, never forthcoming in his speech. He would speak only in response to my questions and then answer as laconically as if language had been rationed out to him. If I asked anything he did not care to answer, he would say nothing but only walk at my side in silence like some savage who had never learnt that conversation is the natural intercourse between people. Still I persevered in meeting with him, for when we were together, Victor's presence unmistakeably enveloped me.

During the first several times we met, the obdurate reticence of the man unsettled me even more than his repugnant appearance. Speech came haltingly to him, as if it might be physically painful for him to shape the words he spoke, so much so that at times I felt reluctant to inflict the ordeal upon him. Yet it was also clear that he was no idiot but a fully articulate man. Indeed, his vocabulary was that of an educated person, and punctuated with literary references: once to Plutarch, once to Cicero, once to *Werther*. But often the words he needed simply would not report for service at his command. Perhaps there was some disjuncture between his mind and his tongue resulting from what he called his injury. At times this impediment left him hotly irritated, not with me but with himself. He would grow cross and crusty as he laboured at what he wished to say, grimacing at the effort. Strange to say, I discovered that on these occasions I invariably found the word he sought in my own thoughts, and would seek to supply it. But at such moments, he paid no attention to me until he had himself given speech to the phrase he held in mind.

It was one such occasion that finally yielded some greater intelligence about my mysterious companion. I had asked a trivial question regarding his family, nothing I intended seriously, merely words to pass the time. I asked if his family lived near by. "Like yourself, I have been motherless all my life," he answered in a sullen tone.

"How can you know I was orphaned?" I asked in astonishment.

"One can tell about such things. There is a bond."

Bewildered as I was by his remark, I was delighted to find something we shared. "You are right. My mother died in giving birth. And what of your father?" I asked, the most obvious question to follow.

Here he fell to groaning under his breath for several long moments. "I scarcely know the man. I was . . . I was . . ." And he halted, blocked in mid-sentence, lost in some thicket of his own thoughts. I might just as well have ceased to exist, for he seemed to have not the least awareness of my presence and heard nothing more I said. I could feel the anger that kindled within him as he strove to complete his meaning; he seemed to be at war with himself. Finally he stopped abruptly and, uttering an exasperated growl, stood cudgelling his brow as if to beat his brain into releasing the word he wanted. I pleaded with him not to trouble himself, but he paid me no heed. Suddenly, with no explanation, he turned off the road and clambered up the tangled embankment, leaving me where I stood. I called after him, but he gave no sign of hearing. In a twinkling he had disappeared into the pinewood. Would he come again? I had no idea.

As I stared after him, a word echoed in my mind. *Abandoned!* I knew he had wished to say "abandoned."

What should I feel but insult at such behaviour? Book-learned though he may have been, the man had obviously acquired nothing of the most elemental social graces. And yet my pique quickly melted away into pity. I felt certain this boorish conduct must be the result of his injury. Far more than I took affront at his discourtesy, I feared he might not return. But he did, the next day, making no apology for his rude departure. His first word was "abandoned," the word he had failed to find the day before. He spat it out. "I was *abandoned* by my father soon after I came into the world."

"Then we are both of us doubly orphaned," I said, resuming the broken thread of our conversation as well as I could. "I also knew nothing of my father. He gave me to a Gipsy woman to be reared. I met him only once. He rode off to war and did not return."

"I have since located my father."

"Oh? Then you are fortunate."

"Not fortunate. He disowns me!"

"Then I am sorry."

"You need not be. There was no love between us. The man is a . . ."

Monster.

At his sides, his maimed hands opened and closed with a rage that was only shallowly buried. He frightened me when he was lost in his fury like this; might he, like some frenzied animal, strike out blindly? "Such a simple matter," I said, trying to soothe him. "That a child should know the love of its father. Neither of us has enjoyed that common blessing."

"It is better so. It makes one strong. I would rather be my own master, not needing the love of others."

"Nonetheless, I count myself lucky. I have found others to love me and care for me."

"Because you are so fair! I envy you that. You see what my appearance is. There has been no one to care for me."

"But that is unjust. Your appearance is no fault of yours. It says nothing of your character."

"Can you be so sure?"

"Of course. There is a beauty of the inner person."

"Ha! It will not survive when the ugliness is so unnatural. People turn away; the beauty goes unseen; it dies. And then there is only the ugliness, a lifetime of it. It eats its way to the marrow bone. We become the thing that others fear and loathe in us."

"No one is so ugly. *You* are not that ugly."

"I was made so hideous I should not have been allowed to live. It was my maker's intention that I should not live. I am a . . ."

Mistake.

". . . a mistake."

"God makes no mistake."

"*My* God made a mistake! He made a thing that blights the eye and makes all men my enemies."

I stopped in the road. It was late in the day, and a cool breeze had begun to blow down from the snow-clad heights. We stood now beneath the wreck of an old ash tree that had been oddly riven by light-ning; upright forked branches rose from its blackened and brooding top like Devil's horns there to frighten guilty souls. In the limbs above, Alu waited, as she had in the past. We had passed many times along this way; the scorched tree had become the informal terminus for our walks—thus far, not quite out of sight of the estate's embowered north gate, and then back. Invariably, Adam had worn his handkerchief across his face; he wore it now. *"Show me!"* I said standing before him, my face tilted sharply to gaze up into his that towered so high above me. "Take away this cloth. My eye will not be blighted."

"It will . . . unless you are more than human."

"Nay! I believe I should be *less* than human were I cruel enough to let so minor a thing turn me from you. Have you never met anyone who was human-hearted?"

"There was once a man who accepted me as a friend."

"Then you see!"

"A *blind* man, he was. A blind man looked me in the face and called me friend."

"But I am not blind. Come, Adam! Remove this handkerchief. You may have need of it, but *I* have none."

He wagged his head no most piteously. But he posed no resistance when I reached to fetch the cloth away.

I had steeled myself against this moment lest I should grow faint; I was determined not to cringe, for I knew he was studying my response closely. Thus, when the cloth came away, it was he that flinched in dread anticipation, not I; his heavily-lidded eyes distinctly winced as a cat's do when it fears being struck. The face behind the cover was the unnatural horror I had feared it would be. While reasonably proportioned, it was little more than a death's-head, the cheeks sunken, the mouth a lipless orifice that gaped like an expiring fish to reveal the yellowing teeth within. As if his hair had been torn away by the handful, running sores showed through the black stubble that unevenly covered his massive skull. The fact that his nose was small and delicately shaped only made the remainder of his features seem the uglier. But most curious of all, I now saw that everywhere—upon his brow, across his cheeks and throat—his taut skin was crossed by a tracery of fine lines: these were scars each of a delicate precision, as if his entire visage had been painstakingly moulded and stitched together from flesh of different colours and textures.

If I was not repelled by what I saw, perhaps it was because a furious curiosity took the place of revulsion. This face . . . I *knew* this face. I could not say how I knew it, for I surely had not met Adam before. And yet . . . I broke off wondering, lest he think I was struck speechless. "My God, man!" I asked at last. "What disaster could have caused you such misery?"

His voice when he replied was almost tender. "My poor Elizabeth! You have seen enough, I think. If you do not wish to see more, do not wait for me tomorrow."

He turned to leave.

O, please . . . O, please!

"I will be here, Adam," I called after him.

What the Visitor
Told Me of His History

June ———, 179———

    We meet in a herdsman's cottage that stands, long abandoned, at the edge of the estate's high meadow. I have granted Adam permission to stay here, rather than in the woods. Each time I go to him, I bring provisions. His eating habits are barbarous; he takes up everything in his hands, dropping morsels everywhere. He will eat no flesh, not even dried fish. Cheese, grapes, wine he will take, but only in small portions. He gives grudging thanks for these favours but eats like one who takes no pleasure in what I bring. The food he finds for himself is little better than animal fare and much the same as I ate in the forest: nuts, berries, even wild grasses. I offer to have furnishings brought—a cot, a lanthorn, chairs and table—but he refuses the gifts. In one corner, he has piled some straw to make a bed; he wants no more. Nor will he accept the change of clothes I offer, a few of Victor's cast-off garments; he remains as unkempt and unwashed as when I first met him. He is much like a beast come in from the wild to nest in this ruined shelter for some little time. Alu behaves toward him strangely. For a long while she kept her distance from him, cocking her head and staring fixedly at him as if she were engrossed in deep study. Adam, for his part, paid no attention to her, even when she flapped over him to perch above his head. Then one day he reached out to feed her a nut. Cautiously, she hopped close and took it, allowing him to run his finger along her throat. Afterwards, she sat at his side staring up into his face and chortling under her breath.

I am never certain when I come that he will be here. If he is, we may spend as long as an hour together with not a word passing between us. Yet I never come away but that I feel I know this strange man better. Even his ugliness has become familiar and no longer forces me to turn my eyes away. He sits with me now unmasked and bare-headed, knowing I take no offence at his appearance. Odd how the frightening is in large measure merely the unexpected. I assure him that his appearance has lost its power to disturb me, but he continues to apologise that I must endure the sight of him.

At last, if only to put an end to his unease, I grow bold enough to address this obstacle directly. We are seated on the floor of the cottage with a modest repast spread between us, taking the meal like long-time friends. I ask: "Will you never tell me how you came to be so deformed?"

"You truly wish to know?"

"I do."

He ponders my question a long while. "I have said it was due to an accident. I shall tell you of this 'accident.' It took place while Victor and I worked together in Ingolstadt. Has he never told you of this research?"

"Only once. There was a gathering at our home; he told us briefly of his work."

"What did he tell?" Though Adam's expression remains as stolid as ever, I can tell at once that he is fervidly interested in what I say.

"He showed us some anatomical specimens he had preserved."

"And what else?"

"How they might be made to seem alive."

"And he was not ashamed to do this?" These words he fairly growls at me.

"On the contrary. He regarded this as an achievement."

"What of those who looked on? Were they not repulsed by this display?"

"They, too, saw this as a sort of triumph."

The groan that bursts from him makes me flinch; I back away, fearing he has lost control of himself. Beating at his temples, he cries, "By what right? By what right?"

They do not deserve to live!

"Pray, I would know why are you so unnerved by this."

"Hear me, then, and you shall learn. Ours was a strange collaboration. Victor initiated the work; but without me, it could never have come to fruition; he would never have learnt what he did. For, you see, at a certain point his researches passed beyond mere curiosity. They came to involve great risk both to body and to 'soul,' as you call it. Victor would have been well advised to leave off, but he was unable to do so. He was driven to investigate powers that Providence has wisely entrusted to no human being. I speak of the power over life and death. It would have been bad enough had he limited his study to lower animals, beasts of a lesser sentience that could only suffer mutely, never asking to have justified what was done to them. But at last *I* became the subject of his curiosity; his . . ."

Here he breaks off and falls into a long, brooding silence. I know the word he wants. *Specimen.* At last he resumes, knowing I understand.

"I alone paid the terrible price of his arrogant misjudgement. It is Victor who is responsible for the hideous wretch you see before you. The 'accident' I speak of is nothing less than my very life, all that I have become, all that I suffer. You see why I bear him a grudge."

"But how did this come about?"

"I have said that Victor and I worked together. But much that he did took place while I was mercifully unconscious. Had he left me in that state, it would have been far better for both of us. Had he simply used me and then allowed me to perish without bringing me out of the unfeeling oblivion in which I lay, I would have welcomed that; and his conscience would be untroubled. But he elected to awaken me."

His lips become still, but his voice is in my mind.

> Did I request thee, Maker, from my clay
> To mould me man? Did I solicit thee
> From darkness to promote me?

He wonders: *Do you know these words?* Of course I do. "They are from Milton," I answer, replying to the question he has not asked. "They are Adam's words to God."

"Yes, the first Adam. And I am the second Adam, created by a lesser kind of god, trapped between two natures—man and . . . thing. You say you 'know' these words, but how could you know their living meaning? Not even the poet himself could have guessed the terror of dawning consciousness. That this dark stuff of Nature, once elemental dust, should suddenly rise up to know itself, should speak, question, and aspire! I was your species reborn, dear friend, unwillingly torn from darkness, knowing nothing of what I might have been *before*, there in that time that comes before time. I woke to find myself the flawed creation of a cruel god, a sort of living prank. I was an anarchy of half-shaped matter projected rudely into the midst of life. But I had no mother at hand to soften my harsh entry into the world—not even, as in your case, an attentive midwife to take your dead mother's place. I woke to find myself irrevocably alone. All about me was a confusion of shadow and sound. And in its thundering midst, my mind, though alert to every sensation, was *tabula rasa;* to nothing could I give a name. My own hand before my face was an alien and nameless object. Was this a part of me, or some other creature? What was it for? The chamber I stood in— which I could not even have identified as a 'chamber'—was a dismal, yawning cavern filled with unfamiliar shapes. Moving among them, I collided on this side and that with the furniture that surrounded me. I groped, I fell; sharp edges bruised and lacerated my body. Only the barest animal impulses stirred in the subaqueous regions of my consciousness. Pain I could feel, in every limb and joint—excruciating pain that drove me this way and that. Every inch of my flesh blazed like an open wound; my head burnt with fever . . . yet I was cold to the bone. My frame shook as if devoured by the ague. By dint of little more than primitive muscular reflex, I searched for some way to cover my shivering hide, and finding a tattered rag near at hand, wrapped it about myself. It did little to warm me; chilled more by the shock of my abysmal condition than by the cold, I could not keep my teeth from chattering.

"There is no way you can remotely imagine my state; I can scarcely recall it myself, except as a chaos of wild sensation. The very fact that I now can speak these words places a welcome barrier of articulation between me and that first riot of consciousness when nothing signified its meaning to me.

"Light and dark are the only vocabulary that the beast at the back of our brain understands. Dark is danger, but light calls out, 'Come!' Light is warmth and safety. Accordingly, I struck out toward the only light I could see in that murky chamber. At the end of a corridor I spied a portal filled with the light of day; I dashed through it to find that it opened into the dazzling immensity of the daylight world. Why I decided to go forward into that whirling confusion I cannot say. I reeled with dizziness and, knowing not which way to run, ran, nevertheless, until exhaustion overtook me. After that . . . I remember little of what happened; memory had not the words to set down what I experienced. I cannot say if I wandered for a day or for months. Time itself had no meaning for me. Does a rock count time, or a wave on the sea? Do the dead know anything of time pasing?"

I attend him closely, hanging upon every word, but I understand little of what he is telling me. "And you hold Victor responsible for the amnesia you suffer?"

"Amnesia! But what had I to remember?"

"I mean your life before you knew Victor."

"*Before* . . . You cannot realise the horror that word holds for me. *Before is nothing.* Darkness, emptiness, the abyss."

"You cannot recall your identity, your family . . . ?"

"There is nothing to be recalled! I am something on the other side of death, cut off, marooned from memory. Oh, how shall I make you understand?" He falls silent.

Adam . . . who are you? The words are in my thoughts. I do not speak them aloud.

"You would know who I am?" he asks.

"Yes."

He rubs fiercely at his brow. "Soon, then," he mutters.

June ———, *179*———

At times, even the herdsman's dilapidated cottage is too confining for him; he grows restless, eager to be in the open as if he feared he might be set upon. We walk out farther in the woods together, though always choosing seldom-travelled paths; Adam has learnt to hide himself from the sight of others. If travellers approach or if we come upon shepherds driving their flocks, we conceal ourselves behind a rock or tree until they are gone and the way is deserted once again.

He knows of many secret places where we can spend entire days unseen; he fancies that when he takes me there, it is his hospitality. He brings me fruit and nuts and clear spring water. He has asked if I will go with him a few days' distance to the place he regards as his true home— among the caves near Montanvert. Dare I go with him?

June ———, *179*———

Sometimes when I am with him, I feel once again close to the heart of Nature as I did in the forest. His presence does not disturb the elevation of my thoughts—for it does not seem to be a human presence. I am sure he exchanges secret conversation with Alu; I have seen the two of them deeply concentrated upon one another, the bird cocking her head as she does when she hears an unfamiliar sound. I have seen him staring intently at an ibex perched above us on the rocks, and the beast looking back attentively. Is this what draws me so inexorably toward him, that he seems half-animal? Is it his extraordinary innocence I admire? Surely there is more of pristine Nature in the man than I had found in any speaking being I have met. And still at other times I fear he may turn wild and pass beyond my control. Many times I must remind myself of the moment when I stared into the eyes of the lynx, not knowing how she might respond.

This morning we meet early and set out for the day; he leads me to a crystal mine from which Mont Buet is distantly visible. For some time we sit in silence watching the yellow lightning dart about the mountain's cloudy crown. We do not speak for a long while, but I know that thoughts are building in his mind. I remark to myself how in his every aspect he reminds me of this shattered landscape where he seems so much at home. He, too, is vast and shapeless, as if he had merely fallen together by accident from a miscellany of parts. I sense sometimes he is struggling inwardly every minute to keep his frame from disintegrating. Often the avalanche leaves behind mountainous ruins like this, bringing down a heap of slag and glacial rock that will lie for centuries until the elements smooth it over and cover it with soil and vegetation.

"You have asked who I am," he says at last. "I cannot find the words. But there are other ways to speak." Reaching inside his jacket, he draws out a soiled cloth packet. "You recall, when I told you of the chamber where I first woke to the light, I spoke of a rag that I snatched up to wrap about myself. A chance act, it proved to be no trifling incident; it became the key that unlocked the secret of my existence. The rag was a smock. See, here it is. Days later I discovered things in one of its pockets. They were at first as meaningless to me as all the rest of the mad, muddled world; but in obedience to some instinctive urge, I kept them by me. And in time, they spoke to me."

Unwrapping the filthy garment, he takes from it a pair of tattered linen gloves; once white, they now bear every manner of stain. I notice how delicately he handles these things that seem no more than rubbish to me. I see there is something more wrapped in the smock. For a single panicky moment, my eyes play a trick upon me. I flinch, believing that what I see there is a forceps. Adam sees my response. "Yes, you are right. Just as you were scarred in your birth, so was I. This is the claw that left its mark upon me. Do you recognise it, Elizabeth?"

The object is nothing like what I believed I saw. It is a small narrow knife. I know its name only because I have learnt it from Victor. "It is a surgeon's scalpel, I believe."

He lays the blade between us on the floor. "And do you know what it is used for?"

"To heal the body."

"Say, rather, to *torture* the body!" he suddenly roars out. "It is an instrument of villainy. Here, now, let me tell you my story as no words can." He reaches out his hand to take mine. I stare down at his palm. Twice the size of my own, it is a patchwork of stitchings and scar-tissue. When we first met, I should have cringed to see this grotesque imposture of a hand extended toward me. Now I can look down upon it with pity. Though his hand is disproportioned, there is no mistaking the strength that lies within it; can I trust it will not maul me? I lay my tiny hand in his; he closes his grip upon my fingers gently; and so for the first time we touch.

Elizabeth . . . fair one!

I am startled to feel the blood race to the roots of my hair. Not with fear. The contact is strangely rousing: daring, dangerous, and intimate— like touching a lion's paw. I have entrusted myself to inscrutable strength and wait to see what will follow.

He presses my hand down flat upon the knife and his hand over mine. As he does so I notice a small, faded mark on the back of his right hand. I have noticed this before, but have not looked at it closely. Now I do so, and my heart turns cold. It is a picture: the tattoo of a ship's anchor, and below it a banner that bears the name "Mary Rose." I look up to ask him about this design; but before I can gather my thoughts, a bell-like vibration echoes in my ears, so near that it makes me dizzy. Not a sound, but a pressure of the air trembling all round me. My vision blurs as if I had grown drunk. The room spins; the walls vanish; I am in another place, dark, dank, and noisome. My hand presses upon a sweated wall of rough stone. The air is almost too foetid to breathe. At the centre of the shadowed space, I see candles suspended from the ceiling in an iron ring; they exude a pall of yellow light. Within it stands a man, his back turned to me. He is deeply absorbed in some project. I cannot help but approach; through no effort of my own, I glide forward across the stone floor. When I am close enough to see, I want to cry out! There on the table lies the hideous phantasm of a man stretched out; he lies naked and quiescent as a corpse, his flesh the livid colour of the grave. His frame is but half there. One shoulder carries no arm beneath it; one leg ends at the knee. His face is a wreck of mouldering tissues folded back to reveal the whited bone of the skull. The man who works over the corpse is lost in the task of stretching a sheet of skin across the exposed sinews of the jaw and throat. Carefully, carefully, he shapes the flesh to the skull, cutting here and there, drawing at the musculature, polishing the bone. He labours with delicacy, like a sculptor of the living frame; but this is grotesque to watch. "Stop!" I wish to shout. But I have no voice. I turn to hide my eyes from this nightmare vision. A second table blocks my way; I see on it . . . God in heaven! what is this? A heap of animal ruins, beasts that have been cut asunder—and parts that I can see are not from beasts. Am I in some mad slaughterhouse? I wonder. I must escape! I rush to a door, but find it locked. Turning, I see that the man who labours at the table has stopped. He looks up as if he has heard a noise in the chamber. I turn my eyes away, I do not wish to see his face—

Look! You must look!

Struggling not to look, I come to my senses to find I am lying weak and shivering against Adam's breast. My hands are fisted in his jacket as if I might fall from some great height if I let go. He seeks to comfort me, but his touch is odious. The scent of decay that clings to his person is more than I can bear. I draw back. In spite of myself, nausea grips my throat.

"This is how I learnt of my origins," Adam tells me. "Things speak to me. The blade, the garment speak. The gloves revealed their history. They told me of him who had used them. I put them on and my hands become *those* hands. Before I possessed the gift of language, these pictures filled my understanding."

"In God's name . . . who are you, man?"

"Ask rather *what* I am."

"Then *what* are you?"

As you have seen.

"But I do not know what I have seen."

"That I am . . ."

"What?"

. . . a made thing.

I stare uncomprehendingly. "Made . . . ?"

. . . not born.

"But that is not possible." I reach out reluctantly to take hold of his hand; I turn it over to study the back. I see that I have remembered correctly. There is a tattoo of a ship's anchor.

"This mark . . . where did you acquire that?" I ask.

"I have no recollection."

"You were perhaps a seaman once?"

"Never. The picture is not mine."

"Then whose?"

"Will you not understand?" he moans impatiently. "The *hand* is not mine. *Nothing* is mine. There are times when all the flesh and sinew of my body cry out to me with the voices of other beings, the dead that live again in me. This hand, this shoulder, this finger . . . this brain. As if I walked through a graveyard, and from every grave I could hear the muffled voices speaking their names. Can you imagine what it was like to learn what I am? A thing? An artifact?"

"Truly, I cannot understand."

"You *saw!* Do not pretend you did not see."

"I saw Victor . . . I believe."

"And me! You saw me as Victor made me."

I have learnt that his eyes, like those of an animal, are deprived of human expression. They can but gaze blankly. And as with the beasts, one feels the greater pity, knowing their feeling must be locked away. If he hurts, one must feel the hurt with him; it will not show outwardly. If he sorrows, one must feel the sorrow; there will be no tears. What I feel now in his presence is an unbearable anguish.

"Stop!" I cry. "Please, no more!" At my cry, Alu, who waits at the entrance of the cave, takes flight and calls out in distress. My eyes burning with tears, I seek to follow where she leads, out from the cave and down the path. I nearly pitch headlong over the precipice, but Adam is there to save me. He holds me fast, and leads me slowly down the way we climbed. On the long walk home we do not speak. It is after nightfall when we reach the estate. He stops at the south entrance, signalling me to go ahead. I turn and bid him good-night; he does not speak, but his voice follows. It is in my thoughts. It is in my thoughts when I arrive safe at the château. It is in my thoughts that night as I struggle to fend off sleep, lest I should dream. Again and again the question: *Can you truly love him?*

June ——, 179——

"Can you truly love him?"

"I am his betrothed."

"Must you be?"

"Our union has been destined since our childhood."

"He has wounded you."

"How can you know this?"

"He has scarred us both."

"I have forgiven him."

"Not I!"

"I beg you . . ."

"Useless to ask." *I am not of your kind.*

"You cannot learn mercy?"

"I have read your books, the high principles and noble sentiments. Much that I find there I view as might a visitor from another world who knows nothing of your needs, your passions. My mind is like some dumb machine that can but mimic your mental habits; despite all the books I have studied, I know less than a peasant child who understands what it means to laugh and to weep. I have never laughed, nor can I shed tears. But there are things great Nature herself teaches, primitive truth the same everywhere for all beings. 'An eye shall be taken for an eye, a tooth shall be taken for a tooth.' *This* I understand. This is the justice of the beast. Do not, I warn you, expect me to have more than the understanding of a beast. 'A life for a life.' That is the iron balance."

He speaks these words with his eyes fixed on me. Cold. Fierce. This is not an expression I have seen before, but the impersonal gaze of a hunting animal that spies its quarry.

June ——, 179——

A curious and confounding experience. We are seated on a mossy ledge; far below the Arve thunders through the narrow gorge. The vista faces out toward the Dent du Midi; there an ocean of angry, dark clouds has piled up against the mountain and in it, the lightning plays, cutting scores of crooked paths between the sky and summit. Adam stretches out his hands toward this distant scene as if he might reach into the clouds. A moment later and I see upon the tips of his fingers a faint blue fire. The ghostly flame spreads to envelop his hands and arms and at last, gathering about his throat and shoulders, becomes a kind of nimbus surrounding his upper body. I gaze into his face, always so coldly impassive; he wears an expression I can only describe as quiet ecstasy.

After several moments he turns to me, his face glowing with the blue light. "It is my blood," he says.

June ———, *179*———
"There is a woman that troubles your thoughts. I can tell you this is needless."

"What woman?"

"You worry that Victor loves another. You think this is, perhaps, what keeps him away so long."

"How can you know my thoughts?"

"Is it not so?"

"Yes."

"You have no reason for fear on that account. *That* woman does not exist."

"You are certain of that?"

"There is a . . . female. But she shares no portion of his love. Quite the opposite."

"What then?"

"I say: You have no need to fear he loves another. Whatever love the man is capable of bestowing, it belongs to you."

"Who, then, is the other woman you speak of?"

"Ask me nothing more. Only believe what I say."

And I do. I have come to accept Adam's uncanny powers. Our thoughts are no secret from one another. At first I felt stripped bare before him, my every fleeting reflection exposed to his mind's eye. But his temperament is so coldly curious, so impassive that I have come to endure his scrutiny as I might the glance of a dog or horse before whom I stood naked.

June ——, 179——

Today, where we walk beside one of the high glaciers, I grow chilled. Adam removes the chamois-skin he wears and places it round my shoulders. "I did not kill this," he tells me. "I found the beast already dead and tore away its skin."

I make no answer. We walk several paces farther. "I could never kill a beast. Beasts are innocent; they are clean. Only man is vile. A man I could kill." He casts a sidelong glance at me as we walk. "Could you kill, Elizabeth? Could you hate enough to kill?"

He asks this question of me slyly, as if he knows the answer. "I do not wish to talk of killing."

"Can you imagine a vengefulness that will be appeased only by blood?" His voice has grown dark and ominous. I look away, but feel his eyes on me. "Can you imagine killing one you love for vengeance?"

I will not speak, but I am certain he knows the answer.

June ——, 179——

At last, news of Victor!

I am scarcely able to steady my hand as I write these words, so fiercely do hope and fear fight with one another in my breast. Yesterday, a courier delivered a letter for the Baron. It was from a certain Thomas Kerwin. Mr. Kerwin writes from the village of Glenarm in Ireland, where he is a magistrate. The town is on the eastern coast, not very far from Belfast. He reports that Victor is before him as an accused man awaiting trial. Having been shipwrecked near the village and there run afoul of the law, Victor has been imprisoned for a crime not specified in the letter. Following his arrest, Victor was brought before Mr. Kerwin for interrogation and was then committed to the town gaol. Soon after his confinement, Victor fell gravely ill—indeed, too ill to stand trial. Finding the Baron Frankenstein's name among Victor's papers, Mr. Kerwin was persuaded to think of his prisoner as something more than a common miscreant; accordingly he took it upon himself to write to the Baron of his son's dire condition. The good judge strongly urges that some member of the family be sent to stand by Victor in his coming trial, if indeed he ever proves strong enough to face the ordeal.

Merely to know that Victor is alive is cause for rejoicing; but I am sobered by the thought that more than two months have passed since this missive was written. Has Victor survived his illness? Has he stood trial? And on what charge, with what punishment prescribed? We can know nothing until someone is sent to find out. I have pleaded with Father to let it be me. But he is adamant that he must make the journey. Debilitated though he is, he feels that he alone can wield the authority that this perilous and unpredictable situation demands. "It may be necessary," he declares, "for me to buy the whole village out from under these savage Irishmen in order to save Victor's neck—if indeed he still lives to be saved. If need be, I shall bring the force of the British garrison in Belfast to bear upon this matter, for I am not without influence even in that God-forsaken corner of the world." And straightaway he begins to plan his journey, first of all arranging for a prodigious stock of gold to be shipped to Liverpool for his use. The emergency lifts his spirits; he is rejuvenated by the expedition before him, his first distant journey in more than three years.

Today, when I meet Adam, I tell him at once of the good news. He is neither surprised nor pleased. I almost believe he knows beforehand what I have to tell him. "I cannot imagine what crime Victor is accused of that he should be so long imprisoned."

Murder.

"Murder! Great God, is he then in danger of being hanged?"

"He will return to you. With *this* crime he is not justly charged."

"And his illness?"

"He has already weathered the worst. He lives, never fear."

I no longer question such declarations. I accept that by some gift of clairvoyance Adam knows all that he claims to know, and especially where Victor is concerned, with whom he shares a peculiar bond. But when I ask for more details of Victor's condition, he turns sullenly silent. "Are you pleased to know that you will see him soon?" I ask.

"We shall not meet, not here," he answers.

"After you have waited so long?"

"I did not come to meet him."

"Then why . . ."

You!
"Why me?"
Be warned! Be warned!

July —— , *179*——

Three weeks now since Father left. This morning I receive a brief letter from him. It is dated from Calais. He writes that he has chartered a packet boat for the Irish coast and will set sail on the morrow. This missive was sent eight days ago. He may by now have reached his destination; he may already know if Victor still lives. Though Adam assures me that Victor is alive, I would read the words from Father.

A strange new air surrounds my meetings with Adam. I know our acquaintanceship is approaching its climax. I do not welcome that fact. I feel secure with Adam only when we are in one another's company, when I can study him closely and tell him what is in my heart. Though we are together each day, we speak less now . . . with our lips we speak less. There is less need of speech between us. Each time we meet, he displays more moodiness and discontent. Even so, I crave his company, for I am needed by him as no one has ever needed me. There is something of the beast in him, but also something of the child—a nature more genuine, more sensitive to pain, more capable of hurt than that of any person I have known. This is surely odd to say—but I find I am becoming the mother to him. I have dreamt of him as my own lost child, for at last I recall where I have seen his face before. I am sure this was the visage I saw eerily prefigured upon my unborn babe the day I buried its tiny remnants in the woods; his is the face my overwrought imagination gave to the child Victor fathered upon me.

Today we sit by the pond where in the past Victor and I came to bathe. Adam idly floats the heads of violets across the ripples. So simple an act, but enough to pass the day.

I cannot understand the visions he has shown me of his life. I cannot understand what he means when he says he is a "made thing." That fact lies hidden in the dark cave of his memory; I entered there once, but not again. He has promised me that he will not take me to that place again unless I ask.

"Why do you say 'union'?" he asks. "When you speak of marrying Victor, why do you say 'union,' never 'marriage'?"

"It was the word Mother used."

Mother?

"Victor's mother. My mother. She spoke always of union. She believed that we should be one soul."

"You wish that? To share his soul?"

"Yes."

"Even if he is . . ."

Cursed.

"I do not believe as you do."

"But if you did, would you share his curse with him?"

He knows the thought in my mind. It is *yes.*

"Then you do not remember your own Holy Book. It did Eve no good to share her husband's curse. She did not purify his sin. Rather, his sin corrupted her."

"If that were true, even so."

"You would follow and be his comfort—even into damnation?"

There is in his voice a note of true concern that sounds more urgently than his hatred for Victor. He fears for me.

"There is a bond between us. I believe it has been there from the first moment we met. To break it would cost my very life."

Your very life. "And I, who am more truly like Adam than any human creature since the beginning of time—I have no mate to share my exile. That is little enough to ask." Then, turning fierce. "Do you find it repugnant, that I should dream of having a companion?"

"No—" But it is useless to deny what he has already read in my thoughts.

"I think you do. How do you picture her? Yes, she would be a filthy mass like myself. For what female would share my life besides one as hideous as myself? That disgusts you? Ask what your own kind looked like in the eyes of *your* God. But did He not agree to make you man and woman together? My creator was not so kind. I have been irrevocably excluded from the company of all living kind."

"You know that you have a friend in me." I speak the words to assuage his misery, but I misjudge. Angered by the revulsion he discerns in my thoughts, he thrusts his face near to mine.

"Think, now, of another prospect. If it were in your power to relieve my loneliness, would you do so? Would *you*, fair Elizabeth, be . . ."

. . . *my mate?*

For a long moment, his eyes, so chill and alien, search mine for the answer I have not the courage to give. "Say! If Victor's life depended on that sacrifice . . ."

All at once, my mind floods with the sensation of intense shame—not mine, his. He turns his face away, rises from where he sits, and blunders out of the cabin, growling in anguish. I do not summon him back, but sit sick at heart, watching him stumble blindly across the high pasture until he is out of sight. Even then I am certain I can hear his howling in the distance.

July ——, 179——

"Tomorrow will be a happy day for you." These are Adam's first words when we meet the following morning.

"Why do you say so?"

"You will know soon enough. Before the noon hour on the morrow. My time with you is brief. There is much I would say before we part."

We are at the crystal mine. A fair, fine day. The glacier-sea below us is a magnificent desolation. Above it, the *aiguilles* reach to pierce the sky, catching the sunlight in cascading prisms. We watch the smoke of a distant avalanche ascend; it is too far off for us to hear its thunder.

"Do you recall the other day," he asks, "you said you would share Victor's fate, even if it meant damnation? Did you mean what you said?"

"Yes."

"Then attend me." He takes the filthy bundle from his shirt, unfolds it, and picks out one blood-stained glove. This he lays upon the ground between us; then he reaches to take my hand. "I have promised I would not show you the pictures I carry in me—unless you assented. Now I would have you learn one last thing. It will require courage; but if we part before you learn of this, you will never understand why I have sought you out."

Reluctantly, I place my hand in his. For a moment he holds it in a soft grip. Then, bending forward, he touches his lips to my fingers. I cannot keep myself from cringing inside, but I fight back any expression of my feeling. I let him press my hand down upon the glove. Once more I see the faded tattoo. I raise my eyes and fix them steadily on his; there I read a sorrow vast as the abyss that parts us from the stars. I steel myself to staring into it, though I grow dizzy with the effort. There is something I wish to say . . . something that must be said, but the words elude me. Instead, I hear his voice echoing in my thoughts. He is saying, *Forgive me.*

And then my mind melts into his.

When I wake, there is the fading echo of a voice crying out, crying out. My own voice, lamenting what I have witnessed. I return to my senses shaken and perspired, my dress clinging to my quivering body as if I have awakened from a fever. I am as breathless as if I have been running. I know I have been running. But I am in my room upon my bed!

A face looms into view above me. Francine is at my bedside, her expression grave, but bravely smiling. She reaches to brush the hair back from my brow. "You were found on the grounds, my dear. You were wandering in the north vineyard too distraught to speak. Felix found you there and brought you home. Are you hurt?"

"Was I alone? Was there no one with me?"

"No one other than Alu."

"There was no man to be seen?"

"A man? Why do you ask?" A shadow of alarm darkens her face. "Were you assaulted?"

"No, no."

"Dear Elizabeth, tell me what has happened!"

"Why are you here?"

"Charles and I have come with the Baron. We have good news for you. Victor has returned to us."

I Learn of Victor's Misadventures

As soon as I showed myself clear-minded enough to grasp her words, Francine recounted how Victor and the Baron had arrived in Geneva the day before. Both men had alighted from the Swiss *diligence* so fatigued with travelling that they could scarcely stand on their own legs. But Victor's condition was the worse; he was so wasted he had not the strength to continue the journey that day even as far as Belrive. For this reason, he and Father made their way to St. Pierre, where she and Charles took them in for the night. There they stayed waiting for the chaise to be sent the next day to fetch them. Francine finished with a gentle warning. "You will find Victor greatly changed, like someone returned from the wars. He has been through some ordeal he cannot explain. But so, too, have you, I think."

In my anxiety for Victor, I waved aside her concern for me. What could I say, in any case, to account for my devastated state? How could I speak of Adam, and of what he had shown me? She would think I was reporting a nightmare. "Take me to Victor," I said, struggling to draw myself up from the bed.

"You are not strong enough."

She was right, but I insisted with all the power of my will. She summoned Charles, who waited in the hall, and the two of them all but carried me from my room.

What she had told me of Victor was true. His pale and feverish aspect made him seem a tormented ghost. The Baron and Celeste were at his side, she applying cooling compresses to his brow and consoling him as well as she could. I could not be sure the man who stared at me as I approached the bed would recognise me, so distracted was his gaze. It was not until Victor spoke my name that I knew his mind was alert.

As frail and dazed as I was, I drove myself to maintain my clarity of mind. I fell upon him and embraced his emaciated frame. Our tears spoke for us; nothing more needed to be said. I kept him closed in my embrace until sleep overcame him and Father led me from the room. Once outside the door, he told me what he knew of Victor's misadventures.

Returning from his mission in the Scots Highlands, Victor had been caught in a storm and blown far out to sea. After drifting for several days, he had shipwrecked on a wild stretch of Irish coast, near a fishing village where, just the day before, the corpse of a strangled man had washed ashore. The backward villagers, distrustful of an outsider, and especially of one who looked as disreputable as Victor, forcibly escorted him to Mr. Kerwin the magistrate, before whom he was openly accused of murder. In his weakened condition, Victor could make no protest; he soon fell ill and lay helpless for weeks in a gaol so unwholesome that it would not have served as a stable. There Father had found him when he arrived in Glenarm; it then took weeks longer to extricate Victor from the archaic legal machinery in which he was caught up. Were it not for the Baron's obvious wealth and prominence, Victor might still be languishing in his wretched cell, or might long since have been marched away to his execution.

As Father related this story, I could see an invincible fatigue advancing upon him. A shadow fell across his eye, and his voice blurred. At last, he begged me to help him to his room where he might find some rest. This was more than the weariness of the returning traveller; it was the merciless lassitude of age claiming the last of his life's energy. With this strenuous adventure, the light had gone out of him. As I led him up the stairs, I knew as well as he that this would be the last of his exploits in the great world beyond Geneva; he had depleted himself in the effort to bring his son home safe. But it was not exhaustion that kept him from saying more about Victor's long sojourn; with respect to that, he simply had nothing to tell. In all their long returning trip, Victor had avoided speaking of the expedition that had taken him to Scotland. He would say nothing more than that it had been an "experiment," a hazardous one, which had at last failed.

Father fell back upon his bed and seemed to sink rapidly into torpor. But when I had finished covering him, he reached out with a frail hand to stop me. "You must marry soon," he said in a weary but urgent whisper. "I fear he has formed another attachment. Do not let him slip away from you."

Poor Father! His guess was both right and wrong. Right in suspecting that my lover had formed another attachment; right, too, in believing there was a woman involved. But how wrong in thinking this woman might be the object of Victor's *love!* Adam had spoken the truth in telling me that the woman—the *female*—over whom I fretted was no rival for Victor's affections. Rather, she was a heartless project of his fevered imagination. I knew this, for I had seen it with my own eyes. Adam had shown me. This was the vision I found still glowing before my eyes when I woke where he had left me at the edge of the estate. This was the vision that had sent me wandering wildly and blindly over the grounds until Felix found me and brought me home.

It was only after I had put Father to bed and returned to my room that I allowed back into my mind that final revelation, Adam's farewell gift to me. I sank down upon my bed so helplessly weary that I scarce found the strength to draw my next breath. Yet when I placed my head on my pillow, I did not sleep, nor could I be said to think. My imagination, unbidden, possessed and guided me, gifting the successive images that arose in my mind with a vividness far beyond the bounds of revery. I saw, with shut eyes but acute mental vision, a place—a squalid chamber, little more than an abandoned hovel, with unplastered walls and a thatched roof collapsed at the corners. I saw the implements of a hastily improvised workshop scattered here and there about the room, the whole lit by a hanging oil lamp that cast a sickly yellow pall over everything. I saw a man, the pale student of unhallowed arts—Victor, as I knew full well—concentrated fiercely upon some task. I saw, strapped down before him upon a platform of rough wooden planks, a human frame, or rather its crude simulacrum. It was a scene such as I had observed in the first delirious vision that Adam had instilled in my mind's eye. But there was a difference I perceived at once. This time, the ruined shape that lay beneath Victor's hand was *female*. Spread out as it was, naked to the eye, with its limbs obscenely splayed upon the table, its sex could not be mistaken. Perhaps because I shared the creature's sex, I winced at its vulnerability—and so hastened to assure myself that this disproportioned heap could not possibly be a living body. No, it must be the mouldering remains of some terrible calamity. But why, then, was Victor poring over it so attentively? Was this perhaps some awful autopsy he was performing? Or a clinical dissection? His labour seemed more frenzied than that. He seemed in fact to be tearing at the carcass, wielding his knife savagely, as if he sought to kill what was already dead. How ugly a spectacle this was! Though I wished to turn from it, Adam's more potent will held me witness. I was to see what he had seen, and see it to the last.

And then, as Victor's blade rent the innards of the corpse more viciously still, I saw . . . I was *sure* I saw . . . the thing, the female there upon the platform, twitch and convulse. Yes, there was no mistaking what I saw: it—she—was straining against the bonds that held her. This must, I thought, be some ghastly physiologic reflex, a final seizure of the moribund flesh. But in the next instant that feeble consolation was snatched from me. For suddenly the woman's eyes blinked open! She lay staring in blank astonishment toward the ceiling. More terrible still, her mouth gaped. Not dead but awakening to her fate, she began to whimper and mewl in bewilderment, then squealed, and squealed again with the panic of a tortured animal. Victor, undeterred, continued all the more maniacally at his task, ripping frenziedly at his helpless captive. If I could have reached out to stop him I should have; but my rôle was only to watch as if through a wall of glass. There was no question but that he was seeking to destroy this woman. His knife was rooting in her breast, seeking to cut her heart away. Deaf to her anguished cries, he tore at her heedlessly. And when at last he realised that, for all his effort, he could not put an end to her, he reached to knot his hand in her hair, and roughly drew her head up toward him. For a frozen moment they stared into one another's eyes; she, in her anguish, bared her teeth at him and emitted a hiss of rage. He, ignoring her, laid his murderous blade to her throat and cut one last time. Even then, when Victor's knife had done its terrible work, Adam would not let me turn away; I was to endure one last shock. As Victor let the lifeless head drop back upon the table, a shaft of light glanced across the window. There I saw a face staring in: Adam's face, twisted with horror and anguish at the deed he had seen. Crashing his fists through the glass, he reached in to seize Victor; but then drew off. His eyes ablaze with hatred, he spoke a final word, then turned and vanished in the night.

Had there been any doubt in my mind why Adam should will me to see this scene, the question was answered in that moment. All was clear. I knew the mission that had guided him to me. I had brought back from my delirium the words that told me what the iron balance portended.

I shall be with you on your wedding night.

We Are Married

The final pages of this memoir, all drawn from Elizabeth Frankenstein's diary, are of so distinct and extraordinary a character as to require a word of explanation, and perhaps of apology.

As the reader will have noticed from the preceding sections, at a certain point, soon after she suffered her miscarriage, the author of this memoir began to manifest distinct signs of mental instability. This, followed by the shock of encountering the fiend, was clearly more than her delicate constitution could withstand. As I write these words, I realise that I am the only surviving human being who can recall this grotesque being from living memory; no one else can know the terror of standing in the presence of something so unnatural. That a fragile young woman already burdened by moral vice and emotional travail should have broken beneath the strain is, for me, entirely credible. But this leaves us to wonder how much of what she reports about the latter part of her life can be taken as truth. Even I cannot judge, for we deal here with the outpouring of a mind running riot. The hallucinations Elizabeth experienced just prior to her marriage are surely symptoms of incipient dementia. Yet I allow for the possibility that madness may sometimes attain to second sight. I can see no other way to account for the fact that the contents of the final revelation communicated to Elizabeth by Adam correspond precisely to what Frankenstein confessed to me in his narrative. His report was less detailed; but that he created a second creature, a female, intended to be the fiend's mate, and that he subsequently destroyed her—this may be taken as fact. But may any of the rest be trusted?

I have taken pains to make this section of the work as legible as possible; the reader should know, however, that this required a considerable exercise of editorial discrimination. I wish to Heaven the author had spared me the task by simply cutting her narrative short. If her account lacked this last section, we might lose a few details of the story, but we should be able to finish this work with a kinder judgement of its author. For the pages she went on to write display deepening mental deterioration. This is dramatically evidenced by the very look of the memoirs. The writing grows hasty and erratic, at times not recognisable as Elizabeth's hand; odd designs, sketches, and scribbles cover entire pages, often blotting out the written text. Several pages have been removed in whole or in part, usually roughly, leaving some jagged remnant. As for the content: this posed an almost overwhelming challenge. Everywhere the language falls into appalling carelessness, wandering from the subject or breaking off in mid-sentence. Phrases and whole passages are inscrutable; and finally there is an abundance of sheer gibberish, concocted of alchemical references and Biblical lore, which defies rational analysis.

Much of this, the sad ranting of a distressed soul, I have spared the reader, paring the final portions of this memoir down to those scattered passages that can be given at least minimal coherence. Even so, the final paragraphs presented a dilemma. I felt impelled to preserve Elizabeth Frankenstein's last words, written just moments before her death, even though they record little more than the agonising extremity of her psychic collapse. This is not the image I would wish to leave in the public mind; but I have allowed editorial responsibility to take precedence over other considerations.

August ——, *179*——

So there will be a wedding. Because Father wants it. Because I am supposed to want it. Because Victor can no longer delay it. Because everybody expects it. Because Adam has willed it. But we will have no children!! I will deliver no babies over to the claw!

I am sleeping poorly . . . indeed, I am not sleeping at all. Long after the witching hour I am still awake. I fear that sleep will bring back the scene that Adam imposed upon my memory. My mind goes round and round. . . .

August ——, *179*——

The toll of Victor's ordeal shows hideously in his appearance and in his erratic conduct. He moves through the house like a hunted animal, seemingly afraid to turn a corner or enter a room. From the hour he wakes, he vacillates between bouts of paralysing fear and bleak despondency. Night brings him no peace; he tosses in his bedclothes, frequently ranting with nightmare. His hallucination of the dark Other has returned; again, he wishes to be watched over. Unable to sleep myself, I am at his side whenever he needs nourishment or comfort.

I wish we were lovers together in the night stealing forbidden pleasures before our marriage. But it is all I can do to mimic loving care; the temperament in which I take him in my arms is deeply compromised. Though he does not know it, I share the secret that makes his life so wretched. I know the crime he carries in his soul, and this changes everything between us. The scent of the charnel-house permeates him.

Can you truly love him? Adam's question will not leave my thoughts. Once there would have been no doubt that my answer was a wholehearted yes. But now, whenever I think of Victor, I cannot blot from my mind the image Adam has shown me. Nor can I dismiss it as a gruesome fantasy; Victor's own misery is all the proof I need that this terrible event indeed happened. What else but such an atrocity can account for his agonies of remorse? I cannot say with any philosophic authority whether the thing I have witnessed Victor kill was a living soul or some subhuman monstrosity. It is enough to know this creature was the companion Adam passionately set his life and hope upon having. He intended to take her—a "made thing" like himself—with him far beyond the neighbourhood of man. I heard her last piteous cries; I saw her struggle to live until her mortal frame was cut in twain. This Victor did before Adam's watching eye. Perhaps there is no human law to judge such an act, but there is a law of the biologic constitution; it governs by spontaneous revulsion. Under that law, Victor stands condemned in my heart. Though I love him still, I love him against the grain of what I know. I love him knowing him to be a murderer and perhaps worse—the enemy of Nature and of Nature's God.

And I, who am more truly like Adam than any human creature since the beginning of time—I have no mate to share my exile.

With every passing day, Father grows more impatient in pressing for our marriage. The more Victor hesitates in acquiescing, the more certain Father becomes that he has formed another attachment. If Father knew of my own reservations in the matter, he would not press me so hard; but I can do nothing more than plead my concern for Victor's health. "Nonsense!" Father replies. "Nothing can do the wretched fellow more good than marriage and a long journey with his bride. He is little short of a shattered wreck."

Father's declining health lends his request the urgency of a dying man's last wish. I quickly resign myself to accepting the marriage as inevitable; toward this end my life flows as surely as the streams run from the mountains to the sea. When Victor joylessly asks, joylessly I answer *yes*. And the wedding date is set for the last day of August, three weeks hence.

Eve, we must suppose, was *born* Adam's wife. Or was she married secretly to Adam by God? Was she so much as asked?

August ——, 179——

Very rainy morning, then damp heat through the day. Slept poorly. A question plaguing me all night: Why did the New Jerusalem need neither sun nor moon? I would not wish to live where there was neither sun nor moon. In the night, all the household asleep, I light a candle and steal downstairs to the library so I might read this passage. It says the city had no need of the sun and the moon; "for the glory of God did lighten it; and the Lamb is the light thereof."

Still, I would prefer the sun and moon. Why does it teach we do not need them? I do not believe these words. I think they would deliver us over to the *sol niger.*

Newton believed that the Great Work might be a prophetical cipher hiding the true meaning of Scripture; but what if the opposite is the case? What if Scripture holds the key to the Great Work? How can one tell which of two things stands as metaphor to the other?

Much bustle about the house. I am passing through the strangest interval. . . . Victor and I seem to stand like living statues at the centre of a busy scene. All around us people make preparations for an event in which we are the focus of attention; congratulatory visits are received every day; our wishes are constantly sought out and acted upon. Plans are made on all sides for a festive occasion in which everyone intends to take joy. But none of this touches us, none of this. We are statues; what seems certain and tangible happiness to others, we both know might dissipate into an airy dream, leaving no trace but deep regret.

The wedding will take place at the château; it will be performed by Charles. The party that follows the ceremony will surely be the happiest hour this sad house has seen in many years. For Victor's sake, Father desires us to take a prolonged tour. Father is dying; he wishes us to be away when he dies. He wishes our happiness, not our mourning. We are to depart early in the afternoon for the quay, then by boat across Leman, and thence to a villa near Lake Como that Father has made part of my inheritance. Victor and I will spend our first night in the matrimonial bed at Evian, at the inn there which commands such a magnificent view of both the Jura and Mont Blanc.

My sleep grows more disturbed each night. Indeed, I do not sleep, but lie in a sort of waking trance. Even the laudanum soothes my mind no longer; I hear sounds . . . a strange thunder somewhere behind the mountains. . . .

August ——, 179——

Slept ill. A windy, coldish day. Again last night, the sounds. Not sounds—a cacophony as loud as cannon-fire; but there are no reports of battle near by. The noise drives me from my bed to find the source. It seems to be in the sky. I stare from the window, but there is nothing there, not even the wind moving. I ask at breakfast if others have heard the same; all say no.

An unpleasant odour in the air this morning: something like burnt lamp oil, but more pungent—stronger out of doors than in. Perhaps a fire among camphor trees . . .

August ——, 179——

I lie late, fatigued as if I had walked from dusk to dawn.

Last night, again, sleep would not be wooed. My head is in a ceaseless whirl through the night. *If time were a river, would it not carry us forward more easily than back?* I have no idea why I spend time thinking of this.

I am bedevilled again in the night by noises that seem to descend upon the roof from the heavens . . . great clashing sounds of metal, like a hundred carpenter's saws, their teeth rasping against one another, but vastly magnified. If metal could scream this would be its voice. An iron voice. I go to the window to look out. The stars are not there. They have been replaced by numbers. The entire sky has been written over with glowing numbers.

If time were a river . . .

"The Book of Nature is written in numbers," Father said. But the stars are very much more beautiful.

I hear the clocks throughout the château chime twice, first one, then another, then another farther off. I return to my bed and start in to weep, knowing the stars have been taken away.

I must try

. . . .[1]

---

[1]A page torn out here. —R.W.

August ——, 179——

Victor has given me back the miniature portrait that Mother painted on her death-bed. "I shall draw you in your pride and strength," she said, "a woman who is her own master."

I think my mother was a prophet. I think she saw the death of the world.

I am not this woman any longer. I am not Elizabeth. I am Lilith, first to suffer at the hands of Man.

August ——, 179——

A dismal morning. My head aches. I do not rise till late. I saw great objects moving across the sky; these are the source of the sounds. Not birds, dead things gliding in air. Immense things made of metal. I have seen drawings of ascension balloons; but these are nothing like. This is what I have seen——[2]

When I call to mind what I saw last night, it is not as one remembers a dream. I do not think I dreamt. I did not dream, but it could not be real. Not a dream, not real. My mind spins round.

Francine visits. We talk of my trousseau; I am to wear Mother's bridal veil and raiment. I take little interest. Francine tells me I look drawn; she worries for me. "You have done the right thing," she assures me. "You will make Victor happy and he will make you happy." I ask her if Charles has ever preached on "the great voice that spoke like a trumpet." I ask: What was this "trumpet"? She cannot say. I ask: What would St. John have called a timepiece if such had been revealed to him? What would he have called an atmospheric engine? What would he have called Signor Galileo's telescope?

August ——, 179——

Since I have been with Adam, my mind wanders. But where is the mind when we are driven "out" of it? Seraphina once asked. I cannot remember what she answered. Where is my mind now?

[2]At this point, the author has covered the page with a strange design: miscellaneous numbers amid which float a myriad of awkwardly shaped crosses repeated over and over. There is no indication what this might signify. —R.W.

Last night I wake to find myself flying like a bird above the Jura. I look down and into the Earth. I can see *under* the Earth. I can see a great ring of fire under the Earth. I see men in a hollow ring of fire, toiling under the Earth like feverish trolls. Not miners, they are not miners. They have other means of light—not like miners—not lanthorns, nor candles. They have set the inside of the Earth afire. They are surrounded by fiery colours. I enter a tunnel in the Earth. The air crackles about me. The air is filled with electricity, it burns against my skin. The electricity has escaped into the world! It is everywhere. I ask what these men are doing, toiling a thousand feet beneath the Earth. A voice tells me: "They are seeking the Stone." Another voice says: "They know the names of all things." Another voice says: "They are taking the world to pieces."

I look round. Every man I see looks like Victor.

This is not a dream. I do not dream any more. I do not sleep. I cannot sleep.[3]

I will wear Mother's bridal veil; that is settled. I will marry, but there will be no union. Victor has killed the One; there can only be the Two. And between the Two there shall be strife until the strong have killed the meek.

In the midst of the throne were four beasts. And the first one looked like Victor. And the second one looked like Victor. And the third one looked like Victor. And the fourth one looked like Victor. And the voice that was like a trumpet spoke, saying, "The Stone has been found. And its name is Division Forever and Death Everlasting."[4]

August 29, 1797

Troubled sleep. I seek my helper three times. It does no good; my mind fights off slumber. There is something happening under the mountains. I think the mountains are crumbling. I saw a great crack open

[3]The next page half torn away. It contained a drawing. What remains of the image is a meaningless tracery of random lines. —R.W.

[4]The next three pages written over and largely illegible. The scribblings include alchemical symbols, a few pornographic images, unidentified faces, and fantastic animal forms. The only legible portion is a list of the tribes of Israel. It contains several errors. E.g., the list includes a "Tribe of Victor of the Scalpel" and a "Tribe of Isaac of the Royal Gold." —R.W.

in them last night and the fiery light show through and the sound of the world being rent asunder in all its parts. There was no sign of this in the morning. The mountains hold the invaders out. The mountains are falling to pieces. The invaders have made tunnels under the mountains.

Tomorrow I must be married.

Morning, August 30, 1797

The worst of nights, the sky filled with the crying out of the metals, Seraphina told us how the metals suffer in the fire, how they howl! The iron voice proclaims the agony of the metals. The metals do not wish to serve. One day they shall rise up against us.

What are they doing, the men beneath the Earth? Do they know what they do? They have found the secret of the *prima materia.* They toil day and night beneath the Earth to reshape the world as they would have it. They have invaded the womb of the Earth. They need no women. The men will make their own children. Their children will be *made things.* Adam was a made thing. Adam was the first of the new male species. Adam was . . .

"I say we shall have no more marriages!"

Mother, forgive them! For they know not what they do.[5]

The house is filled with wedding guests. They have come to witness our union. Our trunks stand ranged in a row in the entrance hall, packed, locked, and corded. I must be brave, I must be gay. I will wear Mother's vapoury veil. They are waiting for the virgin who brings the bridegroom her purity to be defiled. I am no virgin. My purity was ripped from me. There are no virgins at this wedding. There are no virgins left in all the world.

And the dragon stood before the woman which was ready to be delivered for to devour her child as soon as it was born.

Victor and I shall have no children! I will insist on it.

---

[5]The next page illegible. Again, alchemical symbols, including this time a hermaphroditic figure labelled "Victor" and "Elizabeth." Under it the words "Abomination of the Earth." —R.W.

Victor shall perish and he shall have no children.

I shall perish childless.

Adam shall perish, but though he has no mate, he shall have children.

Made things, the children of Adam.

And they shall inherit the world.

And they shall devour the Earth.

Evian: Evening, August 30, 1797

Two hours on the lake. The sky clear, the air mild. A divine day! How happy and serene all Nature appears! But all the way, Victor watches behind us, as if we are being pursued. He sees nothing, but I know what he fears. Useless, useless to watch.

I, too, have reason to look back. High above our sails, I see a black speck against the bright sky. It is Alu, flying in great, slow circles. I had said my farewell to her that morning and set her free to find a new mistress; but she was not to be discouraged from keeping watch over me. How far will she follow? I wonder.

Evening descends gently upon the world; for a brief period, as if by an act of transient grace, we are treated to as sublime a scene as this noble, mountained land can offer. The Alps are in repose: a race of sleeping giants. But as we approach Evian, where the lake broadens, foul weather waits for us like an enemy in ambush. A sky black with clouds gathers behind the mountains. Lightning flashes ominously in the distance. The entire eastern end of the lake is storm.

As swiftly as if an evil Prospero has swept his wand over the waters to summon up the tempest, the weather breaks. From behind the Dent d'Oche, a measureless torrent thunders through space; the rains rage across the face of the tossing clouds, moving more swiftly than the flight of the vulture. The lake heaves, the sky turns fiery violent, hurling spears of lightning upon the hilltops; torrents descend. From above I catch the sound of a faint, shrill cry as it blows by on the wind. Alu's final message: an anguished warning. Gazing upward, for one brief moment I see her struggling in vain against the battering gale, then lose her in the swirling mist. Farewell, then, faithful friend! This is how we part, sundered by the raging elements.

We disembark at Evian, and, blinded by rain, race for the waiting carriage that will take us to the inn that stands upon the heights. We arrive soaked to our skins, our luggage drenched; but no sooner are we within the door than Victor excuses himself, saying he has some business with the boat. He sends me to our room to change, taking care to instruct the inn-keeper to lock the door upon me when I am safely settled. The inn-keeper's wife, a stout, good-natured woman, leads me to our chamber and deposits my valise in the corner. She crosses to the bed and dutifully turns down the covers, as she might for any guest. With a sly smile, she pats the down coverlet and tells me this is the finest bridal bed to be found on the lake. When she has finished laying a fire, she stops at the door to say, "How special a night this is for you, my dear. And may it be the first in a long and happy married life!" Then, as instructed, she closes the door and turns the key in the lock.

As soon as she leaves, I search our luggage to find this book, fearing that the rain may have reached it. I find it dry and attach the letter I have prepared. All is done. I am ready.

Then, garment by garment, I let my streaming clothes fall from me and lie at my feet until I stand naked in the centre of the room. I stare long at the great canopied bed that fills most of the chamber. I think: *Tonight, were I any other newly-wedded woman, I would be meant to lie in this bed as naked as I stand now, wrapped in my husband's passionate embrace, learning the lawful delights of the flesh. Tonight, were I any other woman, I would stand at the threshold of a lifetime's fulfillment as loving wife and mother. But this shall not be for me. I shall lie upon this bed like the sacrificial lamb awaiting the expiatory stroke. And I shall not rise to see the light of day again.*

Victor is carrying a pistol; he sought to hide it from me, but I saw it in his luggage. Victor is beset by fear; he cannot conceal it. I think he is searching the house and grounds this very moment. He knows our danger; he thinks he can defend me. He would lay down his life to defend me. He cannot defend me.

My head whirls. Since this morning, I have felt adrift.

The storm drops thunder and the deluge on our heads; it beats upon the world as if the Earth were its drum. I gaze from the window, watching the crooked fire dance madly among the clouds; now and again the lightning reveals the dome of Mont Blanc as clearly as if this were midday. It is as if the heavens were cracking open and the flame of the Empyrean flashes through.

I have this brief time, this hour . . .

I am impelled to write.

I will leave these words.

These are not my words.

These are . . .

These are not . . .

I see the death of the world.

I see great machines in the womb of the Earth.

And I see the mountains crumbling.

And I see the lightning chained and made a slave of men.

And I see great Nature humbled.

And I hear the sky roaring with an iron voice.

And I see the Earth sprout a deadly garden of billowing fume, by tens and by hundreds great blossoming flowers of fire.

And I hear the electricity speak with a million voices.

And I see the men building cities that have no need of sun or moon.

And I see the men turning from the Earth's fair face to seek new worlds in the void. I see them lifting into the void.

And I see the void devour the hearts of men.

And I feel the deadly chill of the void descend upon the Earth.

And I see the men conjuring their fantasies out of captive matter.

And I see the men making creatures of their own imagination.

And I see the men breeding without women.

And I see monsters bowing down to their makers and rising up against them.

And I hear the rapping at the window and know who is there.

And I hear myself greet my belated wedding guest.

And I hear myself ask for the mercy of forgetfulness.
And I see myself lie down upon this bed
I see myself stretched upon this bed
I see myself a naked offering
I see myself the last woman on Earth
I see . . .[6]

[6]The remaining pages have been removed. —R.W.

EPILOGUE

Readers will recall from Victor Frankenstein's original narrative how Elizabeth met her death at the inn at Evian on that fateful wedding night. Shortly after the words I quote above were set down, Elizabeth was discovered dead in her bedroom. Her throat had been crushed. The first to find her was Victor. He had been occupying himself exploring the inn and its grounds, taking what precautions he could to defend himself and his bride when, as he reported, he heard a scream from Elizabeth's room. Upon unlocking the bedroom, he spied his wife's murderer looking in at the open window and fired upon him. The inn-keeper, his family, and other guests responded at once to Victor's orders that they search the grounds for the killer, but they found no trace of an intruder. Accordingly, when the search ended, Victor fell under immediate suspicion of having himself committed the murder, which remains an event of legendary fame in the vicinity.

In the summer of 1821 I was able to locate a daughter of the inn-keeper who had welcomed the newly-married couple to Evian and taken them in from the raging storm. A child of twelve at the time, she vividly recalled the nightmarish incident that ensued. When asked about the fiend that took Elizabeth's life, the woman unhesitatingly asseverated that she, like her parents, had always regarded the creature as a figment of Victor Frankenstein's fancy. She knew of no one who had heard the slain woman scream; those who converged upon the room were brought there by the gun-shot. Her firm belief was that Victor was the murderer, that he had throttled his bride in some mad fit of jealousy. The fact that Elizabeth's corpse was found unclothed in a room to which only he had access made this seem a crime of passion pure and simple.

Sad to say, this woman's belief remained the prevailing conviction among those who remembered the crime; though he was never arrested or tried, Victor could not prove his innocence in this matter. Even Baron Frankenstein, who succumbed to a stroke less than a week later, may well have gone to his grave believing as others did: that his son's hands were stained with Elizabeth's blood. Victor's fantastic tale of a murderous and monstrous being loose in the world had nothing to support it. This is what finally swayed me to record whatever I found in Elizabeth's memoirs that might help clear Victor Frankenstein's name. Since I alone in all the world can attest to the existence of the creature who took Elizabeth's life, I hope these few final pages, flawed as they are by the incipient madness of their author, will mitigate the suspicion that continues to surround this tragic man. Whatever crimes may be justly charged against Victor Frankenstein, let the world know that it was not his hand that ended his bride's life.

Within a few days following his father's death, Victor fell into a delirious fever, from which he was weeks recovering. When at last he was able to rise from his bed, he resolved to revenge himself upon the wretch who had destroyed his life. So began the hunt that was to lead him for the next two years across deserts and tundra, from the Mediterranean to the Black Sea—and finally to the far polar North. There, in the autumn of 1799, our paths intersected in that frozen sea; and there he at last found someone patient and pitying enough to record his story. No sooner had I completed that task than Victor Frankenstein, worn and afflicted with many sufferings, died in my embrace. A day later, just as the ice broke and our ship began to move south, the fiend whom Frankenstein had pursued across the globe burst in upon my cabin to claim its maker's Earthly remains. Its promise to me was that both creature and creator should be consumed in a common pyre at the world's northernmost extremity. My last vision of the wretched thing was its parting salute from the ice-raft that bore it away into darkness and distance.

How many years now part me from the extraordinary interlude I spent in that ice-bound solitude, dutifully writing out what I took to be a madman's tale. Why I should have done so I cannot to this day understand, unless I was summoned to the charge by providential power. The place was strange; but stranger still was the symbolic condition in which I resided for those several days. I shared the world of the dead with a damned soul. I did not realise it at the time, but that Arctic zone, forbidding, inhuman, and sterile, epitomised Frankenstein's legacy more fully than any place imagination might have invented. It embodied that icy nether region of Hell to which Dante consigned God's greatest enemy. In the poet's view, not even the bloodiest sin committed out of lust or anger equalled in horror the calculated act of malice for which the Arch-fiend stood eternally condemned. Once an angel of light, Satan had employed his intellect to rise up against his Maker. Did Frankenstein's fate, I have often wondered, foretoken a future in which a cool and unfeeling Reason would seize upon bountiful Nature and transform it into a similar desolation?

ABOUT THE AUTHOR

As a child, THEODORE ROSZAK was never permitted to see a Frankenstein movie. His parents thought he might find it too disturbing. Perhaps that lent the story the fascination of the forbidden. Over the past twenty years, he has taught several courses dealing with Mary Shelley's *Frankenstein*, which he has come to regard as the central myth of modern society. He has explored the demonic side of science and technology through many of his books, among them *The Making of a Counter Culture*, *Where the Wasteland Ends*, *The Cult of Information*, and *The Voice of the Earth*. His novels *Bugs*, *Dreamwatcher*, and *Flicker* might also be described as Gothic tales about computers, psychiatry, and motion pictures. A Guggenheim fellow who has been twice nominated for the National Book Award, he is professor of history and director of the Ecopsychology Institute at California State University, Hayward.

ABOUT THE TYPE

This book was set in Centaur, a typeface designed
by the American typographer Bruce Rogers in 1929.
Centaur was a typeface that Rogers adapted from
the fifteenth-century type of Nicholas Jenson and
modified in 1948 for a cutting by the
Monotype Corporation.